"You'll find dazzling imagery, boldly evocative descriptions, larger-than-life heroes and villains, and, at the same time an imaginative yet all-too-real tale that will take your breath away. I'd love to see Paramount—which made *Eye for an Eye*—turn *Wrath of God* into a movie."

—ERIKA HOLZER, AUTHOR OF *Eye for an Eye*

"*Wrath of God* is a towering, transcendent epic and efforts to categorize it make not much more sense than arguing about whether Homer's *Odyssey* is a sea tale or a historical novel or a poem. It is all of the above. So is *Wrath of God*, and I am flabbergasted by its brilliance."

—WARREN MURPHY, *New York Times* BESTSELLING AUTHOR OF *The Forever King* AND *Grandmaster*

"In *Wrath of God* the author displays a novelistic cunning and courage quite unlike anything I've read. Using several genres—western, science fiction, fantasy, historical—he merges and transcends them all, while simultaneously giving you a hell of a read. This is one Wild Bunch I'd love to saddle up with—and one author I'd definitely turn to again."

—KEITH FERRELL, EDITOR, *Omni*

"A marvelous adventure, bold and bracing. The novel works because of the pounding narrative, the heart-stopping scenes of battle and endurance, and some memorable characters, especially the women. (Old Katherine Magruder reminds me of formidable Scots and Irish warrior-women in my own lineage.) *Wrath of God* is fun—a wild roller-coaster ride that will have you screaming yet unable to stir from your seat. But, like all good stories, it also extends our sense of what's possible."

—ROBERT MOSS, AUTHOR OF THE *New York Times* BESTSELLERS
The Spike, Death Beam AND *Monimba*

"I finished *Wrath of God* the other night and frankly I was a bit overwhelmed by what it accomplished. It manages to transcend boundaries, jump fiction's fences and be something on its own. It is one hell of a book."

—DAVID HAGBERG, AUTHOR OF *Critical Mass* AND WINNER OF
THREE AMERICAN MYSTERY AWARDS

"An extraordinary novel that has the kind of surging power and breadth of theme that makes it bestselling material. It compares very favorably with such epic bestsellers as *Jurassic Park, Fatherland,* and *Footfall.*"

—JOHN FARRIS, *New York Times* BESTSELLING AUTHOR OF
The Fury AND *Fiends*

"I read the entire book in one Saturday sitting, starting at 10:00 A.M. and finishing at 4:15 P.M., and found it fascinating. *Wrath of God* is 'good versus evil' at gut-level intensity, coupled with classic military maneuvering, Machiavellian plotting, realistic scenes of torture, suffering at the foot-soldier level, an evil woman, a young heroine, some John Wayne–type heroes, and the wonderful irony of endangered (even *extinct!*) species coming to the aid of the most dangerous species of them all. In short, *Wrath of God* is a great read for anyone who likes a dash of fantasy, a scoop of science and a bucketful of historically accurate, savagely realistic violence in a fast-moving thriller."

—KEN GODDARD,
New York Times BESTSELLING AUTHOR OF *Balefire* AND *Prey*

"I'm impressed, I'm amazed, I'm dazzled. *Wrath of God* is a novel for all seasons and for all readers who yearn to be gripped by a book and pulled headlong into its pages. How do I describe this book? Audacious is the word that leaps immediately to mind. For fans of Clancy, Koontz, Follett, Heinlein, or L'Amour, *Wrath of God* will feel like home. Novels like this don't come along very often, and readers are starved for them. *Wrath of God* should be a very big book."

—F. PAUL WILSON, AUTHOR OF THE BESTSELLING NOVEL, *The Select*

"An extraordinary novel, a tour de force of the imagination. I've read a good many apocalyptic, post nuclear war novels and *Wrath of God* is, by a league or two, the most ingenious and fun to read."

—DALE WALKER, COLUMNIST, *Rocky Mountain News*

"Every once in a while, you read a novel that makes fiction seem brand new again. *Wrath of God* is such a book. It blends high adventure with unflinching realism and shocking violence, then heats the mixture to a fever pitch. More than just another thriller, it is a work of powerful passion, personal poetry, and profound ideas. *Wrath of God* is a thunderous assault on history, conceived on the grandest possible scale. When you are done, you will view our past and our future with a different eye. *Wrath of God* will make you think, feel, care—and leave you changed."

—*Mystery Scene*

Wrath of God is a classical novel, bringing alive the universal clash between good and evil in the affairs of God and men. It is full of archetypal figures, men and women of great power, paragons of good and of evil, heroes and devils, monumental figures facing monumental challenges in an ultimate showdown—all couched in the gritty, fully imagined reality of constant action. It's a historical novel that draws a cast of characters from across the reaches of time and brings them together to a thunderous climax. . . . A universal story full of love and loss and heartbreak and heartmending."

—DAVID NEVIN, AUTHOR OF
THE *New York Times* BESTSELLER *Dream West*

WRATH
OF GOD

ROBERT
GLEASON

HarperPrism
An Imprint of **HarperPaperbacks**

HarperPaperbacks   *A Division of* HarperCollins*Publishers*
10 East 53rd Street, New York, N.Y. 10022

Grateful acknowledgment is made to Daniel Ardrey for permission to include *African Genesis* by Robert Ardrey. Copyright © 1961 by Literate S.A. Reprinted by permission.

A trade paperback edition was published by HarperPrism in December 1994.

Cover illustration by Michael Herring

First mass market printing: December 1995

Printed in the United States of America

HarperPrism is an imprint of HarperPaperbacks. HarperPaperbacks, HarperPrism, and colophon are trademarks of HarperCollins*Publishers*.

❖ 10 9 8 7 6 5 4 3 2

To

HERBERT ALEXANDER

1910–1988

Time-when and for-all-tomorrows

SPECIAL THANKS TO

Susan Gleason, the finest agent I know
John Silbersack, friend and editor
and to
James P. Gleason,
1908–1965
my father

ACKNOWLEDGMENTS ◀━━━━

       I am indebted to Richard Dooda, for twenty years of friendship; Linda Braun and Steve Pagel, Mark Levine and Jim Demaiolo, who make all things possible; Susan Rowan, for her help and kindness; Jay Hyde, for that terrific day at Tor; Bill Lardie, who is a terrific individual; Bill Golliher, who has always been there; John Nelson, one of the finest people I know; Mike Garner and Jane Love, for making me feel like family; Ann Peters and Joan Ryzner, for looking after John Farris and for selling books like there is no tomorrow; Debbie Moore, who knows airports, books, and everything else; Cathy Cadek, who makes Levy so awesome; Chip Crowl, who knows SF, blues and thanks to Hugh and me, the Chicago underworld; Larry Price, who rules our libraries; Greg Meader, who has taken such superlative care of my authors and me; Gene Meader, who has also spent several decades now looking after my writers, me and of course Tom D.; Karen Gifford and Becky Rose, who have now glimpsed the deep dark heart of tarot; Robin Halverson, Beth Perialas, Jeannie Bailey and all their wonderful, wonderful friends at Anderson; David Moman, Don Pennington and Larry Adams, for introducing me to the wonders of Dreamland; Lee Spellman, who makes New York—New York; Nick Ursino, Juanita Roberts and Larry Moser, who sell books by the zillions; Jenny Smith and Kerry Cook, for all those hilarious, tarot-filled lunches; Steve Borjes, who shares my vast affection for Charly Vining; Don

Hay, for all those old, old Pocket Books memories; Coy Taylor and Craig Hardin, for putting up with my prison stories; Carolyn Ignatuk, Cathy Gibbs, Pat Hinger, Janet Newman and Joanne Milakovic, for all those great times in Michigan City; Erik Sakariassen, who carries the West in his heart; Mark Gustafson, for looking after Big Ralph and my compadre, Hugh; Kathy Akins and Doug Mote, who helped me get through Houston; Freddy Valenzuela and John Jarrell, for helping me survive El Paso; Jerry Sanders, who knows the best books and the best barbecue in all of Dallas; Ray Countryman, who shares my passion for Lucifer's Hammer; Dennis Loreque and Paul "Ski" Konarski, who share my passion for baseball, books, and tarot; Mike Smith, for caring about writers; Mel Grossman, who helped me out when I was lowly Jackson Cain; Vance Lee, for a decade of support and a very special evening in Rock Center; Deborah Pearson, for looking after Mike and Rog; Maria McKnight and Ruben Lopez, for scheduling so many great events (and for looking after Mike and Rog); Bob and Gen Logren, who, with Cheryl and Ted Harrison, have shouldered the awesome burden of looking after Ralph Arnote (who needs a lot of looking after); Ron Bankston and Chela Sanchez, who look after more writers per square foot than anybody I know; Karen Rembold, Ted Majerek and Mike Gilbert, for looking after my home-town; Charlie P., for looking after Detroit City; Shirley Grove, Mike Puglie, Jeff Wardford and Ken Wellborn, who also look after Hugh Holton; Pam Branchini, for looking after us all; Donna Ginter, for taking care of my Montana writers; and of course Wild Bill Parnell.

AUTHOR'S PREFACE

After reading *Wrath of God*, people sometimes ask me how I came up with characters as unspeakably evil as Tamerlane and Legion. I guess it all began with my father. He was a prosecuting attorney in Michigan City, Indiana, a steel town on the northern edge of Gary. The Indiana State Prison was located a few blocks from our home, and my father had sent a lot of men there. When I was quite young, my mother would walk my older sister and me over to the prison.

My mother would say: "That is where your father sends bad people," and from the way she said it, I understood that there were some very bad people in this world.

I later got to know some of the inmates. During my last two years of high school, my friends and I played over a dozen tennis tournaments in the prison. These were all-day affairs, and since there was only one tennis court, we had a lot of free time. We spent those off-court hours walking the big yard, hanging out with the cons.

Their most distinguishing trait was their utter plausibility. They came across as decent and caring, incapable of wrongdoing. I even suggested to our neighbor, Doc Weeks—the prison doctor—that locking these men up was a waste of taxpayer dollars.

"Try remembering their serial numbers the next time you play them," was his only comment.

I played there a few weeks later and this time memorized their numbers. Doc Weeks pulled their file jackets for me. They were rapists, murderers, strong-arm robbers. The most ingratiating of the lot had chopped up his wife with a meat axe in their bathtub, then filled it with acid. The stench had brought in the cops.

Another colorful character in *Wrath of God* is the fanatically religious torturer. When people ask me about him, I'm forced to admit he also lived in the neighborhood—and was the prison torturer.

He was civil enough. In fact, he was a student of the Bible, a born storyteller, and he never stopped grinning. Even when he was mad—and he had a terrifying temper—he grinned.

He worked down in the punishment cell in the prison's basement. The recalcitrant convicts were brought to him there, and he'd work on them one at a time for a half hour.

He used to brag to us: "I can whip any man in the Indiana State Prison—young or old, big or small, white or colored. I take off their cuffs, put on the kid gloves, and never leave a mark on them. I just cuddle with them for a while."

In *Wrath of God* I nicknamed my torturer, "the Cuddler."

My father did not believe that good would necessarily triumph over evil. In his all-time favorite novel, *War of the Worlds*—which he actually read aloud to my sisters and me—the human race is almost exterminated by an evil civilization only to be saved in the end by blind luck. At the time Wells's vision of the future seemed extreme, but within a few years the Russians sent up Sputnik, and we were told that both countries could now obliterate the world in less than thirty minutes.

My father felt that Wells's vision had been vindicated—except for the part about blind luck.

In case you haven't guessed my old man was very entertaining, and we loved him very much.

Years later when I became a New York book editor, I bought and edited a book called *The Mote in God's Eye*, which Robert Heinlein and many others hailed as the greatest SF novel ever written. *Mote* has a marvelous apocalyptic dimension to it as well as some extraordinary alien viewpoint characters.

I later pointed out to its authors, Larry Niven and Jerry Pournelle, that no one had ever done an end-of-the-world alien invasion novel with alien viewpoint characters. They put together a treatment.

The treatment contained an asteroid, which the aliens used as a super-bomb. They dropped it in the ocean, where it cracked the earth's mantle, spewing zillions of tons of magma into the sea. The salt water came down as saltwater rain in temperate zones, destroying the topsoil, and as ice and snow in polar regions, inaugurating an ice age. The asteroid destroyed civilization and most of the human race for thousands of years to come.

I said something like: "Stop the presses! I've got a book that's gonna blow this town wide-open. Forget the alien invasion. Let's do a novel about the asteroid."

They roared like gored water buffalo but eventually did the treatment. The asteroid became a comet, and the novel became *Lucifer's Hammer*. Next they wrote *Footfall*, the alien invasion novel, and both books became *New York Times* bestsellers.

Over the years I've published a number of their apocalyptic thrillers. They consider me their "partisan of the apocalypse."

During the 1980s I worked for Tom Doherty at Tor Books as a consulting editor, which gave me time to write novels on the side. My first books were thick, heavily researched westerns full of real historical characters, and I was doing pretty well at them. Then one day I read a book by Harold Bloom about Tamerlane the Earth-Shaker. The book portrayed him as the greatest warlord in history. He drove the Khans all the way back to the Mongolian steppe, conquered most of the known world, and once erected a mountain of a million human skulls.

I got to wondering whether we could whip Tamerlane in a fair fight. I became so obsessed with the idea I couldn't concentrate on my westerns. My western-writing career came to an abrupt end.

Keeping the fight fair took some doing. Tamerlane's horde was a horse-borne army, so I brought back George S. Patton, Stonewall Jackson, and Amelia Earhart to fight him. Today's officers, I came to believe, wouldn't understand old-fashioned warfare. It also wasn't fair for me to annihilate Tamerlane's horde with tanks and missiles, so I had to destroy all our high-tech weaponry.

To level the playing field, I decided to nuke the world.

My friend, the late Herb Alexander, was especially helpful. An author and scholar, he'd been the publisher of Pocket Books for thirty years. He'd also served under Patton, had flown Curtiss-Jennys and was an enthusiastic admirer of Thomas "Stonewall" Jackson. He helped me select and research my cast of characters. He was in many respects the most impressive man I've ever met.

But I still needed a leader for our side.

I've admired many old people, Herbert included. Old age takes guts, and some old people have more guts than a slaughterhouse floor. So I wanted an old person to redeem our country, one who'd fight a circle saw and who wouldn't know how to surrender.

My mother was not a bad prototype. She comes from a long line of Finnish iron-miners. She has love in her heart, but like those miners, she has iron in her fists. I worked in the steel mills for a lot of years, knew some pretty tough people, but none tougher than my own relatives.

She's moved to L.A., and one day I'm with her in her backyard. She's in a rocking chair with a twenty-two pound marmalade cat sprawled on her lap—the biggest cat I've ever seen. The sun is sinking through the L.A. smog, a huge crimson ball, throwing off shafts of red, yellow, purple, and gold. My mother is rocking.

My mother would make a pretty fair Katherine Magruder, but I am not certain about her feline friend. Sure, the Citadel has lost its will, its way, its heart—sort of like that fat beast on her lap—but I don't see America as a marmalade tomcat.

A bald eagle, on the other hand, who's forgotten how to fly, that's not bad. Perch the old bird on the rocking chair's arm, then we can have two old women in a rocking chair, staring out over a barren crimson desert into our country's setting sun. Two old women, waiting for Tamerlane's horde and the trapdoor to drop. Their backs are to the wall, and there is not much left to hope for. But there is iron in their backbones, fire in their blood, and they are not defeated. They will whip Tamerlane—or die trying.

I get out a piece of paper and start to write. . . .

*There, they sit, two old women—on the same black
tideless rock in the last eternally crimson evening—drowsing, wondering, teetering, over and over, again and again.
Just Katherine Magruder and Betsy Ross—two ancient
relics of a long-dead past, rocking, endlessly rocking.*

Under hell's shadow.
At the brink of Time's abyss.
Against the fall of night.

WRATH
OF GOD

What if a weapon had done this deed? What if I held in my hands the evidence of antique murder committed with a deadly weapon a quarter of a million years before the time of man? What if the predatory transition should be susceptible to proof, and accepted as the way we came about? Could we afford to surrender in such desperate hours, as those we now live in, our belief in the nobility of man's inner nature?

I asked Dart how he felt, from a viewpoint of responsibility, about putting forward such a thesis at such a time. I said that I understood his conviction that the predatory transition and the weapons fixation explained man's bloody history, his eternal aggression, his irrational, self-destroying, inexorable pursuit of death for death's sake. But I asked would it be wise for us to listen when man at last possessed weapons capable of sterilizing the earth?

Dart turned from his window and sat down at his desk; and somewhere a tunnel collapsed, a mile down, and skulls jiggled. And he said that since we had tried everything else, we might in the last resort try the truth.

—ROBERT ARDREY, *AFRICAN GENESIS*

Somewhere in the sands of the desert
A shape with lion body and the head of a man,
A gaze blank and pitiless as the sun,
Is moving its slow thighs, while all around it
Reel shadows of indignant desert birds.
The darkness drops again. . . .

—WILLIAM BUTLER YEATS,
"THE SECOND COMING"

PART I

Those that should have remembered
forever . . . remember no more.

—VACHEL LINDSAY,
"THE EAGLE THAT IS FORGOTTEN"

Dawn in the Citadel.

An old white-haired woman in a rocking chair—rocking, endlessly rocking.

She stared at the desert dawn, tired and dismayed. The astonishingly large bald eagle—perched on her block a dozen feet away—ruffled her hackles, cocked her sleepy head, and glared at the old woman with a surprised widening of the eyes.

It was long past the woman's bedtime, and—as if to remind her—the dawning sun blazed above the eastern rimrock, throwing off dazzling shafts of red and orange, yellow and gold. In the distance a cock crowed, and the sun cast long straggling shadows over the desert chaparral.

The old woman's lap was strewn with dispatches, which had been sent to her by her grandson, all the way from New Anchorage—in what was once Alaska—down to her homestead in the Citadel, capital of New Arizona.

She peered wearily at the mess of papers. She could not believe it was happening again. Not now. Not to them.

Raising her head, she stared out over the hot, featureless land. This part of the Great Sonoran Desert was deeply fissured by crimson canyons and arroyos but otherwise empty and dry.

The old woman glanced at her friend, Betsy Ross, the pinioned bald eagle. She smiled, but the smile faded quickly when the old woman focused on the bird's sharply hooked beak and sickle talons. *It is the desert's way*, she thought. *Nothing survives here that does not tear or claw or bite.*

Even the plants came armed, sporting virtual forests of hooks and knives: pointed mesquite, spiky maguey, the ten-foot yucca with its base of razor-sharp, bayonetlike leaves.

She lifted her gaze. The first vulture was climbing the high, hot, mountain thermals. He hung there abeyant, etched against the flawless sky, keeping his lonely deathwatch. With blood-crusted beak, black snaky neck, and spread wings, he glided on the rising drafts, describing wide, lazy circles.

Suddenly, a hawk shrieked, winging over the rim-rock, a diamondback dangling in its talons. A spotted night owl hooted her piercing cry—which some said presaged death—and a pack of coyotes yapped and yelped. The locusts droned, and the flies began their interminable keening. In the distant rocks, the lone rogue puma, which had ravaged the countryside for two long months, ululated loud enough to wake the damned.

Here in these infernal desert canyons and arid mountains, life was hard. Survival was struggle, to subsist was to fight, and nothing was safe, nothing.

Until it was dead.

Again, the old woman rocked and stretched. Yes, she thought, you endured much these last eighty-odd years. You saw the world as it was, and you saw it knocked to its knees by a nuclear holocaust, and you saw it begin again. You saw the desert bloom, and industry revive. You saw tractors jerk and putt and come to life. You saw farmers till, artisans strive, students learn. You saw a semblance of civilization start and sputter, something you and your late husband, Frank, and your dead daughter, Marge, built on your backs with brains and sweat and blood.

You saw the world in all its wrath and wonder, and you think that maybe, just maybe, it will be worth it once again—the pain and sorrow and suffering.

Then *this*. She glanced at the dispatches strewn willy-nilly around her forever tottering rocker.

Yes, she thought, *it is true*.

Nothing is safe, nothing.

Until it is dead.

2

It was still early morning when the two guests arrived. George and Evelyn Bundy came from up the road. Both were in late middle age and graying and wore the same lightweight white cotton clothes, common to the desert country. Evelyn had her first grandson slung across her hip. They came around the side of the house and let themselves in through the backyard gate.

George yelled, "Hi."

Betsy Ross was the first to react, giving them a quick, querulous glance. The old woman looked over her shoulder and nodded.

"To what do I owe this special visit?"

"Last night Jeffers contacted us about your grandson's dispatches," George said.

"He thinks you're overestimating the dangers in New Anchorage."

The old woman snorted hoarsely.

Betsy Ross ungraciously ruffled her nape.

"George, a huge horse-borne army is surging out of Asia. They've obliterated everything in their path, and now they've turned east toward the New World. They'll do the same thing here. They should make landfall up there any day now."

"Jeffers is still disturbed about this arms buildup you recommend," George said, "this call to battle. Last night at a council meeting he got pretty rough."

"'Paranoid fascist' was one of his milder insults," Evelyn said.

A pair of bifocals dangled from the old woman's neck. She put them on and began riffling a stack of her grandson's dispatches. Pulling one out, she read aloud:

"'This is no migratory mass like the Goths or the Huns but a disciplined, determined army bent on conquest. Their dominion is imperialistic, slaveholding, Islamic, and genocidal. Militarily, they are indomitable, having smashed Europe, Asia, the Middle East, and the Middle Kingdom with effortless ease. Everything in their wake they leave shattered, tortured, torn, and dead.

"'They have mastered not only firepower-and-mobility, but firepower-*in*-mobility. Their soldiers are incomparable horsemen and archers, who specialize in lightning assaults, mass arrow volleys, and ingenious siege machines. They possess an efficient messenger and signal system, utilizing both semaphore and heliography. Their superb control-and-command allows them to coordinate armies as much as two hundred miles apart.

"'Their main weapon is fright, and they strive to paralyze the opposition through terror. They render the remains of human captives and polish their leather armor with the grease.

"'Brutality in their camp is commonplace and horrifying: After their conquests they set endless towers of human skulls soaring against every skyline—an unmistakable warning to whatever straggling survivors happen by.

"'Torture is a matter of public policy. Captives are routinely crucified, flayed alive, parboiled in oil, spread out among horses which are then flogged to the four cardinal directions, broken under the scourge, and subjected to "the Death of the Thousand Cuts."

"'The Horde is ethnically diverse—an unwieldy polyglot army composed of almost every race, color, and breed. Over twenty thousand strong, the Horde contains Russians, Moslems, whole divisions of Chinese, as well as many from Champa and India. Their war shaman—a woman named Legion—claims lineal descension from the horned winged demon, Beelzebub. They have convinced their followers that Beelzebub has sent them on a special mission—to purge the Kingdoms of Earth in advance of his Coming. And if they have not defeated their foes before his arrival, then true hell will follow. For all of them.

"'Their leader, Tamerlane, claims to be the reincarnation of the famed Turkistani general.'"

The old woman looked up and peered over her bifocals. "I hope that's not too much overreaction for you?"

George looked away.

Evelyn smiled politely.

But the old woman was still mad.

"Suppose my grandkid's right? What will you do then? Abandon the Citadel?"

"Jeffers thinks Darrell's prone to exaggeration."

Katherine winced.

"What's wrong?" Evelyn asked.

"Jeffers. Whenever you say his name I hear the sounds of Rome burning, men dying, Attila laughing."

"He can be amusing," Evelyn said.

She got up and handed the grandson to Katherine, who began rocking him on her knee.

"Just don't try smiling around him. He'll steal your teeth."

"Yes, but he does have a point," George said. "Ever since you got these dispatches, it's as if someone pinned an Avenging Angel badge on you."

"Only God does that."

"You sometimes act like you and He are awfully close."

With considerable effort, the old woman bridled her temper.

"It's just that I've seen men like Tamerlane before. I've seen the blood in the water, the skull beneath the skin."

"We know. You were there. You were back east when the warheads hit. And you crossed the entire country to get here. You saw it all."

"There are some terribly violent people in this imperfect world," the old woman said.

George reached over and touched Katherine's arm. "We always loved you, Katie. Frank, Rachael, Marge, all of you. Your mother used to bounce us on her knee. When we were kids." He paused to watch the old woman bounce his grandson.

"Mom made you godmother to all her kids," Evelyn said. "You're godmother to half the kids in the territory."

The old woman nodded. "But I'm old now. That's what you're trying to say."

She got up and Betsy Ross followed their progress with angry, protective eyes.

"Will you watch out for Jeffers?" Evelyn asked.

"Tell him to watch out for me. I'm on my way."

"He's entering politics, you know," George said.

"Local geek is not an elected office."

"Katherine," George said, "this is serious."

"You be serious. I've seen that boy do things that would embarrass Martin Bormann."

"Who was Martin Bormann?"

The old woman's silence spoke volumes.

For awhile they said nothing. Evelyn burped their grandson; George chucked the boy under the chin.

"Still you push, Katherine," George finally said with a sideways glance.

"After what Rachael's son sent me—"

"Rachael's dead, Katherine."

"Now I needed that, George. I needed you to tell me."

"Maybe you did, because you lean. People don't like it."

"Maybe you don't either."

"You ought to ease up a bit."

"Maybe you think I'm dead already. The old lady, she just doesn't know enough to lie down yet."

"I'm just saying you mess with Jeffers, you'll come back bloodied. Underneath that slick surface his heart's the heart of an iceberg."

"And he's got no soul at all," Evelyn added.

The old woman's eyes flashed with mean merriment. "I've spit in death's eye a thousand times."

"I know," Evelyn said. "'And never known fear,' right?"

"And never lost my Gandhi-like humility."

"Who was Gandhi?" George asked.

"I don't really know. A strange little blighter, when you got down to it. Used to claim evil was some kind of shuck."

They were clearly disinterested in the inestimable Gandhi.

Taking her grandson up from the old lady's hip, Evelyn asked: "Think little Donavon here will be a doctor like Frank. He could go to the med school and study all those specimens Frank collected."

"Jeffers mucks this up," the old woman said, "your grandkid might *be* one of the specimens. Or end up decorating one of those skull towers."

"Jeffers is spoiling for a fight," George said.

"With *you*," Evelyn said.

"Tell him to bring his lunch."

George leaned forward to kiss her cheek.

Betsy Ross spread her full ten-foot wingspan, and, with a shriek, arched her creamy head and hooked yellow beak high above the flapping pinions. Her scream was truly terrifying.

"You better give that girl some raw meat," George said, genuinely awed.

"Maybe I'll feed Jeffers to her."

She turned and walked toward Betsy's block, cooing softly.

It was time to soothe her ruffled friend.

3

Dusk in the Citadel.

The old woman in her chair, rocking, endlessly rocking.

Betsy Ross, perched on her block, studying her with fixed curiosity.

The old woman's mood was bleak and cold, and for the first time in twenty years, she succumbed to self-pity. She knew it was pointless but still she gave in. She stared at the westering sun, blazing above the rimrock, and let the deep despair wash over her. Soon the dried-up scrub appeared darkly sinister—twisted and portentous as midnight witches in some hideous *Walpurgisnacht.*

Even the far-off mountains—floating in and out of focus in the heat haze, like ghost ships lost at sea—even these appeared bathed in pathos, shrouded in sorrow. Often, to the old woman, those distant peaks seemed so near she could reach out and touch them, even though she knew they were nearly a hundred miles away. But this night they seemed to hang beyond the horizon's rim, beyond the grasp of time itself.

Beyond the reach of God.

With an effort she shook off the self-pity. It was old age creeping up on her, she thought. Yes, and the pain and dread of being eighty-four.

She allowed herself a moment of self-indulgence. With heavy-lidded eyes, she pondered the consequences of Tamerlane's dreams—soaring towers of human skulls set against the skylines, cities obliterated, entire cultures put to the torch. Everything she had worked for, shattered, stupefied, dead.

> *Where gods have fallen,*
> *Vipers rule,*
> *Violence the coin of their realm.*

So it had come to this: The Sword-Arm of Islam, a vast army which had crossed six thousand miles of Eurasia to threaten her world.

God only knew what horrors awaited her friends. Especially with men like Jeffers vying for command. No, this would be one long black night for their weak and timid souls, a hair-raising pilgrimage through the Outer Dark.

Even Betsy Ross was frustrated. She stared at the old woman, irate, quizzical. Hopping off her block, she strutted across the yard and flapped up onto the rocker's armrest. As the eagle perched, Katherine reached into her pocket and took out a morsel of raw liver, wrapped in rawhide. She held it for Betsy, who daintily pecked it out of her hand.

What man has stature on a wracked and bleeding earth? the old woman wondered idly. No man she knew, and certainly not a scarred-up relic like herself. She wasn't even sure who she was anymore. A watchman on the wall or a voice crying in the wilderness? Was she sounding alarms in the night or wailing for a world that could never be?

She glanced back at her old ranch house of thick

adobe bricks, its red tile roof and organ-pipe chimney,
now emitting a pungent plume of woodsmoke. In
between his duties at the hospital, Frank had built
that house, and for some time she had kept a picture
of him over the fieldstone fireplace. But Frank had
been so heartbreakingly handsome it made her soul
crack even to think about him. Every time she looked
at his picture, she was possessed by the suicidal desire
to join him, grave by grave, in the sun-scorched
churchyard, where none came to visit save the dust,
the buzzards, and the wind.

Six months after his death, she interred the photograph in the old cedar chest and never took it out again.

She looked at the bird perched on the armrest.
While other birds circled over the countryside, riding
the high mountain thermals on extended wings, her
own bird limped and flopped in pathetic circles on the
ground.

More and more, Betsy Ross seemed an apt symbol
for the Citadel.

Looking at her crippled friend, the old woman felt
a rush of anger. It swept violently through her, flush-
ing out all the petty doubts, hesitations, and self-pity.
Frank, her mother, Marge, Rachael, they had built the
Citadel—the territory itself.

Those that should have remembered forever . . .
remember no more.

She stifled the impulse to tears. The Iron Lady,
Jeffers had once derisively dubbed her, and she could
feel it now—the pure elemental ore, all the iron in her
backbone and brimstone in her blood, welling up for
one last show of strength.

Those that should have remembered forever . . .
remember no more.

She would change all that. She would make them remember the way it had been—and make them care. As for Tamerlane and his army, if they wanted the Citadel, they would have to pay for it in blood. She would see to that, and in the end she would stop them. Somehow, somewhere, she would put them down. For keeps.

She would work out a plan.

She would find a way.

4

There they sat, two old women—on the same black tideless rock in the last, eternally crimson evening—drowsing, wondering, teetering, over and over, again and again. Just Katherine Magruder and Betsy Ross—two ancient relics of a long-dead past, tottering back and forth, back and forth.

Two old women, rocking, endlessly rocking.

Under hell's shadow.

At the brink of Time's abyss.

Against the fall of night.

PART II

Swift is the reckoning of Allah.

—THE KORAN

The man in the round yellow tent woke to the scream.

That any sound should arouse him was astonishing. The man had been up for two straight days and nights—surveying his troops, studying his battle plans—and had collapsed onto his *daiwan* cushions only two hours before, radically exhausted.

Nothing short of hellfire and Armageddon should have awakened him.

Screams were something the man was used to. He'd heard death cries in countless lands. He heard them twenty years before when his *bedouin* were but a handful of bandits robbing the *caravanserai* crossing the Black Mountains and the Pai-Mir, those soaring peaks called Takht-i-Suliman, or Solomon's Throne. The crazed cry tore through his ears as he plundered the wealthy trading parties, traversing the Great Salt Steppe and traipsing over the "Roof of the World." He heard it when he slew the nation of Kashtahk along the limitless expanse of the Gobi—which travelers call the Great Silence—and again when he breached the rocky ramparts of Eurasia. He'd heard its shriek when he razed Egypt,

Sumeria, Judea, and Turkistan, the white dunes of
Jazirat al-'Arab and the red sands of the great
Nefud, and again when he sacked Damascus,
Constantinople, and the sovereign realms of the
New East—Champa, India, Mesopotamia, the
Middle Kingdom—and had followed the awful cry
through the smoking rubble of Europe.

He heard the same crazed howl everywhere—from
the Black to the Yellow seas, from the Straits of
Malacca to the perpetually frozen lands of the north
called Nouvo Sibir, or New Siberia. Even as he took
his flotilla of caiques and schooners, barges and
galleons across that narrow strip of wind-whipped
sea called the Bering Strait. He heard the strangled
scream, once again, as his ships went under and half
his men slipped below those pounding polar seas.

In truth, he'd heard the hellish howl every place
he'd gone. It had been his staunchest cohort, his
closest companion, his loyalest friend. He'd heard
it as the men had died of thirst in the scorching
sands of the Sumerian cradleland, or when they
had been skewered by broadheads in the Khyber
Pass or hacked to pieces on the arid Persian wastes
carving out his bloody domain.

The scream had even followed him here to the New
World—had followed him always—had been his
secret sharer, his most intimate ally, his hope, his
prayer, his dream, his life.

Even this night, hundreds of captives bellowed in
agony as they hung from bloody gibbets high above
the *bok*, or camp. They howled their torment to the
camp dogs below, gathered in yapping packs, baying
at the crimson cages overhead.

Still this scream was different. Soaring above the

camp's din, it transcended the yelping hounds, snorting mares, and his soldiers' bloody oaths.

The scream had begun without prelude. Wrenched out of the lungs, in an earsplitting crescendo. It hung on and on and on and on, till it finally became somehow detached, strangely eerie, a thing apart. It was as if it ceased to be a voice but had become something grotesquely inhuman, in-animal, the screeching wail of a huge machine run amok, pushed beyond all limits and starting to explode.

It had obviously emanated from the Cuddler's tent—the residence of the Horde's chief torturer. Old Mustafa put a distinctive signature on his handiwork. There was nothing in the *bok*, in the gibbets, or on the battlefields to equal his craft.

If precision was beauty, the Cuddler's exquisitely turned-out artifacts were an *oeuvre*.

And it now appeared this latest work was his most terrifying secret.

Still—even with the scream ringing in his ears—the General could not gauge his reaction to it. For, in truth, the man took neither pleasure nor comfort in the Cuddler's infinite skill. The man viewed these feats with stoic indifference. His was an intellect governed by tyrannical cynicism, elaborate rationality, savage self-control.

Even so, there was something special about that last death cry, and the man—always attentive to genuine artistry—recognized that the screech had gotten to him.

That was something new. Despite the General's unbearable weariness, he pulled himself to his feet. Slowly, he strode to the opening of his vast pavilion.

If the man's thoughts seemed abnormally detached,

one had to consider the circumstances. They were extreme. He was in charge of the most violent army of his time, an invincible war machine which was potentially as dangerous to itself as to its foes. He was as concerned with keeping his own people in line as he was with fighting the enemy. Soldiers who were recruited for valor and barbarism—who routinely flayed men whole and drank their blood from skulls—could hardly be constrained by a fortnight in the guardhouse or even the *chou-da* scourge.

They required the skills of a specialist.

And his specialist now had something new.

The man eased the tent flap open, and stared out over his *bok*. His ancient timepiece said it was midnight. His men would be up for the night, eager for the battle at dawn. He wondered whether he should visit them.

He had no need for camaraderie. In all his years as a desert warrior, he had never needed friendship. Not from men, not from women. He did not trust loyalty. He trusted fear, and he tolerated the company only of those whom he could break.

Of course, if he chose to visit them, he could not go down in full regalia. For better or ill, the Scourge of Allah and Beelzebub's Rage could not wander about like a common *bedouin*. As soon as he was recognized, all would fall before him—prostrating themselves in *salaam* and supplication, beating their foreheads at his feet.

He glanced at the black hooded cloak in a pile of garments to the rear of his tent, near the slitted exit. Once before he'd donned the cloak and ventured among his troops incognito.

He wondered how his men had reacted to the Cuddler's latest triumph.

He carefully draped himself in the dark cloak, wrapped a black woolen scarf around his face, and slipped out the secret slit.

Into the cold and the night.

2

The tall *bedouin* in the black hooded cloak strolled through the teeming *bok*, the largest tent city in human history. On he walked, past thousands upon thousands of round, clay-smeared tents dotting the hills around New Anchorage. Quietly, he strode past the thousands of cross-hobbled and roped-off war ponies, past the huge crackling campfires and their rising pall of pungently fragrant woodsmoke. On and on and on, he slogged—through the ecstasy and the tension of the camp, through his men's mounting eagerness for the battle to come.

Around each of the twenty thousand tents were staked not only horses but half a dozen dogs—shepherds, wolfhounds, and mastiffs. When one of them got too close, the black-cloaked man gave the hound a taste of his double-plaited shot-loaded whip-spring quirt.

On he walked. Everywhere he went, there were his men, veteran soldiers in black *caftans*, polishing their stiff rawhide armor and iron breastplates, honing their knives, shaping bows, mending horse gear. Most of them swilled the everlasting *kumiss*, that bitter brew of mare's milk and blood which they had learned to drink on the Asian steppe. They gulped draught after draught, toasting the coming battle, swilling the heady stuff from gourds and leather sacks and human skulls.

The stranger encountered only men, for the women were kept apart. His strict *bok* code declared women to be "Satan's vipers," "hell's serpent," "the devil that seduced Lucifer" and, therefore, they were concealed by the eternal *purdah,* that high dark screen behind which "Satan's vipers" lived, labored, and died. When rarely they materialized outside the pale, they were draped head to foot in their heavy *aba* robes, their faces masked by the inscrutable *chador* veil.

But even as the man strolled through this exclusively male Horde, it was clear that they had not banished women from their minds. The men—when not swearing bloody oaths or toasting death—talked of little else. Even as their gaze turned toward the valley below— toward the high walls and fortified gun towers, the jutting earthworks and vast concertina coils of encircling barbwire—even then the men's talk turned to women.

Mostly they spoke of Tamerlane's woman—the Lady Legion.

Passing one *yurt,* or tent, a tall angry *Janizary,* who had been addressing a gathering of soldiers, called him aside. Offering him a sack of *kumiss,* he said:

"My friend, the debate on our Lord's Lady—the one called Legion—rages on. I say she is no woman at all but a lamia, an evil *jinn,*"—demon—"who provokes men to insane feats of lovemaking after which they collapse in exhaustion. She, then, turns from a beautiful *houri* to a grotesque serpent and devours them whole. Do you not agree?"

"Why else would she appear swathed in poisonous vipers?" the man in the black cloak asked. He referred to her infamous ability to charm snakes.

"You see?" the man shouted to his comrades. "The man knows." Turning to Legion's tent, he raised a leather sack of *kumiss* and proffered a toast.

"Lady, in thy serpent prison-house, some pity show."

After draining their drinks, they turned to the stranger. He had not touched his beverage.

"You do not drink to our Lady?"

"You say one day she shall turn into a snake and eat our Lord whole."

"But our Lord is Master of Thrones and Crowns, the Scourge of Allah, and Beelzebub's Rage. Our leader can never be killed. Not even by those below," the *Janizary* shouted, pointing to the heavily fortified redoubt below.

"Who would not drink to that?" the stranger agreed.

He lifted the huge leather sack and with both hands drained it in four gulps, the bitter *kumiss* dribbling down his cheeks and cloak.

The soldiers greeted his retort with raucous cheering.

And as they returned to toasting and boasting, singing and laughing, the man drifted away from their fire.

3

It was a strange night, and how long he strolled through the *bok* he could not say. The more he dwelt on his terrible voyages across the Bering Sea—and pondered this strange new land—the more puzzled he became.

Up here, beyond the camp, far up the steep hill to

the north, he could clearly see the strength of the enemy garrison below—the high white walls, luminously bathed in moonlight, the heavily fortified gun towers, the earthworks, the plowed-up perimeter, the concertina coils of barbwire.

Then he remembered, once more, that all his siege engines had sunk beneath the waves in a violent polar storm during the last strait crossing.

The truth came to him in full. Here, alone on this hill, he acknowledged his mistake. This was not his kind of war. He hated battles of attrition. He was a *bedouin.* Hit-and-run, surprise and mobility. Not only fire-and-mobility but fire-*in*-mobility, that was his creed. He was a horse soldier, and his was an empire conquered in the saddle by an army on the move.

In the face of a prolonged siege he did not even know whether he could control his own men, let alone kill this fortified foe.

He had not always lacked belief. In his youth he had burned with Allah's Word. Emulating Mohammed, he had spread the Faith by fire and the sword, converting as he slew.

"Thus sayeth the Prophet," his Imam would roar at their beaten foe, "'their faith was of no use to them when they beheld our punishment. For they shall make their beds in Hell, and above them shall be coverings of fire! In black smoke, amid pestilential winds, in scalding water, they shall eat of the devil's tree. It riseth up from the pit of hell; its fruit is the head of Satan and the damned shall eat of it and fill their bellies with boiling oil.'"

Where had it all gone? His passion? His Faith?

The last one was easy. He knew precisely where and when it had left him.

After the siege of Constantinople, accompanied by his

new consort, the Lady Legion, he had made the sacred hajj *to Mecca, the Ka'bah, the holiest place in all the world, the cube-shaped Ka'bah, which lodged the Black Stone.*

After completing the sevenfold circuit and sacrificing their camels and sheep, they entered the shrine. Allah's Rock lay before him.

"Kneel," Legion whispered behind him. "Beg Allah's blessing. Kiss the sacred stone."

But he could not stoop. He could not humble himself— not even before the True God.

The *Mullah*'s cry shook him from his revery. Scaling a *muezzin*'s prayer tower, the holy man now thundered *The Koran* to his *bok*.

> *RECITE thou in the name of the Lord who created;—*
> *Created man from blood coagulate:—*
> *Recite thou! For the Lord is most Beneficent,*
> *Who hath taught the use of the pen:—*
> *Hath taught Man that which he knoweth not. . . .*

A harsh arctic wind swept across the hillside, blowing in off the Bering Sea, drowning out the *Mullah*'s words. The General pulled his *burnoose* tightly around him, and glancing up at the hilltop, he studied the newly constructed skull-tower above him.

For the first time in his life, the leering skeletal grins—rather than lifting his heart—filled him with dread.

He turned and faced the north. Memories. Memories of freezing mists that rolled in off the polar strait like silent thunder, of tortured icescapes bathed in quicksilver and the ghostly glow of arctic moons.

Memories.

Memories of northern lights flaring in bars along the horizon's rim. Of white nights on pounding polar seas. Of waves crashing and bows cracking, holds flooding and men drowning. Of cities sacked and women raped. Of children wailing and nations dying.

And Legion laughing.

He stared up at the lofty tower—at its eternally grinning death's-heads and sheer steep walls. He trudged the rest of the way up the hill, in full view of the smirking skulls, and in the tower's lee shielded himself from the arctic blast.

How many towers?

How many dead?

How many more?

He stared down at the camp. In one corner of the compound he saw a fiery blue blaze. He had seen it countless times and knew instantly what it was: A naked man—his face, no doubt, taut as a death mask—had been tied to a stake, doused with oil, and ritualistically burned. The kindling at his feet roared into red-orange flames while the body was shrouded in brilliant blue fire. He could see it all. The man screaming, the hair flaring, the blue purity of the body's gemlike blaze as it literally exploded out of itself, black smoke billowing up, the stench of scorched flesh and charred hide and crackling hair, all of it followed by a hideous echoing scream, ululating high above the camp's din.

The man gazed on the spectacle below and felt nothing.

Nothing.

Until he contrasted it with the earlier scream from the Black Tent.

Yes, that scream had been something special.

Contemplating the earlier scream and staring down on the sprawling might of his camp, his old confidence returned. No one could match him. He knew that now. He already was the greatest general in history. Legion, who in her youth had read all the volumes in the famous library of Constantinople, could attest to that. No one throughout the length and breadth of Persia, Arabia, Europe, the Middle Kingdom could equal him for courage and cunning, for conquest and dominion.

In fact, staring down at the New Anchorage redoubt, he wondered if defeat would ever come—if he would ever face a people fierce enough to halt his horse-borne juggernaut or the warrior brave enough to end his desperate dream.

The thought intrigued him. A soldier strong enough and clever enough to take his life. How would he respond to such a man? He would not be a hated foe. A warrior that brave, that clever would be— would be—

A brother-by-blood?

A secret sharer?

No, he realized bitterly, a warrior to rank with Saladin, with Suleiman the Magnificent, with Mohammed on High.

With himself.

But these thoughts were madness. Pulling his black cloak tightly around his shoulders, he shrugged off the bizarre notion and started down toward his tent.

It was clear—Legion had assured him—that the fighter strong enough and clever enough to take Tamerlane's life did not exist.

PART III

We have come here not to mourn that such men died but to praise God that such men lived.

—GEORGE S. PATTON,
ARMISTICE DAY, 1943

September 25, 1918
The Meuse-Argonne Front
France

The Meuse-Argonne Front at dawn.

The creeping barrage of artillery fire, which for the last seven hours had been feeling its way up the field at forty-meter intervals, was now thundering past the Axis entrenchments.

It was time to send his men over the top.

But instead the Colonel paused behind his parapet. He raised his night glasses and gazed into the dark fog of no-man's-land, at the endless aprons of barbwire barricading the *Boche* trenches.

The *Boche* had had four full years to fortify their earthworks, and they were now the most formidable in Europe. Over a million men waited there, squatting behind their artillery pieces and machine guns, wallowing—like his own soldiers—in the same putrid trenches, listening night and day to the same echoing whine of the same shrieking shells.

Dying men in a dying hole in a dying world.

Dying in catacombs, in candlelit dugouts, in sand-bagged ditches hewn from Fricourt chalk or Ardenne's clay or shoveled out of the flooded swamps of Ypres.

The Great War, the newspapers called it, but to the Colonel in his deluged dugout there was nothing great about it. Even as the men waited for him—hunkered down on their duckboards, backs against the trench walls, slumped over their scaling ladders, even as they waited—still he paused.

In truth, the man did not like this war, and he dreaded ordering his troops over the top in massed human wave assaults. The tactics made no sense, and he felt as if he were marching his boys into meat grinders, into gaping graves.

All around the Colonel men inspected and rein-spected their rifles, recited "Hail Marys," blew on their chilled fingers, and prayed. One million, five hundred thousand of them, lined up from the Aisne to the Meuse River, strung out along a thirty-mile front, while—from the English Channel to Red Russia, from the Low Land Sea to the Italian boot—another twenty million men in another twenty thousand trenches per-formed the same inevitable rituals and marched to the same inevitable deaths.

Lowering his binoculars, the Colonel glanced up and down this patch of hell. He nodded to his sergeant, who shrilled two short blasts on his whistle, and the men queued up at their scaling ladders. He lowered his binoculars and watched the young Alabaman beside him pray one last "Our Father," cross himself, and kiss the crucifix strung around his neck. Mounting the scaling ladder, the boy crawled over the parapet. Thirty feet from the trench, he dropped in front of the jump-off tape and waited for the zero hour whistle.

A little whiff of death makes us brothers in the night, the Colonel thought gloomily.

It was time, but still he waited. In front of him and his troops were a dozen crisscrossed aprons of double-woven, quadruple-hooked, eight-gauge wire—the barbs as thick as their forefingers. Those who were not shot on their own wire, or blown to bits negotiating the fog-shrouded shell-pocked muck called no-man's-land, would face even more barbwire.

And these coils would be backed by ten thousand Maxim machine guns, manned by the teeming *Boche.*

Each yard gained would cost him five thousand lives.

Once more, the Colonel raised his binoculars. The field, covered with premorning mist, vibrated in and out of focus. Still other details stood out. The fog rolling in off the Meuse; the vast cloud banks of milky smoke rising high above the *Boche* artillery; the birds flapping and warbling over this devastated moonscape, occasionally roosting on the splintery wrecks of shattered trees, or perching on the coiled barbwire, or foraging around the count-less water-filled shell craters.

In bloodcurdling contrast, sniper rounds cracked and ricocheted off gun mounts and helmets. Mortar and shellfire whined unceasingly. Shrapnel exploded and canisters of mustard gas crashed, the airy saffron-colored coils twisting like yellow snakes. Its writhing threads hung above the field in the pale fog, eternally suspended.

"Fix masks," the Colonel said to his orderly.

The sergeant shrilled three staccato bursts on his whistle, and men up and down the Front fixed masks.

The first rays of dawn streaked over the horizon, and the Colonel knew it was time.

Get them moving, he thought, *before the* Boche *barrage creeps back.*

Still he resisted the impulse to send them across the field. Even when he heard a German machine gunner across the wastes issue a handcrafted invitation. The gunner rapped out on his gun the famous American rhythm, *"Shave and a haircut—two bits!"*

He glanced once more at his chronometer. 0429 hours. In sixty seconds his tanks would roll out of their camouflaged embrasures. Without him.

The thought was wrenching. Ordered to remain at his post, he would be standing there, in the boot-high muck of the Com-Trench, while his tanks charged off into what his superiors hailed as the last battle in the last war. The war to end all wars.

Again, the rains came, ringing against his helmet like some perverted parody of the anvil chorus. Another creeping barrage swept up the battlefield over the trenches, forty meters at a time, saturating the world with its blazing breath and fragmenting shrapnel, pitting the smoking earth with fiery craters, a dozen feet across, another dozen deep and then departing.

0430 hours.

His tanks were rolling. Without him.

He'd known what he would do all along. He realized that now.

Blowing the whistle, he did his duty and saw the men over the top. Now he would find his tanks—somehow, some way.

"We're going after our tanks, Sergeant Angelo," he told his orderly.

"I figured we might, sir. Any ideas on how to find them? They started out nearly ten kilometers from here."

"We'll follow the sound of the guns."

"There's a lot of guns to follow, sir."

"Then we'll go where they're the loudest."

The Colonel hit the scaling ladder and clambered out of the trench, three steps at a time.

2

By the time he crawled out from under the twelfth and last apron of barbwire, his tanks had a thirty-minute head start on him. He and his orderly took off at a trot.

The shellfire was intense, but still the Colonel tried to remain upright, deliberately making himself visible. Shouting encouragement to the men, he tried to set an example.

By midmorning, the rain subsided, and the land grew quieter. The casualties were spread across the Front by the hundreds of thousands, and the Colonel could now hear their screams with sickening clarity.

And then the creeping barrage caught up to him.

Their own barbwire was barely a hundred meters to his rear when the bombardment struck. It was heralded by a parachute flare, igniting brilliantly over the field, followed by a high thin wail. His orderly yelled:

"Get down!"

And flung himself face-first into a muddy shell crater, which already contained two other doughboys.

The Colonel struggled to keep his feet.

He didn't like it standing erect—waiting for the shells and listening to the screams—but he was determined to set an example.

Then the full barrage hit. It seemed to strike as a single shot, a vast blinding roar. The earth shuddered, as if coming apart at the seams. He fought to stay on his feet, like a fighter refusing to take the count, but then fire-belching canisters were detonating millions of shell fragments, and down he went again, tumbling, his mouth filling with mud, rolling back into the crater with Angelo and the men.

Fighting to clear his head, he clambered out of the hole and forced himself to his feet. Staring through the whitish smoke, it seemed as if he were the only soldier still standing.

He stared at the *Boche* lines. Creamy smoke drifted over the enemy entrenchments, swallowing up guns and horizon, veiling the crimson sun. Slowly, through the smoky pall, ghostly figures emerged. To his left, the Colonel saw one soldier doubled over, clutching his abdomen, struggling to contain intestines which were falling out of a hole the size of a trench helmet. To his right, another was writhing in his blood, clutching at a shattered leg. Another, in a crater directly behind him, was fumbling for eyes, which he could no longer find. A fourth floated facedown in a flooded hole.

There were draft horses on the field, used to haul up artillery. These were dead or maimed, and the caissons they had hauled were twisted, smoldering wrecks.

The smoke cleared a little to his right, and another span of horses came into view. This team thrashed on the ground, while neck and chest holes bubbled blood. Two other horses—which had actually borne officers foolish enough to mount them—were now upfield. One of them—a headless bay—foundered on spastically spraddled legs. A walleyed dun bucked and crowhopped in hysterical circles. Legs and boots were still in the stirrups but the bloody saddle was empty.

The Colonel looked down and saw his orderly peering up at him from the bottom of the crater.

"All right, men," he shouted above the battle's din. "On your feet. You won't find the *Boche* down there. Get on up! We have a war to fight."

His orderly crawled out of the shell hole and struggled to his feet. He waved the men on and followed the Colonel, who was already trudging off into the smoke. A dozen ashen-faced men fell in behind him.

On they trudged, behind their muddied leader and his petrified orderly, jumpy and shaken, like an army of ghosts.

PART IV

When the stars shall fall . . .
When Heaven shall be stripped away,
When Hell shall be made to blaze,
Then every soul shall know what it hath.

—THE KORAN

The woman in the General's
tent lay back on the gaudy *daiwan* cushions. The night
was cold. She pulled her black satin dressing robe
tightly around her shoulders and gazed on the plush
surroundings—on the drapes and pillows of crimson
Shantung silk and jet black *pongee,* on her master's
collection of glittering *Shimshir* swords and Damascus
daggers and double-arched compound bows, on his
array of halters and saddles, of quirts and spurs. She
marveled at the marble-topped mahogany table with
its silver vase—containing one perfect red rose—and
its dazzling triptych mirrors.

Studying her reflection, she decided she looked
good, very good—at least ten years younger than her
actual age of thirty-six. Letting her black silk dressing
gown fall open, she continued her appraisal.

She started with the shapely legs, following them
from the tips of her toes to the silken sweep of her
thighs, over the sleekness of hips and abdomen to the
hard flat stomach. She threw open her gown, the better to scrutinize her loins and limbs.

A search of her slender throat revealed no wrin-
kles—hopefully they were still years away. She smiled,

and when her smile reached her wide-set onyx eyes,
they shone.

She took a deep breath and let it out slowly, saving the best for last: the great cascading mass of jet
black waist-length hair, which, regardless of *bok* pro-
hibitions, she wore long. Staring into the mirror, she
realized, once again, that if she had any real claim to
beauty, it lay in these raven-hued tresses. They
framed the milky skin, the wide-set eyes, the sultry
mouth, the angular aquiline nose and made them all
glow.

At least, she hoped they did. Tonight, her beauty
would have to launch ships, foment wars, and raze
the topless towers of Ilium.

2

When the flap opened at the
rear of the tent, it was her Lord. Lowering her gaze,
she leaned across the cushions toward him.

She felt uncommonly erotic. Her latest cycle of
nightmares had not been populated by demons and
gargoyles but had taken a lecherous turn, including
sensual images and carnal cravings.

She stretched her moonlit body across the pillows.

Tonight, she would need every possible edge.

If she were to allay her Lord's suspicions.

If she were to keep her secret safe.

She waited for her Lord to discard his dark robe
and cross his palatial pavilion. Looking up, she struggled to meet his gaze. She could not do it. In truth,
she feared him.

With good reason. She had risen to power in an age universally accepted as *gehenna* on earth, when people fought and starved amid rubble, ate the surviving rats, and then devoured one another.

She had watched her own people turn increasingly barbaric until her master had invaded. She had watched him emerge virtually out of nowhere, out of the devastated Turkistani steppe. She had watched him sweep through Persia, the Near East, and Eurasia like a hot black wind, leaving in his wake only whirling dust witches, the bones of the dead, and his soaring skull-towers, set against every hellish horizon.

She had wanted him more than anything—more than life itself.

She first came to desire him when he defeated her consort, the crown prince of Constantinople. The shah, refusing to give up his gold hoard, had waged war. To Tamerlane this was the ultimate insult. Storming the gates and sacking the capital, he found the shah with his bride, trembling on their marriage bed. She watched with shuddering wonder as he melted down the shah's gold hoard in front of them, then poured it down the crown prince's throat.

She knew then she had to have him. She knew it for all time. The rare artistry of his rage, the breathtaking beauty of his cruelty had touched her to her soul.

She now raised a sack of fine Shiraz wine with both hands.

"May you drink it like a Christian."

It was only when he drank that she forced herself to gaze into his steel-hearted killer's eyes. *Yes,* she thought, *I would crawl through hell for him.* He was more than her lover, her tyrant, her Lord. He was Destiny itself.

She gazed at him with trembling eyes.

She had to hide her treachery one more night.

They lay side by side. In silence.

"You are quiet, my Lord."

"I am uncertain as to the redoubt."

"Do not fear, sire."

"Have you seen the wire coils strung around the fortress?"

"Yes, my Lord. It is called barbwire. It is strung in what is known as concertina coils. It was once common in Europe. It is amply described in books."

"But that thick? That sharp?"

"I know it well, sire. Eight-gauge, double-woven, concertina wire with four barbs. Remember, I found the cutters for you? They will slice through it like a *Shimsir* sword slashing your enemies' throats."

"Still I fear it."

Fear. He used the word again. She was stunned. This was an emotion she did not believe he possessed. She attempted to tease him out of his trembling.

"My Lord, you scare me. Who knows what my master might do in this terrible mood. Mewl and pewl like a frightened babe? Or might he murder men and rape women? Even those closest to him?"

"I have not raped you yet."

She smiled provocatively. "The night is young."

"The night is old. I am old."

He clasped his hands behind his head, and staring across the *yurt*, looked away.

But the lady had a remedy for such indifference. She clapped her hands three times and a manservant entered, bowing, scraping, and salaaming. He also had with him a round wicker basket, three feet across and two deep. Inside were a matching pair of six-foot timber rattlers.

"Can't you do that somewhere else?" Tamerlane asked, irritably.

"Does my Lord fear snakes too?"

"No, but I dislike them. They are cold, slimy, and possessed by *jinns*." Demons.

As if on cue, the rattlers buzzed ferociously. Peering over the basket's rim, they spit and hissed at him.

"And poisonous?"

"Yes! Poisonous!"

Legion languidly entwined her pets around her limbs.

"I find them lovely, my Lord."

He winced as the hissing male rattler buzzed and writhed around her left thigh.

"It's part of their charm, sire."

As her Lord looked away, she allowed herself a small smile. He could not know that she'd secretly raised them from the egg, extracted their poison sacs, blunted their fangs, and trained them as pets. Nor could he know that the timber rattler, once domesticated, was quite docile.

"You know why I do this, sire. When I address the *Ordu* at dawn, my serpent-friends must writhe around my waist and arms. You want the *bok* to know I am Legion, descended from the loins of Beelzebub, spawned by the Everlasting Night? You wish them to know I am lamia? The witch-goddess who destroys men with passion, then devours them whole? The fact that you subdue this lamia nightly truly proves that you are the Scourge of Allah, Master of Thrones and Crowns. Such stories raise your manhood to the demonic, to soaring heights, to—"

"Enough," he said, staring at his lady with frank

disbelief. "As our Cuddler proclaims, 'Cursed is any house where a woman's voice is heard outside its doors.' And, here, the tent flaps are open."

"Suppose I refused your order, my Lord?" she teased. "Would you give me to Old Mustafa? To be carved into his much-dreaded thousand pieces? To be broiled on his gridiron?"

"Our Cuddler calls you 'the devil that seduced Lucifer.'"

"He is a pork-eating infidel and not of the True Faith."

"You only say that because you have not converted him to *your* faith. Only because he refuses to believe in your demonic father, Beelzebub."

"The others believe, my Lord. They fear my father's fiery face, smoking horns, and blazing blood-red eyes. They especially fear his eyes, for they are truly hideous. And when he comes, on that last day, comes thundering out of the sulfurous smoke of the Everlasting Night, when he comes to scourge the earth, you shall not—"

"Stop! I take your word. The vision is awful. But at the moment, I must worry about the redoubt. What if we lose? What if the Horde is destroyed on the wire and the walls?"

Again, she felt it, not only the weird stirring—which caused the tent tassels to tremble and her master's mares outside to snort and blow—but she felt once more her own carnal cravings.

"I feel, my Lord, that we've made a skull of the earth. Around its throat we string not gems but dead worlds. I say we kill for killing's sake. *That* is why we must take the redoubt. To fail, thus, is to fail our blood, to deny our destiny."

"Which is?"

"To scourge the earth. Not for the sake of Allah and the Prophet, but for Beelzebub, for the Everlasting Night."

"*The Koran* tells us: 'There is no God but Allah and Mohammed is His Prophet.'"

"I am no slave to Allah's book, my Lord, nor are you."

"Does the Prophet not speak *history?*" he said.

Here was an opening. A chance to bring up the boy.

"*We* are history—not the dead hand of the past."

"History is excrement."

"Not for us, my Lord, not with a scribe."

"A what?"

Good. He was confused. He did not know.

"Our spies did find him out, my Lord. He keeps a hoard of notes and diaries. All about us, Master. He watches and studies our every move. He schemes to send them south—to friends in other lands."

"To the Cuddler with him, then."

"Nay, sire." She feigned fear. "He writes a lyric prose and speaks a wealth of tongues, including ours. He knows the lands we know not of. This lad will prove his worth."

"He's a treacherous spy."

"He is a *scribe,* my Lord." Her voice rose. "Scribes take no sides, hold no beliefs. They merely *write.* They drink in words like wine, then vomit them out."

"You really want this boy?"

"He writes, my Lord, like angels sing."

"Methinks our Cuddler wants him more."

Walk soft. Your Lord suspects.

"Christ Jesus had his Gospels. Mohammed his

Koran. Krishna his holy *Gita.* We write our words on water, sire, on thin air."

"On the bones of the foe. We write them in words that even rocks remember."

"My Lord, your words and deeds are Eternal Truth. They must be graved immortal, on granite hard."

"Then bring on the boy. Let's view this ink-stained wretch."

"Yes, my Lord, but gentle, please. He is a callow youth. He does not know your wrath."

She clapped her hands twice. Instantly, the scribe was produced by a salaaming guard.

To everybody's horror, the boy stood ramrod-straight, staring into her master's eyes.

Her Lord was speechless.

Secretly, she delighted in the boy's fearlessness— and in his exquisite face. He was a handsome youth— eighteen, no more. His hair pale yellow as summer wheat—cheeks white and smooth as mare-fresh buttered milk. His eyes were clear as glass, blue as God's Own Heaven, and he flouted her master's wrath.

She broke the awful silence. "You are in the presence of Allah's Scourge. Tremble, boy, and obey."

The boy continued to stare.

The guard rose, salaamed twice in obeisance, then punched the youth in the back of the head. The boy's legs buckled, and he dropped to his knees.

"It's clear this youth has not met our Cuddler," Tamerlane observed.

Suddenly, a noxious stench of scorched hide and burning hair drifted through the pavilion.

A hideous scream echoed through the camp. It possessed an eerie earsplitting shrillness.

"What was that?" the boy asked suspiciously.

Because thou lovest the burning ground
I have made a burning ground of my heart
So that thou, oh Dark One,
Mayest dance. . . .

Tamerlane quoted somberly.

"It is an ancient hymn," Legion said.

"Yes," Tamerlane said, "since my Sister-in-Darkness revels in the burning ground, I oblige her with our Cuddler. He occasionally adds Greek fire and the Autumn Stone to his ministrations."

The boy cleared his throat. "You still haven't told me what you want."

"We've seen your dispatches," Tamerlane said. "It is clear you wish to write. You shall have your chance."

"I've told my Lord you have the epic touch, the very thing we need. We wish a scribe close by. A writing wretch to note our every thought, our every deed."

"You'd trust *me* to record your memoirs?"

"You have something better to do?" Legion asked.

As if on cue, the scent of burning hair and hide spread through the tent. Again, a scream tore the midnight darkness apart.

The youth glanced nervously around the tent. "Apparently not."

"We play by certain rules here," Tamerlane explained. "The rules are relentless."

Legion studied him. "My friend, where you come from, the meek inherit the earth and peacemakers are divinely blessed. Here, life is hard. The meek are forever accursed, and our Cuddler deals with the peacemakers."

"I'm not sure I could cut it. The memoirs, I mean. I only write what I feel."

"In that case you shall not feel very well," Legion said.

Again, as if by magic, the victim howled and the stench of burning flesh filled the tent.

"I've died and gone to hell," the boy said bleakly.

Again the smoke, the screams.

"We've never left," Tamerlane observed.

"In our *bok*," said Legion, "there are only three possible states. You may belong to the quick, to the dead, or to the Cuddler. All that matters to our men is that they do not belong to number three."

"I'd hoped this trip would prove an adventure." He used the English word, adventure.

"What is adventure?" Tamerlane asked.

"Violence and terror," said Legion, "recollected in tranquility."

"Let me assure you, then," Tamerlane said, "this adventure you seek shall be granted you."

More smoke, more screams, more sobbing ululations.

The young man looked anxiously around the tent. "Maybe if I view this experience as educational," he suggested.

"No, my friend," Tamerlane said, "whatever happens here, it shall not leave you wiser."

"Your education," said the Lady Legion, "will not be improved."

"Terrific," the young man said, frowning. He rested his chin in his hands and tried not to glance outside at the Cuddler's tent.

PART V

The great American Civil War must upon the whole be considered the noblest and least avoidable of all the great mass conflicts of which till then there was record.

—WINSTON CHURCHILL,
A HISTORY OF THE ENGLISH-SPEAKING PEOPLES

December 12, 1862
Fredricksburg, Virginia

▰▬▬◄

For just one second the fog
cleared.

The Confederate General on the sorrel war-horse
squinted into his field glass. From a high wooded
hill, he could see his enemy—all 120,000 of them—
an unending army of blue-clad soldiers, snaking over
the Rappahannock bridges toward Fredricksburg.
Their flags and guidons and polished musket barrels
blazed in the morning sun. Even five miles away, the
tramp of their boots was earth-shaking.

What the General stared at was the largest army
ever assembled on the face of the earth.

Still he was undaunted. In opposition to Lee and
Longstreet, he had proposed meeting them at the
Rappahannock and "flinging them back into the river."

"Give them the bayonet" had been his heated
recommendation.

Lee had shuddered. The Army of Virginia was out-
gunned and outnumbered three to one, and instead of

laying off bets or covering flanks, the General wanted "to get out the knives."

The man's unflagging aggressiveness was an enigma. No one knew where it came from. His appearance was temperate. His eyes were invariably somber. Silent, withdrawn, he looked innocuous in his ill-cut hair and beard, his ancient gray tunic—a relic from the Mexican War—and his battered forage cap. In fact, the slovenly officer was hardly distinguishable from his threadbare troops, who were sick and starving, barefoot and shell-shocked.

The General also happened to be the finest brigade-level field commander in military history.

Nothing in his past had indicated such ability. Born of a broken home, he had spent his childhood bouncing from one group of disinterested relatives to the next, transferring from school to undistinguished school.

That the General should rise above his fellow officers was astonishing, for the American Confederacy was a force like no other. A volunteer army, they were for the most part Anglo-Saxon rebels—unpaid and ill-equipped. At the outset of the war, the cream of West Point and the Virginia Military Institute had opted for the Gray Confederate Cause, and it boasted an officer corps of real distinction. Its roll call would include Robert E. Lee, Albert Sidney Johnston, James Longstreet, George Pickett, Ambrose Powell Hill, Lewis Armistead, Richard Brooke Garnett, J.E.B. Stuart, Turner Ashby, Jubal Early, and Joseph E. Johnston.

Yet one man stood apart. The unimposing man on the sorrel war-horse. The man who was so profoundly and unshakably religious, the man who would proclaim his single heartfelt desire was "to be near Jesus and be kind." The embarrassingly shabby man on the tired mount, so devoted to wife, children, and his beloved Virginia. The man who had come to prize the company of Bible scholars above all other men.

The man who had come to be the most vicious killer of bluebellies in the Confederacy.

The General's bloodlust was not wholly unprovoked. On this day, for instance, only hours before, the General had watched with mounting outrage as the Yankees had—for no apparent reason—blown the defenseless town of Fredricksburg off the map.

At one time, the General might have dismissed it. He had witnessed needless annihilation before, and from time to time civilians had suffered.

But it was now clear that the rules had changed. The Army of the Potomac had turned intrinsically lawless, resembling a rampaging mob rather than a military force. The Union army had committed itself to wholesale plunder, ransacking fruit cellars and corncribs, stealing chickens, hogs, cattle, sheep, and horses. Some, it was even reported, had mastered the art of confiscating beehives without getting stung.

Yet none of their atrocities had equaled the annihilation of Fredricksburg. Sitting on the big sorrel war-horse, he watched as General Henry J. Hunt—the most accomplished gunnery officer in the Federal army—posted his batteries on the high ground above the Rappahannock River just across the ford from the town. He had more than 140 guns in line—Rodman three-inch rifles, ten- and twenty-pounder Parrotts, a handful of four-and-one-half-inch siege guns—cumbersome cannon, far too massive for field maneuver but invaluable in terrain such as this. One hundred and forty fieldpieces bearing in on a small sleepy Southern town of no strategic importance.

The General on the big sorrel mount stared through his field glass. The big artillery pieces opened up at a rate of seventy shells per minute, until five thousand rounds had been fired—until a vast creamy cloud of gunsmoke roiled up over the high hills across the river. The haze soon enveloped the guns, the Rappahannock, the town, and then continued on across the open slope.

Next, slanting pillars of pitch-black smoke angled high above Fredricksburg, and the General, who had led troops through everything from the Second Manassas to the Shenandoah, from the Seven Days to Harper's Ferry, had to confess he had never seen such shelling.

Soon, an odd golden haze settled over the village and the hills. The rising sun threw off shafts of crimson and burnt orange and purple, and the smoke from the town was now, incredibly, a thing of beauty. Black smoke columns were spinning aloft, bedecked with dazzling rings, while the shells—bursting over the smoldering town—glowed bloody scarlet in the billowing haze.

Despite his wrath, the General had to lower his glass in blank, dumbstruck amazement.

As he studied the spectacle below, his telescope trembled.

2

The morning settled in slow and hard. As the General continued his vigil, the winter wind off the Rappahannock whistled through his threadbare tunic and rattled the leafless trees behind him.

In the valley below, the endless hordes of bluebellies streamed through the hills and across the water, in columns, blazing with flamboyant flags and glinting gunmetal. The earth beneath his own men's feet shuddered with the route-step of those 240,000 Federal boots as the approaching bluebellies rounded Fredricksburg and lined up on the slopes below.

None of the Johnny Reb fieldpieces could reach them yet, except for the General's one English-made Whitworth. It was a massive breechloader with a greater range than his artillery officers could handle. The General let them try it anyway. They missed the bridges but hit a paymaster's tent across the river. Through his field glass the General observed the results. The wages of an entire corps had been spread across a long barrel-and-plank table. The paper money exploded from the flame-shrouded tent in a fiery tornado, followed by a rabble of stragglers and orderlies who chased the glittering greenbacks all the way to the Rappahannock.

But even the whirling wherewithal did nothing to lighten the General's mood. He still thought the Confederate strategy was wrong. Their chief obstacle—in his eyes—was not the legions of bluebellies below.

The plan's flaw was that it was too good.

Glancing overhead, the General saw the two Yankee observation balloons. Their baskets swayed in the upper-air turbulence, heliographic mirrors flashing signals to the communications officers across the river. The General did not have to crack their code to know that they were reporting on Longsteet's men, who were strung out along his nine miles of four-foot stone wall, up along the ridge called Marye's Heights.

Even if the balloonists could not see his own masked batteries—or his men, who were hiding in their camouflaged gun pits and earthworks, or those who were concealed in the woods far to the rear of his fortified hills—it wouldn't do any good.

The General knew that his own bit of subterfuge was insufficient.

No one would dare to take them on.

The balloonist had to recognize that these hills were unbreachable. No army in all of history had faced a more impregnable position than the one confronting Burnside and his troops.

And no man—not even Burnside—would be mad enough to storm these fortifications.

No, the General realized, more in sorrow than in anger, the only way to fight that army was to meet them at the river.

No one could ever dislodge his men from these hills.

And no one would ever try.

Then, to the General's undying surprise, the Union bugler blew "Assembly" and Yankee troops were lining up at the foot of the hill.

By God, that fool Burnside was going to do it. He was going to march his army up that hill.

PART VI

There were giants in the earth in those days.

—GENESIS 6:4

Dawn in the Age of Dinosaurs.

The time is the Late Cretaceous. It is an elemental world of extreme inhospitality, an epoch when oceans roll over seven-eighths of the globe, and the rest of the planet is little more than subtropic swamp, fiery volcanoes, and shallow salt lakes.

Perhaps least inviting are its scorching floodplains. In the wet season these flats are pounded by torrential downpours, hurricane winds, and rivers overflowing their banks. In seasons of drought, the land becomes a broiling inferno, unarable as brick, hot as the devil's own frying pan.

This is the age when the dinosaurs will die. Late Cretaceous will witness the last hurrah of the Brontosaur—with its huge, elephantine body and snake-like seventy-foot neck. It will see the end of the heavily armored Ankylosaurids and Nodosaurs, the leathery Pterodactyls, the feathered Hesperorni, and the dread Tyrannosaurus Rex, King of the Tyrant Lizards.

The Triceratops will make its final stand. A ten-ton rhinolike beast, standing twelve feet high and thirty feet in length, it has a massive head, from which project three four-foot horns and a huge, razor-sharp beak. Broad of chest, wide of hips, with massive legs and a neck covered by a flaring collar of bony frill, Triceratops is built for thrusting and lunging.

She is the greatest killer of all time.

Triceratops is also the most prolific of the dinosaurs, traveling in herds of three and four hundred. If, in years to come, elephants will prove efficient at stripping rain forests, they are nothing compared to Triceratops.

But drought has struck, and the animal's foraging days are numbered. She is weathering dry spells so severe that whole rain forests wither, lakes and rivers vanish, seas disappear.

Vast deserts now stretch over what was once ocean floor. A rising land bridge joins Asia and North America, over which pass the lumbering herds. Migrations which bring with them parasites and plague.

The dinosaurs are dying, and the last Triceratops— thirty-three in all—stumble across the floodplain alone. Stopping here and there, they scratch at the dried-up streambeds, browse the stunted brush—and somehow continue on.

On and on they wander—through a bleak waste in a nightmarish time. Through twilight of the Gods, the fall of the Great Ones, they roam.

Dawn on the floodplains.

Dawn on the hardpan.

2

Thirty-three Triceratops—a pitiful vestige of the original herd—plodded along. Their skins hung like sacks of parchment. Their opaque eyes were milky white, their hooflike pads split and torn.

The crimson earth over which they trod yielded little. Here and there, a twisted mesquite, a gaunt cactus, some wind-bent brush. Along the horizon's rim, mountains loomed, vibrating eerily in the heat haze.

The going was especially hard on the herd's lead cow, for she disliked her duty. Her mate—the Brindle Bull—had been their previous leader, and she was well aware he had done a better job.

With the Brindle, it was true, they had occasionally run out of foliage. Sometimes they had even been forced to abandon one of the river forests—which they had trampled, torn apart, stripped clean—and take to the hardpan. Sometimes they had gone three, even four days without water and fodder, but they had never experienced anything like this.

The old cow had, of course, endured drought before. They had all seen their waterholes dry up, and even the great saltwater lakes—which had once covered the floodplain like glittering sheets of silver—reduced to muddy puddles. But never before had they seen it this dry.

Still she was determined to keep them moving. She had dragged them from one end of the floodplain to the other—all the way from the drought-stricken valley country in the east to the enormous river canyon just over the far rise—and given the fury with which she continued to prod them on, it seemed she would never let them rest.

But she had her reasons. They had to do with the small mountain of eggs weighing down her belly. Those were the creatures she was really bent on saving.

At last, they reached the chasm's rim. Their leader hoped the great waterway and dense vegetation were still down there. They had to be. This river couldn't be like all the others. It had never been dry. It had never even been low.

But when she looked over the edge she saw *nothing*—nothing but dust, hardpan, and heat.

Even worse, there was no place else to go. The desolate gorge was their shortest route to the distant delta country.

She trotted over to a nearby switchback and, with a trumpeting roar, led them down the trail to the dried-up riverbed, where their long trek toward the delta-lands would recommence.

Toward what she hoped would be water—and life for her brood.

The Brindle would have wanted it that way.

3

A herd of thirty-three Triceratops lumbering over a waterless waste. To the other canyon dwellers they seemed a pathetic lot—thirsty, starving, exhausted—but not to Quetzacoatlus, the Flying Dragon, the Thief of Eggs.

As he rode the high, hot thermals—floating effortlessly on his forty-foot wings—he observed their plight with rapt attention.

The Dragon was well equipped for such study. His bulbous eyes were mounted on huge frontal lobes, and even from his elevation of three and a half miles, his vision was godlike.

He had already noted that the herd's lead cow was minus a mate and heavy with eggs.

Meaning that when she built her nest and browsed, her brood would be exposed.

Still the Dragon was dubious—not out of fear but experience. This was no naive herd beast but a seasoned leader seamed with honorable scars—one wise to the ways of Egg Snatchers. The theft would go hard.

For awhile the Winged Dragon averted his gaze. He scanned the terrain for easier prey—a succulent snake or some well-rotted offal. But then he remembered his sick mate and his diseased hatchlings high up in their mountain roost. His young were desperately ill. Down with the fever, they had vomited up everything—and were dying.

His brood needed something soft and fresh and tender. His hatchlings needed the old cow's eggs.

Quetzacoatlus rode the desert thermals, keeping his lonely deathwatch with wise, all-seeing eyes.

On extended wings.

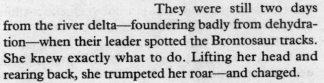

They were still two days from the river delta—foundering badly from dehydration—when their leader spotted the Brontosaur tracks. She knew exactly what to do. Lifting her head and rearing back, she trumpeted her roar—and charged.

The Triceratops were herd animals, who would follow their leader anywhere. Broken, beaten, starving, dehydrated, still they followed.

And one mile up the canyon, the Brontosaur broke out of a sun-dazzled, heat-exhausted daze to find hell itself pounding up her backtrail.

5

High overhead, Quetzacoatlus caught a thermal gust and circled higher. His view was now extraordinary—hundreds of miles in every direction—which enabled him to catch the sudden blur of peripheral motion below.

Despite the sweltering heat, the Triceratops pack had broken into a headlong charge.

The Flying Dragon's eyes widened. From his great height he saw *everything*. He knew what would happen next—something no Triceratops should have known—yet the old cow had figured it out.

The Thief of Eggs was displeased. Robbing the old cow's nest would be no simple task. Any cow cunning enough to spook the Brontosaur would be crafty enough to protect her brood.

The Winged Dragon continued his solitary climb, riding the gusting thermals, higher, ever higher, studying the scene below with keen, carnivorous eyes.

6

Even when the tracks deepened, and the water beneath the hardpan bubbled up, their leader continued to gallop. Calves and cripples might stop to drool, but the old cow knew better.

She knew it was now or never, life or death. If she did not catch the Brontosaur, the herd would never have another chance. The charge had taken too much out of them.

She galloped around a bend in the canyon—then another. The Brontosaur's great strides were deafening—echoing up and down the gorge. Her steps no longer simply cracked the hardpan but left huge, water-filled holes.

Finally, after one more bend, the old cow had an unobstructed view upcanyon. The Brontosaur was foundering, each step a monstrous crash, his massive feet slamming deeply into the riverbed.

As the Brontosaur fought to extricate himself, he stamped harder and harder. Each step was breaking through the pan, sinking him deeper, creating more flooded potholes.

Staring up the gorge at the foundering Thunder Lizard—less than four hundred yards away—the Triceratops realized her herd was going to stop.

They would not back her play. She would have to kill the Thunder Beast alone.

If her brood was to hatch.

PART VII

Time and chance happeneth to them all . . .

—ECCLESIASTES 9:11

PART VII

T. Randall Jeffers stared at the territorial council. There were six members in all. They met monthly in the old mayor's office and sat around the large oak conference table.

"Can we call the meeting to order now?" Jeffers asked.

A tall, angular man with a hawk nose and a hawk's hard eyes, his tone was coldly condescending. Even his clothes conveyed conceit. Unlike most of New Arizona, which wore cotton homespun—council members included—Jeffers favored pre-Holocaust sportswear of gaudy polyester.

"Kate, you okay now?" he asked.

She nodded tersely, but the wadded handkerchief, clenched in her right fist, was spotted with red sputum. Intermittent silicosis—resulting from post-Holocaust smoke inhalation—was a common survivor affliction.

"Then let's get this straight," Jeffers said. "You've got your grandson's New Alaskan dispatches. He says this Tamerlane erects towers of human skulls and presses the few survivors into slavery."

"You left out his supernatural consort, the Lady Legion," Deputy Mayor Horace Sims said. Sims was a short man with owlish glasses and a sly, derisive smile.

"We're talking about hard facts," Katherine said angrily.

"And I don't like your tone," Tom Whirly added, staring at both Jeffers and Sims. Whirly was the local blacksmith and steel puddler. He was a tall rawboned man with big hands and broad shoulders.

"Fine," Jeffers said. "You don't like my tone, fine. It doesn't matter to me what has descended on New Alaska—whether they're the Turkistani Hordes or the heavenly choir. We have time to prepare. Decades. Eons."

"Genghis Khan sacked Asia in under two years," Katherine said. "Darrell claims this Tamerlane did it in less than eighteen months."

Jeffers groaned.

"You may not believe it," said Katherine, "but there's a disciplined army out there, headed for our city gates. And they aren't going to knock politely. One day, they'll kick them in."

"Kate," Jeffers asked, "what *is* your grandson doing up there anyway? Refresh me. I seem to have forgotten."

"Exploring. Gathering intelligence," Katherine said. "For three years Darrell has supplied most of our authoritative information about the continent."

"And now he says we're in grave danger?"

"He does."

"And you believe that *if* Tamerlane gets past New Salt—one very big *if*—he will attack us. We live in the middle of a vast impassable wilderness, Kate. How do you suppose he will cross the Great Sonoran Desert?"

"His officers are *bedouins,* desert fighters. The Sonoran will be nothing to them."

"I still don't see the problem," Jeffers said. "If it

comes to that, I'll handle it myself. I'll negotiate a treaty with him. I'm running for governor of New Arizona, you know. My offer to negotiate could serve as the first plank in my platform."

"You're gonna kill most of your constituency."

"Not at all. I see myself as a stalking-horse for world peace."

"Try Judas goat."

"Try sensible diplomacy."

The old woman furrowed her forehead and sniffed the air. "Is someone burning a tire in here?"

"Your plan to challenge them will only bring back war and pestilence, destruction and death," Sims said.

"They've never left."

Suddenly, it hit her. Her face buried in a linen kerchief, she was coughing convulsively, spotting her handkerchief with clots of blood.

Whirly was up in an instant, his arms around her.

"Okay, okay," the blacksmith said, "it's her silicosis again. Meeting over."

Jeffers and Sims headed for the door.

"She enjoys tilting against windmills," Deputy Mayor Sims observed.

"She is a windmill," Jeffers said.

 **2**

It had been a long summer in the Chiricahua Mountains for Matthew Magruder and his sister, Liz. They and their father, Richard Sheckly, had stayed with a tribe of Apaches. He had insisted that they help with the corn harvest.

The work had been arduous. Matt's sixteen-year-old frame had acquired two more inches in height, another eighteen pounds, and he'd added width to his shoulders. A big kid, he was just a hair under six feet, and with the extra weight was unusually brawny for his age.

It had been a marvelous summer for the both of them—months of wonder and revelation. Faces darkly tanned, eyes smilingly blue, hair bleached yellow as ripe wheat, they were the picture of health.

As they walked up to the council chambers, they saw the door open, and Whirly leading their grandmother out. Following her were the other council members, including Jeffers, whom the kids despised.

Ever since he had arrived at the Citadel six years ago, he'd made their grandmother's existence a special sort of hell.

Then they saw the blood on her handkerchief.

Racing up to her, Matt led the frail old woman toward the infirmary down the hall.

Behind them, Jeffers and Sims were still running their mouths.

"Her arteries must be hard as old bones," Sims sneered.

"Old dinosaur bones," Jeffers said.

"What are you going to do with her?"

"I'm going to paper-train the old biddy. I'm breaking that horse to my saddle, and it won't make for a very edifying tale."

"I can't believe someone hasn't thrown dirt on her yet."

Matt's back was to Jeffers, and his right arm was around his grandmother. For a second he paused, making sure that his sister had her. After that, he knew he was turning, and he remembered to brace his feet and close his fist as tightly as he could—the way his father had taught him—but that was all. The rest was pure instinct. He swung at Jeffers off the pivot, without even seeing him, simply aiming at the voice.

His shoulder stung as teeth shattered against his knuckles.

Then he was over the supine man, his hands around his throat, slamming his head on the floor. His voice was tinny in his ears, as if someone else were talking.

"Speak against her again, one more time, and I'll kill you. I swear before God, I'll kill you."

By this time, Jeffers was bleeding from the nose and ears, as well as the mouth, and it was clear that the boy *was* intent on killing him.

It was only after the blacksmith broke a chair over Matthew's head that he relaxed his grip and they were able to pull him off.

PART VIII

We are done with hope and honor
We are lost to love and truth
We are dropping down the ladder
Rung by rung.

For the measure of our torment
Is the measure of our youth
God help us for we learned the worst
Too young.

—RUDYARD KIPLING,
GENTLEMAN RANKERS

Everywhere the Colonel advanced thousands of men lay spread-eagled in the open or cowered in craters. The corpses were often the lucky ones. The wounded groaned and bawled, tearing at the mud.

The fire was so intense that his own men advanced with their faces averted and their arms raised before them as if walking into a storm.

By the time they reached the enemy wire, half his men were dead, the rest had the eyes of idiots.

In fact, the survivors were now pinned facedown in shell holes. All around him, echoing high above the crash of the guns, reverberated the same inevitable refrain:

"Stretcher-bearers! Stretcher-bearers!"

If there was ever a time for an officer to lead, this was it, the Colonel thought. Ordering his few trembling survivors to keep pace, the Colonel strode purposefully into the machine-gun fire.

Somehow he came out alive and, crossing a small, shell-pocked hollow, he mounted another hill. At the top he found the only other senior officer rash enough to take the field.

Instead of a flat steel trench helmet, the man wore a smashed-down cap. Rather than the olive-drab tunic he sported a red turtleneck sweater, a four-foot muffler, jodhpurs, and black thigh-high cavalry boots burnished to a mirror gloss. In his mouth a teak cigarette holder was rakishly cocked, and his gas mask was conspicuously absent. His only weapon was his riding crop.

He seemed oblivious to the bullets whining past.

He was Brigadier General Douglas MacArthur.

"A truly fine war we're having, sir," the Colonel offered by way of conversation. He tried to stand ramrod-straight, even though the bullets—screeching past his ears—screamed like hornets from hell.

"Indeed. A truly fine war," the General concurred.

But now General MacArthur seemed a little distracted, and the Colonel quickly saw the reason. Another creeping barrage was making its way upfield, forty leisurely yards at a time.

The artillery fire, which they had been struggling to ignore, blew away half the hill, and the seismic upheaval knocked the Colonel to his knees.

MacArthur kept his footing.

Regaining his feet, the Colonel was noticeably embarrassed.

"Don't worry, Colonel, the one that gets you you never see. Or hear."

And then the Colonel saw them, almost out of nowhere, just what he'd been searching for.

Two hundred yards straight ahead, three of his tanks mounted a ridge.

Their appearance seemed miraculous.

"Sir, do I have your permission to join my tanks and take out those machine gun emplacements due east?"

The General studied the Colonel absently. "Splendid idea, Colonel. But of course."

For the first time in months the Colonel felt his spirits rise, his confidence soar.

He headed back downhill to recruit some volunteers.

Standing atop the middle turret, the Colonel led his three tanks across no-man's-land. Two dozen soldiers slogged behind.

If the Colonel seemed overly confident, this time he had cause. He had designed the turreted tank cannon himself and had seen to it that they fired both delayed fuse shells and white phosphorus rounds. The latter detonated not only high-yield explosive but live phosphorus—which ignited on contact with the air and burned at terrifyingly high temperatures.

The spectacle of the Colonel atop his iron coffin— blowing up machine gun nests and spewing white-hot chemical death in all directions—quickly drove the first lines of defense into full retreat.

At first, his tanks seemed unstoppable—until they reached the fourth line of *Boche* earthworks, a long series of seemingly impassable trenches.

The Colonel quickly ordered his men to shovel earthwork bridges across the sandbagged ditches, but before they could begin, the *Boche* regrouped. Opening fire, they blasted the first topside diggers into bloody eternity.

Those who'd only been partway out of the trench dived back in.

The Colonel remained on top of his tank turret. He shouted insults at the *Boche,* then, turning to his own men, he ordered:

"Get back up here and dig this damn bridge."

His men simply crouched deeper in their trench, so he jumped down and grabbed a shovel. He began throwing up the earthwork bridge himself.

Still they cowered in the trench, refusing to help.

The Colonel saw the young Alabaman from his outfit, the one who had kissed his crucifix, crossed himself, and prayed his "Hail Marys" before going over the top.

One of his own men.

Pointing at the boy, he shouted: "You, soldier, you're one of my men. You are *definitely* getting up here."

"Respectfully, sir," the boy shouted back, "it's too damn dangerous up there."

The rest of the troops stared at the Colonel, apprehensive.

His response was instantaneous. Dipping his knee, he swung his trench shovel with both hands, straight over his shoulder like an ax. He laid the edge on top of the soldier's head like splitting kindling. The flat, dented helmet exploded off the man's head at a skewed angle, the chin strap tearing free, the shovel's haft shattering in his hands.

The doughboy slumped to the bottom of the trench, out cold.

The Colonel threw the splintered spade into the ditch and took out his .45. "The next man who refuses to come topside, I'll shoot for cowardice."

That did it, and they finished the bridge. When his tanks crossed the line of trenches, his spirits, once more, soared. He was back on top of his turret with a legion of troops in tow. His tanks flattened the *Boche* barbwire like grass under foot, overwhelming the machine gunners.

Until they hit the last trailing trench lines of the dug-in *Boche* and faced the main body of the Front itself.

His tanks abruptly stopped. Even his own tank driver refused to advance, shouting:

"We're just three tanks, sir."

The Colonel leaped off the tank. With his sergeant in tow, he ordered the rest of the men—crouched behind their tanks or facedown in the nearby shell craters—to fix bayonets and charge. They crouched lower behind their tanks, buried their faces deeper into their shell craters—and refused.

It was then he had the vision.

Up in the clouds, he saw the faces of his forbears in full military regalia.

"Come," they said, beckoning to him. "Come, my boy. It is time to join your blood. It is time to face the fiercest of them all. Tamerlane the Great— the Scourge of Allah, the Sword-Arm of Islam."

His orderly at his heels, he unholstered his .45 and charged directly into the intersecting machine gun fire, less than fifty yards away.

Now less than forty-five yards.

Forty yards.

Thirty-five.

Then twenty-five.

Finally, he was close enough to the *Boche* emplacements—whose hammering guns quickly vectored in on him—that he could stare into their jumping, smoking muzzles. He could watch the ammo belts flapping through the blazing breeches. He could see their ivory knuckles and pointed helmets and the frightened faces of the gunners.

He got off a snap shot with his .45—which took out a boy feeding cartridge belts into the nearest Maxim—and at fifteen yards, a truly spectacular hip shot took out the Maxim gunner to his left.

But now his weapon was empty. Diving into a crater less than ten yards from the Line, he rammed home a fresh clip and pulled back the slide. He leaped howling out of the shell hole and assaulted the lone gunner backing the Maxim to his right. His own lips were drawn back against his teeth in the same simulacrum of a grin crooking the mouths of the men he was trying to kill.

The bullets hit him like sledgehammers. One blew out half his side, another took him through the hip, exiting through his rectum.

He made it to a nearby shell crater, where Angelo struggled to plug his hemorrhaging wounds.

When his tanks renewed their assault and drew the enemy fire, Angelo hauled him out of range.

3

Still the Colonel would not go straight to the hospital. Bleeding profusely, he ordered the bearers to take him to the Com-Trench telephone.

Where he found the General.

From his stretcher he gave him his report.

"We can do it, sir. With just three tanks we played holy hell with the *Boche* emplacements. Sir, with a thousand tanks, with surprise, firepower, and mobility, with ten thousand troops backing me up, I could end this war in a month. In a week."

By then he was delirious. "And I'll still take that Kraut Kaiser on afterward—head to head, Colt to Colt. Just him and me. End all the slaughter with just us two. I owe it to the men, sir. If I'd been a better officer, they wouldn't have died."

He started to cry at the thought of his dead troops, but suddenly, light-headed, he warbled hoarsely:

> *War, he sang, is toil and trouble;*
> *Honor but an empty bubble;*
> *Never ending, still beginning,*
> *Fighting still, and still destroying.*

"You know, General," he rambled, "war is hell, it's bloody awful hell, but God help me, I do love it so."

A doctor was now in the Com-Trench, scissoring the Colonel's blood-soaked uniform and removing it from his body.

Still the Colonel raved:

"Tanks . . . End the war in a week . . . Too much dying . . . Didn't have to . . . End the war in a *night* . . . Tanks . . ."

Staring at the astonishing array of scars disfiguring the man's body—old bullet wounds, long, slashing bayonet scars, burns, and barbwire welts—the doctor was amazed.

"He used to claim he was the eternal soldier. He said he fought in all times past and would fight again in all wars future."

Again, the Colonel moaned: "No, please, no. Not his eyes. Not his eyes."

The doctor found a vein and injected the morphine.

"Pershing called him the classic fighter, Time's own warrior," the General said. "He said he was the finest fighting man he'd ever met. I guess I never understood that. Not till now."

"Only now his fight's coming to an end," said the doctor.

The General was furious. He bent over the Colonel till they were face-to-face and shouted:

"You're not going to die on me. You hear me, Colonel? That's an order. You're not going to die."

The doctor tried to stop him but the General pushed him aside.

"This time, this one time, you're obeying an order. You get me? You aren't dying. You do, and I'll bust you down to buck private. I'll ship your sorry hide home on the next thing displacing water. You get me?"

"The war . . . In two weeks . . . Over . . . With tanks . . ." Then: "His face . . . I saw his eyes."

"Whose face?" the General asked. "Whose eyes?"

"The Scourage of Allah . . . The Sword-Arm of Islam . . ."

The morphine took hold. The light dimmed in the Colonel's eyes, and now the General was crying, something Sergeant Angelo did not think him capable of.

"You aren't dying on me," the General shouted. "That's an order. You hear me, Georgie?"

The Colonel's breath rasped, rattled, ceased. His heart stopped, and his body settled convulsively.

Shouldering the General aside, the doctor bent over the dying man. He hammered his chest with a closed fist. Then, placing both hands on the Colonel's sternum, he rocked back and forth, back and forth.

Hovering over them, the General still shouted: "You aren't dying, soldier! You aren't! That's an order!"

With the seventh pump, breath hissed again in the Colonel's lungs. His heart was back on. Light returned to his eyes. Still the General roared:

"You aren't dying. You hear me, Georgie Patton? You aren't dying. That's a *goddamned* order!"

PART IX

Dark, Dark, my heart, darker than desire.

—LEGION

PART IX

That night Tamerlane and
…e on their cushions. Turning to her,

…e dreams."
…truck her—the urgent stirring, the
…in, horses snorted and dogs yapped
…ed. The camp continued its wild
…noticed.

…Scourge, sire," she said. "Master
…wns."
…warnings on the wind."
…s of a city being sacked."

…s are a tiger's smile, a harlot's
…lack wings of death."
…ry?"

…victory."
…more lurid, more intense.
…*h,* you have witched me, for I
…wear that, if we fail, I will have
…ou Cuddled."

"My Lord, we did not rise out of the red desert and the sweep of the steppe, cross the taiga, the tundra, and the arctic seas to be stopped by city dwellers."

She prayed all would go as before—the way it had that hideous night in Constantinople twenty years before.

The Cuddler's captive, once more, filled the night with hellish howls.

"There go those screams again. What on earth is the Cuddler doing?" she asked.

He shrugged. "You can smell the hair and the hide. He's using fire."

"He has used fire on men before without such screams."

"Do you wish to know *all* his ways?"

"Sire, we know the penalty for learning his ways. He who gazes on the Cuddler's art must take his turn in the tent. Even I, the Lady Legion, am not exempt."

He allowed her an amused smile. "If you must know, he has a new kind of oil vat. He can now raise the temperature of his victims with infinitesimal precision."

Again, the man's screams ripped through the night.

Tamerlane rose irritably and tied his tent flap shut.

"If our Cuddler applied the heat faster," Legion suggested, "the hide would come off in one piece."

"He would not have as much fun."

"But he would have a nice hide."

Tamerlane nodded wearily. "The howls do grow wearisome."

She heard the snorting horses, the baying dogs, and saw the tassels tremble.

Her macabre master, Beelzebub, was making his presence known.

"My Lord, what would you give to have my father, Beelzebub, at your side tomorrow?"

"Lady, I believe you are shaman, tomorrow-teller, royal consort, and wise councilor. But I do not believe you are lamia or goddess, demon-woman or *houri* from hell."

"But if he appeared—with his fiery face, blazing horns that dripped balefire, his giant *roc*'s wings and bloodred eyes hideous from hate and rage—"

"I would welcome him—if he could crush the walls, guns, mines, and coiled razor wire. If your father would join us, then I would follow him, follow *you*, for all time to come."

"I do not wish you in my service, sire. You are Allah's Scourge, Master of Thrones and Crowns. I only wish your trust."

"You once said that to trust was good, *not* to trust was better."

"I also said, 'Preserve thy hate, thy heart.' Perhaps you fear the bloodshed at dawn? The slaughter to come?"

"Slaughter is naught but the violence of creation. Men die that we might live."

"You see no death in killing?"

"Only life. Our life."

"I sometimes fear we move toward hell," she said, suddenly solemn.

"There is no hell."

"Aye, my Lord. It exists, truly. In your cold heart."

"How does it go? Our 'Hymn to Death'?" he asked. "'My nights are ice, my days are fire'?" He struggled for the right words.

She gave him the correct text:

> *The dead self sings, the dead souls dance.*
> *Oh, days of ice and nights on fire.*
> *The dross of death is seared away,*
> *Dark, dark, my heart, darker than desire.*

He nodded appreciatively.

"My Lord, once you said because I loved the burning ground, you had made a burning ground of your heart, so that I might dance." She gazed at the cushions.

"Yes, but you have already danced once, and we greet the troops at dawn. The time for dancing has passed."

"Is not your will eternal?"

He sighed with elaborate weariness. "Then come to me, my Sister-in-Darkness. Let the walls wait."

"And the dancer become the dance?"

"Aye, enter the burning ground."

With voluptuous grace, she stretched across the *daiwan* cushions—toward him.

Slowly, he turned to her.

PART X

How can a man die better
Than facing fearful odds
For the ashes of his fathers
And the temples of his gods?

—THOMAS BABINGTON MACAULAY

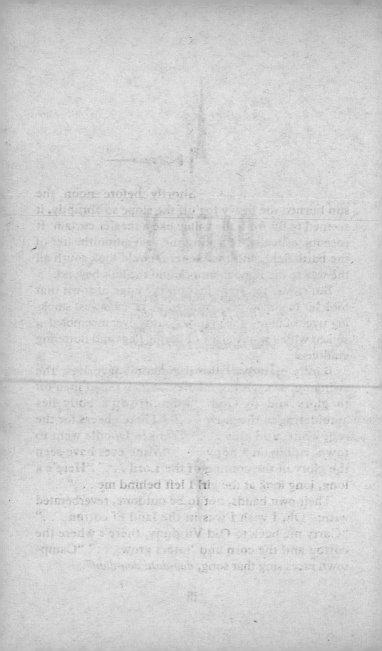

Shortly before noon the sun burned the heavy fog off the slope so abruptly, it seemed to lift from the valley like a theater curtain. It rose majestically, revealing the vast amphitheater of the battlefield, and the General could look south all the way to the Rappahannock and the hills beyond.

But it was the sight just on the edge of town that took his breath away. Gathered there was a vast smoking river of blue—the grandest army ever assembled—spiked with a gaudy array of flaring flags and fluttering guidons.

Bands blared all the regimental favorites, the swinging, swaggering medleys which piped men off to glory and to God: "John Brown's body lies amoldering in the grave . . ." "Three cheers for the red, white, and blue . . ." "Yankee Doodle went to town, riding on a pony . . ." "Mine eyes have seen the glory of the coming of the Lord . . ." "Here's a long, long look at the girl I left behind me . . ."

Their own bands, not to be outdone, reverberated with: "Oh, I wish I was in the land of cotton . . ." "Carry me back to Old Virginny, there's where the cotton and the corn and 'taters grow . . ." "Camptown races sing that song, *doo-dah! doo-dah!*"

There, down in the valley for one shining moment, the General could see it all—all the pomp, pageantry, and wonder of war, war in the grand chivalric style, war in full regalia, terrible as Satan's own wrath, magnificent as God. He saw blue-clad soldiers falling into eights and lined up for miles, all the way to the Rappahannock, flank to flank, slashed guidons and flamboyant flags flapping in the breeze. He saw officers with bared sabers, 120,000 rifle barrels glinting like wildfire in the noonday sun, men marching elbow to elbow, in lockstep, as if on dress parade.

The General glanced back at his own men, most of whom were starving, lousy, barefoot, and frostbit. He ordered his own bugler to blow "Assembly."

Men lined up in their camouflaged gun pits. They quickly gathered around the concealed artillery, which was massed on the knoll of Hamilton's Crossing.

The General had spent long hours studying the trajectories, and as the sun burned away the last few streaks of mist, he gave the coiling blue army below one last look. Then he ordered his bugler to blow "Ready, Arms!" and his artillerists—pulling at trail spikes and cranking up the elevating screws—took aim. At his signal they opened fire.

With his commanding elevation and heavy guns, the General was able to rake the hillside and canal bridges at will. When his rifled Blakelys and twelve-pounder Napoleons converged on the marching Federals, it was as if the bluebellies had route-stepped into a trip wire.

Once the smoke cleared, the entire field of men was writhing in agony on the ground.

Almost immediately the Federal gunners sighted in on the smoke rising above the General's artillery and answered in kind.

The first canister came straight for the General.

He could hear the whine, see the murderous shrapnel sparking and dancing in the air. The shell ripped through the tree overhead—shredding the limbs, showering him with broken branches and debris, then detonating the rocky cliff face behind him. He was splattered with acrid black-powder smoke and a torrent of rock fragments.

Between Confederate volleys a regiment of Federals broke to their right, straight into his flank. The wind changed and a pall of milky gunsmoke enveloped them.

The General saw only smoke, but he could hear the crack of bullets tearing into a nearby tree, the frantic banging of his men's ramrods in their upturned barrels, and the high, thin, unearthly wail of his men in their pits and at their gunnery mounts—the *YIP-YIP-YIP-YAAA-EEEP!* of the Rebel yell—the sweetest sound to his ears on all of God's green earth.

Blinded by the smoke, he nonetheless heard the screams and the gunfire of a thousand charging Federals, now less than 150 yards from his frontline rifle pits.

Just as he ordered his bugler to sound the call to "Fix Bayonets!" the smoke miraculously cleared, and his men opened fire.

He did not see the rest because another Federal barrage arced in on him. It struck with a hellish rumbling as if the earth itself had shuddered, opened, and threatened to swallow him whole.

The General blacked out. When he came to on his knees, he saw that his men had repulsed the Federal assault but not much more.

Then a second bombardment struck, slightly to his

rear, a third fell out of range, a fourth to his left, a fifth exploded high overhead, and the sixth—a nearby ground burst—detonated with enough force to drive him once again to the ground.

God knows he had been under fire before—the Valley Campaign, the Seven Days, the Second Manassas, and Cedar Tavern, to say nothing of Sharpsburg.

But he had never seen anything like *this*.

The whole world was blowing up, leaving him shattered and wasted, windblown and devoid of both hearing and sight. All he could feel was the grass and mud in his mouth, his hands clawing at the blasted dirt, the air around him burning like the scorching breath of hell—and the concussive impact of the shells reverberating in his ears with an unending, head-cracking roar.

Again, he pulled himself to his feet. He stared at the field, astonished. Over four thousand bluebellies lay spread-eagled on the slope, dead or dying, inert or howling. Around him, instead of trees and boulders, there were only the shattered wrecks of splintered tree trunks, their charred broken limbs blazing on the ground, the massive boulders behind him cleaved like split smoking apples or smashed to gravel or pulverized to fire-shrouded dust while his men slowly emerged from their firing pits, shaking their heads in stunned disbelief.

But still they had an answer. One of his gunners pulled the trail spike, spun the elevation wheel, and arced a shell straight onto the big battery that was doing the damage. It hit with a deafening "KA-WHUMP! WHUMP! WHUMPPP!" Inky smoke writhed high above the blasted remains of the battery and powder store. Then, suddenly, a brilliant red-orange fireball rose up out of the pitchy murk, sucking earth and metal into its cyclonic maw. Slowly—ever so slowly—the detonating debris tumbled back to the earth, as the fire below shot high above the battleground, its tongues of yellow flame licking the sky.

The smoke was so dense that the General could hardly make out his men. They drifted through the haze like ghosts. Their faces floated eerily. Their voices were dim and remote in his ears.

A blue-clad Federal missing a hand was trying to bandage a comrade who had lost his eyes to a blast of grapeshot. Farther down the line, through a sudden break in the smoke, the General saw one of his own officers shoot a two-legged mule which had just lost both hindquarters to the Federal shells. A soldier in a nearby gun pit was heaved out of the trench by his comrades, his head blown off.

Everywhere it was the same: bloody horses, bloody guns, bloody men. And the sounds of the shells overhead—the high keening, the thunderous roars, the whispering hisses, and the ear-cracking blasts.

His head was ringing and spinning, his ancient gray tunic smeared with soot and mud and blood. Looking out over the killing ground, he could now see a cloud of dense white smoke rising above the Federal batteries, slowly floating out over the sloping field, strewn with the Yankee dead.

Somewhere in the Union camp their band struck up another majestic march. Drums thumped, brass blared, woodwinds crooned; and another stirring fanfare piped the Federals off to war. A huge blue stream of soldiers strutted up the hill, eight abreast, ready to divide into fours at the two canal bridges, ready to storm Longstreet's stone wall and his own entrenched hills.

But this time the Federals' frontline batteries were reduced to twisted, smoldering metal—silent and torn, wreathed in coils of rising smoke, forever dead.

The General could only stare at them in disbelief. Burnside, he'd thought, was idiotic to attempt *any* assault against this position. But without frontline artillery support?

Yet there they were—flank to flank, garish flags and guidons flapping in the breeze, band music like rolling thunder, officers' sabers blazing in the sun, thousands of rifle barrels gleaming, elbow to elbow, as if to pass in review. In a lockstep toward death.

It was then the General knew Burnside was insane.

Their band struck up, "Yankee Doodle went to town, riding on a pony, stuck a feather in his cap and called it macaroni. . . ."

And his own men pulled at their trail spikes and spun their elevation wheels.

Then slowly, methodically, they sighted in their guns.

◀ **2**

Dusk at Fredricksburg.

The General stared out over the battlefield, strewn with nearly twenty thousand Federal dead— and not a Confederate among them.

The bloodred ball of the sun hung suspended over the westerly hills throwing off streaks of yellow and burnt orange and red-gold, giving a strange amber cast to the unending pall of dust and smoke, mingling with the inevitable fog drifting in from the Rappahannock.

His freezing barefoot men were waiting for nightfall before collecting their much-needed boots and blankets. They waited in the frigid dusk, staring impassively at the bloody field, the eternally wheeling vultures which, lacking their own chivalric finesse and military decorum, rode in on the slowly sinking thermals, floating lazily, dreamily, on massive six-foot wingspans in descending spirals.

There was an awesome power to it all that was not lost on the General. The black swirling gyre of carrion birds—the crimson sun blazing above the rimrock, casting a glow over the bloody ground, its gradual decline bringing forth the first stars of the night—the eerie deathscape, with its rising pillars of smoke, slanting high above the scores of shattered caissons—the dead dismembered horses, fallen by the hundreds, bathed garishly in their own blood, eyes walled with fright—thousands upon thousands of Federals strewn across the field and fragments of soldiers, heads, arms, legs, and torsos, exploded across the hillside—the great clouds of creamy smoke blowing back and forth—the echoing swell of groans, a last ghastly chorus of the maimed, the shattered, and the soon-to-be-dead.

Staring out across that battlefield, the General felt a cold black wind blow through him, winnowing what was left of his heart, savaging his soul, and leaving in its wake a blasted void, empty as the prayers which he now trembled to make, stark and terrible as the God in Whom he now feared to believe.

It was time, he knew that now.
Time to speak his piece.
To Robert E. Lee.

◄ 3

The General stood outside
Lee's tent in silence. It was hard, under the best of circumstances, to gauge the depth of his feeling for his
commanding officer. Respect, affection, unshakable
loyalty, those feelings were always present. But now
there was something else. Something that went
beyond devotion, even beyond awe. Something he
dared not name.

For the first time in their relationship, the General
was afraid.

Perhaps the General had cause, for Lee was a man
like no other. Physically, he was unimpressive. Fifty-
six years old, of middle height, he had a ruddy com-
plexion, a white beard, and dark eyes. He wore only
an old gray coat and a gray felt hat, without insignia.

He was also dying of heart disease.

Yet in matters of faith and spirit, Lee was still
indomitable. His devotion to God was absolute. His
unblinking calm in the midst of chaos unwavering, his
love for Old Virginia—his mystic affinity for her
sacred soil—inviolable. All these things bound him to
the General with hoops of steel.

The foremost military leader of his age, Lee had
been offered the command of both armies. Out of
determination to defend Virginia, he had opted for

the Confederacy, but not without misgivings. For, like the General, he knew he had committed an unpardonable sin.

He had broken the vow.

Furthermore—like the General—Lee had little in common with other men. Neither of them smoked, drank, gambled, or caroused. Neither read novels or attended plays, which they deemed frivolous. Both were opposed to slavery.

But if Robert E. Lee was the greatest military leader of his time, the General was the finest field commander. Lee invariably referred to him as his right arm. Together, they had brought the Union army to its knees.

For if the General knew how to kill, Lee knew how to lead, and it was now clear that the Confederate army would follow him forever, under any and all conditions.

It was equally clear they worshiped him. Once, when the Army of Virginia was rounding a tent where Lee slept on bivouac, an entire corps passed on tiptoe, so as not to wake him.

And his Federal foe regarded him with almost supernatural awe.

The General entered Lee's tent.

The white-bearded old gentleman was bent over his map table.

"Tom," he said, looking up, "I'm glad you're here. I was meaning to come by your tent. I felt I owed you some explanation."

"Sir—"

Lee waved his words aside. "I know. Toward dusk, when the Federals were taking the field, you wanted to attack. But they were out there to carry off the hurt and dying. We can't be animals, Tom. Someday this war is going to end, and we'll have to make peace. We have enough enemies as it is."

"We should have swept the field with bayonets. We should have flung them into the river. The enemy, sir, will be pulling out tonight, getting away scot-free. We should have ended it *now*."

"We did end it. For nearly twenty thousand of them."

"But we left one hundred thousand in reserve. And millions more are still waiting up north. You know that."

"I'm not talking about their soldiers, Tom, but about their hurt and dying. They needed to tend to them. We were right to let them."

"You won't win many wars that way."

Lee's round dark eyes were black as onyx.

"It's the Seven Days, isn't it?" the old man said.

Lee had fathomed his secret, ferreted it out before he could even bring it up.

"You froze, Tom," Lee went on. "Perhaps for the first time in your life. You were supposed to attack, but instead you sat under a tree, refused to give orders to ford the river and strike the enemy's flank. They said you wouldn't listen to anyone, you would not speak, you gave no coherent response at all. And you still won't speak of it."

"I was wrong. You should have court-martialed me. I failed to execute orders. I failed catastrophically."

Lee shook his head. "Court-martial you? My right arm? You can't be serious. All I want to know is what you were doing."

The General shrugged, then his face paled. The corner of his mouth trembled, and he looked away.

"I saw strange things, sir, nightmarish things. Men with long flowing hair, in bloodstained robes, with compound bows strung across their backs. Severed heads and the flayed skins of their enemies hung from their saddles. They came by the tens of thousands, across a windswept plain. They raped women, enslaved men, put people to the sword by the millions, and made mountains of the bloody skulls."

"It's been a hard war, Tom—hard on us all. Especially you."

"This was different, sir, and worse, much worse. And it was in *this* country. In another time, another place, perhaps, but it was done to our land, our people."

"Tom, I have to tell you, Dick Ewell thinks you are insane."

"Only because I court-martialed him."

"But these visions of yours, in the midst of a battle, are hardly reassuring."

"I saw what I saw, and it is still going on. Somewhere, sometime. And I know it awaits me."

There. He said it. He let it out. Finally.

"Think on Christ Jesus. He is your Hope, your Truth, your Light."

"I am no longer sure." Lee was aghast, but the General pushed on. "I also see a world in which He brings neither Hope nor Light. A world which exists in shadows and in death."

"What will you do?"

"I will save that world. For if Christ Jesus cannot help that world, I will."

"How?"

"I am going to that place. God would not have vouchsafed me that vision if he did not want me to go."

"You must put those thoughts behind you, Tom. You have troops here to lead. At dawn."

"Yes, sir." He rose, saluted, and turned toward the flap.

But Lee stopped him. "Think on God, man, think on your soul."

"I no longer fathom this talk of God and of souls."

"Or eternity's abyss?"

"Eternity is *now*."

"And what of death?"

"I've seen the flesh forsake the bone, stone itself struck low with pain. I've felt a weight of wrath that St. Sebastian, plied with bloody darts, might manage to endure but not mere men, not me. I've known the silence and the terror and the dark, and I've been afraid. But death I do not fear."

"You've known war."

"The anvil on which all hammers break."

Lee crossed the tent. He was not a demonstrative man, but he put an arm over the General's shoulders. His dark eyes were solemn.

"You believe me?" the General asked.

"Yes, I do," Lee said. "You will be leaving us soon. I see that now. You have been my eyes, my ears, my right arm." Lee touched his chest. "My second heart. And now I shall be alone."

He and the General left his tent. Beyond the Federal camp, beyond the Rappahannock, the horizon filled with fire. Not lightning but *aurora borealis,* the northern lights, an arctic spectacle unprecedented in southern climes. The lights blazed across the horizon's rim in flaring bars—in blues and yellows, in reds and golds.

"A rainbow from heaven?" Lee asked. "A sign of God's grace?"

"Or a portent from hell," the General said. "I really don't know."

"But you're going to find out. I believe that, Tom."

The General saluted again, then swung onto his horse and headed toward his camp, eyes fixed before him.

Not looking back.

4

It was near dawn before he returned to the high hill called Hamilton's Crossing. His men were awake, decked out in their bloody spoils. When they saw him enter their camp, one of the color sergeants raised a hue and cry.

It was affectionate badinage, which in other times might have amused him.

"How many bluebellies you et for breakfast, General?"

A hoarse cacophony ensued, filled with cries of greeting and ribald halloos. One soldier yelled:

"Nice clothes you got there, General. How 'bout some new shoes?"

He held up a pair of bloody Union boots.

Then came the endless inevitable choruses of his nickname—the one given him by the Richmond papers after Manassas Junction, where, the papers said, he had "stood like a stone wall" against overwhelming odds and had single-handedly rallied the entire Confederate army.

"STONEWALL!" his men screamed and cheered. "STONEWALL! STONEWALL! STONEWALL!"

Glancing around the camp, the General briefly studied the elaborately entrenched earthworks. *Too bad,* he thought absently. He had wanted to get a few more workdays out of those firing pits.

"Orderly!" he called to his first sergeant as he swung down from his horse. "We're striking camp."

"Yes, sir!" the orderly shouted.

General Thomas "Stonewall" Jackson wearily returned the salute, then entered his tent.

It was time to gather up his gear.

PART XI

She was, as ever, the wise old cow—old because she was wise.

Quetzacoatlus was enraged.

Perching on the edge of his cliff face—some eight thousand feet above the desert floor—he glared hatefully at his roost.

The wings of his mate spanned the full forty-foot diameter of the spacious nest. She lay motionless upon the interwoven branches and leaves—dead.

Slowly, painstakingly, he dragged her to the cliff face—tearing half the nest apart in the process—and pushed her over the edge.

He watched her tumble eight thousand feet into the gorge.

But even harder on him was the sight of the two dead hatchlings. They would have been strong males, and now they were finished—nothing but dead, diseased meat.

He plucked them out of the nest's soft core and flung them into the void.

Which left him only the female child. She, too, had taken ill. Now, like her mother and brothers before her, she was vomiting up her carrion—and her fever soared. If he did not do something soon, she would die.

Only the flesh of the Triceratops's hatchlings could

save this nestling. The old cow's eggs were everything to him now. He had to have them. There was nothing he would not do to get them.

He *would* get them.

━━━━◀ **2**

In the bend of the canyon—turning to face his enemy—the big Brontosaur flailed his massive tail, whipping it at his foe with the force of a falling tree.

Still the big Triceratops was undismayed. Stopping her charge, she suddenly hopped over the ground-sweeping tail, executed a right-angle turn, then vaulted it again as it swung back. The massive tail crashed into the canyon wall on its return trip, causing the Brontosaur to reel sideways.

The Triceratops resumed her charge. She hit the left front leg high, impaling it with all three horns, driving it forward.

His leg broken, the beast began to fall. However, nothing that huge topples all at once. For a long moment the Brontosaur seemed suspended in time, taking all eternity to go down. Then the broken leg—which the Triceratops was now driving out of the shoulder socket—exploded. The beast's death roar rumbled up the canyon.

Swinging hard to her left, the Triceratops ripped two horns loose, broke off the third, then jumped free. Backpedaling hard, the tottering Brontosaur loomed above her, then dropped.

The beast's fall slammed the Triceratops sideways.

Dusk.

Four Triceratops had dropped from exhaustion during the charge up the gorge. Six more had been killed dividing up the Brontosaur's remains—far and away the most dangerous part of the hunt.

Though herbivores, Triceratops would eat meat, when starving. At such times herd life turned truly hazardous.

Even their leader had killed an otherwise friendly cow over her half of the Brontosaur's liver.

Night.

Two dozen Triceratops belched and slumbered beside their watering holes.

Only their leader was still up, waiting for first light.

When a thirsty desert dweller slunk close to her, hoping for a drink at her hole, she drove him off with a low-throated growl.

But finally she too slept.

At sunrise she and the herd would be on their way.

Dawn in the canyonlands.

When the last Triceratops moved on up the gorge, Quetzacoatlus targeted the Brontosaur's rotting remains. Folding his forty-foot wingspread, he went into a spinning dive, the wind keening through his pinions.

Sixty feet from the gutted carcass, he opened his wings to their full span and braked.

After gorging himself, the Dragon glared up the canyon.

Only the tender flesh of freshly hatched eggs could save his sole surviving hatchling. All other morsels had been vomited up.

Quetzacoatlus had to have those eggs.

6

When the herd reached the delta and cleared the last rise, the experience was exhilarating. Here was Late Cretaceous in all its glory. The sun flared bloodred over the sluggish muddy river, and great conifers soared. Their thick trunks and leaves glowed with crimson radiance in the humid, pollen-heavy air, every branch bathed in coppery light.

The herd blew long rolling snorts and hurried its descent down the steep mountain switchbacks. Not only did their thirst drive them on, but around the edge of the distant stream grew palmlike cycads, their vast trunks aflame with flamboyant flowers. Down in the valley's heartland, the ground blazed with blossoms, and towering tree ferns sprouted huge sprays of jade green fronds.

Food in the valley as well as drink.

Of course, the herd paid no heed to the thousands of other dinosaurs. A Triceratops herd was never intimidated. Even in their presently diminished numbers, nothing threatened them.

Still their leader paused on the hillsides, ill at ease. Even when the last of the herd passed her by, heading rapidly down the switchbacks, she hesitated. She was, as ever, the wise old cow—old because she was wise.

While her fellow herd beasts thought solely of their bellies, she pondered the darkening sky overhead. Dense purplish clouds, veined by lightning, gathered over the river and thunder rumbled.

She lowered her gaze. She would make her stand here. The hilly soil was amenable to nest-building—mulch on top, alluvial sand underneath—and she was shockingly heavy with eggs, three dozen at least.

She would need a big nest now—thirty feet across, ten feet deep.

She did not have much time. Rain, which earlier that morning had started as a soft sprinkle and grown to a shower, was now a determined storm.

All at once, the black lowering clouds split wide open. Sheet lightning blazed, thunder rolled, and a subtropic hurricane exploded, bending conifers flat against the ground. The rain pounded her in layered sheets, lashing everything and everyone—the river, the forest, her friends below.

Turning her face to the deluge, the old cow bore the storm on her arching neck-frill and did the only thing left to do.

Weary but relentless, she dug her nest.

PART XII

Slaughter is naught but the violence of creation. Others die that we might live. There is no death in killing—only life. Our life.

—LEGION

Dawn in the *bok*.

She had delayed her Lord as long as possible, using every guile, but in the end it came down to the same thing: Tamerlane on his white Arabian mare, she on her black stallion, giving the men their orders.

This day he favored a white flowing robe and *kaffeiah*—not one of flimsy cotton but of flamboyant silks. He wore a necklace of tiny silver skulls. The cabalistic numerals 666 were tattooed on the knuckles of each hand. His robe open to the waist revealed a tattooed circle containing the startling likeness of a horned, bare-fanged Satan, or Shaitan.

His Lady Legion, in her role as war shaman, rode beside him. As he stopped before each of his polyglot armies, she trotted forward to address the troops. For, while he understood their languages, he did not speak them. That he left to his Lady.

He sat back on his alabaster war-horse, while Legion harangued the men. As often as he had observed her, he still found it stirring. Disdaining the *chador* veil, she wore a tight ebony blouse of finespun Shantung silk, with pearl buttons open to the navel. Her rattlesnakes buzzed, hissed, and coiled around

her waist and arms. Her tight black pants of thin
dinghri cotton were tucked into thigh-length riding
boots of rich jet leather, polished to a high gloss and
heeled with six-inch silver rowels, spotted with blood.

She was, to his woman-fearing Muslim warriors, the
incarnation of evil.

Even as the drums rolled and gongs pounded, as
the bells chimed and hellhorns blared, her words
echoed above the din. Speaking first to the Arabs of
their wondrous heaven, she thundered,

"In the Holy Koran, the Prophet promises to all
who die a holy death in battle that heaven shall be eternal ecstasy. Allah's Kingdom is filled with ease, with
figs and dates and wine flowing like golden honey."

Then she spoke of Allah's wrath and Beelzebub's
rage.

"And for those who scorn the Prophet's Call to
Arms, there is another fate. The fires of *gehenna* burn
for you eternal, and your stomachs shall be filled with
devil's fruit and scalding water. You shall meet my
Father-in-Darkness, Beelzebub, Lord of Hell."

At the end of her speech, she cracked the four-foot
double-plaited wrist quirt—already guttered with
gore. To the gasps of their gaping soldiers, she dug in
her rowels and galloped off toward the Indian *Ordu.*

She exhorted them on the horrors of hell and the
hideousness of Kali's fires and on the bloodiness of
their God of Destruction, Siva—both of whom were
now in service to Allah and the Everlasting Night. She
spoke of her father, Beelzebub, warning them of "his
smoking horns and fiery face, his blazing eyes and
horrendous roar, his terrible talons and *roc*'s wing."

"Beelzebub," she shouted "is coming here to scourge
heaven and earth. Worse than hell's own fury, worse

than the Fires of Kali and the tortures of *gehenna*, Beelzebub shall purge all who have not bent to his will."

Next, she addressed the Christian conscripts and to Tamerlane's surprise he heard his own words invoked.

"Slaughter is naught but the violence of creation. Others die that we might live."

Then in midspeech—as he lolled in the saddle, leaned back on his cantle—it happened.

The horses knew it first, and abruptly the men were fighting their reins, struggling to stay in their saddles. The horses reared back, crow-hopped, and arched their backs, while the herd in the remudas slipped their hobbles and stampeded through the *bok*.

But now the horsemen felt the rumbling, too, even as they sawed at their reins.

The earth was coming apart at the seams. The ground shook violently enough to drive most of the horses to their knees.

Atop the hill the quake subsided, then reappeared along the slope. The hillside slanting toward the New Anchorage redoubt buckled and shook all the way down the declivity.

In the valley, the earthquake was equally awesome. The village huts around the valley's perimeter disintegrated, and boulders cracked loose from the hilltop. The tree line was dislodged root and branch, and even from Tamerlane's vantage point—aboard his rearing war-horse—it was clear the disaster was escalating rapidly.

By the time the quake hit the city walls—almost simultaneously with the avalanche—the cataclysm had reached the major fault line. The front wall of the redoubt ripped apart with a thunderous KA-WHUMMPPP!-WHUMMPPP!-WHUMMPPP!

after which all the walls caved in—literally dissolving under the monstrous impact.

By the time the full force of the quake reached the epicentral fault, the city was convulsing. Explosions of black smoke and dust mushroomed over the alabaster walls, accompanied by the howls of animals—which had been brought inside the walls for the siege—climaxed by cries of the maimed, the trapped, and the dying.

Reining in his rearing mount, Tamerlane turned from the cataclysm, and there was Legion.

"What do you think of my father now, sire? Will you follow Beelzebub through all eternity? Will you scourge the earth in advance of his coming? In his name?"

He nodded, speechless.

"Here, my Lord." She handed him the wire cutters. "Wait by the wire for the tremors to cease. I shall meet you in the city afterward with our Scribe. I want him there to record your thoughts. In the meantime, you have a city to sack, men to kill, women to rape. If any have survived."

"Yours in the ranks of death," he said with surprising passion.

He wheeled his horse around, and the Lady Legion watched him lead an army of twenty thousand horse soldiers—his Horsemen from Hell—down the slope toward the wire and the black, smoking rubble that had once been New Anchorage.

◀━━━━ **2**

The Lady Legion uncoiled the rattlers from her body and slid them into their wicker basket. Swinging back onto her Arabian stallion, she paused to study the *bok*. At last, on the far side of the camp, she spotted her man. The Scribe—hands tied behind his back, mounted on a mule—was being led to her by two servants. As they rounded the hill, the servants pointed out the ruins of New Anchorage.

The Scribe looked unhappy.

His ill humor caused the Lady Legion to smile. *Yes, we shall have such pretty times together, you and I.*

He was so proud, so confident of his courage. She knew she could take that from him. The Cuddler could do it in one leisurely night, if she wished.

She did not wish his spirit crushed, but he had to learn the dangers of her rage.

For at those times, my pretty pet, I don't know what to do—whether to maim you, kill you, or eat you whole.

All that moronic rot about wanting a journey, wanting to discover the world and learn the ways of God and man. *Well, my pet,* she thought, *it now appears your dreams have come true. You've succeeded beyond your fondest hopes. You* are *on a journey—one reckoned not in time or miles or degrees of longitude but burned into the soul, a voyage calculated in innocence lost, in lives destroyed, in wisdom put to the sword.*

I am *the journey you so desperately long to make.*

Oh, we shall have such times, you and I. What was your name? Darrell, yes, Darrell Magruder. She trembled pleasantly at the sight of him.

Then her thoughts turned to Darrell's dispatches, his letters home—to his family and those whom he already loved.

Loved more than her.

She recalled hatefully how he revered his grandmother, an old bitch named Katherine Magruder, a white-haired crone with a bald eagle for a pet, no less.

You hold this hag so dear?

Fine, Legion thought, *but one day she will grovel at my feet and beg me to spare her life.*

Ah, Darrell Magruder, what a fine name. I shall teach you much. Oh, I shan't be easy on you. You shall know me in all my wrath and wonder. I shall reveal myself to you as I have done to no one. You shall be the empty vessel into which I pour my hate, my heart, my life.

Staring down at the smoldering ruins of New Anchorage, she noted the echoing screams, the towering flames, the rising pall of dust and smoke and felt a rush of shuddering hate: Hate for those who erected the walls. Hate for the dead and dying who now lay under them. Hate for all who blocked her path.

What woman had more? she mused. Or dreamed more, demanded more or experienced more? Was there a woman of any race in any land, in any time, who would dare to take her on.

To be her enemy?

Her equal?

Her friend?

High above the rubble of New Anchorage, Legion knew that such a woman could never exist. Her father, Beelzebub, would not allow it.

PART XIII

Courage is the price that life exacts
for granting peace.
The soul that knows it not, knows no release
From little things;
Knows not the livid loneliness of fear
Nor mountain heights, where bitter joy can hear
The sound of wings. . . .

—AMELIA EARHART, "COURAGE"

October 18, 1918
Toronto, Canada

A woman in a blood-smeared nurse's uniform pushed a gurney through the fourth-floor corridors. Her eyes were red and unfocused from fatigue. She'd worked for three days without as much as ten minutes rest—let alone sleep—and it now seemed as if she might have to go three days more.

Up the hall, between the rows of doughboys—temporarily spread out on the floor—she shoved the gurney. The men lay on bloody tarps, frayed mattresses, and thin blankets. They waited with despairing fortitude for a bed to be vacated.

For someone to die.

Occasionally one of them would call to her. A hospital wit had named her Nightingale, after Florence Nightingale. Now disabled doughboys called out whenever she appeared:

"Hey, Nightingale, you *positive* you don't have a boy back home?"

"Nightingale, when are you gonna say the word? Let *me* make an honest woman of you?"

"Hey, Florence, how about making an honest man out of *me?*"

This last sally came from a young boy of nineteen—a red-haired RCAF pilot who'd lost an arm to the legendary von Richthofen. The stump festered and he had pains in the phantom limb.

"Only for you, kid," the nurse said easily.

He gave her a big grin, but his face was flushed and spotted with *petechiae*—the livid blotches which always appeared near the end, after they failed the fever crisis. She had known he would not make it when he had begun passing bloody flux, and now she doubted he would last the day.

She bent to mop his forehead, ladled out a dose of paregoric, and, almost without even thinking, began to compose the letter she would write his family.

Not that her attitude was callous. She was professional; that was all. During the last year and a half, she had seen countless doughboys die and had written so many letters to their loved ones that they had become redundant. They had merged into a single letter, and she knew she would have to get to this one soon, before the details of his last days in the ward blurred and were gone from her memory.

She pushed the gurney on up the hall. *His last words were of you and his father. His last moments were filled with a steadfastness and a bravery that made him a credit to his God, his family, and his flag.*

The sentiment was less real than his vivid red hair, his quick grin and easy laugh. *Get those details down before the shift is over,* she thought.

Which shift is it anyway?

She looked at her watch. Five fifty-eight, and for a moment she was not sure whether that was A.M. or P.M. She glanced out the window at the end of the hall and saw that it was still early: The window shade was turning pale gray in the predawn.

Her third straight dawn without sleep and still not a chance to lie down.

She pushed the medicine gurney on up the hall, assiduously maneuvering it between the patients. It had been bad enough before with the streams of wounded, but the recent influenza outbreak had made an intolerable situation impossible.

The Great Influenza Pandemic of 1918 had begun that spring. It had now killed over twenty million people. Not only did it threaten to wipe out every American and Canadian in the British convalescent hospitals, the death, when it came, was terrible—blinding headaches, grotesque swelling, high fevers, explosive dysentery.

So they had rushed their casualties back from Europe—no matter what shape they were in—with predictable results. They brought them back in the holds of ships—suppurating wounds not even half-healed, shattered limbs barely set, stitches ripping out—frantically rushing the soldiers out of France and England before the influenza killed them. And in the process they brought the disease home.

She reached the end of the corridor—the terminal ward. This was the largest room in the hospital, and in it were quarantined the most contagious soldiers.

As the woman approached the door, she took a deep breath. She tightened her mask, then turned the doorknob.

2

The young doctor with the hazel eyes and the close-cropped brown hair had just finished an examination. He'd put a new series of sutures over a dying man's bed ulcer, when he heard the applause.

It was followed by greeting cries: "Hey, what are you doing, Florence?"

"Nightingale! Over here!"

Followed by spontaneous cheering.

He had only worked the lower, noninfectious floors until now, and hadn't met her. He'd heard of her, of course. Everyone had. She was the young American girl. When the influenza struck, most of their help—fearful of the plague—had left, but not her.

Even after the epidemic's second wave—the one which caused most of the twenty million deaths—she had stayed on. By that time, she was running the second and third floors single-handedly, and when the brass finally found three people brave enough to spell her, she volunteered for the newly organized fourth floor—the most dangerous of all the stations.

The first thing the doctor noticed was her walk: confident, aggressive, her back ramrod-straight. Not even three days and nights on her feet could shorten her stride.

That was the thing that got to him—her determination. It was apparent in the way she entered a room, waving to a patient here, nodding to another there, the way she bent to treat the sick and the dying.

The doctor crossed the crowded ward, curious to meet her.

3 ━━━━━━

The doctor followed Nightingale across "Number Four" as she pushed her gurney through the rows of dying soldiers. Death was everywhere: in the stench of carbolic, of rank sweat and decaying flesh. It was in the swollen joints and in the distended bowels, ballooning with blood. It was in the parched, feverish skin—faces and bodies hot, hands and feet ice-cold.

For those who reached this last floor, death was now a foregone conclusion.

The influenza was not treatable. All the nurse could do was keep the men clean, mop their feverish faces, and tell them they were not alone. *In extremis,* she could shoot them with morphia.

Otherwise, there was paregoric. It did little good— and tasted like brake fluid going down—but that was all she had. So she mixed it with camphor tea, wheeled it to them on the gurney, and, three times a day, ladled it out of steaming buckets.

Toward the end of their rounds, the doctor, whose name was Fraser, said: "It makes you wonder how it all started. The influenza, I mean."

"In the trenches. They're squalid enough to breed anything."

"Before that."

"In some other war, some other time. Plague is as old as we are."

She stopped in front of another dying man. He had soiled his sheets, and the liquid in his urinal was bloodied. Pink sputum streaked his cheeks. He gripped his abdomen with both hands.

She glanced up at the doctor. "Morphia?"

Fraser nodded, and she gave the man a shot. Afterward she wiped off the man's face with a damp cloth and changed his fouled sheets.

"You keep the patients clean," he said.

She shrugged.

"No, really," he continued. "I've seen the other floors. They're awash with filth. You've really managed well."

"We could have done better, but the newspaper stories scared away the help."

"You can't blame them."

She said nothing, then stopped the gurney to rub unguent of mercury on a soldier's bedsores and fever blisters. He shivered with ague, his eyes huge with fright. She said, soothingly:

"Try to relax. We'll get you some paregoric. Then you'll sleep."

"Jesus, God. Jesus, God," the man said repeatedly, his body rigid with fever.

After helping her to wrap the patient in a second sheet, the doctor said: "I hear you like to fly."

"Captain Bradly took me up in a Curtiss-Jenny."

For the first time that morning, she smiled.

"You liked it?"

"It was indescribable."

"Do you want to try again?"

"More than anything else in the world."

To their left a young man lowered his sheet and pointed to the sawed-off stump of his right leg. Even through the blood-matted bandages, it reeked of gas gangrene. The doctor paused to undo the gory rags, holding his breath against the stench.

He gave the boy a shot of morphia and a tight smile. He made a note on his clipboard.

"*Schedule for reamputation*" the note read.

The leg had previously been taken off above the knee.

"How many of them were fixed up in Europe," she said, as they moved on, "then returned to the guns and the wire?"

"Maybe this time it'll be over for good."

"It's never over. We never get enough."

"President Wilson is calling this 'the war to end all wars.'" He paused to stare about them. "He must be right. We couldn't go through this again."

"We could do it easily," she said. "Without even breaking a sweat."

"You can't believe that. Not after all *this*." He paused to stare at the carnage around them.

"War just came here to lick its wounds."

4 ◢══════

Fraser did not see the young woman again for three more shifts. By then, she was stretched out on a cot in the emergency ward. Her temperature was soaring.

He put a finger to her throat. Her pulse was erratic. Unfortunately the receiving physician had administered Epsom salts for the fever, contraindicated when there was diarrhea.

Now it was the doctor's turn to change sheets.

"Doctors aren't supposed to do those things," she chided. "That's nurses' work."

"If you find one, let me know."

Her tongue was parched, and her skin so flushed that he gave her both paregoric and pectin.

"Save it, doc," she said, delirious with the fever. "I won't be needing it."

"Think about biplanes."

Fraser began mixing a second dose of paregoric, this one with calcium carbonate.

"Planes," she said dreamily.

He stared into her soft, liquid eyes—eyes so hopelessly young he almost wished he'd never seen them.

"The chart says you're only twenty. You're too young to check out. It's against regulations."

She convulsed violently, and he took a blanket from the overhead shelf. He swaddled her tightly, then added another blanket, then a third.

Her face was breaking out in dark splotchy *petechiae*, the fatal buboes.

"I wrote a poem once. Want to hear it?" she said, her voice rasping terribly.

"Sure." He placed a cold compress on her forehead.

Courage is the price that life exacts for granting peace.
The soul that knows it not, knows no release
From little things;
Knows not the livid loneliness of fear
Nor mountain heights, where bitter joy can hear
The sound of wings.

She began to cough. He gave her more camphor tea with paregoric, then put a finger to her lips.

She shook her head. "You have to let me finish. You'll be the only one to hear it.

She lost her place, and now her eyes were glazing, that same glassy stare he'd seen a thousand different times, in a thousand battlefield hospitals in what seemed to be one crazed eternal war.

A bearded white-haired doctor in a bloody surgical gown approached them.

"Another soldier gone to Valhalla," the old man said sadly.

Suddenly, Fraser was angry. He grabbed her by the shoulders and shook her. "Goddamn it, courage is the price we pay, you just said. Where's all your courage now?"

It seemed miraculous to him that she opened her eyes.

"I saw her again," she said simply.

Keep her going, he thought. *Keep her talking.*

"Saw who? Saw what?"

He quickly prepared an IV of glucose solution.

"The woman in black. She came to me with snakes and whips, riding a black stallion. She's very bad, and she wants to hurt our friends. We can't let her do that. We can't let her hurt our friends, can we?"

"If you die, how can you stop her?"

"But I can't . . . Her friends . . . They're bad . . . Mountains of . . . Skulls. . . ."

Her voice was losing resonance, trailing off; and again, she shut her eyes.

The old white-haired doctor in the bloody surgeon's gown bent over her. "Mountains of skulls, huh? Shell shock, I suppose. Seen too many casualties." He put a stethoscope to her chest. "Doesn't sound like there's much left."

But Fraser wouldn't let go. He shook her by the shoulder again.

"The woman in black with the snakes?" Fraser said. "You say she's evil, wants your friends?"

Slowly, the young woman's eyes blinked, opened.

"You can't stop her if you're dead."

The young woman's eyelids fluttered convulsively.

The old doctor quickly went through her chart, checking for the woman's name. "The woman in black with the snakes? You can't stop her, dead. Do you hear me, Amelia?"

The woman's eyes flickered.

Still the old man pressed. "You cannot stop her if you're dead. Do you hear me? Amelia Earhart, do you hear me?"

Now Fraser, the young doctor, leaned over her: "You said you wanted to fly again?"

The woman's eyes opened. She focused on him.

"Fly," she said softly.

"You can't fly planes if you're dead," the old doctor repeated. "Do you hear me? The woman with the snakes, you cannot stop her if you're dead."

"Cannot . . . stop . . . her . . . if . . . dead. . . ."

Her eyes fluttered again, and she stared at the two masked doctors, standing over her.

Slowly, haltingly, her eyes began to clear.

The old doctor applied more cold compresses to her feverish forehead.

Fraser methodically hooked up the IV.

PART XIV

Turning and turning in the widening gyre
The falcon cannot hear the falconer;
Things fall apart; the centre cannot hold . . .
The blood-dimmed tide is loosed . . .

—WILLIAM BUTLER YEATS,
"THE SECOND COMING"

Dusk in the Citadel.

The old woman, sitting in her backyard, stared at the scrub brush and the dried-up prickly pear in the deepening twilit gloom. She fixed on the barren chaparral with expressionless eyes and tottered back and forth, back and forth.

The bald eagle—with the creamy white crown, the lush gray primaries, and the alabaster tail—perched on her block and studied the old woman. The smoky eyes were narrowed to angry slits. On Katherine's lap was a frayed photograph of her late husband, Frank.

Just at sunset, just as the sun balanced on the rimrock, she heard her back gate creak. Matt and Elizabeth, her grandkids. The old woman gave them a sour look.

"I suppose your sister bailed you out of jail?"

"They said I was released on *your* recognizance," Matthew said.

"Too bad. Kill anyone since you got out?"

"Not so's you'd notice."

"The way you tagged Jeffers, maybe I'd be safer with you back in."

He shrugged. "Haven't killed any old ladies this week."

He suddenly bent over the old woman, giving her a hug, which she acknowledged grudgingly.

"I'm more worried about *you* and Jeffers," Liz said. "You sure he isn't giving you problems?"

"That child? All he gives me is a disgraceful craving for cotton candy."

"What's cotton candy?" Liz asked, puzzled.

The old woman snorted. "You wouldn't like it. 'Pears you two were weaned on pickles."

"What are you going to do about him?" Matt asked, pressing.

She stared at him a long hard minute, then ruffled his blond hair. Affectionately. "Maybe I'll try keeping my big mouth shut."

"Do you know how?" Liz teased.

"Depends. It isn't enough to opt for silence. You have to know what kind of silence to opt for."

"Won't silence play into Jeffers's hands?"

Katherine averted her eyes and stared at the crimson ball of the sinking sun. "Yes, but maybe that's just our way. To be tyrannized by weak neurotics who don't know the difference between what hurts and what feels good."

"Grandma," Matt said, "you told us once that to say nothing, to do nothing in the face of evil was to die a little. And now you want to give up and quit? You can't. It was *Darrell* who sent you those dispatches."

Darrell. God, please. Not Darrell. Let him be all right.

"Yes, Darrell," Katherine said in a tired voice. "If your brother makes it home in one piece, I'll be content. It's all I ask."

"But what he wrote us, his warning—?"

"'Our fathers and ourselves sowed dragon's

teeth,'" she recited dutifully. "'Our children know and suffer the armed men.'"

"Speaking of father," Liz said, clearing her throat.

"Ah yes, you two are back from the mountains and your prodigal father. You certainly look tanned and fit. Lived with his blessed Apaches, did you? Pitched in with the corn harvest? Is he still studying black magic under that gourd-shaking, rain-dancing medicine man?"

"Well, we sort of wanted to talk to you about that."

"There's something I've been meaning to say about your father. I know you love him, and I know his heart's sound. In fact, out of all our kids, I suppose I loved him best. Maybe I loved him too much—expected too much. Old folks sometimes get just as hard as their arteries. But after your ma died, Richard simply up and dropped you two on my doorstep without so much as a fare-thee-well or a by-your-leave. You two deserved more than this bag of bones and that crippled bird over there."

The bird ruffled her snow-white hackles, glared at the old woman, and flapped her wings furiously, spreading them to their full ten-foot span.

Liz walked over to the irate bird, crooning in low, tender tones. She smoothed her alabaster hackles and soft gray primaries.

"You've done fine, grandma," Matt said.

"Oh, I do my best, and I'm not complaining. I want you two here. You children have been the light and pride of my old age. You, me, that crazy bird included, we get along fine—better than dogs and cats in a sack. You three put life back into these old bones. I'll be the first to admit it. But that still doesn't explain a man who abandons his kids and responsibilities for three years. Maybe I'm just feeling sorry for myself, but Frank and I—" she glanced at the weathered yellowing photograph of Frank on her lap "—your father was our favorite, you understand? The one we had that special feeling for. Now I wish I'd taken a knotted plowline to him instead."

"Grandma," Liz said anxiously, "that's what we have to talk to you about."

"Sure, I know. You kids have a right to be sore. It wasn't any kind of life, not having a father these last three years. He's obviously refused to come back home with you."

"We know you have lung problems, Grandma, but somehow you have to make it up to the camp."

Her eyes narrowed instantly. "Is my boy Richard in any trouble?"

"No, he's done something wonderful, in fact," Matt said.

"Remember all those years he spent studying mathematics and physics with that professor friend of yours?" Liz asked.

"Dr. Schonbrun?"

"Yes. Using all that stuff—plus the things he learned from the old shaman, Spirit Owl—Dad's made a marvelous machine. It's got computers, sun-powered generators, everything."

The old woman looked skeptical.

"With it, he can go into the past," Matt explained, "and look around. He can see anything, find anything."

"You're crazy."

"We've seen it," Liz said. "We *know* what it can do. You can see it for yourself. You have to."

"It's a trick of some sort. An optical illusion."

"It's not," Matt said, "and anyway, he's added something new. 'An aperture,' he calls it. He uses it when he goes back into the past. He can reach in through the aperture and take things out."

"What are you getting at?"

"Dad's done it," Liz said, her voice rising. "He's really done it."

"Done what?"

"Don't you understand?" Matt said, excited. "He's opened up a hole in time."

2

An old woman rocking, endlessly rocking, just an old woman and her pet bird. Two old-timers, alone in a barren desert waste, lost and adrift in a world they never made.

Dawn flared in the east, blazing brilliantly. Shafts of red and yellow, purple and gold soared high above the rimrock. In the distance a cock crowed, and the rising sun cast long, straggling shadows over the desert chaparral.

But the old woman was oblivious.

What if—? A hole in time—

The old woman stared at the books, now scattered across the back-yard.

A Stillness At Appomattox by Bruce Catton.

"Courage" by Amelia Earhart.

War As I Knew It by George S. Patton.

What if— A hole in— If it could— In time— If—

She shook her head. No, it's impossible. You're out of your mind.

And so they tottered—just two old women, rocking, endlessly rocking.

What if—? A hole— In time— What—if—?

On and on, they creaked—waiting for the Wolves of Wodin and the trapdoor to drop. Just two old women—endlessly rocking.

At Eternity's edge.

At the brink of hell's abyss.

And Time running out.

Only the dead have seen the end of war.

—PLATO

PART XV

Men are like stars, Young Scribe.
They live, they die, black holes eat them.

—LEGION

The young man in the black *burnoose* allowed his sheaf of foolscap notes to drop to his lap. Leaning back against his heavy *daiwan* cushions, he looked around his yellow pavilion. He was bored.

His *yurt* was littered with collapsing stacks of books, and laid out across his worktable were ink jars, fountain pens, and thick reams of paper. His storage trunks were open, his robes and personal effects spilling out. His sleeping pallet was unmade.

His two *yurt*-mates only added to the confusion. His *Imam*—a Sufi scholar with long gray hair and beard—knelt on his prayer rug and salaamed to the east, intoning repeatedly: "Salaam alakum . . . Salaam alakum . . . Salaam alakum."

His black-robed bodyguard—jailer was a better job description—noisily honed his thirteen-and-a-half-inch Kabar Combat Knife on an oiled whetstone.

"Hey, guys," Darrell said, "I'm working on The Conquest of The World: *A Verse Epic in Three Volumes* by Tamerlane the Great. You know, the *magnum opus* our intrepid leader ordered me to write? Could you try lowering the racket a few decibels?"

Gurney looked up at him, blank-faced. He was wearing a black *caftan* cinched at the waist with a red sash, and his flowing *kaffeiah* headcloth hung below his waist. Finally he grinned. The grin made his black sweeping mustache look rakish.

"We could try," he said.

Gurney continued to whet his knife.

"I do not understand your word, decibels," the *Imam* said, opening his eyes.

"A unit of sound. An earsplitting unit of sound. Seeing as how you two are here to assist me in this masterwork, I thought you could, at least, try keeping quiet."

"Young Scribe," said the *Imam*, "the problem lies in your lack of discipline. You must concentrate harder. The inspiration will come."

The *Imam* bent over his rug and commenced a new round of prayers.

"I need a break," Darrell said. "Let's go for a walk."

Reluctantly, the *Imam* interrupted his prayers. "Young Scribe," Hamid-al-Qadar said, "if you cannot work, you are to study the Ways of the Prophet. Mustafa was quite insistent on that matter."

Gurney's grinding grew louder.

Kicking his feet up on his desk, Darrell stared at the tent top.

"Go ahead, Hamid. Fire away. Educate me on Islam."

The *Imam* stared at him, his eyes expressionless. "We have previously discussed only four Pillars of the Faith. We will now speak of the fifth—the pilgrimage."

"I know all about taking trips," Darrell yawned. "I traveled quite a ways just getting here."

"The trip we speak of, Good Scribe, is a journey of the heart, a pilgrimage in understanding, not miles traveled."

"Which means nothing. I already know more than I want to."

"I speak of the holy *hajj* and the Sevenfold Circuit."

"Yeah, I know about that too," Darrell nodded. "Mecca, the Black Rock. Some *verkachte* meteorite, as I recollect. You bow down, kiss it, and shoot straight into heaven. I got that Pillar covered. Let's go on to the next lesson."

"The pilgrimage we speak of is the Sufi path to Truth, not lessons in a book. Its journey takes a lifetime, and its way stations are repentance, abstinence, renunciation, poverty, patience, trust in Allah, and satisfaction."

"What was that last way station? Satisfaction? You got me there. No way I'm finding satisfaction—not in our Lord's *bok*."

"I speak of a union with the divine."

"Not me. Not here."

"Read this." The *Imam* handed him a leather-bound copy of *The Koran*.

"You're wasting your time," Gurney said, still whetting his blade. "You got a hard-core infidel there."

The *Imam* pointed to a passage, and Darrell read:

When Earth is rocked in her last convulsion;
when Earth shakes off her burdens
and man asks "What may this mean?"—
on that day she will proclaim her tidings,
for your Lord will have inspired her.

Darrell closed the book, and handed it back to the *Imam*.

"I can't get into it."

"Don't let Mustafa hear you say that," Gurney said.

"That old fraud?"

"Not where Allah is concerned," said Gurney. "He may be mad, but he still believes."

"In what?" Darrell asked. "Rape? Murder? Torture? Dismemberment?"

"In the unrivaled oneness of Allah," Hamid said.

Darrell threw his head back and horselaughed.

"What do you believe in, Scribe?" the *Imam* asked.

"For openers, I don't *even* believe in belief."

"You believe in nothing?" asked the *Imam*.

"I believe in what I see, hear, feel, smell, taste."

"Mustafa can extend those senses most thoroughly," Hamid said.

"Listen up, boy," Gurney said.

Darrell merely grunted.

"Our Lord can extend those senses too," the *Imam* said. "You anger him or provoke our Lady, they will teach you things you never even dreamed of."

"Do you know what they tell those who enter the Cuddler's tent?" the *Imam* asked.

Darrell shook his head.

"'When we are done,' they tell their victims, 'you will possess the gift of tongues and speak the speech of snakes and rocks. You will sing songs to dead stars and anthems to dead gods. You will know what lies beyond all worlds and words. You will be eternally wise.'"

"In other words," Gurney said, "some things you don't want to know."

"He's saying you should return to your history, Young Scribe," said Hamid.

"I've got to clear my head."

"Young Scribe," the *Imam* said, "it is raining."

"That's why we have *kaffeiahs*. That's why robes have hoods."

"You are avoiding work," the *Imam* said.

"I need more color and atmosphere—more smell of the powder, roar of the guns."

"In the rain?"

"It's letting up."

"Stay here and write," Gurney said. "Our Lady Legion promised the next chapter to our Lord by tomorrow."

"Too bad for Tamerlane."

"If our Lord hears you talk like that, he'll have you Cuddled," said the *Imam*.

"They say his new assistant is very bad news," Gurney said.

"They should both scare our Scribe," the *Imam* said. "They loathe him."

"Our Scribe must learn to keep his mouth shut around those men," Gurney said.

"And finish his book," the *Imam* said.

"I have this problem with motivation."

"Our Cuddler is a motivation expert," Gurney said.

"His assistant too," said the *Imam*.

"You think they could help me with my poem?"

"No," Gurney said, "but they could hang you by the hocks over a slow-burning fire. They could flay you whole. They could cut you into little pieces and fry them in oil."

"I hear his new assistant's built a rack," Darrell said.

"And something called a strappado," Gurney added.

Darrell gave his friends a wry smile and led them out into the *bok*. All around them were pitched thousands of pavilions, each flanked by tethered horses and yapping dogs. In front of these tents were smoking cook fires, weapons stockpiles, horse gear, *kumiss* sacks.

As if to confirm his friends' warnings, Darrell was instantly confronted by the Cuddler's handiwork. Everywhere they went mutilated men writhed from gibbets or twisted on stakes. These victims were constant reminders of the Horde's rough justice—of its brandings, dismemberments, impalements, castrations—the price it exacted for *Ordu* disobedience.

For most of the men, however—at least, for those not at the Front—life seemed fairly comfortable. Around the campfires, the soldiers drank, smoked, and laughed. Lately, their *bok* had even attracted volunteers.

"What sort of men enlist in this outfit?" Darrell asked the Captain.

"Men with more than one name—some more than a dozen. Men who would kill you for your boots. For the heels. For your word broken *or* kept. Who'll turn you over to the Cuddler the first time you even think about escaping to the Citadel."

They left the tent city behind them and started up a hill overlooking the battlefield. It was a long, steep climb, and its summit was restricted to all but the *bok's* elite. The Scribe had special access.

At the summit Gurney studied the field below.

"There it is, Scribe—the inspiring story our Lady wants you to tell."

"You know," Darrell said, "in the last four months we have not pushed the Mormons back one inch.

That's the real story of this campaign. Unfortunately, our Lord doesn't find it inspiring."

"It is if you're a Mormon," Gurney corrected.

"We signed a treaty with them," Darrell said irritably, "then launched a sneak attack. We slaughtered and enslaved half their civilian population before they drove us back from their city. In short, we raped, tortured, murdered, and generally jerked them around. Still we can't drive their army off their wire."

Darrell raised his field glasses. Despite the gray rainy twilight, he could make out the spectacle below. A series of human wave assaults were battering the Mormon trench lines. Each wave terminated on the New Salt wire, scythed flat by hammering guns.

"Our Lord, we are told, is favored by Allah and the Prophet," the *Imam* said.

"I think the coin spins evenly," said Darrell.

"Not for Tamerlane," the *Imam* argued. "Our Lady says he's blessed."

"Then why does he fear the tortures of gehenna."

"That is also Legion's doing," the *Imam* said. "Such notions give her power over him."

"But not over the Mormons."

"Battle plans can change."

Darrell studied the *Imam* coolly, then returned to his field glasses.

The moon rose, and visibility improved. In the surrounding hills Darrell could see the Horde's convoys, transporting shells to their artillery. In the valley Darrell could now distinguish the no-man's-land separating the two zigzagging trench-garrisons. Beyond the New Salt garrisons loomed their capital city.

Darrell returned his gaze to the *Ordu*'s Front. As usual, the frontline trenches were swarming with conscripts, preparing for their human wave attacks. It was in the rear that Darrell noticed something new. Tonight, their *Janizaries* were pouring into the rear trenches and streaming toward the Front.

The *Imam* took Darrell aside. "Tonight it is rumored we will launch the biggest assault of all, that we will bury New Salt."

"We haven't yet."

"Our Lord has a surprise for them."

"I can't wait."

"I know," the *Imam* said. "Some wounds never heal. But for the moment you have no choice. You must do as you are told."

"I feel guilty just being here. Just being alive."

"And your guilt shall not be absolved," said the *Imam*. "Not here. Not in the *bok*."

"You listen to him, Scribe," Gurney said.

"You must learn the meaning of *salaam*," said the *Imam*.

"I already know it," Darrell said. "It means surrender, obedience. It's the root of Islam."

"It means we have the freedom to *obey*," Hamid said.

"What we're doing is wrong."

"Tonight, there is no right or wrong. Tonight, there is only victory or defeat."

"Who will win?"

"The Old Whore, Death," Gurney said.

Darrell's face was sad. "Legion maintains this is all Allah's will. The *Ordu*, she says, is whipping history into shape—for the True God."

"And for Beelzebub," the *Imam* reminded him.

"Never forget Beelzebub," said Gurney.

"How could I?" Darrell asked. "Our Lady's real big on him too."

"She's also big on our 'history,'" Gurney said.

"She wants you to write that history," said the *Imam*. "Do not make our Lady mad."

They were joined by three guards.

"Our Lady and Tamerlane want you to watch the battle with them," a tall, gangly sergeant said, walking up to Darrell. "The Cuddler and his Englishman will be there."

"Go with Allah," the *Imam* said.

"And the Devil," said Gurney.

"You didn't have to remind me," Darrell told him.

He started down the hill.

2 ━━━━━━

Darrell found Tamerlane on a high summit, studying the battlefield through field glasses. He was flanked by four bodyguards, armed with AK-47's. Like Tamerlane, the men were dressed in hooded black robes.

Legion strolled up to Darrell. She was also dressed in black, but now that the rain had slackened she wore her hood down. Her dark hair hung to her waist.

Darrell stared at Tamerlane's heavily armed escort. He took Legion aside.

"Why so many guards?"

"Believe it nor not, he is in constant danger. Not everyone loves our Lord."

Darrell glanced down the hill. The Cuddler's tent was at the bottom of the slope. A half dozen flayed victims hung from their heels over slow-burning fires.

"I thought our Lord had universal appeal."

"In his line of work you never trust to chance."

The Cuddler and his English assistant, Forsythe, joined Tamerlane. The two Cuddlers wore red cambric cloaks, which hid the bloodstains of their craft but not its black scorch marks.

"What of my Majordomo?" Tamerlane asked. "How did he handle your tent?"

"He didn't," Mustafa said.

"He had a weak heart," said Forsythe. "He died during the third day of interrogation."

Forsythe had an upper-class British accent. His mouth locked in a chronic patrician sneer.

Darrell looked away. He had liked the old man.

"I see our Scribe disapproves," Forsythe said.

"The Majordomo's been with you, sire, since before Constantinople. Next to our Lady, he was your closest adviser."

"He imposed on that closeness," the Cuddler said. "He became impertinent."

"Much as our Scribe becomes impertinent," Forsythe observed.

Mustafa nodded his assent.

"The Scribe does not bother me," Tamerlane said. "And he amuses my lady. He makes her laugh."

"He holds blasphemous beliefs," said Mustafa.

"Writers have no beliefs," Legion said. "They have only words. They use them to write sagas."

"You killed an innocent man." Darrell used the English word, innocent.

"I do not know this word, innocent," Tamerlane said.

"It is nothing, sire," Legion said. "Another word in the English dictionary. It falls between imbecile and lunatic."

"There is no such thing as an innocent man," Tamerlane decided.

"The Scribe," Mustafa said, "does not approve of your war, sire."

"Why not?" Tamerlane asked. "Does not war improve our lives?"

"Not our spiritual life," Darrell said.

"What means this word spiritual?" Tamerlane was irritated by the English words.

Legion burst into laughter.

"It means everyone is a part of everyone else," Darrell said.

Tamerlane was confused.

"It means that peacemakers are divinely blessed," Forsythe mocked, "and that the meek shall inherit the earth."

"Yes, I would like that," Tamerlane said. "If the meek possessed the earth, I could take it from them most easily."

Legion agreed. Calling for brandy tankards, she raised hers in toast:

> *To Beel', of the sacred stones*
> *Our ancient hymn to thee intones*
> *We drink thy blood in loving cups*
> *And break for thee men's bones.*

Tamerlane drank deeply, then turned to the Cuddler.

"Come, Mustafa, tell me more about our late Majordomo—how he took it."

Legion, Forsythe, and Darrell—recognizing that they'd been dismissed—moved quietly down the slope. When they reached the bottom, Legion turned to Darrell:

"You watch your mouth. Our Lord cared for the Majordomo, and still he had him Cuddled. He doesn't even like you."

"Nor does Mustafa," Forsythe said.

As if to underscore Forsythe's point, the Cuddler pointed his finger at Darrell and roared: "He shall learn the way of the Black Tent too, just as our Majordomo learned it. For the Scribe betrays us, sire. I swear by the Dark Trumpet and the Last Day, things will go hard. We will all be gathered into the Fiery Pit—into the place called Armageddon—unless you give me the boy. Allah and the Prophet demand his blood. He plots to bring us down."

"Our Lady might not always be here to protect you," said Forsythe, "and when that day comes, Mustafa will ring your chimes like church bells."

"Why does he hate me anyway?" Darrell asked.

"Since when does Old Mustafa need a reason?" Forsythe laughed. "He's stark-staring mad, and he will not sleep till you're howling on his coals."

"What about you?"

Forsythe's sneer was dazzling. "The truth is I don't like you much myself."

Again, Mustafa thundered at the Scribe:

"We shall touch you, boy—down to the well of the foul womb in which you were born, to whatever Bitch of Babylon gave you birth."

Mustafa returned to Tamerlane.

Forsythe slapped Darrell on the shoulder. "Well done, sport. You've got him hopping tonight. I especially loved your speech about spiritual love. Everyone-is-part-of-everyone-else. You are bloody marvelous, you know. Imagine, spouting that 'Jesus saves' drivel to Tamerlane. To Tamerlane of all people! Utterly priceless. You know I may actually miss you."

"You sure make a guy feel at home."

"We subscribe to the gospel of violence, friend, and you don't. That's all it is."

"Guess who wins," Legion said.

Darrell said nothing.

"There's no other way," Forsythe said. "You waltz in here babbling all that peace and love nonsense—what do you expect?"

"Generosity?"

"Oh my," Forsythe said, "the item's long out of stock."

Legion's eyes flashed. "Listen to him, Scribe. He's telling you plain."

Again, Forsythe grinned at Darrell. "You really *hate* us, don't you?"

"I feel as if I've stepped in from another world, another time."

"You never dreamed men like Mustafa existed, did you?" Forsythe said.

"I hear he now has a rack."

"Ask the Majordomo."

"You're just trying to scare me."

Forsythe put his finger in Darrell's chest. "We do scare you, boy."

Darrell looked at Legion. "At least, I still have you."

"Like Forsythe said, I might not always be around."

A blood-chilling shriek tore out of the Cuddler's tent.

"That boy is in serious pain," said Darrell.

"Yours shall be etched on the very walls of hell," Forsythe said.

Legion pointed to Darrell's note case. "Speaking of which, let's see what you've got. Read."

Darrell opened it up. He read aloud:

> *As through some nightmare world we have marched*
> *An army that has died and gone to hell*
> *To fight forever in the pit of death*
> *At war forever never to know peace.*

Legion cut him off. "The whole tone is wrong. The imagery is far too depressing. Our men are heroes and martyrs, not dust and mud. Try comparing them to Saladin and Suleiman, to Allah and the True Prophet."

"I'm not even sure we're going to win."

Legion glanced at her watch. "Really?" She pointed toward the valley. "Then take a good look at the battle down there. A really good look."

Darrell glanced over the rimrock with grim foreboding.

The Big Offensive the *Imam* spoke of was about to begin.

◀■ 3

Conscript Harris followed the Sergeant up the shoulder-wide trench. Behind him, single file, slogged six ragged recruits. They trudged through a driving rain.

Their Sergeant, William Hawkins, was, on the other hand, handsomely turned out. He wore a steel helmet, a black waterproof poncho, and leather boots—something he unceasingly pointed out.

"When we whip these bloody Mormons, you'll

have real outfits too. I know. Last year I was a sorry-ass conscript just like you, but look at me now. I'm living like a lord—plenty to eat and drink, a warm bunk, and women too. I tell you, when we take New Salt, you'll all live like kings."

Harris doubted it. Since his "conscription" he had known nothing but hunger, cold, exhaustion, and terror, and he saw nothing new to convince him otherwise. Whenever he glanced into the dugouts, carved into the trench walls, the Frontline conscripts all glared back with hideous grins, haunted eyes, and the dirtiest faces he'd ever seen.

When the squad reached the Forward Trench—the Front Line—Sergeant Hawkins, again, turned to lecture them.

"Now boys, I'm going to tell you how it is. When the whistle blows, we go over the top. Do you understand? You attack and attack and attack."

"What kind of weapons do we get?" the conscript next to Harris asked.

"I'm packing the only gun in this squad," the Sergeant said, slapping his slung AK-47, "and believe me, I'm the one you men have to worry about. Try turning back, and I'll cut you in two like a buzz saw."

"Don't we get *any* weapons?" Harris asked.

"Just before jump-off, I'll hand out black-powder grenades. Once you're in the enemy's trench, you'll have to bomb your way from traverse to traverse."

The Sergeant paused, letting his speech sink in. All Harris heard in the meantime was the bursting of shells, the screaming of the men, the scurrying of rats, and the chatter of machine guns.

"The Mormons do not accept retreat or defeat," Sergeant Hawkins said, "but this night we'll convince

them otherwise. This time you will be backed by six
divisions of seasoned *Janizaries*—the best his Lordship
has to offer. This is the night we finally break New Salt."

The speech was finished, and Harris dutifully
accepted his burlap sack of grenades.

The Sergeant lined them up on the firing step.

Harris would be the first to go over.

All they needed now was the signal to advance.

And then it came—the shrill, screeching jump-off
whistle.

Harris vaulted the parapet, and the squad followed.

4

*In Lawrence Hardy's night-
mare, it is always the same. He is bent over the sights of
his smoking machine gun. Into his line of fire march thousands of Tamerlane's conscripts six abreast. His 50-caliber
Browning hammers in his hands, back and forth, back
and forth, its barrel blazing.*

*Unfortunately, he cannot stop them, and he knows
why. He has killed them already.*

*Still Hardy is not afraid. In fact, he is relieved. He
knows finally why he is in this war. He is here to learn the
secret behind this endless slaughter.*

He is here to read the faces of the dead.

The man shaking Hardy's shoulder—and waking
him up—looked to be at least sixty.

"Private Donahue, sir. I'm your new assistant."

Hardy made room for the old man in the bunker.
"Seen any action so far?"

"Not yet. You expect some tonight?"

"Maybe." He pointed to their tripod machine gun. "You know how this thing works?"

"Not really."

"You keep the cartridge belts loaded, in line, and the cooling jacket topped off with water."

"That's it?"

"They hit us tonight, that'll be plenty."

"Major Wilson told me it gets rough here. He said I'm your sixth assistant."

Hardy said nothing.

The old man was clearly nervous. "The Major said you 'live close to the bone' up here."

"That bother you?"

"This bunker sure does. The air in here smells like a cage full of dead snakes."

Hardy glanced around the emplacement. He had to admit it was not inviting. A muddy hole, two meters high and two across, barricaded by stacked sandbags.

"Sergeant," the old man said, "the sun's going down now. How will we tell the enemy from our own returning patrols?"

"They cross my line of fire at night, they're *all* enemies."

Suddenly the wind changed, and the stench of the battlefield filled the bunker.

"God, that's awful."

"Wait till we get the machine gun going. Then you get the stink *and* the smoke." He pointed to a rat scurrying past the adjacent water bucket. "Watch out for those things too. Especially if you've got dysentery. The blood and diarrhea drives them crazy. They'll eat you whole."

The wind changed again, and the stink was again oppressive. The private looked sick.

"This is the Great Charnel House of War, my friend. You'll find that smell everywhere—in your boots, your bullets, your water, your bread. Here. Have some of this." Hardy popped the cork from his whiskey canteen and handed it to him.

Donahue took a swallow. He gagged. "That's hard liquor."

"It better be. I traded two boxes of 50-caliber ammo for it."

"You swapped machine gun bullets for booze?"

"Stay up here long enough, you'll sell your soul for it."

Donahue forced down another swallow, then handed it back.

"What did you do before the siege?" Hardy asked.

"I was a classicist. A Greek scholar."

"That sounds practical. Did those books say anything about fighting Tamerlane?"

"No, but I read how the Spartan few fought the Persians at Thermopylae."

"How did they do?"

"The Spartans fought a delaying action—one that gave the Greeks a chance to regroup. They were all killed."

"You think that's all this is? A delaying action?"

The old man shrugged. "History might see it that way. Maybe we're just buying time for the Citadel."

Hardy glanced back at the trench behind them. It was clogged with the wounded. They were knee-deep in bloody bilge and black rain.

"Do *they* know they're dying for your so-called history?" Hardy sneered, pointing at the wounded.

"You shouldn't make fun of them."

"I don't see why not."

"They've earned our tears," Donahue said. "They fought eye-deep in hell."

"I'm fresh out."

"They're worth them anyway."

Hardy stared at the scholar, incredulous. "In that case, why don't you dig this bunker a little deeper. Our sapper squads get lazier by the day." He handed the old man an entrenching tool.

"You're really expecting action?"

"Just don't toss the dirt out the same place twice. The snipers triangulate on it."

The old man took the entrenching tool and began to dig. "Those men back there, they *are* worth our tears."

"Save your tears for yourself, old man. Before this night's over, you'll need them."

5

Major Harun Al-Rashid of the *Ordu* Sapper Brigade squatted in a muddy mine shaft and stared up at the dripping ceiling. He was squarely underneath the New Salt Command Bunkers. For the past four months he had supervised the construction of six such tunnels, and now he paused to consider his most recent contribution.

He'd spent six weeks packing the last quarter mile of these shafts with black powder; at 0200 hours they would set it off. By then, he and the gas battalion would be topside, where they would blanket the New Salt Com-Trenches with chlorine gas.

He looked at his pocket watch. 0147 hours. Thirteen minutes to go.

He stared downshaft. He was looking at three miles of black tunnel—clumsily braced with sagging cross-beams and groaning shoring timbers. The shaft was filling with water, and the ceiling was coming down in chunks.

Major Rashid looked up to find his chief engineer, Lieutenant Abdul Salam, staring at the detonator and shaking his head.

"What is wrong?" Rashid asked.

"This detonator's wet," the Lieutenant said. "The wiring may not work."

Rashid could barely hear him above the roar of the cascading water.

"It does not inspire confidence."

"What of these gas masks?" Abdul held up his muddy respirator. "If the chlorine doesn't kill us, the clogged filters will."

"I'll be happy if we aren't buried alive."

Major Rashid looked at his chronometer. 0135 hours. Eleven minutes to go.

As if on cue, the rain of black sewage accelerated. The stench was awesome.

"The sinks have flooded," said Rashid.

"Eleven minutes before zero hour," Abdul said, "and we're drowning in their dung."

6

After crawling under the last belt of *Ordu* wire, Harris found himself in a long line of conscripts. They all marched toward the Mormon guns.

Everywhere it was the same: Thousands of conscripts, slogging forward, heads down, wave after
wave. Haggard faces were black with muck and their
eyes hugely white.

The terrain was bad. They slogged through quag-
mires and shell holes, over bloated bodies and deluged saps. The stench was unnerving.

Harris was less than two hundred yards from the
Mormon wire when an artillery round almost took
him out.

He came to in a flooded shell crater, puking up
muddy water. Another conscript was dragging him up
the slope.

"Time to go back up?" Harris asked weakly.

"Why? You want to die?" the conscript asked.

The man had a point. Machine gun fire hammered
the rim mercilessly, splattering his upturned face with
filth.

"The fire here is nothing," the conscript said.
"Wait till you reach the aprons."

"The wire detail cut it. That's what the Sergeant
told us."

"Not a chance. I was with the wire detail." The
conscript held up a pair of wire cutters. "We were
driven off."

"The wire's not down?" Harris was shocked.

"It never is. The Mormons patch it up faster than
we can cut it. Those Mormons are hard-core. They
don't scare, and they don't care. We're never going to
take those trenches."

Harris stared at the top in silence.

Kearny tossed him the shears. "You want them, take
them. The damn things never work right anyway—
especially in the dark."

"But we have to reach the wire. If we don't, the Sergeant'll shoot us."

"And if you get there, the Mormons will."

"But the Sergeant is closer. He'll shoot quicker."

"That's a fact."

"Don't you care if you die?"

"Not anymore. "

To their rear they heard the hammering of the Sergeant's machine gun.

Kearny glared at him.

"Sergeant Hawkins wants us to charge the Mormons like lions."

"Not on purpose I won't."

They both stared at the crater's rim, which was still being riddled by nonstop machine gun fire.

Another body plunged into their hole, where it floated facedown. The water quickly turned red.

"I heard the Mormons actually volunteer for combat," Harris said.

"I did too," Kearny admitted grudgingly. "I worked in one of Tamerlane's nitro plants as a lab assistant. The fumes were so strong they tarnished the guards' guns and blinded half the shift. Once in awhile the nitro would go off."

"It must have been bad."

"The Lady Legion didn't think so. She set it up. It was her idea."

"You saw her?"

He nodded.

Harris was impressed. "How long have you been with the Horde?"

"Since they sacked New Seattle."

"You must have seen some things."

"Enough to make Satan weep."

"Why do we do it?"

"Have you seen the way the *Janizaries* live?"

"Those stories are lies."

"I've seen their feasts and orgies. Rice of every color and flavor, lambs stuffed with walnuts, almonds, pistachios, barons of beef, pheasants, turkeys, and jellied tongues. Whiskey, wine, beer, women. Things can change for us."

"At present," Harris said, studying the machine gun fire up-top, "our prospects don't look good."

His newfound friend nodded. "You're right. Anyway, I'm just interested in today."

Suddenly, the Sergeant's machine gun was hammering behind them—hard.

"We don't have much time," Harris said.

They crawled to the top of the crater and stared at the Mormon lines—at thick belts of wire on which were spread-eagled thousands of conscript dead. Beyond the wire stretched New Salt fire trenches, fortified by more wire belts and densely stacked sandbags.

The machine gunners hammered the ground around them.

"Time to saddle up," Kearny said.

They clawed their way over the crater's rim and crawled toward the wire.

7

Lieutenant Mann and his squad were fixing the Mormon wire when he saw them—wave after wave of conscripts coming straight at them. The first line was at least a thousand men long. He knew that the bags lashed to their wrists were packed with grenades.

For months Mann had heard rumors of a massive assault, which would be backed by the *Ordu*'s seasoned veterans. But so far they had not risked it.

Not until now.

"Okay," Mann said, breaking silence, "it's time to earn our pay."

"What pay?" the new recruit asked, confused.

Mann ignored him. "Corporal, give me your extra pistol and ammunition. Fix what wire you can as you fall back. If you fail, the trenches'll be overrun."

"What are you going to do?" the new recruit asked.

For the first time that night Lieutenant Mann smiled.

"I'm going to buy us some time."

8

To Gunner Hardy's astonishment, just as the wave of enemy reached the second belt of wire, a lone Mormon officer angled toward his bunker. If he had not recognized him as Lieutenant Mann, he would have cut him to pieces.

He was glad he hadn't. Twenty minutes earlier, his scholarly assistant had been blasted out the bunker by a 105. He now lay facedown in the mud eight feet from his machine gun's muzzle.

So much for Thermopylae.

So much for Arts and Letters.

The Lieutenant scrambled into the bunker and squatted beside Hardy. Hardy handed him his whiskey canteen, and Mann took a deep pull.

"That tastes like Life itself."

Hardy jerked it out of his hand. He helped himself to a snort and shouted: "Here they come."

Hardy swung the big gun back and forth. Mann kept the cooling jacket filled and the belts in line.

While they changed barrels, Hardy pointed to the men he'd shot.

"None of them ever thanked me."

"That's 'cause they don't like you. I don't like you much myself."

By now the wire apron was weighted down with so many bodies its crisscrossing pickets were ripping loose. Finally, the apron shuddered and collapsed.

"Aw, hell," Hardy groaned.

Mann shoved a fresh belt into the breech, pulled back the bolt, and replaced the smoking barrel.

"Lock and load," he shouted.

The next wave scrambled over the collapsed wreck.

The gun traversed back and forth, back and forth, and the *Ordu* conscripts collapsed on the second wire.

"You know what your predecessor said?" Hardy shouted above the hammering gun. "He said we were the Spartan few at Thermopylae, civilization's last best hope. He claimed we'd be remembered by history. I said save that talk for the Citadel."

"Or for those men there," Mann said, indicating the piles of corpses littering the back of the trench.

"He had them figured too," Hardy shouted. "He said they were worth our tears."

"Why?"

"Because they walked eye-deep in hell."

"What's that got to do with us?"

"He didn't say. That 105 nailed him."

"There it is."

"Yes, there it is."

Now the number 2 belt was straining under so many bodies it, too, heaved and fell. Mann topped off the cooling jacket, shoved in another belt, and screamed:

"Lock and load!"

The last belt was eighty yards from the bunker—too far for lobbing grenades but close enough for the traversing machine gun. There, the conscripts piled—by the dozens, then the hundreds, higher, higher, higher.

Until an ear-shattering blast hurled them almost out of their bunker, everything going up in fire and smoke.

Hardy had spent a lot of time in this war and had seen a lot of demolition, but nothing like this. The blasts seemed to be going off in stages, throughout the entire trench-garrison. They began with a *ka-ka-ka*, which quickly merged into a steady protracted *kaaaaaaa*, which then merged into a *kaaaa-whummm-mmp-kaaaa-whummmmppp!* which finally blew into a rumbling, gut-churning WHUMP!WHUMP! WHUMP!WHUMMPPP!

Next came the whirling clouds of black smoke. They rose overhead, sucking everything out of New Salt—guns, wire, canteens, blankets, cartridge belts, tools, helmets, boots, men—breaking up the maze of trenches into a maelstrom of shards and fragments.

Then the billowing clouds metamorphosed. Six fireballs rose out of their murky depths with torturous slowness, burning off the black smoke, till high above the blast they merged into a single ball, spectacular as the sun.

The heat was terrible. As the fireballs faded a smoky hailstorm of dirt and debris hammered at Hardy's bunker.

When Hardy was able to evaluate the damage he realized that half of New Salt had been obliterated. Little remained but dust and ashes, falling from the sky.

Suddenly the *Ordu* conscripts screamed *en masse*—a crazed YIP-YIP-YIP-YIPPPINNNGGG!—as they charged the trench lines like banshees from hell. Hardy was shocked from his daze.

"The wire," Mann screamed. "Watch the wire."

Hardy looked around to see the next wave of conscripts vaulting the number 1 apron wire. He pounded at the traversing screw with his fist, simultaneously wheeling the big gun in a 120-degree arc. He dropped two dozen conscripts on the wire less than fifty yards away. Their combined weight bent the entire belt of wire.

"Change the goddamn barrel!" Hardy screamed.

Mann shoved an extra barrel into the breech and loaded a fresh belt. Hardy pulled back the bolt and vectored on the next wave scrambling over the corpse-littered wire.

The big gun raked the waves of conscripts, piling them one on top of the other until they were stacked four high.

9

Major Al-Rashid's brigade was clambering out of its hole just as the six shafts blew. Everywhere he turned, Mormons were doubled over with smoke inhalation, clogging the trenches.

Rashid immediately ordered his battalion topside—

up onto the narrow land bridges dividing the trenches. He led them straight toward the Front, gassing the trenches as they went, cutting off the Mormons' lines of retreat, shooting anyone who crossed their line of fire.

By the time he reached the front lines, conscripts were storming the trenches, and New Salt was about to collapse. There wasn't much for Rashid and his men to do, so he marched them up the Fire Trench's parapet just to keep an eye on the fighting.

It was only when they reached 12-Bunker that Rashid stopped and stared, dumbstruck.

The Major had fought every step of the way from Alaska to New Seattle and had seen a lot of carnage here in New Salt. But he had never seen anything like this. The last six wire belts in front of 12-Bunker were piled high with conscript dead, and the ground between the belts was a bloody swamp.

The number 1 belt was the worst. There, the bodies had formed a small mountain, and the ground from the wire to the trench line was stacked with the dead.

The lone machine gun still hammered.

Rashid ordered his men to lower their weapons while he went up to look. The gunner and his assistant had been driven out of their Forward Bunker into the Fire Trench and were now defending the narrow ditch, back to back. The assistant gunner had just emptied his 9mm into the mass of attacking conscripts while the machine gunner—his chest and shoulders looped with crisscrossing cartridge belts—blasted anything that rounded the traverse.

Rashid was impressed. He watched as the assistant gunner hurled his empty 9mm into the face of the closet conscript. Grabbing an entrenching tool from the parapet, he swung it like a battle-ax, holding the *Ordu* at bay.

Major Rashid screamed in his loudest parade-ground voice:

"CEASE FIRE!"

He underscored the command by emptying his AK-47 between the machine gunner's legs.

When the man stared up at the Major, he found himself looking into six other automatic rifles.

"This war's over," the Major said. "You two out of the trench."

The conscripts heaved the stunned Mormons topside.

"Lieutenant," the Major ordered, "take these two into custody."

"Shouldn't I just shoot them?"

"Hell, no. We lost some good men blasting our way out of that mine shaft. It's time to replace them."

"With what?"

"These two. They just enlisted."

The conscripts were speechless.

"Friends," the Lieutenant said, smiling, "you just joined the *Ordu*."

10

Darrell waited with Legion and Tamerlane on the high ridge, watching the battle below. Eventually the Cuddler and his assistant joined them.

As Darrell studied the massive chain reaction of detonating powder kegs, he felt and saw each of them blow—blow and blow and blow and blow.

He had never seen anything like this. The *whump-whump-whump-whumps* went on and on and on, merging into one earth-shaking *KA-WHUMMMPPP!* blanketed by a roiling cloud of black smoke, which was then consumed by a red-orange fireball levitating high above the earth.

Still some of the trenches stayed intact. They had been stormed so many times they were now cauterized by new dugouts and aprons of barbwire.

Nor had their control-and-command been demolished. Behind the Frontline earthworks, the New Salt generals were dug in deep—in reinforced cellars, heaped high with dirt, virtually bombproof. There, fighting still went on—at the very center of the garrison—amid a hailstorm of charred debris tumbling from the sky.

Through his binoculars Darrell saw the gas crews and shock battalions emerging from their holes. They quickly gassed and machine-gunned the trenches,

"Under the eye of history," Legion said to him, "none of this matters. Men are like stars, Young Scribe. They're born, they die, black holes eat them."

"Are you suggesting our Lord is a black hole?"

"No, but his father is Allah."

"I thought he was a werewolf," Darrell muttered.

The *Ordu* batteries blazed in the hills, and the smoothbore trench mortars below were moved to almost point-blank range. They fired two-, three- and four-inch bombs in a dead-flat trajectory at the Mormon lines.

The whole world seemed to be on fire.

"I still can't see them giving up," Darrell said, "living in chains."

"The Normans domesticated Saxony. Rome razed

and salted Carthage, then subdued Gaul. The Mormons are mortal. They will be broken."

"Just so some of their generals survive," Forsythe said.

"Why?" asked Tamerlane.

"Torture one man, terrify a thousand."

Tamerlane nodded. "We will save some generals for you."

"Think of it as history," Legion said to Darrell.

"History writ in blood," Darrell said.

"Don't you feel a certain primitive delight?" Legion asked, clapping Darrell on the shoulder.

"What happens to the ones who surrender?" Darrell asked.

"They are in the Kill Zone," said Tamerlane. "We lock and load."

Darrell, angry and repulsed, was unable to take his eyes off the scene below.

That night Darrell worked in his tent until dawn—adding to his notes on Tamerlane's battle plans.

Would he ever find someone brave enough and cunning enough to smuggle them out?

Would anyone in the Citadel ever read them?

What would happen to him if the notes were discovered in the camp?

It would be the Cuddler's tent for sure.

He tried not to think about that one.

In the flickering light of his candle, he continued to write.

PART XVI

He who lives more lives than one
More deaths than one must die.

—OSCAR WILDE, *THE BALLAD OF*
READING GAOL

PART XVI

1

Two children and a white-haired old woman climbed a steep mountain trail on muleback. The day was hot, and the switchbacks narrow. Their mules were starting to falter. Falling rock or a buzzing rattler would spook them over the edge.

The children dismounted. The boy led his grandmother's mule by the cheek strap. His sister led the other two mules.

By late afternoon the trail wound upward over a series of stone benches—irregular steps of granite shelf rock. Yucca and prickly pear gave way to clumps of bear grass, then stands of greasewood and piñon. Above the piñon were forests of ponderosa pine.

The heat was unrelenting. Their mules were lathered to the hocks. Every breath was painful.

In the end, they lost all sense of time, distance, and direction.

2

When they reached the forest country, Apache sentries came out. These were stocky, long-haired men wearing breechclouts and leggings, thigh-high moccasins, and buckskin shirts.

The trail flattened, and the children swung back onto their mules. Rounding a cluster of barn-sized boulders, they entered an encampment of brush wickiups. Children, squaws, and yapping camp dogs surrounded them. They smelled old hides and woodsmoke.

A man on a big bay approached them, bareback, from across the camp. Though he was white, his buckskin garb was Apache.

The old woman eyed him suspiciously. He halted in front of her. His paint bristled at the mule smell and pulled back, snorting.

The old woman scowled. She couldn't help herself. He angered her.

He was her son, Richard Sheckly.

3

Dusk in the rancheria.

The old woman, her son, and her two grandchildren sat inside Spirit Owl's dome-shaped lodge.

"I'm glad you could make it up here," her son said. "I think you'll be impressed with what we've done."

Katherine ignored his remarks and studied the brush wickiup. Twenty feet in diameter and fifteen feet high, it was supported by mesquite poles, bent together at the top, then thatched with maguey. The ground was covered with skins.

Weapons and gear were strewn around the lodge. There were sheath knives, buckskin blankets, two rifles, arrows fletched with hawk feathers, ringed with black bands, and black, compound bows.

The old woman looked up at her son.

"The children claim you've opened up a hole in time."

"Enju." Yes.

"What is this *enju* stuff?" the old woman snapped.

"Grandma," Elizabeth said, "you promised you'd watch your temper."

"I was until he started with that *enju* nonsense." She turned to her son. "Can't you at least address me in my own language? I *am* your mother."

"I haven't forgotten."

"Then what am I doing in this—this—this wigwam?"

"It's not a wigwam," Matthew said patiently. "It's a wickiup. You know the difference."

"Yes, but what I still don't know is what I'm doing here. Richard, these children of yours tell me you've invented a Time Machine. That's obviously insane. The Los Alamos scientists worked on Time Penetration for decades. They had the best technology in the world, and they came up with nothing. But I'm supposed to believe that you—living on mesquite nuts and pemmican, working with little more than pencil, paper, and a broken-down computer—have succeeded where they failed?"

"The Los Alamos experiments helped me enormously," Richard said. "Their scientific insights were indispensable."

"Then why did they fail?" she asked.

"They relied on reason. They dwelt solely on the empirical characteristics of space-time. It was a fatal error."

"But you didn't make any errors," the old woman said. "You've always been smarter than everyone else, haven't you?"

"I never said that."

"I'll say it," Elizabeth said. "I think Dad's real smart."

"What's more, he's not only opened up that hole," Matthew said, "he's brought things back."

The old woman glared at them.

"I haven't got much," Sheckly said. "Up to now I've had difficulty aligning my spatial coordinates with their fourth-dimensional counterparts. I haven't been able to project the aperture with any precision. Since the ocean covers most of the globe, I've only retrieved salt water and prehistoric fish. They did not do well in these desert mountains."

Matthew handed his grandmother four specimen jars. She stared at their contents distastefully.

"They look like dead guppies," she said.

"I'll do better next time," Sheckly said. "My computations are more precise."

"What's the Indian have to do with all this?" the old woman asked.

"Spirit Owl has extended my awareness, offered me insights into divinity which have enabled me to perceive the greater whole. His heightened sensibility, which applied to the Los Alamos studies, facilitated my breakthroughs."

"He helped you open up this hole?"

"I could not have done it without him."

"What's he doing now?"

"He's spent the last nine days performing purification rituals before the holy cliff higher up the trail."

"What's so holy about a little red rock?"

"Apache tradition holds that many-seasons-past a lightning bolt split the cliff face. When the Indians examined the site, they found the petrified remains of a 'three-horned devil' imbedded in the rock."

"Dad thinks there's an old dinosaur fossil in there," Elizabeth said.

"And I think you're all crazy," the old woman said. "Drugs, fasting, and dehydration will induce hallucinations. I'm going to get all three of you down from these mountains before you harm yourselves further. I won't sit still for any primitive peyote rituals."

"But I wanted to show you—"

"Shut up!" Katherine shouted. "I won't listen to any more of this lunacy. To think I let these children come up here for the summer. Richard, if I find out you've harmed these children, I'll have you locked up. I'll—"

"Grandma," Matthew pleaded, "can't you even look at what Dad's done? For five minutes? Just this once?"

The old woman ignored him. "Richard, if you've—"

"Grandma!" Elizabeth shouted. She crossed the wickiup and stood over the old woman. "Do you hate Dad that much? You won't even let him show you what he's done?"

A young Apache girl entered the wickiup's crawl hole.

"Spirit Owl is ready. The sacred ritual begins at once. No one is allowed off the mountain until it is over."

Richard Sheckly got up and followed her out the crawl hole.

"What is happening?" the old lady asked.

"Spirit Owl has declared that the Spirits are in harmonious concord," Elizabeth said, "and Dad is going to help him open the hole. No one knows when we'll have this opportunity again."

"We are leaving this mountain *now*," the old woman said.

"It's too late," Matthew said. "The Apaches wouldn't let you back down that trail, even if it were possible. Which, as you'll see, it won't be."

"Why?" the old woman asked.

"Just watch," said Matthew.

"Grandma," Elizabeth said, "you're in for the surprise of your life."

◄ 4

At the edge of the sacred red cliff, Spirit Owl danced and chanted. The dance was in no way enjoyable. He was into his ninth straight day of purification rituals and was in serious pain. His muscles burned, and every breath was pure hell.

First had come the sacred sweat baths, and even these had been torturous. He'd sat in a hide-covered wickiup, stripped to the waist, in front of a fire. Beside it, in a shallow hole, were piled round, smooth stones, heated white-hot. A wrinkled crone named Cat Mother periodically splashed water onto them, filling the tightly sealed wickiup with scorching steam.

"Tell me," Cat Mother had said, "does the holy heat teach you true-knowledge?"

"I learn that heat hurts. I learn that old hags are less sensitive to the pain than men like myself."

Cat Mother had laughed heartily. "More hot rocks! Hurry!"

A young girl had brought in several more. Cat Mother poured water over them, and the steam billowed.

All he experienced was fatigue, thirst, and blurred vision.

Still he continued his wailing dance. His incantations held no more meaning for him than the Martian moons, but he chanted them anyway, the canyon reverberating with their singsong trills and vibrant tremolos.

The old hag strode up to him.

"Your eyes roll back, old man," she taunted. "I see only whites. What's wrong? Are you tired?"

"Shut up, pig," Spirit Owl said.

"Pig, am I now?"

Her laughter shrilled through the night. "Lift those knees, old man. You'll never open your hole that way."

"Go to hell."

"Ah, what's wrong, pretty one? Do you thirst?"

Again, her laughter screeched.

"Shut up, I said."

"Louder. I can't hear you. Chant louder—if you expect to split Time like a thunderbolt."

The old man hurt, but still he knew she was right. He lifted his legs higher.

In truth, the ordeal at the Pole had been much worse. That ritual had been so bad even Cat Mother had opposed it.

"Great wisdom can be learned at the Pole," she'd said. She'd underscored her point by touching the livid ridges of scar tissue along his back. "But can any amount of wisdom be worth such sacrifice?"

He had admitted he did not know.

Cat Mother sprinkled the hoddentin, *the sacred pollen, to Above, Below, and to the four cardinal directions.*

Meanwhile Spirit Owl slipped out of his moccasins and medicine shirt.

She pinched the flesh around the trapezius muscles, gradually slipping an awl under each muscle. She then inserted skewers through the awl's channels.

Spirit Owl had not moved.

Cat Mother lashed the skewers to the hanging rawhide ropes.

She took hold of Spirit Owl's legs, kicked away the block, and the old man hung suspended.

His back was hideously humped, but his rolled-back eyes remained fixed on the Red Horns in the cliff face.

Spirit Owl entered his trance.

Yes, that had been the hard part.

For it was at the Pole that the Three-Horned Beast had disclosed his Truth.

And Spirit Owl's course had been revealed.

All that was left for him now was to dance and to dance and to dance.

And to chant.

"Lift those knees higher, old man," the hag shouted. "Bellow out your sacred song. Where do you think you are? In a *pindah* rest home? You dance for the gods, old one, and they do not favor lazy, fearful, stupid dancers."

Her cackling laugh echoed through the night.

"Dance, sing, croak your guts out. Sing, I tell you, sing!"

5

Katherine Magruder stood in the mouth of a nearby cave. She studied the dancing shaman with mounting anger. She could not believe her son and grandkids had done this to her:

Put her on a mule and sent her up the trail, to this so-called sacred cave by this so-called sacred cliff to watch an insane old man bellow and dance. And listen to his senile assistant cackle.

Even worse, the wrinkled hag was now carving Spirit Owl up. With an ornately jeweled silver knife she slashed his arms, side, and legs till the old man's blood splattered the ground.

And still his dancing continued. He sang and prayed, danced and wailed.

Now the crone prepared a monstrous fire. She put tinder on the bottom, oak in the middle, and green, fresh-cut piñon on top. The tinder and oak caught right away, then mixed with the green woods. The smoke spiraled high into the air.

Despite the shrieking winds the smoke hung high overhead, motionless as stone. Then it became black, denser, more ominous. It seemed to metamorphose into anvil-shaped thunderheads, then swirling tornado clouds.

Thunder boomed. Sheet lightning blazed bone white across the sky. Funnel clouds twisted through the canyon, and the rain came down in slanted sheets.

The old woman had seen much in her eighty-four years. She'd seen fireballs blaze, the nuclear clouds rise over the desolated earth. She had seen refugees by the millions—burned and broken, starving and diseased—clogging the highways, swarming the charred rubble that had once been hospitals.

But she had never seen anything like this.

Katherine and her grandchildren stood in the cave's mouth. The storm raged, yet the fire soared higher and higher, untouched by the downpour.

As Spirit Owl danced around it, the flames flickered eerily in his mad eyes.

The old woman now felt his power.

Lightning bolts dislodged boulders from the peaks, hurling them into the crimson gorge.

Rain crashed, the thunder boomed, and the wind howled into the night.

◄■ **6**

Katherine did not emerge from her cave till dawn. She was too stunned, too confused. She was no longer sure where she was—or what was happening.

Even the canyon was different. The sky was cloudless, the wind dead still, the cliff face bone-dry. The storm had done little more than settle the red dust.

Spirit Owl squatted on his heels, his back to the gorge. His slashes were healed, little more than thin white scars.

What is happening? the old woman wondered. *Are you going mad?*

Her grandkids came out of the cave, yawning, unperturbed.

My God, she thought, *they've seen it before. This is for real.*

Again, she looked at the old man. He was staring at the cliff face—at the imprint of the Three-Horned Beast—except that the old man's eyes were rolled back.

He was still in his trance.

Her son squatted in front of his antique computer. It was powered by a portable generator. He worked the console assiduously.

Suddenly, Spirit Owl leaped to his feet. He resumed his chanting dance, the singsong tremolos trilling eerily.

Light flickered on her son's monitor, and the old woman went over to look. The screen turned a brilliant white, then the light forked and flared repeatedly like chained lightning. It flashed into an arc of crackling alabaster flame, then a dazzling globe, then a miniature sun. Throbbing, it exploded into a white-hot supernova.

The light subsided, and her eyes adjusted painfully. There was a picture on the monitor.

A sultry steaming predawn river wound through a subtropic rain forest. The jungle landscape was filled with palms, buzzing insects, and strange-looking tree ferns. Her son focused on a pile of gnawed bones along the shore.

Her grandkids were now on each side of her.

"There was a flood earlier," Elizabeth said. "This is all that remains."

Her son panned to the desolated shoreline. There were a lot of gnawed bones. This was a very hungry riverbank.

Slowly, her son panned to the treetops.

7

Dawn in the Late Cretaceous.

The sun, on Richard Sheckly's monitor, flared bloodred over the rain forest. Punching his keyboard, Sheckly panned to the rain forest below. Here and there he paused for a close look at a tree—a thick, dark, needle-bearing evergreen, a great towering red-wood, a lush weeping cypress, an occasional spruce or salt cedar. One spectacular cycad glowed crimson in the pollen-heavy air. Each of its jade green fronds was sharply delineated, awash in coppery radiance, its branches aflame with flamboyant flowers.

Sunlight slowly flooded the jungle.

Sheckly panned to the river. Hundreds of batlike creatures glided above the water's surface, their wingspans two to three feet long, their pointed beaks fanged.

Now and then, a larger predator surprised them. A Pterodon dived for his breakfast, scattering the other airborne beasts in several frantic directions. Moments later, he rose, his thirteen-foot wingspread fully extended, a thrashing Baptanodon dangling in his beak.

Sheckly turned on the sound. Three stereo speakers vibrated with the croaking of frogs, the buzzing of insects, the distant rumble of footfalls. These were followed by heavy splashing and a thunderous roar.

Sheckly panned upriver.

A massive dinosaur lumbered toward them. He seemed to be two beasts in one—the body and legs of a bull elephant, a seventy-foot anaconda for a tail and neck.

The Brontosaur moved downstream with a stiff, swinging gait, browsing the water's edge. When he lifted his legs, Katherine could see his feet were quadrapoidal. When the Brontosaur put weight on a foot, it expanded, then contracted when the weight was lifted. Like the modern-day elephant, this creature seldom mired.

He paused by a cycad. Its top blazed with brilliant flowers, and he began to crop the higher, untouched buds.

What fascinated Katherine was not the dinosaur's bulk but his diminutive head. Hovering atop the long boomlike neck, it was in constant motion. It rose and fell, rose and fell, as if hoisted and lowered by cable chains.

The Brontosaur needed to keep busy. There was not much to browse. The usual supply of water reeds and cycad fronds—as well as the river's animal life—had been devastated by the recent flood. The beast would have to leave the sanctuary of the river.

The Brontosaur clambered up a beach. His massive feet made sucking noises and left huge potholes in the muddy sand. Between these footprints, his tail excavated a deep ditch.

He headed straight for a clump of palmlike cycads, their trunks aflame with brightly hued flowers. Raising and lowering his boomlike neck, he cropped the foliage.

Suddenly, Sheckly panned to three other observers. They were two dozen yards away in a stand of conifers. He moved in for a close-up.

There was no mistaking Tyrannosauri rex. Even half-concealed by the trees, the beasts looked ferocious. Bipedal, they had massive torsos, two short arms, and almost human hands, but with razor-sharp talons arching out of the thumbs and forefingers. Their total body length stretched over forty feet—from the ends of their jaws to the tips of their tails.

Sheckly panned to the heads, which were six feet in length. Each slavering jaw glittered with a hundred serrated fangs. They twisted impatiently at the hips and rocked back and forth on their heavy tails. They obviously needed great self-control to stand and wait.

But they did hang back—waiting for the Brontosaur's approach. From cedar to cycad to tree fern, he browsed, moving closer to them, farther from the river.

The Brontosaur was less than a dozen yards away when he spotted their pack. With a trumpeting roar, he wheeled about and raced for the river.

The three Tyrannosaurs bounded from cover and quickly caught him, less than ten yards from the water.

The first Tyrannosaur attacked his tail, locking onto it with both talons and jaws. The second threw himself on the Brontosaur's back. The third circled around and hit him from the front.

Still the Brontosaur refused to go down. He dragged all three of them toward the water, his voluminous footprints flooded with blood.

The river was swollen, and because of their sharp, narrow feet, the Tyrannosaurs knew they would mire and drown.

The two on his back and tail let go, but the one in front now found their roles reversed. The Brontosaur bulldozed him into the stream.

The river came instantly to life. Carnivorous fish circled the two beasts. Scavenging dinosaurs lined the banks, while overhead, scores of carrion-feeding Pterodactyls swarmed and wheeled.

A Panzercroc—with a six-foot head and fifty-foot body—rested on a nearby sandspit. He opened a sleepy eye. The prodigious killer blinked twice, pushed up on his four stumpy legs, and slithered into the river.

The Panzercroc sculled straight for the mired Tyrannosaur. It was dinnertime, and the croc had had a very hungry week.

8

Sheckly located the Tyrannosaur's two surviving friends on the shore. They glared at the river, their jaws and chests drenched in blood, their prey escaping. It looked like they would have a hungry morning.

One of the Tyrannosaurs suddenly looked at the hill behind them.

Sheckly panned to the summit. The dinosaur there was ten feet high, thirty feet long, and shaped like a rhino. Out of her face and forehead arched a high, bony frill, and from her nose and brow extended three four-foot horns.

Trembling over her circular crater, the Triceratops looked exhausted.

Sheckly panned to her sloping, craterlike nest-hole. Six feet deep and forty feet across, it contained three dozen thick-shelled eggs, each the size of an elongated coconut.

The mother was laying them in perfect concentric circles.

Sheckly panned to a side shot of the Triceratops. She was little more than bones and parchment. Her rib cage protruded under her muddy brown hide, and her eyes squinted shut against the pain of expelling the eggs.

If she was aware of the Tyrannosaurs, she did not show it. With her bony frontal frill, her trio of horns, and the agility of her bowed, flexible forelegs, she was seldom in danger. It was a desperate predator, indeed, who stalked a Triceratops.

Which was apparently the Tyrannosaurs' plight.

They inched their way up from the river, hoping to catch the Triceratops off guard and sneak in behind those lethal horns.

The mother had just released her last egg when the first Tyrannosaur attacked. He charged from the left, while his partner lunged from the right.

Wheeling around, she gored her first attacker laterally, disemboweling him. Turning back toward her other attacker, she struck again but this time missed. Sidestepping her thrashing tail, the Tyrannosaur leaped onto her back. Digging in his arching talons, he sank his serrated fangs into the only vulnerable spot on her body—the soft nape, just behind the bony frill.

Each time she exhaled, he tightened his massive six-foot jaws. Inexorably, he pulled her throat skin up around her trachea, choking off her windpipe.

Her neck began to crack.

With thirty tons of Tyrannosaurus Rex straddling her, the Triceratops retreated into her nest-hole. With her last breath she spread-eagled her brood.

Quetzacoatlus—the Flying Dragon, the Thief of Eggs—was already tearing out the liver of the Tyrannosaur's fallen friend.

Her eggs would be next.

Light flickered on the adjacent cliff face. It forked and flamed, flashed repeatedly, then exploded into a white-hot nova.

The light flared, died, then all was still.

Katherine gazed on a circular two-foot hole in the cliff face. There was a sweltering rain forest, buzzing insects, and stench of bloody death within the circle.

The aperture was directly in front of the dying Triceratops's face. The old woman was nose-to-nose with her. Above the Triceratops's frill were the blazing eyes of the Tyrannosaur. Both beasts were covered with gore, and the thirty-foot nest-hole, in which the mother foundered, was filling with blood.

Nonetheless, the mother hung on, staring through the hole in time at Katherine.

Their eyes locked.

Slowly the Triceratops pushed herself up off her stomach. Pawing the ground inside the crater, her left forefoot located an egg.

She rolled it up the long slope of the nest-hole.

It was the rankest egg Katherine had ever seen— covered with dirt and afterbirth and splattered with blood—but to the mother it was clearly precious.

With the egg near the top of the nest, the Triceratops paused, closed her eyes, and died. Her body slumped, settled, and collapsed.

All was still.

Except for a single leg spasm, which sent the left foot flying. It flipped the egg out of the nest, through the hole, and into the old woman's outstretched hands.

The hole faded, shrank, and was gone, leaving behind three petrified horns and a wall of red rock.

The old woman stared at the thing in her fingers, covered with feces, mud, and blood—a fresh-laid, still-warm Triceratops egg.

9

That night Katherine and her grandkids sat in Spirit Owl's wickiup. They waited for her son and the old shaman.

As they waited, Katherine looked on the Indian's

lodge with new eyes. The weapons and totems, the horse gear and buckskin blankets—all smelling of woodsmoke, burning sage, and old hides—had taken on special meaning.

At last, her son and his father-through-choice entered the hut's crawl hole. Matthew and Elizabeth stood up.

"Grandma has something she'd like to say," Matthew said. "To both of you."

The old woman glared at him, silent.

"She's supposed to say she's sorry," Matthew said, "but she doesn't know how."

"You have to admit it, Spirit Owl looks pretty good," Elizabeth said. "Doesn't he?"

"He always did," her grandmother said.

"You two know each other?" Matthew asked. "How long?"

"Time-when," she said, then repeated the words in sign talk.

"And for-all-tomorrows," Spirit Owl said aloud and with his hands.

The two men sat on buckskin blankets opposite Katherine.

"Your son says you want me to reopen the hole," Spirit Owl said.

"You've seen Darrell's dispatches," Katherine said. "We need something from before the Great Destruction, something that will stop this Horde."

"It is always the same," Spirit Owl said, "with the *pindah lickoyee*," the white-eyes. "You dread the barbarians, the earth-shakers, so you make terrible weapons. Then you go to war."

"Maybe," the old woman said, "but you will also face this Tamerlane. Here. In your rancheria."

"Suppose I said *nada,* the war you seek is inside of you?"

"That's great," she said. "You can use that line on Tamerlane when he's burning your village and raping your women."

"I admit I was intrigued by your grandson's dispatches," Spirit Owl said. "In one letter he spoke of the Islamic *gehenna.* Tamerlane's consort, the Lady Legion, seeks to unleash this holy hell on earth and your grandson thinks she might just do it."

"I wouldn't go that far," Katherine muttered.

"I would," said the shaman. "Do you know why the Apaches fear the owl, whose cry portends death?"

"I suppose they don't want to die," the old woman said.

"*Enju,* because our own Spirits have described for us this Underworld. It is a Dead Land—one similar to Legion's *gehenna.* Our sacred *gans,* our Daughter-of-the-Water and the White-Painted-Lady tell us it is possible to unlock the gates to this Inferno—to inflict this hell on earth."

"I'll give you this much," the old woman said grudgingly. "Tamerlane skins men whole."

"What is it you need from before the Great Destruction?"

"If we expanded my son's power and gave him real computers, could you bring back howitzers, machine guns, tanks?"

"I can bring back nothing unaccompanied by a soul."

"Could you bring back people?" the old woman asked.

"*Enju,*" yes, the old shaman said.

"What will happen to their bodies in the other world?" Katherine asked.

"Which bodies?" Spirit Owl said.

"We each have many bodies and reside in many worlds," her son said.

Katherine shrugged. "The people I'm thinking of won't care. They're about to die anyway. Painfully. Frightfully. They'll be happy to come here."

"Why do you want to bring back dying people?" Elizabeth asked.

"We aren't kidnappers," the old woman said. "We aren't robbing anyone of a life unlived—only a death undied. We're giving them a second-time-around."

They stared at the old shaman. His eyes were rolled back, entranced. They waited a long time.

Finally his sister-through-choice—the old hag—worked her way through the wickiup's crawl hole. She carried a buckskin bag under her arm. She emptied its contents in front of Katherine. It was full of soft dead leaves—and one dinosaur egg.

The old shaman opened his eyes.

"I can open the hole three more times. Under one condition."

"I was afraid of this," Katherine said.

"Before I open the hole, you must hatch this holy egg."

The old Indian and his hag got up and crawled out of the wickiup, leaving the Magruder clan alone with a big dirty egg, resting atop a pile of dead leaves.

"My God," Katherine said. "What am I going to do now?"

10

Two days later the old woman sat in her backyard rocker, reading *The Pickwick Papers*. The deepening twilight brought a chill to the red desert. She pulled her shawl tightly around her shoulders.

She stared at the egg. It lay in a basket of mulch on a nearby table. She was not optimistic.

Hatch that thing? she thought. *Never happen.*

The old woman hadn't been a farm girl for nothing. She knew from experience that incubation wasn't that simple. You just didn't stick these things in the oven and turn it on. The process was subtle. A little heat here, a little chill there. You had to maintain a balance.

You also needed communication. The mama and the hatchling had to talk. One of the things the hatchling told the mama was whether it was too hot or too cold. The mother had to respond, and the hatchling had to feel loved. Not enough mother love, you'd get a neurotic hatchling.

And who would want a neurotic dinosaur?

The old woman studied her newfound friend. It was getting cold now. She added a handful of dead leaves. Maybe their decomposition would keep the hatchling warm. If it got any colder, she would take it inside.

She looked around her backyard. Betsy was not on her block. A neighbor had brought over a goat's head, which the bird was now tearing to pieces. She didn't even bother pulling the brain out of its open base. She plucked out the eyes with two pecks, then ripped off the pate with her sickle talons. Within seconds, the skull was split as if cleaved by an ax.

Betsy was up to her eyeballs in goat's brains.

Katherine's son and two grandkids entered the back gate. They pulled up chairs and sat beside her. For awhile they watched Betsy worry the goat's cranium. Finally her son spoke.

"We're never going to hatch the egg this way."

"I know."

"We did some checking in the old library," Elizabeth said. "Seems like Triceratops was a herd beast. His mother did more than just drop the eggs and run."

"You don't mean she wet-nursed them," the old woman grumbled.

"No, but she did nurture them," Matthew said.

"I suppose we could try one of those four-foot Mexican iguanas," Katherine said, leaning back in her rocker, "or a Gila monster. They might relate to it."

"No way," her son said. "They have cold blood."

"You mean our Triceratops has warm blood?"

"*Hot* blood," Elizabeth said. "The bodily processes alone are enough to keep it warm-blooded. As it gets bigger, its problem will be keeping cool."

"Where are we going to find a hot-blooded dinosaur big enough and mean enough to rear a Triceratops?" the old woman said, scowling.

Her son and grandkids turned toward her eagle.

Betsy Ross had reduced the goat's head to a few bloody bone fragments. There was nothing left for her on the ground, so she bird-hopped up to the picnic table's bench, then up to its tabletop, then onto her block. After all those goat's brains, her crop was the size of a football.

Betsy Ross ruffled her alabaster nape and cocked an eye skyward. It had been a good meal. She shook her white wedge-shaped tail and preened her snowy breast with a scarlet-crusted beak. After awhile, she stopped preening, drew up a leg, and shut her smoky gray eyes.

"Where do we find a hot-blooded dinosaur big enough and mean enough to rear a Triceratops?" Sheckly reported. "We turn to its closest living relatives. Like that old lady dinosaur over there, the lineal descendant of the Pterodactyl, the one with all that blood on her beak."

They turned to stare at the big, feathered dinosaur. Sensing the sudden attention, Betsy Ross glared back at them, her smoky eyes turning yellow with hostility. She was angry at having her after-dinner nap disturbed.

"Betsy, old girl," Sheckly said softly, "you're about to become a mama."

The next day Katherine and the kids took Betsy Ross for a buggy ride. When they returned, the hooded Betsy Ross instantly sensed that something was wrong. She began tearing at Matthew's glove, straining against the jesses.

There in the middle of the yard stood Betsy Ross's old nest—ten feet in diameter and five feet high. In its center was a small soft circular cavity, ten inches across and four inches deep, lined with rabbit fur, leaf mulch, and lichens—containing one Triceratops egg.

Richard Sheckly put on a gauntlet. Taking the jesses from Matthew, he slipped the hooded bird onto it.

"How did you retrieve that nest?" Katherine asked.

"Before we left the rancheria, I had some Apache friends take it down from the red butte. They lowered it in pieces, reassembled it, then brought it back here. I figured if the egg was in *her* nest, she might ignore all the other things wrong with it."

"Such as its size?" Katherine said.

"Look, it's our best shot," said Sheckly. "Eagles are extremely maternal. They're famous for adopting owlets and baby hawks, even sparrows."

"Liz and I read that one," Matthew said, "tried to hatch a golf ball."

"Sometimes I think I did," Katherine grumped.

Sheckly approached the nest, with Betsy Ross balanced on his gauntlet. Wrapping the jesses around his wrist and forearm, he removed the black hood.

Betsy's head jerked back. It was her old roost. There was no doubt about that—the one she and her mate had built. She seemed to recognize everything—the interwoven cornstalks and maguey, the scraps of red cloth, the rabbit fur lining the nest-hole.

It was *her* nest, in *her* territory. There was also no mistaking that there was an egg in it. An awfully big egg, it was true, but still an egg. And she was genetically coded to brood eggs—any and all eggs—which happened into her nest.

She emitted a low, gurgling cry and gripped the gauntlet so hard Sheckly's knees buckled.

She wanted off the glove.

Sheckly leaned toward the nest and unfastened the jesses. Betsy Ross hopped onto the nest's edge. She studied the huge egg a long moment, as if calculating the correct angle of approach.

With a jaunty rolling gait, she sauntered up to the cavity. Spreading her pinions to their full ten feet, she spun around and lowered herself onto it.

Her imperious eyes narrowed to smoky gray slits.

Betsy Ross—queen of all she surveyed—sat regally on brood.

12

Late that evening, Sheckly returned to the backyard. It was a bright clear night. The moon was three-quarters full, and the sky blazed with stars.

He sat in his mother's rocker and stared at the bird. She was perched on the nest's rim. Raising her eyes from her egg, she met his gaze, recognizing him instantly.

The two of them went back a lot of years.

Sheckly knew what the Destruction had done to the raptors. Fallout had not only poisoned their air, it had fouled their food and water. Everything the other birds suffered, these birds of prey received in spades redoubled. That even a few of these species survived was miraculous.

As for Betsy's breed, no one counted on their return. For over four decades—long after the owls, hawks, and vultures had restocked themselves—eagles were nowhere to be found. Even Sheckly had written them off—until that golden morning when the Citadel had discovered Betsy and her mate circling overhead.

The male, Patrick Henry, had a nine-foot wingspan, a huge yellow beak, and a snowy-white head that glistened in the sun. Betsy Ross—with her ten-foot wingspread—had been the largest female anyone had ever seen. With radiant hackles and alabaster tail, she'd been breathtaking in flight.

Sheckly watched her hop off her nest and hobble across the yard toward him. She stopped to tear at an old rabbitskin, using it as a toy. Compared to what she'd been, she was a sorry spectacle indeed.

He tried to shake off the sadness of memories past. He hated looking back. He'd seen what the pain of nostalgia had done to his mother. It had turned her from a happy, vital woman into a bitter harridan, but he could not help himself. He'd been responsible for bringing the bird here.

In his mind's eye he could still see Betsy Ross as she had been—she and her mate, soaring above New Arizona, performing their intricate courtship rituals. They'd wheeled upon the hot mountain thermals, higher and higher, now and then coming together, almost touching, then quickly drifting apart, in ever-widening, ever-rising spirals.

Once he'd climbed a nearby peak and positioned a high-powered telescope. There, he studied their nest life atop a nearby butte. Betsy had hatched the young and tended to the nest, while Patrick Henry hunted, returning each dusk with a skinned-out carcass in his talons.

The eaglets were hysterical at feeding time. Chirping, flapping, and fighting, they consumed prodigious amounts of carrion. Soon the base of the red butte was covered with diamondback rattles, jackrabbit hindquarters and lizard-skins, prairie dog bones and eagle down. It was a true eagle paradise.

Until the disaster struck.

It occurred late one dusk while Betsy was pecking out

morsels for the eaglets. Patrick had taken his stand on the far rim of the nest. He was making his toilet, carefully removing loose feathers and down, preening his alabaster chest with his red-flecked beak.

The arrow took him straight through the center of the chest, pinning him to the crimson crag.

Betsy's ten-foot wingspan was instantly at full spread. Three swift beats, a powerful back kick, and she launched herself high above the spire, a full forty feet over its top.

The second tri-bladed broadhead skewered her left pinion near the carpal joint, slashing the shoulder nerve plexus.

She tumbled helplessly, crashing on top of the red butte.

Now Sheckly watched as Betsy Ross dropped the rabbitskin and headed back toward the nest. She flapped and hopped onto the bench, from there to the tabletop, then up to the next.

She brooded on the egg.

Some prenatal communication, he supposed. The hatchling probably complained it was getting chilly.

He remembered the two Apache boys who had shot the eagles, how he'd gone to their rancheria, filled with rage.

Spirit Owl had taken him into his wickiup.

"What is it you really want?" the old man had asked. "Retribution? The boys punished?"

"I want to know why they did it."

"They thought that by killing the birds and plucking their tail plumes they would steal the eagles' medicine."

"That was a terrible thing," Sheckly had said, "killing the birds for their feathers."

"Enju," agreed, the old man said. "An act of wicked pride. But what do you want?"

"I want the eagles back, dead or alive. Since the red butte is on Apache land, I will need your tribe's permission to scale it."

"It torments you?" Spirit Owl said. "The idea of the male still hanging there, impaled on the rock? And his mate, shot through the pinion, alone on that peak?"

"I just want them down."

The old man handed Sheckly a black falconer's hood and a pair of jesses.

"What are these for?"

"You must cover the bird's head with the hood. The leather jesses you tie to the feet."

"You think I'll have trouble with two dead birds?"

"The female is still alive."

Sheckly studied the brooding bird. *Well, old girl,* he thought, *was it worth it?*

Betsy Ross stared back at him, her smoky gray eyes angry and unyielding.

I should have guessed the answer to that one.

At dawn, he had begun the climb, and the first half of the ascent wasn't bad. Sheckly was an experienced rock climber who had spent much of his youth—to his mother's distress—scaling the cliffs and peaks of New Arizona.

But the upper half—around four hundred feet—got rough. The butte became vertical as a plumb line, and hard sandstone gave way to the flame red pillar crowning the butte, a crumbling column striated with friable layers of ocher clay and pink laterite. From there most of the crimson rock face was too porous to drive in a piton, and the handholds he dug with his pick were virtually useless.

He had no way to anchor his line, and the strain on his hands and arms was agonizing.

After awhile his memories of the climb dimmed. He did remember dragging himself over the edge of the vast circular nest. Standing on the outcrop, he tore the spread-eagled male off the tri-bladed broadhead and flung him over the side of the butte to the Apaches below.

By then Sheckly was so drugged by pain and exhaustion, he couldn't recall scaling the last two hundred feet. All he remembered was his hands bleeding, and then he was pulling himself over the summit.

The red sun flared in the west, then sank below the mountains. He would be spending the night up there.

Suddenly, he saw her. She was directly in front of him, less than six feet away. What struck him were her blazing amber eyes. Not even two days and nights on a desert peak, without food or water, could put out their fire. Hurt and drastically weakened, she remained indomitable.

He removed the black falconer's hood from his backpack and approached her from her blind side. Slipping the falconer's hood over her head, Sheckly lashed the leather jesses to her feet. Then he drove a piton into the red rock and anchored the leather cords.

Next he took a small bag filled with cotton balls and pieces of liver from his pack. He soaked them thoroughly with water from his canteen and inserted them into the hood.

Betsy Ross ate.

At dawn, with her head and talons bagged, her wings trussed to her sides, he tied the bald eagle to his back.

He began his descent down the scarlet spire.

He watched the bird hop off the egg. She perched on the edge of the nest and waited. Must have gotten a signal. Suppose the hatchling was getting hot. *Well, I hope you know what you're doing,* he thought without enthusiasm.

She turned and met his stare. He felt the heat of her eyes.

Her smoky amber eyes had lost none of their imperial fierceness.

*I know you accept me. After all, I brought you down.
And you accepted my children and my mother. But will
you accept that hatchling, if it ever makes it out?*

*I'll never understand you. I don't even know what's
wrong with your wings. Why won't you fly? We never
found any physical damage. Did you simply give up?
Found a nice easy life here with my mother and the kids
and that pond.*

*You and my mother—two of a kind. You even sit on
the arm of her rocking chair.*

Two old women.

His eyelids grew heavy and finally closed.

Richard Sheckly slept.

13

As for Katherine, she was
counting her dinosaurs before they hatched. The day
Betsy Ross accepted the egg, Katherine hauled her
grandchildren into the Citadel's main library. She
lined them up, like soldiers, in front of the card cata-
logue files.

"I want to know *everything* about our Time
Travelers," she said. "Their mental and medical problems, their family histories, their favorite books,
movies, music. What they ate, how many hours they
slept, what kind of clothes they wore. I want to know
what shames them and what makes them proud."

"You want footnotes too?" Matthew said.

He did not relish spending his summer in the
library.

"No," Katherine said. "There's not enough time.

When you're done, head back up to that sacred cliff. Take a high-speed minicam with you. Your father won't have the power to reopen that hole, but he'll be working out his new coordinates and tracking these three people on his computer monitor. You can tape some footage of them off the monitor."

"We're making home movies of history?" Elizabeth asked.

"If we intend to use half the Citadel's electricity, we'll need more than just fairy tales. We'll have to *show* the council something. Now get to it."

"Sir, yes, *sir!*" Matthew shouted, sarcastically snapping to attention.

"Anything else, *ma'am!*" Elizabeth bellowed, mimicking her brother.

Their scowling grandmother did not return their salutes.

14

Three and a half weeks later Matt and Elizabeth were back in the Citadel with their notes and videotapes.

Katherine set up a meeting with Clement Lamont. He was her oldest friend, a fellow council member, and the Citadel's chief magistrate. Tall, wiry, with closely cropped iron gray beard and hair, he favored black suits, black bow ties, and was humorless as a mortician. He was one of the few people left who had personally experienced the Destruction.

Together, he and Katherine controlled enough votes to push her energy request through the council.

They each had a pile of notes outlining Katherine's time travel plans, specifically which people she planned to bring through the hole in time.

"Say all this Time Machine stuff is true," Clement said. "I still have reservations about the three you want to bring through that hole." He riffled the stack of notes in front of him. "Your first general, for instance, sounds awfully sophisticated. He commanded whole armies, entire fronts. His later years sound like armchair generalship, push-button warfare. We're a tiny outpost, not a Great Power."

"Clement," Katherine said, "the kids have our men on videotape. Let me show you what they look like, so you'll have a better sense of who they were and what they accomplished."

Elizabeth turned on the VCR. The monitor showed a freeze-frame of a man holding a pistol in his outstretched hand. The shot changed to an angle over the man's right shoulder—and the action commenced.

His gun jumped, and a Mexican soldier fell from his horse.

"What's going on?" Clement asked. "A frontier shoot-out?"

"It's our push-button general," the old woman said. "He's just shot one of Pancho Villa's leading Colonels, one-on-one."

"We're talking *war*, not frontier gunfights."

The monitor cut to World War I. The soldier—now a Colonel—wore a doughboy uniform and a pancake helmet. He was going over the top.

Shells splattered mud and shrapnel in all directions. Men fell all around him, riddled by machine gun bullets, blown to bits by artillery fire.

Still the Colonel advanced, crawling over the

corpse-strewn concertina wire, slogging through the watery shell craters.

"Does that look like an armchair general to you?" the old woman asked.

"Duly noted."

The tape cut to 1939–40. The General was training armored assault troops in the Southwestern desert.

"Familiar country," Clement said.

"It is. The General trained his tank corps near here."

"He's a desert warfare specialist?" Clement asked.

"He's an expert on every kind of warfare," Katherine said, "including amphibious assaults."

She cut to ships at sea—and the invasion of Sicily. There, on the beach, his men faced their first enemy fire. Instead of advancing, however, the terrified soldiers dug in, and refused to budge.

Suddenly, there was the General. Shouting orders, waving troops forward, he seemed to be everywhere at once. He sighted in mortars, even fired rounds himself, driving his men, cursing them, moving them up the beach.

In the next scene those same troops were marching through Palermo, victorious.

On and on, the General's troops rolled—the Saar Campaign, Bastogne, the Bulge, the invasion of Germany.

The old woman read off his stats:

"In his last campaign in Europe, during 281 days of intense fighting, he liberated 81,522 square miles, including 12,000 cities and towns. His own casualties totaled 160,692 while he inflicted 1,443,888 casualties. He took a total of 1,280,688 prisoners. Very simply, he has conquered more territory in a shorter period of time than any general in history."

"Why would such a man help us? We're hardly the NATO Alliance or the Roman Empire."

"He wasn't real happy with his last war," Katherine said. "He felt we'd beaten one tyrant, replaced him with another, and that all the suffering and dying had been in vain."

The monitor then cut to a limo crashing into an army truck. The General was slammed headfirst into the front seat, breaking his neck.

The next shot was a freeze-frame of him in a hospital bed, in spinal traction. His neck was immobilized by steel hooks, driven up under his jawbone, then cranked tight.

The monitor showed freeze-frames of his funeral cortege in the rain.

Then of his cross in the Luxembourg cemetery.

A lingering close-up of the cross.

"Sure, he'll come along," Katherine said. "He's got nowhere else to go."

Matthew whipped out his harmonica and treated them to several bars of "Dixie."

"What's that for?" Clement asked.

"To get you in the mood," Elizabeth said.

The monitor cut to another battlefield—full of Union bluebellies and Confederate graycoats.

"What we are seeing," Katherine said, "is the first major battle of the American Civil War—two hundred years ago."

The scene was surreal. In the hills overlooking the battlefield were the town and farm folk of Virginia and Maryland. They wore their Sunday best—frock coats and top hats, gingham dresses and bonnets. They had food hampers, binoculars, and were seated on blankets. They clearly perceived the War Between the States to be a picnic.

The monitor returned to a green rolling battle-ground. Grayish white smoke drifted over the field. The monitor zoomed in on a Confederate Brigadier General in a frayed uniform and an old forage cap.

"Our General's men have the high ground, but they're being shelled and stormed by a force three times their size."

The monitor cut to an overhead shot of the battle.

"As you can see," Katherine said, "the rest of the Confederate Army is in full rout. Only the General's brigade holds its ground."

Scene by scene he was shown turning the tide of battle. At last, his outnumbered troops were driving the Yankees from the field.

"I take it this General has seen a lot of action?" Clement asked.

"Take another look."

She ran more of his battlefield footage, preceding each scene with the name of the conflict.

"Slaughter Mountain."

"Winchester."

"McDowall."

"Malvern Hill."

"Second Manassas."

"Fredricksburg."

"Antietam."

Her footage of the Antietam cornfield was horrendous.

Now Katherine moved in for a close-up. The General was in the Wilderness Woods. It was night. The forest was burning, and the General was shot off his horse.

Katherine froze the next frame.

A surgeon's bone saw was amputating the General's arm.

In the next scene the General raved on his deathbed:

"Order A. P. Hill to take the right flank . . . Major Pendleton, go see if there is higher ground between Chancellorsville and the river . . . Where is Pendleton . . . ? Tell him to push on those columns. . . ."

Then there was more incoherent raving followed by:

"Let us cross over the river and rest under the shade of the trees."

Slowly, his body settled.

"He'll like it here just fine," the old woman said.

Liz cleared her throat. "New tape?"

"Yep."

A woman swung down from an open-cockpit biplane. She jerked off her leather flight helmet and eye goggles. She would have been pretty, but that her hair was severely bobbed and the white goggle-circles around her eyes clashed comically with her sunburned skin.

"She knows about prop planes?" the Councilman said.

"Everything."

There followed scenes of her barnstorming stunts, of her cross-country air races and transoceanic flights.

Katherine cut to footage of her crashes—as she stalled engines, blew tires, snapped safety harnesses like banjo strings and catapulted out of cockpits. The old woman showed her pancaking planes into trees and sandbanks, flipping planes end over end in rainstorms. Planes caught fire, ground-looped, lost their wheels, ended upside down, with the pilot hanging from her harness.

"This is just to show you," Katherine said, "that breathing life back into our rickety old planes will not be any day at the beach. It will require real courage."

"You sure she'll want to do it?" Clement asked.

The footage shifted to the woman flying over the ocean in a twin-engine Lockheed Electra.

"This time," Katherine said, "she's trying to circumnavigate the globe."

On the monitor the plane's engine began to sputter. It was obviously running out of gas—and headed toward the Pacific.

"Her navigator was a lush," Katherine said. "He got them lost, and they missed their stop-off in Hawaii."

"She crashed in the Pacific?"

"Worse."

What followed were freeze-frames of the woman crash-landing in the jungle, where she was captured by Japanese soldiers, tortured, and incarcerated in a concentration camp.

In the final sequence she was bent over a tree stump and decapitated by Japanese guards.

"Why did they do all that to her?" Clement asked.

"They thought she was a spy. They were preparing for war and were a little paranoid."

Katherine flashed to the woman's Lockheed going down on the Pacific atoll.

"I plan on stopping the action right here."

She hit the freeze-frame.

The plane froze in time—inches above the island rain forest.

"The way I see it," Katherine said, "her options are extremely limited."

15

That night, when the old woman returned from the council meeting, she found the kids and her son standing in the backyard beside the eagle nest.

"We have the votes," Katherine told them. "The Citadel will supply us with enough power to get those computers going."

"Now all we have to do is hatch that dinosaur," Matthew said, looking into the nest.

"That eggshell looks harder than Arkansas bedrock," said the old woman, shaking her head.

"Well, if the hatchling does break out," Elizabeth said, "we'll know it's one tough kid."

Betsy Ross, who was standing nearby, hopped up to the egg, roused her hackles, and eyed it with obvious skepticism.

She took her time stretching and refolding her pinions.

"It better be tough," Katherine said. "Just look at its mother."

"Something tells me," her son agreed, "it's going to have a very *un*permissive parent."

16

The next morning the egg started to tremble.

Betsy Ross, who was perched on the edge of the nest, glared impatiently at it. The rest of them stood there and gawked.

"My God," Matthew said, "that was quick."

"Maybe Mother Nature did things faster in the Late Cretaceous," his sister said. "What do you think he's doing in there?"

"You see where the egg's blunted at one end?" their father said. "That's the air pocket. The hatchling has to tear through the amniotic membrane and find its oxygen in there."

The infant squawked inside the egg. "Urk-urk-urk!"

"Sounds like the hatchling's broken through," Sheckly said.

The chirps escalated: "Urk-urk-urk!"

Betsy Ross's crude call-note came back: "Ka-EEEK! Ka-EEK-EEK-EEK!"

"Well," Sheckly said, "looks like it's time to drill."

As if on cue, the hatchling screwed an egg tooth through the blunted end of the shell, guaranteeing an air supply. It began drilling a series of holes through the egg's longitudinal axis.

Betsy Ross was getting nervous.

Sheckly wrapped her jesses around his forearm. Taking a deep breath, he planted his feet.

"Who knows what Betsy'll do when she finds out what's inside?" he said.

"You mean she might kill her baby?" Elizabeth said.

"It won't look like any eaglet *she's* ever seen," he said.

The shell started to split along the line of drilled-out holes dotting the longitudinal axis and Betsy's eyes narrowed. She emitted a strident screech, and her snowy white hackles lifted.

Sheckly tightened his grip on the leather jesses.

"Dad," Matthew said, "are you sure about eagles adopting hawks and owlets and all that stuff?"

Before his father could answer, the top of the egg lifted off.

Out clambered a baby Triceratops, a Lilliputian replica of its full-grown mama. Two of the three facial horns—the ones projecting just above the eyes—were disproportionately small, but in every other respect its minuscule features were adult, right down to the body and the bony frill projecting up out of the forehead and over the neck. It opened its turtlelike beak and emitted a greeting cry, revealing two rows of teeth. Each wide, stumpy foot sported a trio of talons.

Betsy Ross's pinions flapped to their full ten-foot span. She shot straight to the end of her jesses, high above the nest, almost wrenching Sheckly off his feet. The backyard reverberated with her screams, and Sheckly, unable to hold her back, was dragged over the nest's edge.

Her wings settled, her hackless lowered. She emitted a soft, strangely melodious "Ka-EEK! Ka-EEK-EEK-EEK!" totally undinosaurlike but somehow tender and maternal.

"Take the jesses off," the old woman said. "Can't you see she wants to be with her kid?"

Obediently, her son freed the jesses. The hatchling, which had raced, in trembling terror, back under a piece of eggshell, stuck its head out.

"Urk?" it questioned.

"Ka-EEK! Ka-EEK-EEK-EEK!" Betsy answered impatiently.

The old woman walked up to Betsy. She tossed a piece of liver into the inner nest. Betsy bird-hopped up to it, stomped on it with a talon, and began shredding it into tiny morsels with her other foot. She picked one up and raised the tidbit over the hatchling's frill.

The diminutive dinosaur threw back its head, opened its tiny beak, and accepted the morsel.

"Urk," Katherine went, mimicking the baby's call-note perfectly.

The hatchling, still chewing the morsel with double rows of well-developed teeth, lifted its head and stared at the old woman. Recognizing its greeting cry, it answered:

"Urk-urk-urk."

Katherine responded. "Urk-urk-urk!"

There followed a long litany of greetings and answers.

Richard Sheckly looked at his children and burst into laughter. "Do you know what happened when your grandmother returned the baby's call-note?

"What?" Elizabeth asked.

"Our baby just found a second mother. Your grandma's going to wet-nurse a dinosaur."

17

Dawn in the mountains.

In the mouth of the cave, the old woman waited.

She'd been upset for a long time.

Among other things, the trip up the mountain had been bad. Spirit Owl had insisted they begin the ritual at once, arguing that it might be his last chance to find the Sacred Spirits "in perfect alignment, in harmonious concord."

*So as soon as the infant had hatched, they started out.
They climbed the mountain at reckless speed, their mules
lathered to the hocks.*

*Yes, everything, so far, had been bad. The climb was
exhausting. Spirit Owl's Sun Dance was hideous. The night
before, the wind, the rain, the lightning and thunder were horrendous. Katherine finally collapsed in a corner, praying:*

Not the bombs. Please, God, not again.

*But there were no bombs. In fact, at dawn it was as if
the storm had never been. The sky was cloudless and clear,
the day windless, the red dust dry as old bones.*

And her son was patiently working at his keyboard.

Richard now appeared ready. Every erg of the
Citadel's power was channeled into his computers.
He had his coordinates aligned, and Spirit Owl's
dance had reached a wailing crescendo.

Suddenly, light flickered on Richard's computer
monitor. It turned dazzlingly white, then forked and
flared, soared into an arc of searing flame and
exploded into a supernova.

The fire faded and died.

A picture formed. A limo on a highway in Germany
turned onto a dirt road, on a collision course with an
army weapons carrier. The truck sped closer.

Lightning flared and flamed on the cliff face, then
dimmed and was gone.

In its place was a hole—seven feet high, four
across.

Katherine walked up to the cliff and stood directly
in front of it, staring into a long murky tunnel.

A dot appeared in the distance, grew larger, until
she at last discerned its shape.

The shape was that of a man.

A man was passing through a hole in time . . .

18

The General in the black
limo had already died. In fact, since that moment it
seemed as if his whole life was being replayed, like a
motion picture running backward. He witnessed his
death on the hospital bed, the traction hooks locked
under his jaw, the ambulance rushing him to the hospital. Then the snapping of his neck, the crash and—

Stop-time.

Freeze-frame.

Something weird happened.

He felt his soul depart his body, like a silk kerchief
plucked from a magician's sleeve, and he was floating
through space and time.

Then he was in a black tunnel—with a dot of light
at its end. An enigmatic Indian in a buckskin breechclout and leggings was leading the way, waving him
on. Otherwise, he was alone.

Was he dead? Dreaming? Had he had a stroke? He
shuddered at the thought. *Please, God, not a stroke. I
know I've been hit on the head a lot but not a stroke. I
couldn't take lying around, doing nothing, sitting on the shelf.*

On and on, the General walked. The old Indian
was still looking back at him, waving him forward.
No point in not going ahead. He'd always maintained
something like this would happen. Hadn't he claimed
he'd fought in all battles, in all places, in all times?
That he had razed Carthage and sown its fields with
salt, that he had served under Caesar in Gaul, that he
had slogged the long road back from Moscow with
Napoleon? Hadn't he always seen himself as the eternal soldier who had returned repeatedly—always in

times of violent struggle and earthly upheaval—to save his people?

Well, if nothing else, the General was properly dressed. Six feet two inches tall, he wore a stainless steel helmet with four gold stars blazoned across the front. His tunic had four stars on each of the shoulder loops, as did his collar tabs. They were also on the butts of the two pistols, strapped to his hips—a nickel-plated ivory-handled Colt .45 automatic and a Smith & Wesson .357 Magnum. He was wearing tan riding breeches, which bloomed at the thighs but tapered tightly into his black, knee-high cavalry boots, shined to a high gloss. His cavalry crop was tucked under his arm.

The General was glad he looked good as he passed through the blinding wall of light. On the other side he was met by a white-haired old lady in a pale cotton shift. She stared at him with blank astonishment. Not giving an inch, he returned her stare with a hard, unyielding gaze and cracked the crop against his boot.

After all, he was George S. Patton.

◄■■■ 19

       Sheckly left Patton to his mother and kids. While they gaped and stammered at the General, Richard punched new figures into the computer.

This time the monitor focused on a dark battlefield. There was so much smoke, Sheckly wasn't sure what he was screening.

But Spirit Owl was. His wailing dance accelerated, and soon lightning bolts blazed over the hole. When they subsided, far down the dim tunnel a dot appeared. It swelled, gradually taking form. Spirit Owl was bringing through the hole not simply a man but a man and a horse.

Sheckly began to crank up the power, not knowing how much amperage he would need. The computer chugged and grunted, clunked and wheezed, registering its protests.

The hole expanded.

The man and the horse approached . . .

20

The gray-bearded Confederate General, passing through the hole in time, rubbed his left shoulder. He was surprised that it no longer hurt.

Suddenly, he realized why.

The amputated arm had miraculously returned.

So had his old VMI forage cap, his Confederate uniform, and his heavy black boots. He was also packing his good Navy Colt and was riding his best horse.

He patted his mount's neck. Old Sorrel was the bravest war-horse the General had ever had, and it was a good thing he was with him now. Their present situation looked bad. The visibility was nil, the horse's footing nonexistent, the tunnel weird, and their future doubtful.

Luckily, Sorrel had someone to follow—the Indian scout leading them. He was stripped to the waist, wearing a buckskin breechclout and leggings. A strange-looking brave, he appeared to be at least a

hundred years old. Well, he seemed to know where
he was going.

So be it. Wherever he was taking the General, he
was meant to go. God must have wanted him there.
God had always held a special destiny for him. The
General believed that implicitly. Now. Always.

Reaching into his saddlebag, the General found a
lemon. He'd always favored lemons. They not only
prevented scurvy, he liked their taste.

Sucking on the lemon, he peered up the tunnel.
There was now a spot of light at the tunnel's end.
Guess the old Indian knew where he was going.

Now he was leaving the tunnel and entering a blaze
of light. It hurt his eyes and dazzled Sorrel's as well.
Reining him in, he shaded the horse's eyes with his cap.

Finally, his eyes adjusted. Where did that Indian
go? There he was. He sure was ugly. He was wailing
and dancing, his knees pumping up and down, his
rolled-back eyes fixed on the sun.

Who was that old lady? The two kids? What was
this? A desert canyon? Was he in Mexico? Was going
to have to refight the Mexican War?

Where was he?

Oh well. He'd find out soon enough. Putting his
cap back on his head, Thomas "Stonewall" Jackson
swung down off his horse.

21

Katherine and the kids could
gawk at General #2 but not Sheckly. He didn't have
the time. He was at work on Traveler #3.

Spirit Owl wailed and danced, Sheckly's coordinates fell into place, and again the monitor came blindingly to life.

The monitor focused on a plane at sea. Cutting to the interior of the cockpit, Sheckly panned out over the blue Pacific. Unfortunately, there was no time to sightsee. The twin-engine prop plane was sputtering and jerking, almost out of fuel.

In the distance was a jungle island runway, toward which the plane was limping.

Suddenly, Sheckly was in trouble.

"Hey," he shouted to Katherine, "we've locked onto the whole plane. Spirit Owl's trying to bring a twin-engine Lockheed through that hole."

"Good," she said, "we can use a bomber."

"But I can't make the aperture big enough."

"How big can you make it?"

"I don't know. You want to rip a permanent hole in Time? A tear big enough to fly a plane through?"

"That seems to be Spirit Owl's plan."

"We may never get it closed again."

"Richard," she shouted, "I want that plane."

Against his better judgment, he punched new parameters into the computer.

"We're blowing the boilers," he shouted to his mother.

Lightning blazed around the sides of the hole. Slowly, it expanded from ten feet to more than fifty.

The roar of his overtaxed generator and the whining screech of his computer were rivaled only by Spirit Owl's trills and tremolos.

Then everything was drowned out by the deafening roar of the plane. It was flying at them, full tilt, crammed into the tunnel so tight that its wingtips brushed the very walls of Time.

"Oh, my God," Katherine yelled, "here she comes."

They all hit the ground just as the plane roared toward the hole.

22

           The woman in the airplane had nothing to fear. She had seen enough horror to last a thousand lifetimes.

She still remembered how lost and out of fuel, she and her navigator had been forced down on a remote Japanese island—where she had been starved and tortured.

Her final memory was that of being bent over a tree stump and having her head hacked off, bushido-style, with a none-too-sharp sword.

Her head had bounced with a thump, next to her navigator's.

At which point, Time reversed itself.

So the woman piloting the plane was not worried about her destination. The world had already tortured and killed her. What more could it do?

Among other things she felt good. Her head was back on her shoulders. She was bathed, well fed, uninjured, and all decked out in her flight suit. Whatever came up, she'd be ready.

She did not even mind that Fred Noonan, her alcoholic navigator, had, a while back, uncorked a fifth of Black and White.

"When the going gets tough, the tough get drunk," he'd said. And he did not stop till he was sucking air.

He wouldn't have been much help sober. The present

weather conditions were unlike anything she'd ever seen. The engine was silent, and the propeller blades still as death, frozen in Time.

If it had not been for the ancient Indian, sitting on the plane's nose, waving her forward through the black tunnel, she would have felt hopelessly lost. But he seemed to know where they were going, so she stayed at the controls.

Meanwhile the pinpoint of light in the misty distance grew larger.

Most important, she was no longer afraid. That was a relief. Fear was not something she'd been intimately acquainted with. In fact, her husband, G. P. Putnam, had sometimes wondered if she was not defective in that respect.

"Pathologically brave," he'd once called her.

The Japanese had shown her where such bravery led.

Well, too late for that now.

It was time to get back to work. The speck of light was growing quite large.

Maybe you're approaching Heaven's Gate, she thought. Odd way to enter. In an airplane, an old Indian sitting on the plane's nose, your navigator, Noonan, drunk as a lord.

Oh no, now he was singing:

> *When your back's against the wall.*
> *When your towns and cities fall.*
> *Black powder and alcohol.*
> *Black powder and alcohol.*

I sure hope God has a sense of humor.
The speck of light was rocketing at her, and it

didn't look like the Pearly Gates. *Maybe you're headed for Hades,* she thought.

No, you've been there already.

The light was blinding, so she lowered her sun goggles. She was piloting her plane not onto a jungle landing strip or into a watery grave but through a hole in time. Barely squeezing through, the engine, to her surprise, leaped noisily to life. She only had a half dozen people for an audience, but she still decided to put on a show. She performed two barrel rolls, then dipped her wings.

Her engine sputtered.

You're running on vapor, girl. Time to put this crate down.

She was flying over a vast crimson canyon, and the only flat landing space—about four hundred yards from the hole—had a dozen brush wickiups on it. She shrugged. *You seem to be the ones who brought me here. This is what happens when you invite a pilot to lunch.*

She made a rough two-wheel landing, taking out half of the brush huts.

"Say, Tonto—or whatever your name is—where the hell am I?" she shouted at the plane's nose.

Only Tonto wasn't there.

Figures.

However, there were two kids, a couple of soldiers, a bunch of Indians, and a white-haired old lady coming toward the plane. Who knows what *they* wanted.

She unsnapped her safety harness and pulled herself to her feet. She kicked open the hatch.

That damned Noonan.

He was now out cold.

She caught a glimpse of herself in a side mirror. Her hair was bobbed, and she had on a leather jacket, a khaki flight suit, a white scarf, and sun goggles. She raised the goggles and grimaced at her white eye-circles.

She headed down the gangplank. Before the props spun to a jerking halt, she was already walking away from the plane toward her onlookers, without looking back.

This was clearly a woman who had the right stuff.

This was Amelia Earhart.

23

Night in the mountains.

The three Time Travelers sat around a cook fire in front of Spirit Owl's wickiup. After finishing their meal of venison stew, they draped themselves in blankets. Katherine handed Patton a bottle of 1811 "Year of the Comet" Napoleon cognac.

"It's probably the last *litre* left on earth," she said. "If you'd do us the honor."

Sheckly gave Patton a Swiss Army knife and five earthenware mugs.

"I can see this is a special occasion," Patton said, decanting the cognac.

Katherine smiled. "We hope to enjoy many special occasions together."

"I'm not so sure," Patton said. "I still can't tell whether you people are for real, or whether this is some bizarre debriefing trick."

"Debriefing?" Stonewall asked.

"It's twentieth lingo," said Katherine. "It refers to the gathering of military intelligence."

"For instance," Patton said, "if Katherine and her

son here started pumping me about atom bombs, I'd know I was really in Russia, getting debriefed by red agents."

The old woman gestured toward the vast deserts below. "George, you of all people ought to know this isn't Russia. You reconnoitered these red deserts twice—when you chased Villa into Mexico and when you trained that North African tank corps in '42."

"I can't remember every rock and tumbleweed," he said.

"Would you remember the Grand Canyon?" Richard Sheckly asked. "Or Monument Valley? We can take you there."

"Okay," Patton said. "I get the picture. We're in the U.S."

"Speaking of which," asked Amelia, "what happened to it?"

"You remember that atom bomb we spoke of?" Katherine asked. "After it was built, the United States and Russia constructed powerful delivery systems for it—rockets and rocket-powered airplanes called 'jets.' Soon other nations had the bomb as well—tens of thousands of them. Eventually the nations used those bombs."

"But someone built a stronghold," Patton said. "The Citadel, you called it. And you survived."

"My mother built it," the old woman said.

"She must have been a wise woman," Jackson said.

"She always denied that," Katherine said.

"She said she could merely recognize the obvious," said Sheckly. "That was all."

"What was obvious?" Amelia asked.

"Too many nations had too many nuclear weapons," the old woman said. "She was especially concerned when certain Latin American and Middle Eastern despots acquired them."

"Middle Eastern nations?" Jackson asked.

"What was once the Ottoman Empire," Sheckly explained.

"My mother had information that two of those Mideastern powers were planning a nuclear apocalypse."

"They saw it as God's will," Sheckly said.

"Apparently it was," said Jackson.

"It seemed so preposterous that at first no one believed her," the old woman said. "Then when the weapons hit, there was nothing anybody could do. Moscow and Washington were hit first—eliminating their control-and-command—after which the rest of the weapons were launched almost automatically. Everybody blamed everybody else, and they were taking no chances. It was as if we and the Russians no longer had control of our own weapons."

"Then everyone the world over piled on," said Sheckly. "Nations hammered each other with everything they had."

"Are there any of these nuclear weapons left?" Amelia asked.

"I don't know," Katherine said. "I'm not sure they'd work if they did exist. There were a lot of them though. Sixty thousand at one point."

"It must have been pure hell," Patton said.

"The famines and plagues that followed the Destruction were even more lethal than the bombs," Katherine said.

"The world, in many respects, has been a very unsafe place," Sheckly said.

"But not for the Citadel?" Patton asked.

"Not for now," said Katherine. "My mother had the time and will and money to prepare. She stockpiled everything we needed in underground caches. Books sprayed with insecticide, computers and software, microfilmed libraries, weaponry and ammunition, food, medicine, machinery. She also stockpiled people—doctors, farmers, craftspeople. She even talked scientists from Los Alamos into moving down here."

"Have your people made much progress in rebuilding this world they lost?" Stonewall asked.

"Our people have seen too much famine and plague and barbarism," the old woman said. "Most of them are exhausted. If they can eat, sleep, stay dry, survive, they're content."

"I can understand people like that," Amelia said. "What I can't understand is *us*. What are *we* like? Are we the same people we were back *there*?"

"You're a pilot, Amelia. Look at the stars overhead," said Sheckly. "Pegasus, Aries, Andromeda, Virgo, the Big Dipper—all wheeling around the Pole Star. They're the same. Why should you be different?"

"The trip through Time didn't change our bodies?" she asked.

"Time and matter are one—the same substance," Richard Sheckly said. He pointed to a nearby pine tree. "Isn't that tree there part of Time? Isn't duration as much a part of its existence as its so-called matter?"

"The tree is not *in* Time," Katherine said, "but *of* Time."

"Then what is matter?" Amelia asked.

"Before the lab at Los Alamos was blown up," Sheckly said, "the scientists there tried to answer that question. They broke matter down into its tiniest units, its smallest building blocks. At matter's most fundamental level they learned that matter was not matter at all but ghosts."

"Ghosts?" Jackson was incredulous.

"Specks of nothingness," said Sheckly. "One scientist called them 'spots of Time.'"

"I ask for explanations," Jackson said, "and you give me poetry."

Sheckly's smile was sympathetic. "There was once a man named Erwin Schrödinger who investigated all this craziness. He pointed out that if, at the nucleus of being, nothing is real, then in the universe it must also be so. He proposed to test his hypothesis by sealing a cat in a black box. From outside the box, a trip lever would drop a cyanide pellet into acid. Poison gas would then fill the box."

"You mean they killed the cat?" Amelia asked.

"No, they never did it," Sheckly said. "Obviously the cat would have died."

"So Schrödinger was wrong."

"No," Sheckly said, "all the experiment would have proved was that in *our* universe the cat would have died."

"In another universe the cat lives?" Patton asked.

"Yes," Sheckly said, "Schrödinger maintained that the cat is *both* dead and alive, and *neither* dead nor alive."

"In other words," the old woman said, "we're all in the Land of Schrödinger's Cat. Somewhere you are dead. Somewhere you have never been. Somewhere you will never be. Somewhere you are all of the above."

"But here we are alive?" Amelia asked.

Katherine touched Amelia's hand in an uncharacteristic display of tenderness. "Here, you are alive. Through the work of my son and that old man *there*." She pointed toward Spirit Owl, who sat by himself on the other side of the rancheria.

"Somewhere? Somewhen? Somehow?" Jackson said, throwing up his hands.

"At the nucleus of being paradoxes thrive," Sheckly said.

"General Patton," Matthew said, "I've read you believe in reincarnation."

"I do."

"Dad, is that possible?"

"In Schrödinger's universe, it is both possible and impossible."

Amelia gasped, Jackson groaned, but Patton, throwing back his head, roared with laughter. Getting up, he walked to the cliff face. He rapped it with his knuckles.

"Thus I refute Schrödinger."

Now Katherine laughed. "You're a fine one to talk, George Patton. You just walked through a wall of rock."

Patton rapped the rock again.

"So be it," he said. "Somewhere I may be dead and alive *and* neither dead nor alive. Somewhere I may be just as deranged as Schrödinger's crazy cat. But all I care about for the moment is here and now. I'm alive, kicking, and you know something else? I'm happy as hell."

"Why are you so happy?" Amelia asked.

"Because this Magruder clan has gotten me everything I could ever want."

"Which is?"

"They've found me somebody to fight."

"How did you know?" the old woman asked, glancing around. "Did somebody here tell him?"

"Of course, no one told me. I've known I'd face those Saracen hordes, time out of mind—since before I was born."

"You know him too?" Jackson said. "The Warrior? The one I dream of?"

"And the lady in black?" Amelia asked. "The one with the whips and snakes? She's in this too?"

"How did you three know?" Katherine asked.

"Don't you get it, Kathy Jane?" Patton grinned. "We're all in the Land of Schrödinger's Cat—not in Time but *of* Time. Since history's dawn this fight's been brewing."

"You knew in advance," Richard said, stunned at the implications.

"That's why we're here," Jackson said.

"And I say it all sounds great," Patton laughed. "Just what the doctor ordered. A knock-down, drag-'em-out donnybrook. If Amelia's buddy, the lady in black, wants to play, I say bring her in. We'll deal her a hand too."

"I was afraid you might be upset when you learned why you were brought here," Katherine said.

"Hell, no!" said Patton. "This is where it gets *interesting*. You'll never know how it warms the cockles of my heart. I've been wanting to lock horns with old Tamerlane for a bear's age."

"My sentiments exactly," Jackson said.

"Something tells me I'm going to hate this war," Amelia grumbled, staring at the distant stars.

Something tells me, Katherine thought, *you're right. My God, are you right.*

PART XVII

Their false gods availed them nothing.

—THE KORAN

Darrell Magruder stood outside New Salt's high white walls. There was a charred hole, forty feet high, where the main gate had once been. He and his black-robed friends—the *Imam* and Captain Gurney—eyed it suspiciously.

The rains had passed, and the final downpour, sluicing the blood and powder smoke off the walls, had left them clean and without sin.

Darrell thought the walls looked pretty good—except for the severed heads and black vultures leering down on them from the wall tops. Tamerlane's slaves had spent the morning lining the heads up. The hundreds of dark-winged vultures, wheeling over the city, now descended on them in steady deliberate spirals.

The *Imam* took his arm. "Young Scribe, your Lady has summoned us. We must go."

Darrell continued to stare at the wall top.

"Get a grip on yourself," Captain Gurney said. "You've never seen a city put to the sword."

"I don't see why I should start," Darrell said.

"You don't have a choice," said the Captain.

"Our Lady wants you to witness our handiwork," the *Imam* said.

"She said you should view it as an 'adventure,'" Gurney said.

"'Violence and terror recollected in tranquility' was the way she defined adventure," Darrell said.

"She once told me torture was 'an expressive art,'" the *Imam* said.

"She's expressed that sentiment often," Gurney said.

Darrell nodded. "With astounding clarity."

Reluctantly, he entered the blasted gate.

2

The man, who climbed out from under the pile of naked women, was gasping for breath. For several weeks he had sampled the most beautiful ladies New Salt had to offer. He was now exhausted. When he clapped his hands, his purple-clad eunuchs escorted the naked women out of his tent.

Alone, staring up at his yellow tent top, Tamerlane threw himself back on his cushions.

"By Allah," he moaned, to his high yellow tent top, "I do not know which is more tiring—slaying our enemies or servicing their women."

He doubted whether he would ever service another woman again.

He needed sustenance, then sleep—lots of it. Clapping his hands, four dark-haired slave girls, dressed in purple pantaloons and long purplish veils wheeled in carts laden with delicacies—wheels of cheese, hammered silver pots overflowing with rich black caviar, thick chunks of *paté*, roast beef and chicken, sausage and stuffed marrow, stuffed lamb and stuffed ribs, peppered rice, *kunafa* swimming in honey, fritters, almond cakes, and ice buckets of chilled champagne.

They fed him till he nearly burst.

He was leaning back on his cushions when his *vizier* entered, bowing and salaaming. The man's black *caftan* and turban matched his long beard.

"Rise," Tamerlane said, impatient for sleep.

"Sire, the Mayor's wife begs for a second chance."

"Send her to my soldiers. Let her beg them."

"Your concubines say she is most repentant. They tell me you will not be sorry."

"The most beautiful *houris* in all of Allah's paradise could not tempt me now."

"Your concubines have starved and chastised her. She is ready to do *anything*. They say she will surprise even you."

"All these Mormon women have done is surprise me—week after week after week. What possible surprises could the Mayor's foul hag have in store?"

"Allah requires that we be merciful, my Lord. Afterward, when our soldiers have their way with her, she can reflect on your kindness."

Tamerlane nodded. He propped himself up on his cushions, and his *vizier* brought the woman in. She knelt naked before him.

Tamerlane had forgotten how beautiful she was. Her hair was black as the underside of a raven's wing, and she wore it long. Her eyes, dark as obsidian, were framed by a generous mouth and high wide cheekbones.

"Here, child," Tamerlane said, "eat." He held out

candied dates and a goblet of champagne. She crept closer and ate from his hand.

After awhile he tired and gave his *vizier* an irritable nod. He reached down to take her away, but instead of leaving she clung to Tamerlane's feet.

"If you know what is good for you," Tamerlane said, "you will go."

She looked up, and for the first time she met his gaze. "Mercy, my Lord."

"Ask it of my troops. *Vizier,* take her away."

"Please, sire, a chance. For my children and husband, if not me."

Over her shoulder, Tamerlane noted that her arched bottom was a lurid crimson.

"Who did this to her?" he asked his *vizier.*

"Your concubines, sire. They said she was a rude, ungrateful girl."

"They were right. She is most unruly."

"Please," she asked, trembling.

"I am most tired."

"A chance. Just one."

"You refused me once. Why should I accept you now?"

"Please. You will not be sorry."

Waving his *vizier* away, Tamerlane nodded wearily. "We shall see."

3

"Where are we meeting our Lady?" Darrell asked as they walked up Temple Street.

"At the Great Mormon Tabernacle," said the *Imam*. "Our Lord is dealing with New Salt's leaders there."

"You wouldn't want to be them," Gurney said.

Darrell didn't want to be anybody in New Salt Lake. All around him black-clad soldiers sacked the town. They swarmed the streets, carrying off anything they could get their arms around—stuffed chairs and sofas, typewriters and toilet seats, books and clocks, cameras and cookstoves.

For the most part, these goods were loaded into wagons and hauled back to the *bok* to be divided up. Other more personal items, including whiskey, food, and New Salt's women, were consumed on the spot.

Especially the women. Everywhere Darrell turned, half-naked women were being chased screaming through buildings, up avenues, or down streets by drunken gangs. In virtually every alleyway, twisting queues of soldiers took their turns at spread-eagled females.

Nor were New Salt's men immune from the violence. For several weeks they had been systematically massacred, till now only a handful were left. In fact, when one was flushed from hiding and killed, it was a rare occurence. Darrell saw only one man decapitated—just as he crossed Temple and Sixth—and was grateful that he'd only witnessed that one.

But evidence of the earlier slaughter abounded. Throughout the city, the streets were blackened with blood and skull-towers soared.

In fact, crossing the intersection of Seventh Street and Temple, they walked under the shadow of one of these spires. The rotting edifice loomed high above the city, almost seeming to touch the low-lying

clouds. Flies plagued its base, and vultures circled its
peak and sides. Its death's-head stench was indescribable.

"Our leader's got a real gift," Darrell said, putting a
handkerchief over his nose and mouth.

"As a soldier?" Gurney asked, quickly covering his
nose.

"As an architect."

"His towers do possess a certain rough charm," the
Imam said, also struggling to ignore the stink.

"Raw realism," Darrell decided.

"Primitive power" was Gurney's opinion.

"These Mormons brought it on themselves," the
Imam offered, as if by explanation.

"Because they fought back?"

"No, because they were infidels, *and* they fought
back," the *Imam* said.

"The infidel he tortures hard," Gurney said.

"Torture one, terrify a thousand," said Darrell.

"Exactly so," the *Imam* agreed.

They headed up the steps of the Great Mormon
Tabernacle. A score of black-robed *Janizaries* were
gathered in front. Machine guns were slung from their
shoulders, and their slaves turned a goat on a spit.
The men drank sacks of contraband wine.

"Brace yourself, Scribe," the *Imam* said.

The first thing Darrell noticed when they entered
was Forsythe. He stood behind the sanctuary's main
altar, a mitre high on his head. A long, flowing cope of
crimson silk draped his shoulders, a crozier in his fist.
In a singsong basso he presented a devil's eucharist to
several hundred ragged victims seated in the pews.
They were, for the most part, generals and city offi-
cials, waiting to be sentenced.

"*Sint mihi dei Achoerontis propitii*," Forsythe orated. "*Per Iehovam, Gehennam et consecratam aquam quam nunc spargo, signumque crucis quod nunc facio, et per vota nostra, ipse nunc surgat nobis dicatus . . .*"

Darrell glanced around the vast stone vault. Everywhere, he saw pews overturned, church property vandalized, walls desecrated and defaced.

Then there were the torture victims. Hundreds were already stretched on racks, hung from strappados, smoking on gridirons, flayed, blinded, castrated, impaled, their screams merged into one awful howl.

The Cuddler, impervious to the din, strolled from victim to victim. He instructed his assistants on the finer points of torture—tightening a thumbscrew here, turning a rack wheel there, widening a flay, applying an ember, gouging an eye.

Darrell finally spotted her Ladyship, standing in a circular alcove. She was wearing black pants and thigh-high boots, heeled with silver rowels. Her crimson *caftan* was cinched at the waist with a thick leather belt heavily encrusted with gold and jewels. As she studied the spectacle around her, she idly cracked her boot tops with a wrist quirt.

Behind her, a curved stained glass window depicted Brigham Young preaching to the multitude. The noonday sun filtered throught the colored glass, spreading a garish rainbow of reds, blues, yellows, and greens over Legion. The effect was not beatific.

When he reached her, he noticed their Lord had just entered the sanctuary and was berating Mustafa.

"What's wrong with our Lord?" Darrell asked Legion.

"He believes that New Salt's former Mayor is holding out on him—hiding a vast treasure hoard as well as munitions caches. He blames it on the Cuddler."

Darrell was incredulous.

"He feels Mustafa is too old for the job," Legion explained. "He's telling him he's grown feebleminded and lazy. He's threatening him with some of his own medicine."

Darrell could only gape.

Legion pointed to the Mayor with her quirt. A dozen feet away, he was stripped naked and stretched on a vertical rack. The Cuddler, who now returned to his work, began filleting the Mayor's rib cage. The horizontal bones quickly gleamed ivory white against the man's bloody chest, but the Mayor endured the torture, tight-lipped.

"The Mayor's pretty tough," Legion admitted. "Even when we sent his wife and daughters to the pavilions, he refused to crack."

"Pavilions?" Darrell didn't understand.

"Our Lord's brothels."

Again, Darrell was speechless.

"Maybe the Mayor doesn't know anything," Gurney offered.

"Our Lord is unconvinced."

"Suppose he's wrong?" Darrell asked.

"What does it matter?" Legion said.

Tamerlane joined them. "The Mayor rambles incoherently about the Citadel. He says it will never fall."

"He's crazy," Legion said.

"What about the Citadel, boy?" Tamerlane asked the Scribe. "Is the Citadel as strong as he says?"

"I haven't seen it for five years. I really couldn't say."

"What was it like? As dangerous as New Salt?"

"Not really."

"What does the boy tell you two?" Legion asked the *Imam* and the Captain.

"He speaks mostly of his grandmother," the *Imam* answered. "She's their leader."

"He says she is old," Gurney said.

"She has a bald eagle for a pet," said the *Imam*.

"The great Genghis Khan trained eagles as falcons," Legion said, "and he flushed his quarry with cheetahs."

"The old hag is dangerous," Tamerlane concluded.

Leading them to the flayed Mayor, Tamerlane yanked the man's head back by his hair.

"What do you know of this Citadel?" Tamerlane asked him.

"You'll never make it . . ." the Mayor slurred disjointedly. "Deserts . . . Weapons . . . Never . . ."

Tamerlane turned to Darrell. "If you are holding out, boy, it will go hard."

"I don't know what he's talking about."

Tamerlane started to summon his Cuddler, but Legion stopped him.

"Have the boy write a report—everything he knows about the Citadel," she said.

"He says he knows nothing."

"He's a Scribe. He only knows what he writes."

"What do our scouts say of their leader?" Tamerlane asked.

"Our scouts report that she still runs the Citadel."

"The Scribe will write his reports," Tamerlane said, "and we will send more scouts."

"In the meantime we must pillage," Legion said. "*The Koran* vouchsafes our men four-fifths of our plunder, but our New Salt booty has been neglible. We must redeem their loss—for the good of *bok* morale. Everything north of the Citadel must be sacked."

"I did not think New Salt would hold out so long," Tamerlane admitted. "By the time the city fell, there was very little left."

"Their people are sorry now," Legion said.

"We will make them sorrier still," Tamerlane said. "We will plunder their friends, raze the nearby cities and towns."

"Excellent," Mustafa said, without bothering to look up from the Mayor.

"Then we will turn toward the Citadel."

"There will be be mountains to climb," Legion said, "deserts to cross."

"Cities to burn," Tamerlane said, "women to rape."

The thought made Legion smile. Turning to the Mayor, she patted his cheek. "Speaking of which, your wife pleases our Lord. She was most . . . affectionate."

"And a superior whore," Tamerlane agreed.

The Mayor's lips pulled back in a feral snarl.

"Why does he not break?" Tamerlane asked Forsythe, who had joined them.

"He thinks Joseph Smith will save him," Forsythe sneered.

"*La ilaha illa Allah*," Old Mustafa boomed, still carving up the Mayor, "*Mohammed rasul Allah*." There is no God but Allah, and Mohammed is His Prophet.

Legion fingered Forsythe's crimson cope. "By the way, you *are* in the wrong church. This is Catholic attire. That was a Satanic eucharist you were presenting."

"I would have dressed as Brigham Young, but he lacks sartorial splendor," Forsythe said.

"The proper élan," Legion agreed.

"He is, very simply, too *boring*," Forsythe said.

The sneering Forsythe leaned over Mustafa's shoulder, till he and the Mayor were nearly nose-to-nose.

"Say, old stick, what about our Prophet, the venerable Mohammed? Why not offer him a few prayers? Maybe he'll rescue you."

The Mayor spit bloody sputum in Forsythe's face.

Forsythe continued to sneer, even as he wiped the crimson spittle from his face.

"Big mistake," Gurney said.

"Real big," Legion concurred.

"You ruddy Yanks are rude," Forsythe said, "and now I'm going to teach you a *nasty* lesson in humility."

"Not very smart at all," said Legion, shaking her head.

"You are about to enter the nethermost pit of hell," Forsythe said. "That old man and I—" he pointed to Mustafa "—will introduce it to you personally."

"Which can happen to you as well," Legion said to Darrell, "if you do not tell our Lord what he wants to know."

"I already explained I haven't been back in five years."

"Who cares?" Legion said.

"Our Lord wants it in writing," said Gurney. "Something he can use."

"Something truthful," Legion said.

"If you lie to him, sport," said Forsythe, "he'll break your bones for marrow."

"How did I get into this?" Darrell said to no one in particular.

"Write," the *Imam* said. "Write as if your life depended on it."

"It does," Gurney noted.

"Write fast," said Forsythe. "It does not pay to keep our Lordship waiting."

That night, Darrell sat at his tent desk. He stared at a stack of blank paper. He did not know what to write. The Citadel's weapons were sixty years old and his people desert dwellers, few in number and far between. They had not practiced war in decades.

New Salt had been the Citadel's last, best hope.

On the other hand, the old woman was still alive. Legion had said that, and if Katherine was alive, there was a chance. If anyone could find a way to beat the Horde, it was she.

What the old woman needed was time. That was what he had to buy her.

Slowly, Darrell picked up his pen and went to work.

A plan was beginning to form.

PART XVIII

Peace is going to be hell on me.

—GEORGE S. PATTON

Sitting in her backyard rocker at dusk, the old woman studied her four time travelers. They seemed to be adjusting.

Betsy Ross not only accepted Harry, she was now a doting mother—almost paranoically protective of her hatchling. That very afternoon, when Stonewall had attempted a shortcut across the yard to get a cup of sassafras tea, he had been driven off by piercing screams and thrashing pinions. He and Patton now sat in a remote corner of the backyard, swapping war stories, giving Harry and his mother a wide berth.

Surprisingly enough, Betsy Ross had accepted Amelia. She had even deigned to perch on her gauntleted wrist—perhaps the implicit respect of one downed flyer to another.

At the moment Betsy and Amelia were playing with Harry in the backyard wading pool. Harry was now the size of a fat pit bull—but with horns and a big bony frill arching over his head. All three were engaged in a splashing contest. Betsy Ross, with her powerful pinions, was, to Harry's trumpeting embarrassment, whipping them both.

The old woman studied the Generals. Patton looked the most at ease. He'd seen the dawn of the nuclear age one hundred years before, so he was not overwhelmed by the Great Destruction.

Jackson's adjustment had been more difficult. Since his arrival, he had spent most of his time in the Civil War section of the Citadel's main library. Stonewall could not get over the fact that the South had lost. He was despondent over what he termed "Lee's complete misapprehension of military strategy," and he viewed Reconstruction as a nightmare.

"Those Yankees didn't just defeat us. They burned us down to bedrock and sowed our fields with salt. Like Carthage. Didn't they understand they were crippling their own country?"

The twentieth century also baffled him.

"That nuclear war, followed by the famine and the pestilence, was all described by John in Revelation. But John said there'd be a City of God afterward. 'A New Jerusalem,' he called it. What happened? Where did it go? Why was there no Second Coming? Was Revelation wrong?"

"Maybe God just hasn't gotten around to it yet," Katherine had muttered under her breath.

Amelia, however, was the most troubling.

"I'm a pacifist," Amelia said stubbornly. "Under no circumstances will I ever wage war."

Katherine's crack researchers, Matthew and Elizabeth, had missed that one.

"No matter how terrible the foe," Katherine had asked, "or how honorable the cause?"

"I just don't have it in me."

Katherine was not without sympathy. She'd *seen* the Manhattan Crater hours after the bomb hit. Then she crossed the country—on foot, at first, later on a motorcycle. She'd seen the violence, the famine, the plagues. She fought on the Citadel's barricades, driving off the swarms of plague-ridden refugees. She was hardly naive about war.

Well, Katherine thought, *you're the one who dragged her through that Time Tunnel. You never asked her whether she wanted to come.*

Anyway, Betsy Ross liked her. If nothing else, Amelia could help Betsy baby-sit Harry, which was going to take some doing.

The old woman stared at Harry with narrowed eyes. He *was* shooting up fast. His appetite was prodigious—up to eighty pounds of roughage a day. All around his wading pool were piles of corn fodder.

Even now, Betsy Ross was thrashing him with her pinions, telling him it was time to eat.

There was no question as to who ran that family. Betsy Ross was the head mother. She told him when to play, when to rest, and when to eat. At night when he got cold, she was the one who spread-eagled him with her pinions and kept him warm.

If only Betsy Ross could take Amelia under her wing.

2

After supper Katherine joined George and Tom on the front porch. Tom sipped apple cider while George peacefully smoked a cigar.

"As far as I can see," Jackson said, "you have no

real laws, monetary system, or police force—all of
which restricts our ability to raise an army."

"We do have one good fighting force," Katherine
said, "Major Thompson's Border Rangers. He gets
lots of horse and cattle rustlers south of here. Some of
those bandits get pretty rough."

"That would be a start," Jackson said.

"Maybe," the old woman said, "but I have to tell
you the Major's no Sunday picnic. All those border
people are hard-nosed. They aren't about to abandon their own homes to any bandit gangs in order to
help us."

"You say this Thompson's tough?" Patton asked.

"More guts than you could hang on forty miles of
line fence."

"A good leader?" Jackson asked.

"A born leader," the old woman said. "The sort of
man others just naturally look up to. Those I knew
who served under him would've followed Thompson
straight to hell."

"His people obey orders?" Jackson asked.

"They have to—the kind of business they're in,"
the old woman said. "One of them gets caught south
of that border line, the bandits get out hot coals and
knives."

"What happens to the bandits the Rangers catch?"
Amelia asked.

"They trim the trees with them."

"Without a trial?" Amelia asked, joining Katherine
on the porch glider.

"It's a rough game they play down there."

"You think they'll join us?" Jackson asked.

"I don't know. They don't offer their allegiance
easily."

"Maybe if Tom and I go down there and tell this Thompson about Tamerlane," Patton said. "Explain the facts of life to him."

"I know the Major," the old woman said. "You don't tell him anything. He's the kind of man you have to *show*."

"Then what do we do?" Jackson asked.

"I've already sent my grandson Matthew down there."

"Katherine," Jackson said, "Matt's a good boy, but he's barely sixteen. If Thompson won't take from George or me, why would he take from a boy?"

"Because he's a Magruder," the old woman said.

"What's that supposed to mean?" Jackson asked.

"It means he'll *do* something."

3

It was dusk when Matt Magruder caught up with Major Thompson and Captain Connolly. They were at the Ranger camp, sitting around a fire. They wore broad-brimmed Stetsons, collarless shirts, and denim pants. Except for the silver stars pinned on their shirts, they looked like middle-aged cowhands.

Major Thompson listened politely to Matthew's proposition. Captain Connolly grinned the whole time.

Matt finished. For a long time the only sounds were the stamping of the nearby remuda, the creak of saddles, and the jingle of bits and spurs.

"Your grandma wants me to organize a force," the Major finally said, "and take on that army up in New

Salt? Well, I got some men, and that Horde makes it this far south, I suppose we'll fight them. But I can't see my men packing up, heading north, and abandoning their loved ones. This here's mighty sudden country."

"If you don't stop Tamerlane up north," Matt said, "you'll have to fight him *and* the bandits. Right here."

"If it comes to that, we'll do it," the Major said. "But it will be here, not up north."

"What I don't get," Captain Connolly said, "is why his grandma's sending us you."

"I told her I wanted to serve under Major Thompson."

The two men just stared.

"I heard it was an honor."

"It's a job is all," Captain Connolly said.

"Still I'd be obliged."

"You wouldn't be serving under me," the Major said. "You'd be serving under Captain Connolly here. If he'd have you."

Matt met Connolly's stare.

"People told me serving under the Major was an honor," Matt said. "Nobody said anything about you."

The Captain stopped grinning. "Your grandma teach you to ride a horse and sling a Colt—or just mouth off?"

"I'm a fair hand."

Captain Connolly glanced at the Major. "Well, he's big enough. We're heading south, and we're short a man."

"We get south of here," the Major said, "a man gets cut off, them Mex bandits'll stake him out on cat-claw and anthills."

"I'll keep up."

"Captain, it's your decision," Major Thompson said.

The Major walked over to the remuda. Matt counted over sixty mounts in the corral—bays, paints, pintos, grays, two chestnuts, several roans, and one stunning Appaloosa. The Major roped out the Appaloosa. It was the sort of horse a man could have traded the whole remuda for.

When he looked back at Captain Connolly, the man's eyes were expressionless.

"Raise your right hand."

Matt raised it.

"You swear to serve in the Border Rangers without recompense and to obey without question all commands from Major Thompson and myself, so help you God?" Captain Connolly did not wait for a response. He rummaged in his saddlebags and came up with a silver star. "You can pin this on. I don't have no Bible to swear you on, but I'll take your word."

"You never heard my word."

The Captain glared at him. "Well, do you give it?"

"I do."

"You're sworn into the Border Rangers."

"May God have mercy on your soul," a voice said behind him.

Matt turned around.

"This here's Lieutenant Rowdy," Connolly said.

The big rawboned Lieutenant wore a dirty scoop-brimmed Stetson, a black drooping mustache, and crisscrossed bandoliers. He rode a pinto and led the Major's Appaloosa by the *mecate*. He carried a roping saddle over his pommel.

"I don't know who you are, kid," Lieutenant Rowdy said, "but the Major wants you on his horse." He dropped the extra saddle at Matthew's feet. "Also on this."

"I got a saddle."

"Take this one tonight," Captain Connolly said. "You may need the heavy horn."

Matt measured and adjusted the stirrup leathers. He saddled the Appaloosa, tightened the cinch, and swung on.

Captain Connolly, who'd just roped and saddled a rangy dun, rode up to him.

"Why's the Major giving me the 'Paloos?" Matt asked.

"We're bringing back two thousand head—real longhorns. You don't get them kind up Citadel ways. That pony there's the best cuttin' horse you ever seen."

"Looks like some kind of show horse," Matt said.

"Give him a loose rein and let him do the head work," the Captain advised. "He's forgot more about punchin' beef'n you'll ever know."

"You know the old debate," Rowdy said, "'bout which is meaner, a grizzly or a longhorn?"

"No."

"Get unhorsed," Rowdy said, "you'll find out."

Captain Connolly handed Matt a wrist quirt. It had a leaded stock and two heavy lashes of plaited rawhide with three-inch poppers on the ends.

"You drive the strays back toward the herd with this," the Captain said.

"Use the poppers," Rowdy said. "Them bandits'll think its gunfire. Put the fear of God in them."

A fourth Ranger rode up to the three. "Best not lose the quirt neither. It's also the Major's. God only knows why he's givin' you all his stuff."

Matt stared back at him, silent.

A fifth rode up. "That's the Major's mount, boy.

You bring him back galled or windbroke, the raven's'll breakfast on your eyeballs."

He reined his horse around and headed south with the rest of the company.

"These men don't like me much," Matt said to Rowdy.

"They can't figure why the Major's saddlin' us with a shorthorn," Rowdy said, "and givin' him that 'Paloos to boot."

"He's a Magruder," said Captain Connolly.

"Figures." The rawboned Ranger stared at him, shaking his head, then spit downwind. He kicked his mount into the other Rangers' dust.

When Matthew looked back at Captain Connolly, they were the last two men left in the camp. Connolly was giving him his derisive grin.

"Why did *you* take me on?" Matt asked.

"I figured the Major wanted you. He never would've roped out that 'Paloos for himself."

"Why did he do it?"

"You don't know?"

"Know what?"

The Captain sneered, spurred the dun around, and headed toward the river at a high lope.

Matt followed him into the water.

4

The sun dropped below the rimrock, and inky thunderheads eclipsed the stars. Matt Magruder rode with Captain Connolly and the Major.

"Kind of a bad night for a border raid, isn't it, Major?" he asked.

Captain Connolly snorted hoarsely.

"Those longhorns are moving fast," the Major said. "We don't catch them tonight, we'll be trailing them to Argentina."

Lightning flared, and for a moment Matthew could see the terrain. The *llano* was covered with thickets of prickly pear and fissured with crisscrossing arroyos. Matthew hoped his horse knew where he was going.

He also wished his backside didn't hurt so much. He couldn't seem to adjust to the roping saddle or the horse's irregular gait. Here, the 'Paloos jumped a cutback. There, he sidestepped a yucca. Once a buzzing diamondback. Matthew's rump felt like the saddle had grown teeth.

5

Shortly after midnight, in the dry wash country down by the Gila River, lightning flickered. In the feeble light they spotted their Apache scout. He was kneeling at the base of a small rise, careful not to silhouette himself against the skyline.

The Major kicked his mount toward the scout. Matt and Captain Connolly followed at a more leisurely pace.

"Who's the tracker?" Matt asked the Captain.

"An Apache named Horse Ears. He's one of old Spirit Owl's grandkids."

"Is he good?"

"Let's say you wouldn't want 'im doggin' your trail."

"Do anything besides track?"

"Best demolitions man I ever seen. Given the scarcity of dynamite, that's a valuable skill."

"You picked a hell of a night for him to trail beef. I can't see anything."

"Horse Ears don't need eyes to track. He can smell, hear, 'n' taste a trail."

They found Horse Ears and the Major rein-standing their mounts. Horse Ears was kneeling. This was one trail Matthew could also smell. Cow manure.

"We intersected their trail here," Horse Ears said. "They're about an hour's ride due south, probably camped by the Gila River."

"They sure won't want to cross it tonight," the Captain said.

"We'll circle east," the Major said, "rest and water our own stock, then hit them on the flank. We don't want to drive those cows into the river either."

"We'll have a hard enough time getting them back north without fording and refording that Gila," said Horse Ears.

"Captain," the Major said, "you pick a half dozen men to drive the herd away from the Gila. We'll bring the boy with us. The rest of the men can deal with those rustlers."

"Yes sir," Connolly said.

"We'll swing wide," the Major said. "If we want to surprise them, we'll have to stay clear of their outriders."

The scout swung onto his spotted pony. He headed southwest into a nearby arroyo.

"We got slickrock canyons down here, boy," Captain Connolly said. "That's a real maze he's leading us into. You stick close. I don't want the Major losing that 'Paloos."

Matt followed the Major and the Captain into the gorge, the rest of the Ranger company close behind.

◀━━━ 6

Lightning flashed along the riverbank, and Matt was able to study the herd. There were fifteen hundred longhorns spread along the Gila, and another five hundred on the other side. The snorting and stamping of the cattle were now a monotonous rumble.

"Whatever you do, don't get off that horse," Captain Connolly said. "Them longhorns'll charge a man afoot."

"Yes sir."

"Give the 'Paloos a loose rein. He'll slip in and out of those horns. You'll make out fine."

"What about the bandits?"

"They're camped two miles north of the herd. Horse Ears, Lieutenant Dwyer, and some of the boys will settle up with them. Assuming these stampeding longhorns don't finish them off first."

"You sure they won't hear us?"

"They couldn't hear Armageddon all the noise them cows are making."

"What about their outriders?"

"They couldn't hit the broadside of a barn from the inside with the doors shut. They ain't never had enough powder to learn. You just worry about them longhorns."

Captain Connolly swung off the bay and loosened his cinch.

"Your saddle could turn," Matt said.

"We may be going into that river. Try it with a tight cinch, the 'Paloos won't be able to blow the water back out his nose. The 'Paloos drowns in that river, you'll drown too, what with all them cows."

As Matt was letting out his latigo, Rowdy rode up.

"Just stick with us," Lieutenant Rowdy said. "You get separated, you won't be missed till first light, when we're back in camp."

Matt swung onto the 'Paloos, and they headed east along the river.

7

An hour later they met the herd along the water's edge. All Matt could see were white eyes and flashing horns, giving the herd an eerie look, as if they were not cows at all but friends from hell.

Lightning flared again. Matt could now see that there were really three herds. One herd was south of the Gila. The other to the north was split by a red-clay ridge that ran perpendicular to the river.

The Major, up ahead, cut loose with his horse pistols. The Rangers, following his lead, opened fire and drove the herd north, away from the Gila.

Matt fired his own Colt and got his portion of the herd moving north—but not in a straight line. The herd's southern perimeter zigzagged, and the cows closed in around him and the other Rangers. Almost immediately they were sucked into the herd's middle and driven south, prodded on all sides by horns.

Thunder boomed and rolled. Sheet lightning blazed. The rain hammered them in layered sheets.

Meanwhile, his Appaloosa dodged the spinning horns, working his way south of the surging herd.

Lightning blazed, and Matthew spotted Connolly and the Major. The Captain was exiting the stampeding steers along their western flank. The Major was trapped on the red ridge bisecting the herd's middle.

Lightning flared, and again Matt saw the Major. The colliding herds were crushing his ridge on both sides. He and his mount straddled a collapsing mound of clay.

Lightning flared again, followed by a tremendous thunder crack. The sky split in two, and lightning bolts blasted the herd south of the Gila. They stampeded north into the water.

The thunder boomed like cannon fire, and, again, lightning split the earth, but this time *north* of the longhorns. Its bolts stopped the north herd dead in its tracks, turned it around 180 degrees, and stampeded it straight into the path of the Gila herd, which was now almost out of the river.

Matt gave the 'Paloos a slack rein and hard spurs, driving him into the milling steers. He was less than thirty yards from the trapped Major. In the lightning's blaze he saw the Major's foundering roan, her eyes huge as saucers, the ridge crumbling beneath her.

Matt roweled the Appaloosa as hard as he knew how. He brought the quirt down on its flanks, again and again, the poppers cracking above the stamping steers like pistol shots.

Lightning flared, and, to his horror, Matt saw that a black-and-white stud bull from the Gila herd was colliding with the southbound herd. Caught in the middle, he was mounting what was left of the Major's rise.

Coming up behind the Major's foundering mount, the stud bull rammed her from behind, unhorsing the Major, then gutting his horse. Clambering over the fallen roan, the bull went after Major Thompson, who was already staggering up the disintegrating ridge.

Running out of ridge, the Major turned to face the attacking bull, his Colt drawn. Matt saw the muzzle-flash, but the stud bull's head was down. The rounds ricocheted off the bony plate between the bull's horns. The bull butted the Major repeatedly, worrying him with his horns.

When Matthew reached the ridge, he drew his own Colt. His first three rounds missed, but by then his 'Paloos was pinned against the rise, and he was able to take aim.

The bull—now raking the Major with his horns—was less than four feet away, and Matthew shot him through the back of the head. When the bull turned to face him, Matthew shot him between the eyes.

The bull took two steps to his right, one to his left, then tumbled over the ridge.

"Get up!" Matthew screamed.

Pulling himself to his feet—bleeding from his ears and nose, his left arm dangling uselessly—the Major staggered toward the Appaloosa. Matt emptied his right stirrup and held out an arm.

"Swing on," he yelled.

The Major grabbed his hand, then raised a boot toward the empty stirrup.

The ridge collapsed under a sea of steers, and the Major went down with it, between Matt and the fallen bull.

The 'Paloos was foundering under the crush of three colliding herds. Matthew had one round left, and there was nowhere else to go. Wrenching the reins hard right, he shot the 'Paloos in the back of the head. As the horse fell toward the bull, Matt jumped free.

The bull, the remains of the ridge and the dying 'Paloos formed a crude triangle.

Matt shouldered the bloody Major under the Appaloosa's belly. Cutting the latigo, he flung his roping saddle over the Major, then threw himself over the fork.

After awhile Matthew thought he saw sheet lightning though he could not understand how since his eyes were buried in the stirrup leathers.

He heard thunder, and his mouth filled with blood.

There was more thunder, more lightning, more rain. Again, the red clay shook, and for awhile it seemed to Matt that he was drowning in blood.

Salt rose in his mouth. Afterward it seemed he could smell the sea and ride its waves as they plunged and fell.

Then he heard their silence, felt their blackness, savored their death.

Then he knew no more.

8

Back in the Ranger camp the only man who could look Matt in the eye was Captain Connolly, and he continued to sneer. The rest of the men were respectful but silent. It was as if they did not like being in the boy's presence.

Matt hung around camp for a week, nursing his concussion, cracked ribs, and separated shoulder, but also waiting to see whether the Major made it.

When Major Thompson came out of his coma, Matthew decided it was time to move on. There was work to do at the Citadel.

His last morning, Captain Connolly rode up on his dun, leading a pony by the *mecate*. It was another Appaloosa.

"What's that?" Matthew asked.

"The Major's other 'Paloos. Marge had a brother, didn't you know?"

"Marge?" Matt said, confused. "Marge was my ma."

"She was also your horse—the one you shot. You didn't know her name?"

"I didn't even know she was a mare. Guess I took her for a gelding."

"They don't teach you much at the Citadel, do they?"

Matt shrugged. "What's this one's name?"

"The boys around here call him Darrell. Not to the Major's face though. You can call him Stony. It's what the Major calls him."

"This some kind of joke or something?"

"Boy, they *don't* teach you much at the Citadel."

"I asked you a question."

Connolly's sneer was gone. "The Major and your late ma were supposed to be married, only she didn't cotton to it much down here. She left him for your old man. The Magruder clan was never real popular after that."

Matthew was speechless, but Connolly continued:

"I never saw much in her myself. Or your grandma for that matter." The Captain hocked and spit downwind.

"Tell the Major I didn't come down here for no horse."

Matt swung his saddle onto his bay.

Captain Connolly pulled it back off.

"You watch your tongue, little boy. You ain't too big for a hidin'."

"Said I didn't come down here for no horse." He met the Captain's stare.

Captain Connolly shook his head in disgust. "You still want them Rangers? That it?"

"The Major wasn't interested."

"He's got a lotta hard bark on him. So do most of these boys. They don't forgive, and they don't forget. The Major don't either, you get right down to it."

"Then there it is."

"Yeah, there it is. And after what you done for him I don't suppose I could round up more than two or three thousand men myself."

Captain Connolly picked up the boy's saddle and swung it onto the 'Paloos.

"And don't go spittin' on the Major's present here. Down this way people take that hard."

The sun rose over the eastern rimrock, casting long, low shadows over the red desert.

Matthew cinched up the slick-fork and swung onto the 'Paloos. The horse blew and snorted twice, shying bites at his new owner.

Matt dallied the bay's *mecate* twice around his pommel.

"Said before, didn't see what the Major fancied in you Magruders. Guess I do now."

Captain Connolly slapped the Appaloosa's rump with a coiled lass-rope.

The Appaloosa broke into a high lope, and Matthew headed north, toward the Citadel, without looking back.

9

Four days later, the old woman—seated on her front porch with Patton and Jackson—spotted Matthew riding up the street.

"Well, gentlemen," she announced, "the Prodigal Son returns riding one of Major Thompson's Appaloosas."

"I wondered what happened to him," Jackson said. "The telegraph's been down for nearly two weeks."

"Beautiful horse," Patton said. "Wonder how Matthew ended up with him?"

"You wouldn't understand," Katherine said.

"Try me," Patton said.

"Oh, I guess he just reminded the Major who he was—in case the Major forgot."

"You're right," Patton said. "I don't understand."

"What's that supposed to mean?" Jackson asked her.

"What I told you before. He's a Magruder. The Major just forgot it for awhile."

She watched as Matt took off his new Stetson and waved it at her.

"Gentlemen, I can tell you something else."

"He got himself a new hat?" Jackson said. "I can see that. He's not wearing his tan Plainsman's anymore."

"He's got something else too. All of us do."

"What?" Patton asked.

"A new army."

The old woman swung down off the porch and went out to meet her grandson.

10

Though the Generals now had an army, they were seriously short on black powder. And to fight the Horde, they definitely needed guns.

The night after Matt returned, Patton and Stonewall visited with the old woman on her back porch.

"Kathy Jane," Patton began, "even though you've never invoked it, the Special War Powers Act grants you wide authority in 'emergency situations.' I think it's time to declare the current situation 'an emergency.'"

"This place has always been an emergency, George."

Patton leaned forward. "Katherine, am I going to have to make a speech?"

She sighed. "This is the Citadel, George, not Parris Island. You can issue all the orders you want. It's another matter to make them stick."

"You can try anyway," Tom Jackson said. "You have the army to back you up."

"You have us," Patton said.

She gave them a long, uncomfortable stare. "The first order of business then is to find Elizabeth a job. We'll call her 'Secretary to the Committee.' We have to do something to keep her from going off mountain climbing, time-traveling, or whatever with her insane father."

Elizabeth was instantly summoned to the meeting.

After she located writing materials, Katherine brought up the second order of business—the problem of the Citadel's arms shortages.

"I know you two have armies to run, but they're not running very far without ammunition and transport. I want you to take some time off and visit our defense industries."

"I was hoping martial law would handle those problems," Jackson said.

"Our people don't know the meaning of the word *law*, let alone *martial*," Katherine said. "You've got to go to them in person, show them what you want, draw them pictures if necessary."

Jackson averted his eyes.

"Katherine, among other things we're going to need gasoline," Patton said.

"We'll pay a courtesy call on the oil fields. A year ago we hit black gold forty miles southwest of here. It's not much by our old standards—just two hundred barrels a day, not two hundred thousand. Under ordinary circumstances it wouldn't even pay for the rigs, but now it's life and death."

"So why are my tanks low on fuel?" Patton asked.

"We have nothing to pay the help with. We've commandeered all the oil, so the riggers and refiners are working for free."

"We could print more money," Patton said.

"That's what we've been doing," Katherine said. "That's the only reason we've gotten as far as we have. We've been paying people off in Confederate money—no offense Tom."

"What else?" Patton asked.

"You'll need gunpowder, which means we have to visit the guano pits for the nitrates to make it. Our nitrate production has virtually stopped. We have to get it going again."

"You want us to inspect bat droppings?" Jackson asked.

"That's right. They're precious as life."

"They *are* life," Patton said.

"'Between feces and urine are we born,'" the old woman quoted gloomily.

"What's the problem in the pits?" Jackson asked.

"For some reason no one wants to go down there," Katherine said.

"I can't understand why," Elizabeth mumbled, assiduously taking her notes.

11

A few hours later Katherine was at the door of Elizabeth's room shouting: "Rise and shine."

Elizabeth turned, groaning, to her clock. 0330 hours. These people had no mercy.

On her chair—instead of her blouse and skirt—was a khaki uniform, size three.

"So you're drafting fourteen-year-olds now, huh, Grandma?"

"General Grandma to you," the old woman snapped. "Shake a leg or you'll be late for the war."

"Yes sir, General, ma'am," Elizabeth grumbled under her breath.

12

Elizabeth rode in the Jeep's backseat with her grandmother, Patton and Stonewall up front. It was a hot bouncing dusty ride to the San

Carlos guano pits—nothing but sand and mountains, cactus and mesquite—and it was nearly 0700 hours before they got there.

They were just in time. The desert mountains were already heating up.

The owner-operator of the guano pit and the munitions works—Elroy Watkins—approached them by the dirt road next to his saltpeter plant. He had close-cropped iron gray hair and a neck red as a lobster. The deeply etched lines crowding the corners of his eyes and mouth gave him a stern expression. His denim coveralls and boots were well-worn. He looked to be at least ninety.

Patton scowled.

"Now don't you make any cracks about his age, George S. Time was you couldn't walk in the same sun as Elroy."

"The time is *now*, Katherine," said Patton.

"I still say he's one of the best ordnance men I ever met."

"Which was probably back in the Pleistocene," Patton said, "when we fought with sticks and rocks. But right now there's a goddamn powder shortage."

"Now, Georgie, don't get me riled. I told you before I do not tolerate profanity in the presence of children."

Watkins reached their Jeep.

"Elroy, those are Generals Patton and Jackson and my granddaughter, Elizabeth."

He nodded. "I suppose you're here to tell me I'm short on my powder quotas."

"We're low on powder, Mr. Watkins," Patton said, "and we just can't let that happen."

Elroy wasn't interested. His eyes were fixed on the old woman.

"Now Katy, before you start hounding me about your powder, you best take a look around. It won't hurt you to learn something."

"I'm always ready to learn, Elroy."

The saltpeter shed was eighty feet long, thirty feet wide, and fifteen feet high. It was filled with a dozen storage tanks. Boiling water was piped out of steaming vats up through the bottoms of the tanks. At each end of these one thousand-gallon tanks was a drainpipe and valve. The nitrate solution seeped out of the screened-off drainpipes into fifty-five-gallon drums.

"We test the runoff with hydrometers. When we get enough high-density solution, we take the drums outside, pour the liquid through ashes into pans, and boil off the water."

"I've seen saltpeter manufactured before," Katherine said.

"What kind of wood charcoal you grind the powder with?" Jackson asked.

"Pine with no knots, cottonwood, some cedar. No hardwoods."

"You smelting pyrite for sulfur?" Patton asked.

"It's cheaper to freight it in from New Texas. They pump live steam underground, then pump it out. It's pure sulfur, and it don't cost hardly nothing. Just shipping."

They walked back outside, and Elroy pointed to the powder mills across the road.

"We use three separate grinding wheels. One for the charcoal, another for the sulfur, the third for the saltpeter. We wet it with water and urine and corn the dough through wire sieves. After it's dry, we rotate it in old cement mixers."

"Okay, so you know how to make black powder," the old woman said. "Let's see those bat caves you have so much trouble with."

"Not yet, Aunt Kate. Got a surprise for you. A new addition. Want you to know I ain't been just jumpin' the duck up here."

"Elroy," she said harshly.

He led them out of the camp. At the rim of the mountain was a big steel Quonset hut.

"Long way from the main works," the old woman said.

"I call this our high explosives department. We make the nitro here. There's acid tanks and other hazardous materials all over the place, so don't sneeze." He glared at Katherine. "Don't raise your voice neither. Put on these cotton masks and safety glasses. Some strong fumes in there."

The interior of the hut was divided by partitions.

"This first enclosure," Elroy said, "is called the acid room."

In the center was a huge cast-iron vat with a tightly sealed earthenware pothead. Two glass distilling tubes ran out of opposite sides into ceramic receivers. Another tube pumped air into the sealed vat.

"Here we boil sulfuric acid and saltpeter. The condensation dripping out of these tubes is nitric acid."

"Elroy," Katherine said, "after sixty years you've finally surprised me. That's the one part of the process we couldn't master."

"What was that?" Jackson asked.

"Making nitric acid," she said. "Certainly not on this scale. With the acid we can make nitroglycerin, gun cotton, dynamite, and blasting gel. It means we no longer have to rely on New Salt."

"Most of their explosives had decomposed anyway," said Elroy.

The old woman walked around the second partition. She glanced back at them and grinned.

"Come and look," she said.

The other half of the shed contained a dozen ceramic storage tanks, round and interconnected by glass tubes. Here they collected the nitro.

"What do you do with it when it's finished?" Katherine asked.

"We turn it into the safest thing we can think of."

Elroy escorted them past the tanks and tubes and nitrators, then around the second partition. There, three lab technicians sat at lab benches. In front of them were big platters of clay and sawdust, which they slowly saturated with nitroglycerin.

"Once it's mixed with clay and sawdust," Elroy said, "it's harmless as mud."

"Until you put a blasting cap on it," Patton reminded them.

"You got gun cotton and blasting gel too?" Katherine asked.

"Right over there. Want a look?"

"Not now, Elroy. What I really want to look at is bat droppings. We have to find a way to get you more saltpeter."

13

Elroy led them up an endless succession of mountain switchbacks, one treacherous trail after another, and there was little in the way of footing.

The men reached the cave in slightly under a half
hour. Elizabeth, who stayed behind with her grandmother, took longer. She moved more slowly, keeping
one hand on the back of Katherine's belt.

Elroy escorted them through a clump of boulders
into the narrow cave entrance. With his lantern pointing the way, they followed behind him with torches.

It was a dark walk through low, dirty shafts. They
had to twist and turn, bend and stoop, to keep from
banging their heads. Elizabeth was amazed that her
grandmother kept up.

Then they reached the sinkhole.

The cavern was dark, but with the aid of their
lanterns, they could make out the interior. Five hundred feet up from their lookout was the roost. The
bats hung inverted from the ceiling.

"Two hundred thousand of them," Elroy said,
"and all of them vampire."

From the colony fell a constant downpour of urine
and feces. It formed a black pond almost a thousand
feet below. The stink was overwhelming.

Jackson handed Elizabeth his binoculars, and she
peered more closely at the pit. There were lanterns
down there, and she could see the pit clearly. It was
seething with rats, snakes, spiders, and centipedes.

Down below, in a dark corner of the pit, Elizabeth
saw a hydraulic hose dangling out of the drink. Its purpose had been to pump guano into the storage tanks
outside the nitrate shed. It was now slack and idle.

"Hard to understand why those men don't want to
work nights," Elizabeth said, breaking the silence.
"Seeing as that's when the bats feed and all."

"Hell, I've given up on nights," Elroy said. "I'd be
happy if they'd just work days."

"Let's go talk to those boys," Patton said.

They met the crew by the saltpeter tanks. They were ill-clothed, guano-filthy men just up from Sonora. Even the desperate poverty of Mexico couldn't get them into the pits.

"I hear some of you men don't want to work down there," Patton said. "Afraid of a few bat bites?"

"They carry plague and rabies," the foreman said.

"Now I personally know that to be a goddamn lie. Bats are the cleanest animals on God's green earth. Rats are the ones that carry plague."

One of the workers complained, "My sister got rabies from a bat."

"Like hell she did. That was a goddamn dog that bit her," Patton said.

"They really don't want to do it," the foreman said.

"That job'd be a damn sight better with some overtime pay, I bet."

"I'm sorry, General," one of the workers said. "Those Citadel dollars aren't worth much anymore."

"Gold is," Katherine said.

The workers were attentive.

"By the powers vested in me by the Special War Powers Act, I hereby nationalize nitrate production. You'll be paid in government gold. As soon as this war's won."

"Who says we gonna win the war?" the worker asked.

Patton answered for Katherine. "I say we will. Before this war's over, I'm going to march up to Tamerlane and shoot that sonofabitch myself."

Eight men signed on for the day shift.

Three even agreed to try the four-to-twelve.

As they returned to the Jeep, Elizabeth whispered to the General: "Bats *do* carry plague and rabies, sir."

"Then I'll come back here and shoot those goddamn bats, too, just as soon as this war is over. Those
men are patriots. Even if they do crawl around in bat
crap." Patton shuddered at the thought. "Jesus, I hate
to think of good men like that getting the Black
Death. Even if we did have to buy their loyalty with
Tamerlane's gold."

14

Katherine had told Elizabeth
to remember everything she saw and "get it down."

"As Secretary of the Committee, that's your job—
to record all the appropriate facts. A dirty job, no
doubt, but someone's got to do it."

Given the pace that Patton set it was miraculous
that Elizabeth was able to record anything. Late at
night when she got to bed she was so tired she could
barely lift her notebook and pen, but somehow she
managed.

Her journal was especially vivid on their inspection
of the oil fields, which they visited the day after
inspecting the guano pits. For this trip they started
even earlier. At 0315 hours they were in Patton's Jeep,
and by 0535 they reached the middle of the fields.

The site itself was little more than sagebrush, cactus, and two dozen wood-frame oil wells. North of the
derricks hovered a big storage tank and three distilling
towers.

Such was the Citadel's oil industry.

At one time work here had been considered prime
employment—so lucrative that labor was restricted to

whites and a few Apaches for some of the hotter day-
time jobs. There had been no need to import
Mexicans.

No longer. The 134 men gathered around them
had seen the inflationary war reduce their wages to
nada. Dressed in dirty, sweat-stained homespun, run-
down boots, and floppy straw sombreros, these men
were destitute.

"With all due respect, ma'am," a lanky rawboned
pipe fitter named Harold Porter said, "the wages
you're paying us don't amount to squat."

Ignoring the profanity, Katherine said, "We
printed too much money. I admit that. At the time we
had no choice."

"We do." The speaker was Charles Wilson, a
sandy-haired, freckle-faced labor steward. "We can
find other work."

"We can also go back to the old ways of getting
paid," Harold Porter said. "Get paid with something
real, something that *means* something."

"Under the old system you bartered services and
swapped goods," Katherine said. "That was no system."

"We traded rifle shells, ma'am," Chris Bunker, a
short, swarthy wheelwright, said. "Maybe that weren't
no system, but they was worth something."

Porter agreed. "A rifle shell's something you can
use. These bills you're paying us with, what we supposed to use them for? Wallpaperin' privies?"

Again, to Elizabeth's surprise, her grandmother
ignored the crudity.

"Their value will come back," her grandmother
said simply. "You have the Citadel's guarantee."

"No disrespect, ma'am," Porter said, "but this here's
the Great Sonoran Basin. Averages less than three

inches of rain a year. The summer heat tops 130
degrees. The buzzards, sidewinders, and Gila monsters
out here die of dehydration. You can't shave after sunup
because the water on your face dries too fast—'fore you
can even put a razor to it. And you're asking us to work
in that heat—to put up derricks and cap off gushers.
You're asking us to scale them two-hundred-foot distilling towers and syphon off gasoline vapor? This here
desert is hotter and drier than Death Valley *and* the
Sahara. This ain't no desert, ma'am. It's the devil's own
frying pan. And you're asking us to work it for *free.*"

"She said she'd make it up to you," Patton said.
"She gave you her word."

Wilson put a finger in Patton's chest. The crowd of
riggers closed in tight.

"You're both old-timers, so I'm gonna show you
some courtesy. I'm not gonna tear up this toilet paper
money in your face. But your time's up. We waited
around long enough for you to hear our side of it.
Now it's *adiós.*"

"What will you do about Tamerlane?" the old
woman asked.

"We'll make out. Mexico's got oil wells," Wilson said.

"You think he's going to stop here?"

"He wants Mexico, let 'em come. If the desert
there don't kill 'em, the dysentery will."

"Might kill you too," Jackson said.

"No quicker than this damn job."

"It's mighty slim pickings south of that border
line," said Katherine. "And our *Mejicano* friends don't
cotton to gringos. They never got the hang of the
Good Neighbor Policy—not after the Great Plague."

"Can't hurt us no worse than we been hurt
already," Wilson said.

"She's been trying to finance a war," Patton said.

"And it don't feed the bear."

"She said she'd make it up to you," Jackson said.

"With gold bullion," Katherine said. "Fresh minted."

"Yeah, we heard all about your offer. Word spread like wildfire out of those guano pits. Might fool a bunch of manure eaters, but not us."

"They're pitching in," Patton said. "The munitions plant's back on line."

"So what?" Wilson said.

"So we'll have bullets and guns," Patton said. "We get enough gasoline, we can whip these sonsofbitches."

"Only sonsofbitches I see getting whipped is us," Wilson said. "With phony money."

"We're offering you a chance to live as free men," Jackson said. "We're offering you the Citadel. Civilization."

Wilson looked at the sun. It was just climbing over the eastern rimrock. "All I see is another scorcher."

"Hot day, no pay," Harold Porter said.

"See you in Chihuahua, old woman," Wilson said. "You, too, Generals. Three months back-breaking labor's all you get *por nada.*"

Suddenly, they could feel it all around them. It started as a slow, chugging rumble, then escalated to muted roar, then erupted into rolling thunder.

A well was coming in. The oil thundered nearly a thousand feet in the air. For a moment the entire derrick seemed to levitate, then shattered at the base like a lightning-struck tree, broke off, and fell with an earth-jarring crash.

Black gold poured down on them, and one of the men shouted:

"It's a gusher."

A couple of them started toward it—to cap it off, to conserve the crude.

Wilson waved them back. "Let it blow. We're makin' tracks. This hole's done played out."

Jackson ignored him. He strode through the black rain toward the capping wheel. It was two feet in diameter and covered with crude. When he grabbed it, it was too slick to turn.

Wilson shouted at him: "This ain't the industrial age, General. No push buttons out here. Takes three grown men to turn them oil-slick wheels."

Patton had joined him.

"Hey, General," Porter shouted. "Try shootin' it shut. With that shiny nickel pistol."

Then, to Elizabeth's undying dismay, her grandmother was slogging through the thick inky downpour to help.

Under the gusher's racket her three friends were deaf to the mob, but that still didn't stop Wilson.

"Go ahead. Try some honest labor. See what it's like—what you get for paying us off with this worthless s——."

He used a four-letter expletive which—due to the detonating derrick—Katherine could not hear. Unfortunately for Wilson, her granddaughter could.

"Take your friends and get off our land," Elizabeth shouted at him. "This is still Magruder property. Clear out. You're trespassing."

"You shut your mouth, little girl. I'm not taking any s—— off any midget bitch. I'll take a latigo to your sorry ass." He unthreaded his belt. "In fact, that ain't such a bad idea. Something to remember us by."

"'Fraid not."

A big Apache in dirty buckskins crossed in front of Elizabeth—the biggest Indian she'd ever seen.

But Elizabeth didn't care. She shouldered him aside and yelled at Wilson:

"I said get off our land. None of you would be here—none of you would even be alive—if it wasn't for that old lady there."

"You little ——." This time Wilson used an expletive the girl had never even heard before.

The Apache hit Wilson so hard, his punch sounded like a pistol shot. When Wilson landed, he bounced.

The Apache turned and looked down at the girl.

"I'm sorry. He should not have shown disrespect to your family."

"I don't care." She was screaming now, beside herself with rage. "I don't care about any of you. You can all rot in hell."

"Still he should not have insulted your clan. I know your father. I am Spirit Owl's grandson."

"Too bad for Spirit Owl. He's got grandkids won't lift a finger for their old ones. I pity the old man."

"It's not like that."

"It's not? Then what are those folks doing right now, clawing at that wheel, capping off the rig? Next they'll refine it for you. What then? Fight your f——g wars?"

It was the first obscenity the girl had ever spoken. And the last.

The four-foot eleven-inch girl turned and strode through the thunderous oil. It was now pouring out full bore, a torrential tidal wave of black gold. The stream knocked her down twice, but she kept going. Saturated to the bone, she joined her friends, grabbed onto the wheel, and put her back into it.

Inch by inch, the slippery wheel turned, closing the valve.

When the oil was capped and flowing into the storage tank, they turned around.

To their surprise, the riggers were back on their derricks and distilling towers.

Wilson was still flat on the ground.

15 ◄━━━━

For the moment Matt and the Generals were pleased. They had their army, and they were heading south to train it.

Katherine, however, was anxious. Harry was now the size of a yearling steer, and getting bigger by the week. When he jumped into their backyard pool, half the water splashed out.

Sitting in her backyard one morning with Amelia and Elizabeth, Katherine said:

"Harry's like a tiger in a litter box."

"You mean a shark in a goldfish bowl," Elizabeth said.

"You're right," Katherine said, "and I should have seen it coming."

"None of us dreamed he'd shoot up so fast," said Amelia.

"Well, we did have precedents. An ostrich is a good-sized dinosaur, and it reaches its full growth in six months. Whales mature in less than two years."

"Harry's growing five times faster than any whale," Elizabeth said.

Their conversation was interrupted by a huge splash.

"Speaking of which, we're going to need more water," Katherine said. "That's the fourth time today he's emptied the pool."

"How about a bigger pen, while you're at it?" Elizabeth said.

"Penitentiary, you mean," Amelia said. "When Harry reaches full size, it'll take a stone-walled prison to hold him."

"We could try Yuma Jail," Elizabeth said.

"We'd still have to feed him," said Amelia.

"How much is he eating now?" the old woman asked.

"Six hundred pounds of roughage a day," her granddaughter said.

"It's those stomach stones," said Katherine. "They allow him to digest *anything*. Grasses, water reeds, cornstalks, tree bark."

"You sure you don't want to try Yuma?" Elizabeth asked.

"Hey, Harry," Amelia yelled to him, "you want to visit Yuma Prison?"

"That still wouldn't solve the feeding problem," said the old woman. "You know how long it takes to hand-pick six hundred pounds of fodder?"

"It's time for Harry to start foraging on his own," Amelia said.

"The exercise would be good for him," Elizabeth agreed, "but we'd still have to build that stone wall around a cornfield. He'd wipe out our neighbors."

"Half the territory the rate he's growing," the old woman said.

"We still have to introduce him to the outside world," said Amelia. "There's no doubt about it."

"It won't be easy," Katherine said. "He's skittish around people outside his herd."

"Once you eliminate his out-group," Amelia said, "you have a fairly skimpy expedition."

"He gets along with you two, Betsy Ross, and me," Katherine said.

"He gets along with horses okay," Elizabeth said. "Probably because they have four legs."

"Where should we take him?" Amelia asked.

"Someplace where there aren't any people," Katherine said. "Liz, you know some red-rock canyons that aren't too far from here? Any with flat bottom streambeds we can pull a buckboard over?"

"One I can think of."

"Any roughage along the creek banks?"

"Sure," said Elizabeth, "if you accent the *rough.*"

"Sounds like Harry's going to be on hard rations," Amelia said.

"Last week I saw him eat a prickly pear," said Elizabeth.

"He could eat sticks and rocks like a hydrophobic dog," the old woman said.

"Let's plan a two-day trip," Amelia said. "Betsy Ross could use an outing too. Maybe we'll find some carrion along the way."

"She can ride in the buckboard with you," Elizabeth said to her grandmother.

"Let's do it," Katherine said. "Tomorrow morning?"

"First light," said Amelia.

"We'll be off like a herd of turtles," the old woman grumbled.

16

At dawn, the four friends started up the Salt River Canyon. Amelia, on horseback, took the lead. Harry followed, browsing the stream banks. Elizabeth and Katherine trailed in the buckboard. Betsy Ross perched between them, her eyes glaring balefully.

The entrance to the canyonlands was modest enough—little more than a crack in a cliff face. Two hundred feet high, it was less than forty feet across. After three miles it intersected a larger fissure, then another and another.

They were now hemmed in by walls of solid rock, two thousand feet high.

Amelia felt like an insect crawling along the canyon floor.

17

The sun was at zenith.

The four friends were threading a maze of gorges, rock sculptures, and massive boulders. The air was scorching and windless. Their stream had shrunk to a trickle. Except for the keening flies and the shrieking locusts, the canyon was dead still. It was time to find some shade, water the stock, and break out the grub.

Amelia was just rounding a bend when she saw the puma. He was on top of a barn-sized boulder. A huge slinky tom, he was six feet from nose to rump. His snaky tail whipped back and forth, back and forth. His head was disproportionately small, and his yellow eyes were frighteningly calm.

Their draft horses were not calm though. Tearing up their breeching, they smashed the wagon tongue and kicked over the buckboard. The old woman was catapulted over the box siding and Elizabeth knocked bouncing off the tailgate, where she was instantly pinned by the backward-flipping wagon.

Trapped under a rear axle, Elizabeth could only stare in horror at her grandmother, who lay in a heap beside a blood-streaked boulder. Their wagon team—reins loose, horse collars flopping—disappeared around a bend.

By now Amelia's mount was exploding. Somehow Amelia managed to hang on, levitating high above the saddle. Then the gray came down. A split second later Amelia slammed into the saddle.

Banging off the fork and the pommel, she was soon on the ground.

At which point Harry charged.

Lumbered was closer to the truth.

The tom, sidestepping Harry's horns with effortless ease, mounted Harry's back and clawed his leathery sides. Slipping his head under the bony frill, he sank his fangs into Harry's nape.

Betsy Ross leaped, yowling, off the overturned buckboard and scrambled toward her son. Flapping helpless at his feet, she could not reach the tom. She couldn't jump high enough.

"Amelia!"

Amelia turned her head and saw Elizabeth. The girl was pinned under a wagon wheel. One of Patton's nickel-plated ivory-handled .45s was in her fist. She chambered a round and threw it to Amelia, who picked it up.

Amelia turned. The tom was watching her now, his gaze steady, unblinking. He was *daring* her to make a move.

Her first round burned the panther's right shoulder, and the second missed entirely. As he jumped free of the trumpeting Triceratops, his third shot also missed.

Now he was on the canyon floor, rocking back on his haunches, less than a dozen feet away. Betsy had chased Harry up the canyon, away from the battle, so Amelia and the tom were alone. The panther stared at her with unmoving amber eyes.

She raised the .45.

Shrödinger's cat, she thought, *that's who you are. Well, you have me now. Erwin, this is one you didn't tell us about—one who broke out of your box and found me.*

Where now, Erwin?

The panther roared and leaped.

In that last heartbeat of eternity the tom was the most beautiful thing Amelia had ever seen.

Which universe, Erwin?

This one?

The next?

None at all?

She shot the big tom straight through the heart.

18

Returning to the Citadel, the four of them were a sight. Amelia—on foot and out in front—was leading a dun-colored dray horse by its dangling harness strap. The old woman was slumped over the animal's neck. Her granddaughter was mounted behind her, holding her up by the waist. Betsy Ross and Harry followed, Betsy perched on his frill, glaring hatefully.

Nor did their moods improve. For one thing they had sustained extensive physical damage. The old woman had serious contusions and a bad concussion. Elizabeth had a broken arm and four cracked ribs. The mauled Amelia had, once more, dislocated a shoulder. Betsy Ross suffered from paranoid exhaustion.

Although Harry's sides had been raked bloody and his neck gnawed, those injuries turned out to be the least significant. His psychological distress was far more troubling. For in the moment that the panther had leaped from his back and charged Amelia, she'd shot Harry too—with something far more lethal than a bullet. She'd hit him with Cupid's arrow.

The old woman had anticipated the contingency. Only two weeks before, she had discussed it with her son on her front porch.

"What do we do if he goes into heat? You ask me, he's probably starting puberty right now."

Richard's analysis was prescient. "He'll probably fall in love with one of us."

"I'm serious."

"So am I. Harry's a fanatical herd beast. You ever notice what happens if we accidentally leave him alone?"

"We don't. Betsy Ross is with him constantly."

"Not that one time she wasn't."

The old woman had hoped to forget that episode. When Harry had been substantially smaller, Betsy Ross had left him sleeping in the backyard under the saguaro. She had bird-hopped into the kitchen looking for table scraps.

When Harry had awakened and found himself alone, he'd turned into a bomb and exploded. He'd butted the back door off its hinges and trumpeted through the old woman's house like a water buffalo in a china shop, looking for his lost herd.

Betsy Ross had not left him alone since.

"Remember those geese Rachael and I used to keep when we were kids," Richard said. "They were dinosaurs, too, you know."

She had hoped to forget that episode as well.

"Herd dinosaurs," she grudgingly acknowledged.

"Yes, a gaggle of graylag geese. Remember who the gander's mate was? Did you enjoy the role?"

No, the old woman hadn't. None of them had been amused—least, of all, William Tell, the gander. Where, when, or how he had fallen for Katherine, no one could say, but he'd definitely swallowed the hook. She had awakened one morning to hear him honking outside her bedroom, and when she had opened the window, he was staring at her, goggle-eyed.

No matter how many times she rejected him, it had done no good. He'd refused to take the hint. For the rest of his unfortunate life, he'd trotted after her.

Whenever she left him, his honking had been horrendous.

Finally one summer she and her late husband, Frank, had taken a two-week trip to inspect a new dam up on the Mogollon Rim. The disconsolate goose had honked continually, could not sleep, had refused sustenance, and had finally died of emaciation.

His death honks, they were told, had been heartbreaking.

No one had taken his demise lightly.

Sitting in the yard, Richard said: "Birds and lizards are notoriously inept at choosing love objects."

"There sure aren't any other Triceratops around," the old woman agreed.

"Frogs not only mistake other species for loved ones, they'll go after rocks, tree stumps, and floating leaves. Doves have been known to fall for stuffed pigeons, even rolled-up rugs. Peacocks have fallen in love with turtles. Remember Konrad Lorenz's jackdaw? The one that used to stuff worms in his mouth?"

"I not only read the book, I gave it to you."

"I'm just saying don't be shocked if it happens."

So she was surprised but not shocked when love came to Harry. It had hit him with almost palpable force—when Amelia had driven the panther from his back and shot the cat dead.

The romance was not pretty. Whenever Amelia left his side, Harry became morose. He would trumpet distress calls. His eyes would grow red and rheumy. He would lose weight, and his once-healthy hide would wrinkle and sag.

Whenever she was near—as she was today, there by Harry's new backyard corral—he swelled with male vanity and chomped cornstalks from her hand. Some described him as "dreamy-eyed."

Betsy Ross, meanwhile, perched on Harry's arching neck-frill and glared at Amelia with undisguised distrust, sensing what Amelia had done to her boy.

The old woman got up from her rocking chair. She walked over to the barbwire corral and leaned on a post. She did not attempt to hand-feed the Triceratops. When Amelia was around, other herd beasts did not exist. Instead the old woman approached Amelia.

"Long time no see," the old woman said.

"Wish I could spend more time back here. That's for sure."

"What have you been doing anyway?"

"I've been seeing the Citadel, trying to get to know some of the people. The truth is I've been worried about our dealings with Tamerlane's army."

"You aren't the only one."

"I've even spoken to Randall Jeffers and his friends."

"That's a job with a lot of downward mobility."

"You don't like Randall much, do you?"

"He's a fourth-rate fool with delusions of grandeur," Elizabeth said, coming up behind Amelia.

"You mean gender," her grandmother said.

"It's not funny," Amelia said. "He's asking for a public hearing in the Citadel's public square. The Collective Association wants to discuss your Military Preparedness Program."

"So I've heard."

"Are you going, Grandma?"

"I wouldn't miss it for the world."

"He wants to debate you at that hearing," Amelia said, "and he's out for blood. While you've been nursemaiding Harry, he's been campaigning for governor. Your 'fascist militarism' is the major plank in his platform. He sees this hearing as a turning point in his campaign."

"You better watch out, Grandma," Elizabeth said. "You know how upset he gets you."

"He's not a bad debater either," Amelia said.

"Does his face still look like unrisen dough?" the old woman asked.

Her granddaughter broke up.

"Laugh all you want," Amelia said, "but he's really

good. And he's gathering support. Some people think he makes a lot of sense."

"What do you think?" the old woman asked.

"I'm a pacifist, Katherine."

"Even against men like Tamerlane?" the old woman asked.

"We're also throwing down a gauntlet."

"By defending ourselves?"

"How?" Amelia said. "The way New Salt did?"

"We'll do it different."

"You really think we're tougher than New Salt?"

"No," the old woman said, "but we do have some things they didn't have."

"What?"

"We have Patton and Jackson. And you. We also won't fight them defensively."

"Terrific. We'll attack twenty thousand seasoned soldiers with two thousand cowboys."

"We have better intelligence than New Salt had."

"Yes," Amelia said, "Darrell's dispatches are informative. Unfortunately, the information's all bad. What did Darrell's last dispatch say? That Tamerlane's transporting all of New Salt's heavy artillery down here plus a small mountain of munitions. We resist him, he'll blow us off the face of the earth."

"He'll do that anyway."

"Katherine, don't say that to Jeffers next week. Not up on the platform. He'll obliterate you. I mean that. He's spoiling for a fight."

"Tell him to bring his lunch *and* dinner."

"I wish you'd duck this one," Amelia said. "Just this one time."

"See that you're there," the old woman said. "This is going to be fun."

19

The next Saturday afternoon
found the old woman and Elizabeth waiting for Jeffers
in the Citadel's *plazuela*. The fort walls and the big
adobe house were freshly gessoed and sparkled in the
sun.

The Citadel's main square was over 150 yards on
an edge and lined with piñon pine and live oak. The
speakers' platform was erected in front of the big
house, complete with two podiums and microphones.

Jeffers, who had issued the challenge, was to speak
first, the old woman second. Over two thousand people had shown up to hear them.

Jeffers and Amelia were the only ones missing.

After waiting three-quarters of an hour, the old
woman—neatly dressed in a white cotton dress, her
only jewelry a simple gold wedding band—went to the
podium without him.

"Since Randall can't seem to find his way to the
Citadel," the old woman said, "I'll get my speech over
with first. It doesn't matter what Jeffers says anyway.
The truth is his plan won't work. You can't cut deals
with tyrants. And if there's anyone out there dumb
enough to think so, they'll get the peace they deserve.
The peace of New Salt. The peace of the Holocaust.
The peace of the grave.

"I know Jeffers and his friends think otherwise.
They tell us that peace can be won on the cheap—
through words, not deeds, with concessions, not
blood. Give the tyrant what he wants, and he'll go
away. After all, the tyrant doesn't want war either.
He's just like us.

"But the Tamerlanes of this world are not like us. You can never give them enough. They will always want more. For their dreams are not of peace but of dominion, and the hymns they sing are not paeans to love but the sirens' song of death.

"You know I promised myself when I stepped up here I would not engage in *ad hominem* attacks on Randall Jeffers. It's been a difficult promise to keep because the hard fact is I don't like Jeffers. I not only think he speaks a lot of rot, he speaks it atrociously. To say he is naive is inadequate. He is suffocatingly stupid, breathtakingly ignorant.

"Worse, he is now managing to waste our time—something we have very little of. Hobbes said that hell is truth seen too late, and at the rate we're going, we are in for orgies of hell. Because to Tamerlane the plundering of this land is not subject to negotiation. His is a *jihad*, a holy war, and the dark gods he serves are no rosy cherubs, strumming lutes and hip harps. They're fiends from the abyss. Just ask the refugees, who have fled here from New Anchorage, New Salt, and all the other places Tamerlane has razed."

The old woman sat down, and the applause was modest.

They were waiting for Jeffers to rebut, but he still had not arrived.

Instead William Crawford took the podium. His black frock coat was sharply pressed and his gray hair and beard carefully trimmed. He read his remarks.

"Randall Jeffers and Amelia Earhart have chosen not to attend what they deem to be a pointless debate. Randall Jeffers has instead asked me to read a simple statement.

"'Katherine Magruder and her two antediluvian

Generals are three anachronisms of an age long past. Their call to arms summons forth only the stench of death, piles of corpses, and dead spectral voices wailing in the wind. Follow the course they prescribe, and the Citadel will be turned into a nightmare world run by pagan warlords, baying at bloody moons, smoking altars, and vengeful gods. Our present dilemma is not one of tactics and strategy, not a problem of proper generalship, it is a situation of stark simplicity. Should we wage a war we cannot win—a war the very fighting of which would return New Arizona to irretrievable desert and destroy forever our last brief vestiges of civilization? Do we wish to go back to a time when nation was turned against nation and brother against brother, when men wore horns and animals' skins and licked blood off swords? When all that was left for their women was to weave winding sheets and shrouds? Do you wish to go back to an age when women were dubbed woe-man by the Anglo-Saxon brutes? When men blamed women for all the evil in the world, kept them in bondage, and decimated the globe? They must not do it again. The death-dealers must not defeat the death-defiers.

"'Therefore,' Jeffers goes on to say, 'the time for useless talk has ceased. Amelia and I are taking our petitions to Tamerlane. We are presenting them to him beneath the Mogollon Rim. There, we hope to begin negotiations which will lead to a lasting peace, one which will vouchsafe New Arizona's prosperity for a generation to come. I'm sure you wish us well.'"

The ovation was thunderous.

Ignoring the ecstatic crowd, the old woman turned to her granddaughter.

"We have to reach your brother and the Generals

down on the border. It's time to mobilize that army.
Now. Every man they can get."

"Isn't that short notice?" Elizabeth asked.

"Darrell is in trouble. More trouble than we can
imagine. Go straight to the telegraph office and tell
your brother. He'll understand."

"What's Jeffers's campaign have to do with Darrell?"

"He's been working for *us*, systematically betraying
the Horde. Amelia knows that. So does Jeffers."

"You think they'll tell?"

"You know Jeffers. What do you think?"

"I think we better get to that telegraph office."

"Let's get that wire sent now. Liz, we're going to
war."

The two women left the platform, ignoring the
excited throng.

20 ◢

That night the old woman
and Elizabeth sat in the backyard and reread Darrell's
most recent dispatch. It had arrived that afternoon
after the so-called debate.

The old woman could not believe her eyes.

Dear Grandma,

*I'm writing this as fast as I can. The situation here
is deteriorating, and I may not be able to get this to
you. I don't know what happened at the Citadel, but
three days ago we heard this rumor that some 1930s
aviatrix and that idiot Jeffers were approaching the
bok, ostensibly to negotiate a truce.*

*Well, as you can imagine, Tamerlane and our
Lady are not preparing any royal reception for them.
Our leaders aren't into diplomatic niceties. They're
going after hard intelligence.*

*Meaning, Jeffers and this Amelia will be sent
straight to our Cuddler.*

I can only assume my cover will be blown.

*I haven't seen this 1930s pilot. Sounds like she's
even older than you are, Grandma. Maybe she's too
senile to rat me out. I have no such illusions about our
old buddy, Randall, though. He'll tell them about my
dispatches quicker than a rabbit can procreate.*

*Sorry, Grandma. I occasionally forget your delicate
sensibilities. Too much time in the bok.*

*But never fear. Hang tough and keep the faith. This
snafu's no fault of yours. Whatever happens, I love you
all. You, Dad, Matthew, even the Baby Dwarf.*

Tell Liz, to me, she'll always be ten feet tall.

Love,
Darrell

The old woman glared at Elizabeth. "I should have
known. I should have guessed she and that moron,
Jeffers, would pull something like this."

"How could you have known?"

"Amelia kept asking me these questions: 'Doesn't
Jeffers have a point? Why can't we reason with
Tamerlane? Isn't it worth a try? If we can avoid the
blood and the slaughter, isn't it worth meeting with
them?' Then she told me she was taking time off to be
by herself. 'To think things over,' she said."

"What were you supposed to do, Grandma? Slap
her in jail? Put her under house arrest?"

"I wasn't supposed to let her kill Darrell."

Elizabeth took her grandmother by the hand. "Maybe that'll teach him not to call me 'Baby Dwarf.'"

The old woman stared at Elizabeth—all four feet eleven inches of her.

"What makes you little ones so tough?" she said.

"Grandma, I'm telling you there's nothing to worry about. Darrell will think of something. He always has. Of all us kids, he was the smartest, the toughest."

"Liz, you're not so bad yourself."

"Come on, Grandma. Let's face it. Of all us kids, Darrell was the best."

"I still say you're not so bad."

"What I want to know is whether *you*'re going to hold up?"

"If George and Tom come through for us, I will."

"Tom and Patton said in the wire they would. They'd lead that rescue party right into the *bok.*"

"Yeah, but I didn't care for that one line there," the old woman said, "where George described Amelia as 'no longer of any strategic value.'"

"He doesn't understand your insistence on rescuing *both* Darrell and Amelia. That could prove difficult."

"I brought that girl into this world. I'm not going to abandon her."

"The General wants to save Darrell. He just thinks Amelia's less important. That's all."

"He's wrong there. Before this is over she'll be 'of strategic value.'"

"You think so?" Elizabeth sounded doubtful.

"You mark my words," the old lady said. "We're going to need that girl."

PART XIX

I have dreamed a dreary dream
Beyond the Isle of Skye.
I saw a dead man win a fight,
And I think that man was I.

—Anonymous,
"The Earl of Douglas"

Darrell McGruder squatted in his pit, studying a pair of brown rats. Nearly a foot long, they had hard red eyes, sharp teeth, and massive rear ends. They'd grown fat off the previous tenants.

"Asses like dogs" was Forsythe's apt description.

Darrell had spent the previous night fighting them off with his wooden slop bucket. The battle had been successful, and he'd protected both himself and his comatose cell mate.

Why he'd bothered saving his companion he was not sure. Jeffers was certainly no friend. When Jeffers entered the camp, the first thing he did was inform Tamerlane of the secret dispatches Darrell had smuggled into the Citadel.

Because of Jeffers, Darrell was in the hole.

Topside, he heard the cage hasp hammered out. The overhead bars were raised. The hole was only five feet deep and six across, so, at last, Darrell could extend his legs. Slowly, painfully, he got up.

Just then a guard flung Amelia back into the pit. Her weight knocked him back into the sewage.

As Darrell lifted the unconscious woman out of the slop, he could see raw red scorch marks through her torn pants and blouse. All her fingernails had been prised out.

"The girl has guts," the guard said. "I'll give her that. Our Cuddler never got a peep out of her."

The guard lowered himself into the pit. He hoisted the unconscious Jeffers topside.

"He'll do better with this one," the guard said as he climbed back out.

Darrell carefully lowered Amelia onto the inverted slop bucket.

"I don't know why you bother with her," Darrell said, looking up. "*He'll* tell you anything you want to know."

But instead of the guards, Legion and Forsythe were standing over them. The smiling Legion—dressed in a black blouse and tight black slacks—had two pet diamondbacks writhing around her shoulders and waist. Forsythe wore a red cambric cowl, scarred with scorch marks.

Darrell stood up, and his two tormentors squatted to face him.

"Tell it to Mustafa," Forsythe said. "He thinks there's always more to find out."

"He may have a point," Legion said. "When Mustafa's done Jeffers will tell us things *Jeffers* doesn't know he knows."

One of the rats began splashing toward the slumped Amelia. Darrell kicked him back across the hole.

"Must be nice," Forsythe said, "cohabitating with rats."

"It's fine for the rats," Darrell said. "They're really great little beasts. I'm surprised our Lady doesn't drop one of her rattlers down here for good measure."

Legion stroked her pets, carefully keeping them away from the pit.

"No-o-o-o," she crooned, "those two rodents might murder my darlings."

Amelia, coming to in her corner, opened a blood-shot eye. "Those rats *are* pretty mean."

"Quite so," Legion agreed. "They are, in fact, the most destructive animals on earth."

As if to underscore her point, both rats scampered toward the stooped Amelia, and Darrell was forced to remove her from her inverted bucket and beat them back with it.

"*Rattus rattus* eats us," Legion explained, "not vice versa. And because they vector plague, they are the greatest cause of human misery in history."

"Outside of our own ferocity," Forsythe said.

"Agreed. But that does not minimize their achievements."

"The little buggers are tough," Darrell had to admit.

"Tough?" Forsythe shrieked. "They're bloody well indestructible. Every disaster that kills us—war, plague, famine, flood—causes them to multiply exponentially."

"They do seem fond of this sewage," Darrell said.

"They delight in squalor," Legion said.

Slowly, Amelia worked her way up the pit wall. "Where's Jeffers?"

"The poor boy's taken your place in the tent," Forsythe said.

"And he's getting the full treatment this time," Legion said.

Forsythe's leather apron, Darrell noted, was blood-stained as well as scorched.

"Why on earth?" Amelia asked.

"I know," Forsythe sneered. "The man is so willing. He positively eats betrayal. I say, he wallows in it. Unfortunately, Mustafa is not impressed. The more Jeffers screams, the more Mustafa thinks he's holding back."

Amelia was clearly dismayed.

"Forget about Jeffers," Legion said. "Look on the bright side of things. Now you two have each other."

"Yes," Forsythe concurred, "a marriage made in heaven—a match to rank with that of Messalina and Caligula."

Amelia scowled.

"Ah, our friend *is* unhappy," Forsythe said. "She's no doubt worried about Jeffers. She's afraid he'll betray her friends in the Citadel. After all, she didn't."

"Yes, and I don't see why not," Legion said. "She didn't approve of their militarism all that much. That's what Jeffers says."

"Oh, she'll have another chance to confess her sins," Forsythe said. "She will face our Cuddler again. Again and again and again. Until our Lord and your Ladyship are sure she's told us all."

"Go to hell," Amelia said.

She then spit at an encroaching rat. To Darrell's dismay, her sputum was pink.

"Good show," Forsythe said. "Mustafa loves spunk. He exults in primitive resistance."

"I'm afraid he's right," Legion said. "Underneath Mustafa's *Koran*-quoting facade, he's pure pagan."

"With a pagan's lust for pain," Forsythe said.

The screams from the tent were now ear-shattering.

"What's going on in there?" Darrell asked.

"Jeffers has just been shod with the iron shoes—

roasted red-hot, of course." Forsythe sniffed the smoke billowing out of the tent. "Mustafa is now straddling him over an iron barrel filled with blazing coals. It's called Loping the Mare."

"Next he will break his bones," Legion said.

The screams were truly unnerving.

Amelia slumped into her corner.

"I say," Forsythe said, "you two don't seem pleased with our little show."

"I could live without it," Darrell said.

"Perhaps you think our Lady here will help you? Slip you a cup of Socrates's hemlock? Hurry death, so to speak?"

"If so, he's a child," Legion said.

"At least, this child doesn't have to write any more poems about Tamerlane," Darrell said.

"No, but you will sing his hymns," Legion said, "and dance in the fire of his shoes."

Jeffers's screams were no longer even human.

"Doesn't your Cuddler like *anyone?*" Darrell asked.

"Oh, he'll be most pleased to see you," Legion said.

"Definitely," Forsythe agreed. "You he'll receive as a brother. He'll deliver you from your chains, show you the purest fires of the Self."

"The lights will burn all over hell," Legion said.

The old man emerged from the Black Tent. His red robe was scorched, and his shoulder-length white hair and beard were stiff with gore. A crazed light burned in his eyes.

"I'm told he sleeps with a whip," Darrell said.

"A cat-o'-nine," Forsythe said.

"That shows a certain narrowness of vision, you ask me," Darrell said.

Mustafa returned to his tent. The moment he entered, Jeffers's screams recommenced.

"Perhaps, but he knows his stuff," Legion said. "Just listen to those howls. And that's how he treats the ones who cooperate. Can you imagine what he'll do to you?"

"You'll be cast down for your sins," Forsythe said. "The stones themselves shall weep."

"You shall know depths below depths," Legion said, "and the very truth of hell."

The next scream shook even Forsythe.

Legion leaned over Darrell and smiled. "You are about to soar on the wings of night."

2

Lieutenant Sadat and Sergeant Assad were now both veterans. It was a good thing for the Ordu too. Their present post—a mountain lookout commanding the vast southwestern *llano*—required the steady nerves of seasoned soldiers.

For some time now scouting reports had warned of possible sneak attacks, and at times like these, nothing seemed impossible. Here in the twilit desert everything was scary, unreal. In fact, if Hardy and Mann stared long enough into the gathering dusk, the parched chaparral itself turned strangely ominous. The distant saguaro now—vibrating in and out of focus—was no longer a treelike cactus but an enemy sentinel, and the squat bushy yucca with its bayonet-shaped leaves not a plant but a battlewagon.

"Do you think anyone will attack us?" Sadat asked.

Assad looked over his shoulder to the north. Behind them, downslope, the camp's trailwise horse herd cropped the grass and mesquite of the Rio Lobo River Valley. The remudas—now containing over twelve thousand head—were a fair indication of the Horde's strength.

"Not unless they're stupid."

"Or insane."

"Or both."

The night wind whistled through the *llano*, and the two men pulled their black *caftans* tight around their bodies.

"Keep your eyes fixed south—on that *llano*," Sadat said. "If any scouts sneak through, the Cuddler will have our hides on a high rack."

Assad grudgingly agreed. He raised his field glasses once more and continued his lookout.

3

Hardy was not the only man who was apprehensive. Major Thompson of the Stonewall Brigade was upset. Flattened against the rimrock, he anxiously studied Hardy's hill through his nightscope.

He ignored the enemy troops camped out on the flats. Those, his troops could handle. Hardy and Mann on the mesa, however, unless eliminated, would quickly spot his advance and report it to their superiors. Furthermore, he needed their hill for his mortar company. Without ample mortar cover the whole operation—including Jackson's three-pronged assault against the Horde's eastern flank—was doomed.

Jackson's three-pronged assault. Something else that made Thompson nervous. One of his officers, after examining the strategy, had pronounced it "suicidal" and promptly resigned his commission.

"You're charging hell with a glass of ice water" had been his opinion.

Thompson didn't think much of the assault either.

He'd been with Generals Jackson and Patton when they had—in strict accordance with the Citadel's constitution—presented their strategy to the council.

The plan had encountered anger and confusion.

"Let me get this straight," Clement Lamont said. "You want to tip our hand to the Horde. Give them a chance to judge our overall military preparedness—our grasp of tactics and strategy, our weaponry, our ability to coordinate assaults. You want to reveal to them our true capability."

"Clement," Katherine argued, "if it were only Darrell, I wouldn't do it either. Darrell can take care of himself. But it's the girl as well. She didn't ask to come here. We got her into this."

"She went over to the other side," Crawford said.

"She was trying to help."

"She was wrong."

"We can't abandon her now."

"Let her fry," Clement said.

To the Major's relief, the old woman had muttered under her breath:

"Like hell we will."

The Major watched at the cliff through his nightscope, waiting for the signal from his Apache scouts that they had neutralized the lookouts.

When the signal came, he would send his First Mortar Company up the slope and lead the rest of his battalion across the *llano,* through the enemy's horse herd, and—if they survived that—straight into the their *bok*.

To fight a ten-thousand-man army.

The Major had his doubts.

Then it happened. He received his signal from the cliff—three flashing torches. The enemy's sentries had been eliminated, and it was time for him to launch his assault. Outnumbered six to one, he was now to attack ten thousand veteran soldiers with barely two thousand recruits.

"Captain Connolly," the Major said, "take your mortar company up the slope. Remember to bring those M-60s too. You'll be expected to defend that position."

"We'll have to," the Captain said.

Connolly buttoned up his gray twill military tunic and pulled his forage cap down over his eyes. As he led his platoon over the rise and into the chaparral, Major Thompson turned to Lieutenant Matthew Magruder.

"Line the men up. We're heading out."

The Lieutenant sent word down the line, and they mounted up. The gray-clad battalion followed them down the rimrock and into the dark.

4 ━━━━━

Horse Ears floated slowly downstream under the tangled leaves of the hollowed-out log. At night, in the black water, he was virtually invisible—as was the blasting gel inside the log.

He studied the rim of the dam two hundred feet away. Another five minutes, that was all. Then he could hook the log to the dam and haul ass, at which point his career in "underwater demolitions" would be over.

Then he saw it. The *Ordu* wasn't supposed to have its patrol boat out—not this late at night—but there it was, closing in fast.

The suspect log would never pass inspection.

He unlimbered the spool of fuse wire from his backpack, crimped it onto the log's blasting cap, then tied it off. Wrapping the towline around his waist, he dived to the bottom of the reservoir, turned toward the dam, and began to kick.

The dynamite-laden log picked up speed.

He hit the dam wall, breathless, but still submerged.

Somehow he relocated the I-hook the Sergeant had screwed in the night before. He threaded the towrope through the hook. Bracing his feet against the dam wall, he pulled.

Topside, the log picked up speed.

Bullets instantly peppered the surface water, the log, the dam wall.

When the log butted against the steel-and-concrete dam, he tied off the pull rope and turned toward the shore, his lungs bursting. Bullets hammered the water overhead.

He kicked as if he were possessed, not knowing which he feared the most—being shot, the pain in his exploding lungs, or the off chance that the unexpected patrol boat would hit the log's blasting cap.

Or the even more terrifying possibility that the demolition team on shore would throw their backup switch and detonate the log by remote control.

Just as he reached the shore, his last fear was realized. The demolition team threw the switch, and everything around him went up in flames.

Even at the bottom of Darrell's pit the detonation was earth-shaking. Amelia was knocked off her inverted slop bucket and pitched headlong across the cell, straight at the rats. Darrell was bounced off all four walls before landing on top of her.

The two rodents, however, were no longer interested in them. Their red eyes blazing, their screams shrilling, they rocketed up the wall of the pit-cage and escaped through the bars.

After getting Amelia back on the inverted slop bucket, Darrell pulled himself to the bars for a better look at the camp.

The camp dogs howled. The horses slipped their hobbles and galloped off. Soldiers leaped over their pit, tearing straight through the Cuddler's yard, and raced south.

Darrell turned toward the cause of their panic. Thundering at their hill—less than a hundred feet from the pit—was a wall of water over fifty feet high.

He squatted beside the confused Amelia and put an arm around her.

"Get set. We're about to be—"

And then the wave hit.

6

When Darrell came to, Gurney was pulling Amelia and him out of their water-filled pit. For several minutes all they could do was vomit floodwater.

Finally, Darrell caught his breath. The water was receding from the crest of their hill, but the rest of the camp was a muddy swamp, strewn with foundering stock, drowning men, and thousands of collapsed yellow tents.

"Where's the *Imam?*" Darrell asked.

"He finally found his *hajj*, his journey's end."

"The flood got him?"

Gurney nodded. "I hung on to the bars, till the water subsided, but he was carried off."

"Why did our fearless leader camp next to a dam?" Amelia asked, slowly getting hold of herself.

"It was for the horses," Gurney said. "They needed water and forage. We have twenty thousand head to look after."

"You *had* twenty thousand head to look after," Amelia said.

Gurney and Darrell suddenly turned to the south. The Stonewall Brigade, which had descended on the camp from the southern hills, was fording the flooded camp and climbing their hill. Patton's troops approached from the southeast. There was no armed resistance.

Patton arrived first on a big bay. His khaki uniform was wet, but the gold stars on his helmet, shoulders, and nickel-plated .45s glittered. He glared at the doubled-over Amelia, who was once more regurgitating floodwater.

"Again, I meet the troubler of my peace," Patton said to her.

Now Jackson—completing the pincer movement—pulled up on Old Sorrell. He swung down off his mount and went straight to Amelia, covering her with his poncho.

"We have to get out of here," Jackson said. "The main force is to the west, requisitioning mounts and matériel. That's why you made it here so easily. But they'll return now—or attack the Citadel. Either way you have to leave." He turned to Amelia. "Can you ride?"

Amelia nodded.

"What about you?" he asked Darrell.

"He's staying," Gurney said. "So am I."

Patton and Jackson stared at the bodyguard.

"There's a munitions dump," Gurney said, "above the floodline. You give Darrell and me two M-16s and a grenade launcher, we might just blow it."

Matt Magruder kicked his Appaloosa forward.

"I'm volunteering, sir."

Darrell looked up. "What do you know? My baby brother. How's Grandma? The Dwarf?"

"Just fine." Matt looked at Patton. "General, I want to stay."

"Not a chance," Darrell said. "He'd never make it. None of you would. That ammo depot is guarded by *Janizaries,* real soldiers. You don't speak the language, and they don't know you."

"It's a job for two men or an army," Gurney said. "And you're needed back at the Citadel."

"You're running out of time," Darrell said.

Patton gave Darrell a hard look. "You trust that man."

"He pulled us out of that hole."

"Why are you doing this?" Jackson asked Gurney.

Gurney stared at the hills beyond and said nothing.

"Back in New Anchorage," Darrell explained, "Tamerlane killed his wife and family."

"Lieutenant Magruder," Jackson said to his adjutant, "give these gentlemen whatever they need."

Matthew collected two M-16s and a grenade launcher from the men.

Suddenly Amelia stood up. "Make that three M-16s. I'm going with them."

"Never happen," Darrell said.

"You can't stop me. I owe the Citadel that much."

Darrell looked at Patton and Jackson, waiting for an order.

"We can't control her either," Patton said.

The two Generals averted their eyes.

Darrell looked back at Amelia. She continued to glower at him.

"There's no way you can stop me," she said.

"Anything you say."

Darrell lifted his elbows and grimaced, as if working a kink out of his back, then he hit her with a short left. He caught her just before she landed in the mud.

Jackson was instantly off his horse, hoisting her onto his own McClellan. He lashed her wrists and hips to it, then swung on behind her.

Patton stared at Darrell. "Your grandmother wanted me to bring you home."

"You'll tell her something."

"I suppose so. Good luck, son."

Darrell looked up to find the Major staring at him. He didn't recognize Thompson.

"Don't think I've had the pleasure, sir."

"Major Eliah Thompson."

"*The* Major Thompson? All the way from Sonora? I *am* impressed. What brings you up here?"

"He loves the Citadel," Matthew said. "Can't get enough of it."

"That's not the way Grandma tells it." Darrell stared at him, curious. "Can't picture you throwing in with us."

"Maybe I'll tell you about it sometime," Thompson said.

"I'm looking forward to it."

"Let's move it out," Gurney said. He looked up at the Generals. "You too."

He grabbed Darrell's arm, and the two of them started toward the dump.

7 ▶

Gurney's captaincy got them past the mountain sentries, but when they reached the ammo dump, they were ordered back down. Still Gurney tried.

"Our Lord has sent us here to inspect the munitions," he yelled at the black-robed guards manning the command post's machine gun bunker. "You'll answer to Mustafa. He will flay you whole."

"The *bok* is under siege," the sentry answered. "No one is allowed into the munitions *yurt.*"

Gurney waved a counterfeit pass at the guards, then climbed under the first wire with Darrell.

"I have a letter of conduct from our Lord."

The sentries fired warning shots.

Gurney fired an answering clip into their chests.

He and Darrell raced through the mine field, clambered under the razor wire, and were diving into the guard bunker, just as the mountain sentries reached the first wire barricades.

Gurney lined up his tripod machine gun. Staring over Gurney's shoulder, Darrell watched as his friend cut down the attacking soldiers. Man after man after man collapsed as the big gun hammered.

"Get that grenade launcher," Gurney yelled at him.

The munitions depot was less than fifty yards away—and big as a barn. The patched canvas tent was stretched over the powder and dynamite kegs like a crazy quilt. The tent's bottom was a full ten feet above the storage pallets and roped to ground stakes. The sides of the black-powder kegs were exposed.

Darrell screwed on the launcher, sighted in the yellow *yurt*. Then hesitated.

They were well within the dump's blast radius.

"You got that thing bracketed?" Gurney yelled at him, the M-60 still hammering in his fists.

Over a dozen soldiers were spread-eagled on the barbwire.

"Lock and load," Darrell yelled back.

"Then let's get it on."

Good-bye Grandma. Good-bye Dad. Brother Matt. Baby Dwarf. Betsy Ross.

Good-bye Citadel.

Where do they go, he wondered idly, when the ghost walks out and leaves the body behind?

He squeezed off a grenade, and as Legion had once predicted, the lights went on all over hell. They started as pinpoints, expanded into dazzlingly brilliant spirals, merged into a single maelstrom of fire, and then the universe exploded into flames.

8

Darrell couldn't believe he was still alive. He was even more amazed when he saw that it was Legion bending over him, cradling his head.

Everything else was charred, smoking rubble.

"I said before you were a child."

"The child in me's dying."

"A child who hurt our Lord."

"And cheated your Cuddler." Darrell's lips forced a smile.

"Yes, and Mustafa will pay for that most dearly. Forsythe too. When you escaped from *their* pit-cage, they were responsible. That, Tamerlane will never forgive."

"I wish I could see it."

"That is not possible."

Darrell sighed. "I'll never be a poet now."

"Yes, you were spared that awful calling."

His throat rattled, and he grew light-headed.

"I escaped your fiery shoes."

"But not your fate."

"Which is?"

"You told me once you sought a journey. You have found it."

"How does it end?"

"In the belly of the beast."

"Tough luck on my part."

"You lost your talisman, your star."

"But not you."

"No, not me."

His breath rasped. He felt light as air, buoyant as

bubbles, as if he were made of Time itself. He was to
soar on the wings of night.

Again, he felt himself falling—

Falling toward—

Falling out—

He tried to speak, but instead of speech, he felt a
sudden rise, another, then another, then nothing—no
rattling gasp, no body settling, no sound at all.

He tried to tell her— Tried—

Oh, Christ, oh—

Oh, God—

Oh—

Oh—

9

The Lady Legion stared at
the dead youth. Still cradling his head, she kissed his
bloody lips.

*What's left for us now? Do we make a hell of the
earth—or work Death's streets like a whore?*

In her clenched fist she gripped the boy's last
poem, salvaged from his former *yurt*.

> *Although I know all roads,*
> *I shall never reach home.*
> *Death waits.*
> *Over the* llano,
> *On the wind,*
> *Death waits.*

He had known all along what he would do. He had

never even tried to escape. He'd stayed instead to spirit out his dispatches. He *chose* to remain—and hurt them all.

Still he had not died in innocence and youth. She'd robbed him of that: That flower she'd plucked bleeding from its thorns.

She recalled their one night together. She had met him by the river and taken him on the wildest of rides. To ravage him, to strip him clean: That had been her purpose. She was Legion, and it was her nature to conquer.

But not that night. She had been mastered—by *him*.

Adding insult to injury, he had told her *nunca mais*, never again. She had laughed, saying who would want *him* a second time, but she knew the truth. He had not wanted *her*.

So she had been pleased when Jeffers had first ridden into camp and betrayed the Scribe. She wanted to see him Cuddled. She longed for him to taste the lash and suffer the wheel's bite, to understand what he had done.

But now, looking at his bloodied face, she knew she had not wanted *this*. She saw instead in his glazed eyes the mirror of her own Narcissus—her True Self.

Here I lie—in love, in hell.

Rage rushed through her veins like fire, and suddenly she knew her course. She would not rest—not while flower bloomed or wind blew free.

Shutting her eyes, she swooned with the violence of her hate—the gentle and the innocent ones, bathed in flames, soaked in tears, helpless in her hands. Her song of death would never cease. Not till she'd made a skull of the earth, not till Hell itself cried out from terror and from truth.

Oh, the Citadel would pay. Of that, she was sure. The fallen tents and flooded valley were of no consequence. Reeking of slaughter, washed in enemy blood, she would rally the Horde like a Scourge, like the fiery wrath of Hell itself.

Her love for the boy lay like Death upon her heart.

Staring at his corpse she felt nothing, wanted nothing—only revenge.

With his shattered knife she dug an unmarked grave.

PART XX

We learn nothing save through suffering
The memory of pain falls drop by drop
Upon the heart in sleep
Against our will comes wisdom
The grace of the gods is forced on us.

—AESCHYLUS, *AGAMEMNON*

In Amelia's dream she is entering the Cuddler's Black Tent. Inside, it is always the same—filled with bloodstained torturers and screaming victims.

They writhe on the rack, under the flaying knife, under the lash. One blond-haired boy, still in his teens, struggles to be brave, while a red-robed torturer prises out his nails.

His mother shrieks in the wheel's teeth.

The view leaving the tent is not much better. Amelia finds more victims. Some suffer in pit-cages, others from gibbets. Two groan under piles of rocks—peine forte et dure. A renegade Indian, strung up by the thumbs from a hanging rack, moves his mouth noiselessly, his eyes rolled back into his skull—every other part of his body motionless, paralyzed with pain. Another man, stripped naked, is spread-eagled beside a hill of fire ants. His body is a virtual mountain of the red insects. They devour his eyes, mouth, and genitals.

In her dream, Amelia is drawn back into the tent by an ear-shattering scream. Inside, she finds Jeffers. Shod in fiery shoes, he straddles the blazing mule.

She attempts to escape, but as soon as she reaches the opening, she meets Mustafa and Legion coming up the hill *toward her. Both are dressed in robes—Legion's black, Mustafa's red. His cat-o'-nine is draped over his shoulder, and Legion is bedecked with her diamondbacks and guns.*

The Dark Trumpets of the Apocalypse sound, and Legion is laughing at Amelia. "There, she is—our child of light, our friend to man."

The Cuddler shakes his crooked staff: "We shall cure her of those delusions quite thoroughly."

Indeed, they shall. His eyes flash, his white hair and beard are wildly disheveled. His charred robes are scorched black by the fiery tools of his trade.

Just as they reach her, the Final Trumpet sounds—the Judgment Call. All across the desert hills and flats, the ground opens up. The Dead erupt from their jagged graves, the blood of their death wounds hard as iron, black as pitch, their eyes hideous with fright.

"This is Allah's day," *the old man rails.* "He comes to flay you to your soul, to cast you howling into hell."

"You tell her, old man," *Legion says.* "Tell her we shall touch her to her core, to the frigid pit of her dark Madonna womb, to the foul hole in which she was born."

Amelia is sobbing in her bed.

"Allah on High," *Mustafa shrieks,* "the Eternal Scourge, the Lord of Armageddon, he's come for you, filth."

"No," *she shouts.* "No, it's not like that. I didn't— It's not—"

The grave grass weeps. More graves erupt. The Dead—hundreds of thousands, millions of them now—point their fingers at her.

Mustafa grabs her by the hair.

Legion strokes her intertwining snakes and laughs.

Even Amelia knows they are right. She is guilty—weighed in the balance and found wanting.

At last, she screams.

2

When Amelia awoke, Katherine Magruder was sitting on the edge of her bed, shaking her shoulders. The old woman wore a beige housecoat, and her short white hair was neatly combed. Her voice was soft.

"Was it the same dream?"

"No," Amelia said. "Legion was with the old man this time. She called me 'a child of light,' 'a friend to man.' The Cuddler said they would cure me of those delusions quite thoroughly."

"Those aren't delusions. We all long for friendship and love."

"Not her. She swore to probe the bottom of my being, 'the frigid pit' of my 'Madonna womb,' she called it."

"The dreams will pass."

"No, Forsythe was right. He told me once that if I survived the tent, I would be eternally wise. I would know 'what lies beyond all worlds and words.' He said I would 'possess the gift of tongues and speak the speech of snakes and rocks.' I would 'sing songs to dead stars and anthems to dead gods.'"

"Your despair is a conceit," Katherine said. "The wheel turns, and we all atone. In the end. If we live long enough."

"Not me. For me, the lights burn all over hell. I know that now."

Katherine laughed. "I still say it's a conceit."

"And I say all the doors are shut."

"But not locked."

Amelia turned away.

"You have company," Katherine said. "For break-fast."

"Who?"

"Our illustrious Generals."

"What do they want?"

"The winds of war are blowing. They want you."

3

Amelia paused in the dining room doorway. The two Generals and the old woman were seated at the oak dining table. Patton and Jackson were formally attired in khaki drill. As a concession to the lost Confederate cause, Jackson allowed himself a gray bandanna.

The Generals rose, and Patton pulled out her chair. Katherine poured Amelia coffee from a fire-blackened pot. She then unrolled a sheet of yellowed parchment.

"This dispatch is from our Lady Legion. I'll cut to the part where Tamerlane offers us peace."

"'We come to you not with the sword of war but with the olive branch of reconciliation. We are both people that have known strife—both victory and sub-jugation, conquest and empire. It is time for all such conflict to end, and for us to live side by side in contentment and peace.

"'Our Lord, Tamerlane, is just. He is not con-ceived—as some claim—by hellfire and violence but by the True God. He is possessed by a spiritual power that partakes of all things and flows through all things. His dreams are not of brute dominion and bloody death but of the interconnectedness of things. He would receive you not as a hated foe but as a brother—and I as a sister. We come not to destroy but to make all peoples one and our fractured lives whole.'"

There was a long silence.

"At least, we don't have to listen to Jeffers anymore," the old woman said.

"What was it he said about war being expensive?" Jackson asked.

"He argued it wasn't cost-effective to fight the Horde," said Patton.

"That was it," Jackson nodded. "He was looking to save us money."

"Tell Amelia what you want," the old woman said to Patton.

"Amelia, do you still remember how to fly?"

"I suppose so."

"Here." Patton unrolled a hand-drawn three-foot by three-foot map of the Citadel and the surrounding territory.

Patton pointed out the Citadel's forces—and the *Ordu*'s.

"During our retreat from their *bok*," Patton said, "Tamerlane routed our western flank. He cut our supply lines and tried to attack the Citadel. He failed to breach the Citadel's perimeter but did take the nearby mountains."

"Tamerlane's got the high ground," Jackson said, "less than eight miles from here. They've mounted their artillery on that eastern hill—Monte de Roca— and our scouts have spotted some communications equipment on the other. We think that mountain contains their control-and-command."

"What do you need?" Amelia asked.

"Aerial reconnaissance," Katherine said, "but we can't get the Electra or Rachael's old Jenny off the ground."

"The Jenny's pretty banged up," Patton said, "and the Electra takes aviation fuel—which we don't have."

"One hundred and eighty-seven octane," the old woman said.

"I can't help you with the fuel problem," said Amelia.

"Can you get the Jenny up?" Patton asked.

"Probably."

"You can handle the recon then," Patton said.

"Those Jennys aren't very sturdy," Amelia said.

"It's a rough flight," said the old woman. "Mountain thermals and low-level flying."

"How rough?" Amelia asked.

"Assuming you can get the Jenny in the air," Patton said, "you'll fly in here." On the map he pointed to the *bok*'s northwest flank. "You'll come in straight over the mountain where they've got all that communications gear and take a close look. Next you'll reconnoiter the camp, then Monte de Roca. We have to know about their artillery, machine gun emplacements, troops, the number and placement of their guns—if they're mobile or fixed."

"You'll have to come in low enough to raise the chickens," Jackson said.

"Another thing," Patton said. "Darrell may have destroyed more powder than we realized. If they're fletching arrows instead of field-stripping automatic rifles, we'll know. We also have to check on Monte de Roca. We have to know what kind of ordnance they've installed, the damage it'll do, and if those guns can reach the Citadel."

"Now is there anything *you* need?" Katherine asked.

"My old navigator, Fred Noonan."

"He's back on the sauce," Katherine said frowning. "He's living in some border town brothel—a real hell-hole. I'd look for a substitute."

"Fred is the only man I know who can get the Jenny's engine turning over."

"Then you've got him," Jackson said.

Patton nodded reluctantly.

"Give me a day to track him down," Katherine said. "Tomorrow morning we'll pay the boy a visit."

4

At sunup Captain Connolly and Matt Magruder were at Amelia's billet in full uniform. Their horses were saddled, and the old lady's buckboard was waiting.

"He's dead drunk in a border town cantina," Connolly said. "Twenty miles south of here."

They had a hard hot ride through some of the most desolate country in New Southwest—nothing but waterless arroyos, scorching flats, and wind-bent sage. It was one stretch of desert, Amelia noted, that nobody had improved with irrigation and fertilizer.

Nor did Alacron improve anybody's disposition. The town was nothing but scorpions, flies, and two peons, *dormir la siesta* in the shade of a filthy jacal. Otherwise, nothing. No breeze, no rising smoke, no horses, no dogs, not even a pecking chicken.

For the moment, Alacron was dead.

They stopped in front of the local cantina.
Matthew tied their horses to the hitchrack, while
Captain Connolly helped Amelia down.

Amelia followed them through the batwing doors.
Even by Alacron's standards, the cantina was grim.
Two tables, three chairs, and a raw plank bar serving
mescal and beer.

Behind the bar was a hard-looking gringo with a
dirty mustache, blood-streaked eyes, and a rank
apron. As Connolly and Magruder bellied up, he produced a bottle and glasses. His smile was full of broken yellow teeth. He nodded toward Amelia.

"Hey, that's a fine-looking gringa there. I had me a
woman like that, I'd be makin' *mucho dinero.*"

"Matt," Amelia barked.

Matt Magruder loosened the grip on his quirt.

Captain Connolly smiled back. His smile was not
pretty. "Hell, compadre, a man with your kind of
looks, he oughta have *muchas gringas.*"

The bartender gave them another obscene grin,
then poured them each a shot. Matt smelled his and
shuddered. The Captain ignored his like it wasn't
even there.

"I'm looking for a man named Noonan," Connolly
said. "Fred Noonan."

"A gringo?"

"Yeah, six feet, blond hair, thirty-five years old."
He showed the barkeep a photograph.

"Never saw him."

"Then I guess we made the trip for nothing, right?"
The barkeep nodded.

Connolly took out his Browning 9mm. He chambered a round and shoved the barrel into the barkeep's mouth.

"You recognize this?"

The barkeep pointed toward one of the back rooms.

They crossed the cantina. Connolly pulled back the blanket draping the doorway, and they entered. It was small and dark. The maguey branches covering the window hole failed to keep out the buzzing flies. The crumbling adobe walls were bare except for the filth and a cracked plastic crucifix. There was no furniture. A heap of rancid blankets and a few empty *mescal* bottles were strewn around the floor.

"What is *this*?" Matt asked.

"An Augean stable," said Amelia.

Finally, Amelia saw something move under the Indian blankets.

Whatever it was, Connolly kicked it.

It groaned, and a foot came out.

Connolly kicked Noonan's exposed foot, and the pile of blankets stirred a second time. Noonan's head appeared. His face was puffy and unshaven, his long hair greasy. He opened a bloodshot eye.

"What are you doing here?"

"Boy," Connolly said, "you live in a pigsty."

Noonan sat up slowly. He fumbled in his shirt pocket for a crumbling hand-rolled cigarette. He stuck it in his mouth. With a trembling hand, he lit the butt.

He coughed hackingly on the harsh smoke.

"What do you want?"

"You're buildin' us an air force," Connolly said.

"And yourself a life," Amelia said.

"I'm doing fine already." He pulled a half-full bottle from under his floor blankets.

Matt broke it with his pistol butt.

"Goddamn you," Noonan shouted, "you haven't got the right."

He dug a second bottle out of the blankets.

Connolly kicked it across the room. It shattered against the wall.

"You're coming home," Amelia said.

Noonan stood and searched the room for another jug.

"There's nothing more to drink, son," Connolly said. "Not now. Not ever."

"That ain't right. You can't do this to me."

"Sure we can," Matt said, approaching him from the left.

Connolly rounded him on the right. "Now listen up, boy. If there's anything I hate, it's a yellowbelly. You hear me? In my outfit, you can't hack it, you pack it."

"I can't hack it."

"I told you, we ain't havin' no yellowbellies in our army," Connolly said. "I won't tolerate a quitter."

"I ain't in your army."

Again, Noonan cast about frantically for a bottle.

"A yellowbellied drunk," Connolly rasped.

"Bartender! Bartender!" Noonan yelled.

Connolly backhanded him across the jaw with his Browning. Matt caught him on the way down, then hoisted him over his shoulder.

Amelia pulled back the drape. They exited the bolt-hole, Matt in the lead, Noonan belly-down.

When they passed the bar, Amelia said to the bartender, "Send his bill to the Citadel. It'll be honored."

"Your friend isn't well?"

"He feels great," Matt said. "He just enlisted."

"Of course, he feels fine," Connolly said. "He's joinin' the goddamned army."

They shouldered their way through the batwing doors.

5

Rehabilitating the old Curtiss-Jenny was not as difficult as building the Great Pyramid or digging the Panama Canal, but it came close. At least, Amelia thought so. There was a hangar to erect, a tool shop to set up, and a runway to be cleared and rolled. They needed machinery—drill presses, metal lathes, power saws, welding tanks, and torches—and they needed spare machine parts. And because Harry could not bear further separation from Amelia, they had to build a corral for him next to the hangar.

They also had Noonan to nursemaid. His shakes and DTs were so bad Amelia finally had to tie him to his cot. There, in the hangar storage shed, he sweated out his recovery.

Most of his hallucinations focused on Patton. He believed the General was in the shed, standing over him.

For hours at a time, he raved at the old man.

"I can't hack it, General," Noonan shouted deliriously. "I'm *not* in your outfit. Understand? I'm heading south. Guatemala, Panama, Brazil. Any place they don't have an army."

They forced liquids on him, kept him clean, but the rest Noonan had to sweat out himself.

Then there was the Jenny. Ten feet high from wheelbase to the top of its single prop, its narrow fuselage was twenty-eight feet long. The wings were fabric-covered, with wooden struts, and each was supported by a twisting jungle of turnbuckled guy wires. The Curtiss JN-4 was cobbled together with wood and

cloth, spit and chicken wire. It had a top speed of
seventy-five miles per hour, an eleven-thousand-foot
ceiling, and carried enough fuel to fly two and a half
hours.

Rebuilding the engine was the biggest problem.
Rachael's crack-up had twisted piston rods, bent
heads, shattered cylinders, and cracked the propeller
shaft. In short, they had to remachine the whole thing.

Katherine sent over a skilled machinist, so Amelia
was able to start without Noonan. He drilled the propeller shaft first, shaped it with a hammer and chisel,
then smoothed it on the lathe.

Boring an engine block out of solid cast aluminum,
he next drilled the pistons and rings out of cast iron.

By then Noonan was ambulatory. He wasn't much
fun to be around—with his cold sweats, dry heaves,
and recurring hallucinations—but he still pitched in.

First he went to work on the prop. It had been so
long since Amelia or Noonan had worked on a Jenny
that neither was sure about the prop's proportions.
But Noonan had researched propulsion systems in a
wind tunnel, and he set one up. In it, he tested airfoil
shapes till he thought he had the right one.

If the power train—the prop, engine, and transmis-
sion—didn't synchronize perfectly with the propeller
torque, the blade and shaft would shatter.

Noonan also devised a crude test for the rigging.
He spread a ton of sand on the wings, balanced each
of his coworkers on the tips, all the while thrumming
and tightening the guy wires. The wings held.

Their biggest problem was overheating. To cool
their engine, they attempted all sorts of homely
devices. Few of them proved effective. Most of the
time, Amelia just ripped away the leather-strapped

cowling, after which the frontal exhaust pipes would spit oil and flame in her face. Occasionally this technique also set fire to the nitrate dope, which they used to glue on the plane's linen covering. These fires ruptured radiator tubes, which scalded her with exploding geysers of steam. From time to time, however, the technique also cooled the engine.

The first flights seldom lasted more than a minute or two, and even under the best of conditions, they were horror shows. The plane bucked and plunged, its wires snapping like twanging banjo strings. Amelia often smashed wingtips and collapsed wheels on landing.

But gradually Amelia could take her up for longer flights, tougher tests. She bounced the Jenny over mountain thermals, through evasive actions so hard the guy wires literally screamed from stress.

It was no wonder that hangar morale sagged. The sight of her coming in for a landing—wheels wobbling on the runway, Amelia's face splattered with oil—gave all of them serious pause. They viewed her mission with grim foreboding.

6

So did another friend. Harry was beside himself. As he circled the split rail corral adjacent to the airstrip, he eyed his mistress with alarm. She had returned to their herd in bad shape—exhausted, emaciated, dispirited—and as far as he was concerned, her condition had not improved.

Nor had his. He had been heartsick over Amelia for

months, and his appetite had fallen off to nothing. He picked listlessly at the piles of roughage in his corral. When he splashed around in his pond, he showed no real enthusiasm. His ribs began to protrude.

Even worse, there was now rebellion in his herd. His parents—the white-haired old woman and his shrieking, wing-flapping mother—were constantly after him. The old one would scowl and point menacingly at the piles of fodder. She would order him to eat, and when he refused—most humiliating of all— shove fistfuls of fodder into his mouth.

However, compared to Betsy Ross's rebuke, that was mild. His winged mother wasted no effort on coaxing or scolding. She simply leaped up onto Harry's arching neck-frill, dug in her talons, and smote him with her massive pinions.

Worst of all, Quetzacoatlus—the Winged Dragon, the Thief of Eggs—had reentered his life. There he perched, just outside his corral, bigger than life.

His herd, of course, should have been furious. They should have destroyed the Flying Demon instantly, but instead, they fussed over it as if Quetzacoatlus were a precious treasure, something to be protected. If it hadn't been for the pointed stakes, slanting in at Harry—piercing him when he got too close—he would have plunged through the barricade and slaughtered the Dragon himself.

Once, in a moment of overwhelming rage, he had actually challenged the sharp stakes. This happened when the Winged Dragon gobbled his mate whole. Seeing her disappear into the Dragon's belly, he no longer cared about personal danger or pain. He rammed the sharp stakes until blood flowed from his thighs and chest. He charged and charged and charged, his battle cry roaring like thunder across the *llano.*

It was clear he had scared the Demon. The beast instantly disgorged his cow, and she came racing back to Harry, terrified.

After that battle, the Winged Demon had retreated to the great cave just beyond the corral. In fact, they had all—to Harry's bellowing rage and pawing consternation—joined the fiend in there. To do what, he could not imagine.

So be it. His herd was in rebellion? All right. One day he would settle up. He would free himself from the impaling stakes and get rid of that Winged Fiend once and for all.

He would set things right.

7 ━━━━━━

It was the day of the big flight—Amelia's reconnaissance of the Horde. For once, however, she was not thinking about the Jenny or weather or wind direction. Nor was she concerned about the enemy guns. She just stood by the corral, trying to calm down her friend.

Since the day they had wheeled the Jenny out of the hangar and onto the runway, Harry had been out of control. She was afraid he'd start ramming the stakes again.

Amelia tried to comfort him. She stood outside the pointed shafts and petted his nose while he munched cornstalks.

She stole a glance at the Jenny—now tethered to its

hardstand—and contemplated the best method for sneaking away from Harry. When she climbed back into the plane, she was sure he would explode.

The wind made the decision for her. The wind sock swung due east, which was what she needed for takeoff. She gave Harry a final pet and headed for the Jenny.

As Amelia swung into the cockpit, Harry's roar was horrendous. The restraining stakes of the corral quivered and cracked with his charges. But there was nothing she could do about that. She gave Katherine a thumbs-up and pulled down her goggles.

Noonan spun the prop. On the third turn, the engine sputtered to life. As the Jenny started down the runway, the hardpack rushed below her in a dusty blur. Amelia felt the new undergear working smoothly, the shocks easily absorbing the accelerating jolts. The narrow-gauge wheels did not wobble.

Then the wind veered—blowing north-northeast. The mesquite and prickly pear at the far end of the runway grew larger, more formidable. She knew she wasn't going to make it.

She ground-looped the Jenny, then taxied back to take off again. She eased the stick forward, building rpms.

This time the nose lifted. She cleared the chaparral, and the ground fell away. Circling the strip, she watched the plane's shadow sweep over the Citadel.

She had come to admire her new home. Everywhere she looked there was land reclaimed from the desert, industry reborn. To the west there were oil rigs and distilling towers, and in the east, forges and machine shops.

Southeast was farmland—fields of corn, beans, and maguey. Here and there she could see the tiny communities that homesteaded those fields—small clusters of adobe farmhouses, the sod roofs interwoven with maguey stalks. Due east, lay the larger, more substantial residences, such as Katherine Magruder's, which was built of split red logs, a shake roof, and a fieldstone fireplace. A fenced-in holstein with a full bag peacefully cropped a clump of grass behind Katherine's house, and the densely green backyard garden bespoke an ample larder. In the valley grazed her longhorns and mustangs and up in the high country, her sheep.

Five miles from Katherine's spread lay the main Citadel village—the town that had grown up around the old fortress. Circling the strip, Amelia could clearly see its hospital, its three schoolhouses, its post office, shops, and two churches.

On the hill overlooking the village was the old white adobe fort itself, with its large library, computer systems, and weapons caches. Now primarily a research center, staffed largely by the descendants of Los Alamos physicists, the fort was—as Katherine liked to put it—the last, best hope of science and civilization.

Patton's tank corps was now directly below Amelia. He was taking them over an obstacle course of potholes, sand traps, wire aprons, and steep hills. To her dismay she observed fewer than fifty tanks—nowhere near the two hundred plus he'd hoped for. Most of them were stuck.

They looked exactly like what they were—junked cars with a little body armor welded on. They had eye slits instead of windshields, cylindrical machine gun turrets on top, but instead of tractor treads, they trundled along on wheels.

Now Amelia was passing over Stonewall's infantry bivouac. Again, their numbers were small, this bunch less than a thousand. They were divided by company, and from what she could see, the troops were green. They still hadn't learned how to march.

Tamerlane's camp lay to the north, between two small mountains. She headed toward the nearer one— Monte de Espinas, the Mount of Thorns.

Over the last ten million years, it had been subjected to too much desert climate: scorching days of heat, nights of subzero cold. The impact was shattering. Even today, one could hear the *crack!* of its fracturing rock face reverberating across the *llano*.

The desert wind had also done its job. It had sandblasted these cracks into mountain arroyos. The crosshatched gorges were now choked with mesquite, prickly pear, and barn-sized boulders. Lately they had been lined with barbwire, boobytraps, and *Ordu* machine gun emplacements.

As Amelia circled the slopes, she saw a heavily fortified bunker complex near the summit. From the looks of the antennae above these command posts, they were communications centers. The hill bristled with machine guns, but there was no artillery.

Time for the *bok*.

She banked due east over the thousands of yellow *yurts* spread out between Monte de Espinas and Monte de Roca. Ever since they'd blown the dam, the camp's three main streams had been jumping the banks. The *bok*'s remudas had abundant water and graze. It was also estimated that after the camp's raiding parties returned from Mexico, their horse herd would number over fifteen thousand head.

Pushing the stick right-forward, she applied right

rudder and slanted over the *bok*'s defensive perimeter—
a zigzagging trench system, replete with forests of barbwire and deeply dug-in machine gun emplacements.
Her eyes searched the perimeter for antiaircraft fire—
for the pale yellow flashes, the puffs of white smoke,
and devastating claps of concussion.

Nothing.

Amelia slowly circled the *bok*. From a thousand
feet up, the thousands of tethered horses were
reduced to tiny toy animals, men and dogs to crawling
bugs.

Stop sightseeing, she chastised herself. *Look for their
guns. Frighten some goddamn chickens.*

Nose down, throttle back, Amelia descended in a
controlled glide. The propeller blade, catching the
sun, flashed sequences of light and shadow in her
eyes, which she attempted to ignore.

She dipped a wing and swung through the middle of
the camp. Coming in at under two hundred feet, she
could see the *Kaffeiahs* and upturned faces of black-
robed men and the veiled faces of those women allowed
beyond their partitions, but still there were no guns.

The men usually kept their weapons near their
yurts, so she dropped another hundred feet for a closer
look. She scanned their cook fires, their piles of horse
gear, and sacks of *kumiss*, searching for weapon stores.

Finally she saw them. In each of the *yurts'*
entranceways was a rack of double-curved bows and a
barrel of fletched arrows, but no guns.

Tamerlane *was* low on ammunition.

Then she remembered what it had been like—
when Darrell had blown the Horde's ammo dump.

*Lashed to Stonewall's McClellan, half-unconscious,
first she heard it—not so much a blast as a shrill roar, an*

*express train screaming through a tunnel, its whistle wail-
ing. Then there was its single visual impression—a white
column of fire soaring thousands of feet into the sky. Pure
fire, that was all. No billowing smoke, no afterflash, just
that one incandescent column, blindingly bright. Then it
vanished as if it had never been.*

*Next came the blast waves—over and over and over
again—followed by a low-throated rumble and a single
thunderclap, which even from forty miles away caused the
horses to buck and snort.*

Darrell had done it: He had destroyed Tamerlane's
powder stores.

Now Amelia banked toward Monte de Roca, staring at it through the struts and guy wires. From two
miles away it was a red mountain, its southwestern
slope bisected vertically by a gaping gorge, an ugly
gash, opened eons ago by volcanic fires below and the
fracturing heat of the desert sun.

The mountain grew until she was under its
shadow. Directly beneath her was the massive canyon.
Its bottom—which stretched nearly two thousand feet
across—was covered with crimson boulders, coiled
barbwire, and zigzagging trench lines. The parapets
and traverses were reinforced with heavy rock and
sandbags. A sentry stood at every firebay, and the
dugouts bristled with machine guns. They were obviously here to stay.

She cruised up the first thousand feet of the sloping
ravine. It was there—halfway up the steep arroyo—
that she saw the first big guns. Tamerlane had
attempted to camouflage them with cut brush, and
she had to fly deep into the gorge for a really good
look. Still, she could see their leering mouths. She
counted three of them. Flying deeper into the canyon,

peering between the whirling prop and the singing wires, she made out others—a total of eleven.

The guns were thick black tubes, eight feet long, buttressed by heavy shock absorbers and bunkered in stone. For every gun she'd counted, she figured she might have missed two.

Amelia plunged deeper into the ravine. Still no gunfire, still no stacks of rifles. Soldiers were now emerging from their quarters. Not one of them packed a sidearm or carried a rifle. Tamerlane's powder was clearly reserved for cannons and machine guns.

She climbed out of the ravine, reconnoitering the hill's sloping summit. More wire aprons, more machine gun emplacements. This—as she had been warned—was their *Janizary* enforcement unit, in charge of the conscripted artillery men below.

If any conscript lost his nerve, these were the men he would answer to. They would definitely have guns.

Suddenly, there they were—the real *Janizaries*, the Death Squads. There were no standing orders against firing guns up here. As soon as these men spotted her, they dragged out their M-60s and aimed them aloft, straight at her, tripods and all.

Shoving in the throttle and nosing down for speed, Amelia pulled back on the stick. As the Jenny's nose came up, she kicked the right rudder bar and chopped the throttle, flipping the Jenny. Halfway around she kicked the left rudder bar. Pulling the throttle back tight against the stops, she banked hard, her right wing straight down, perpendicular to the mountain's base, her left pointed arrowlike at the sky. The *Janizary* bullets slammed through her slipstream.

She came out of a banking roll on the other side of the peak, her wires screaming. She was now flying straight into the sun. The furnace-hot thermals—radiating off the crimson cliff—lifted her like a giant hand.

The Jenny rode them, lurching and shaking. Only when Amelia was past the mountain did she cut the throttle.

She hung there over the summit, feeling terribly isolated. That mountaintop behind her seemed the most miserable piece of rock she'd ever seen. Its eastern face was a sheer mile-high cliff. The western slope housed the Horde's big guns, guarded by their Death Squads.

Before her, there was nothing but a maze of red canyons.

Amelia opened the throttle and, straight into the sunglare, sped from Monte de Roca.

What drew her due east, at first, she could not say. There was nothing but dazzling light and red rock. She couldn't see anything else. Then it hit her. *Neither could the Horde.* At night, it was too dark for them to see, and for most of the morning there would be too much sun.

If Stonewall could find a way through that maze—marching by night, hiding by day—and if he could scale that cliff face, the Horde's artillery was vulnerable.

Amelia stared again into those sun-scorched canyonlands—some two thousand feet below her—where it was said that even Apaches died. She remembered the Generals' orders to avoid them at all costs.

Katherine had told her all about them: They were a vast plateau, created by a tightly packed cluster of ancient volcanoes. Ten million years ago the cluster had burned itself out, and gradually they eroded into tableland. The seismic tremors, the fracturing extremes of desert heat and cold, the endless sandblasting winds had widened all that split rock into buttes and mesas, monoliths and crags.

But mostly she saw cracks. These red furnacelands were split by mazelike fissures, hundreds of feet deep. These gorges transformed the tableland into a maddening labyrinth, infinite in its complexity, stretching from horizon to horizon.

She'd been told not to go down there because thermal winds blew through those gorges with terrifying force. Her eggshell aircraft would never survive.

Still, those canyons faced the Horde's blind side, and if there was a way through them—through a maze that had baffled even the Apaches—the Citadel's forces might surprise the Arabs on their flank.

If Amelia could find a way through the maze.

If she remembered the route.

If she survived.

Amelia stared into the red-rock labyrinth. She'd need a gorge at least a hundred feet in width—one big enough to maneuver in—and there were plenty of those from which to choose. She started to descend.

Suddenly, her headset came to life. Katherine Magruder was breaking radio silence.

"Jackson's on recon south of the arroyos. He's spotted you. He says you're out joyriding. I want you back her right now. Do you read? Over."

"Roger, over."

Amelia ignored the order and continued her descent into the canyons.

The headset was exploding: "Do you read? Over."

Amelia still ignored it.

Now Patton was on the headset.

"Mission scrubbed! You hear me? You're coming back."

She clicked off her radio and studied the sky.

"Weather, fair and cloudless," she said half-aloud, "except for a few scattered cirrus to the north." She listened to the Jenny's racketing engine. "Running rough though. Number one cylinder head sounds a little hot. Time to crack the cowl flaps, right?"

She tore off the leather cowling. The engine instantly splattered her face with smoking oil. She wiped her goggles with a rag.

"Everything A-OK," she mused wryly, "running like a champ."

She throttled down and eased into a glide. Skimming the cliff tops at an altitude of eleven hundred feet, she finally picked a canyon. It was a quarter mile due south and was over a hundred feet in width.

Bucking the updrafts, she inched the Jenny toward it, continuing her descent. When she was directly over the chasm, Amelia leaned on the left rudder and right aileron. Slanting her right wing straight down—perpendicular to the earth—she sideslipped into the abyss.

Her concentration was total, and it seemed to her that she could visualize everything at once, in detail. When she ducked a jagged outcrop to her left, she saw a scorpion crab-walking along its top, its tail arched, the stinger poised. When she flushed a raven off a fallen rabbit, she could see the bird's flight with utter clarity—its flapping pinions, its wedge-shaped tail feathers, its talons and beak. Broken deadfall spilling down the talus slopes was visible—with its jagged corners and sharp stone edges. Mesquite growing laterally out of the canyon wall was so vivid that she could see the leaves, the nuts, the branches, every individual thorn.

Amelia was high. It was as if her mind were racing at the speed of light, and she could do anything.

She could negotiate blind curves almost without looking, somehow make rapid-fire decisions as every turn, every landmark mapped in her mind.

She did not even feel in a hurry.

She had all the time there was.

She was leaking Time.

8

After an hour and a half of cruising the canyonlands, she no longer felt fast or smooth or smart. Her vision was blurring, and the shimmering heat waves in the gorges vibrated in and out of focus.

The force of the thermals was, at high noon, relentless. The 130-degree heat, the dehydration, the exhaustion, the cramped cockpit, the narrow nine-hundred-foot canyon walls had made her more than delirious. She now questioned her sanity.

As proof of madness, Amelia noted her delusions. During the last half hour she'd come to believe there was a larger pattern to the winding chasms, that they radiated from a central seismic fault line like the twisted spokes of a wheel. The canyonlands weren't random at all. There was a plan to this matrix, and she thought she had it mapped.

But she could not find a passageway out, a way home. It was clear to her now—what she should have known all along—that Katherine had been right. She never should have entered these canyonlands. Here in these crimson fissures, she would die.

Amelia was surprised that it did not bother her. She felt no terror, no anger, not even loneliness.

In the distance she swore she saw a shade tree.

It was a mirage.

So was the pond.

In fact, the canyon floor looked as if it had once been a river. She laughed. That was crazy. A river in these deserts.

Still she followed the old streambed. *Follow it home, Dorothy,* she thought. *Follow it back to Kansas.* Amelia knew she had finally lost her mind.

Did old Mustafa do that to you? Legion? Tamerlane? Whose insanity is this?

You're martyred to a madness not your own.

All she could see were red canyon walls and the shimmering heat haze. All she heard was the knocking engine and the shrill whine of the struts.

What is it, little girl? This coming out of prison? This life after death? This—?

Her head drooping, Amelia was about to pass out when the engine caught fire. Smoke scorched her eyes and throat; burning oil seared her face. Her left wing burst into flames. Torn fabric flapped in the air like a blazing guidon.

It was a small miracle the fabric hadn't caught fire hours ago.

Time to land this crate, she thought. She cut back the throttle, pulling it all the way to the stops and set the friction brake. The Jenny yielded to the loss of power, sinking, sinking over the sandy streambed. Amelia slowed her twisting descent, holding her off, holding her off. She felt the wheels touch. They were starting to ground-loop when the Jenny's nose smashed into the rocky bed. The fuselage flipped end over end, her chest and crotch tearing at the leather harness.

She had the brief sensation of hanging upside down, crankcase oil dripping in her face. Then everything around her turned black as the burning oil seeping under her goggles.

9

Jackson needed a full hour to scale the canyon's hundred-foot wall, and the work was hard. His khaki uniform was soaked with sweat, his hands trembled. Over forty now, he felt gnarled, hard-used.

When he reached the top, he pushed his gray Confederate forage cap far back on his head, revealing matted gray hair and a wet, dusty forehead. He untied his gray bandanna, wiped off his face, beard, and the back of his neck. He stared at the land around him.

This far up, he had a clear view of the Sonoran Desert—its maze of rugged buttes and crimson canyons.

Suddenly, he caught a blur of motion. He couldn't believe it. There was the Jenny. Flames were gusting from under her engine housing, her left wing was on fire, and her fabric flapped like a fiery pennant. She bucked the thermals, out of control. She seemed to be moving in slow motion, almost swimming through the heat haze, pieces of her breaking up, spinning and drifting and tumbling away in the wind. Then she went down, disappearing from sight. He thought he heard a muffled crash, did see a cloud of dust and smoke rise above the canyons, but that was all. His heart sank.

In battle he had been fearless to the point of embarrassment, but now his terror was palpable as pain. He realized he had fallen in love with Amelia—with a willful, rebellious girl.

He remembered the ride back from the Arab camp, holding her on his McClellan. Amelia was shaking, bleeding, half-unconscious, yet he was the one who trembled.

Oh God, don't let her die.

Jackson pulled himself together. He lowered himself over the canyon's rim.

◀━━━ 10

When she came to, the first thing she saw was Tom Jackson. He was a hundred yards upcanyon on Old Sorrel, leading a company of Rangers. Since she was hanging inverted from her safety harness, the men and their mounts appeared to be upside down.

Hot oil splattered her goggles, and she knew she looked a fright. She tried to reach for her belt knife—to cut herself free from her safety harness—but she was having trouble. *Damn,* her shoulder was dislocated again. Maybe Jackson could put it back in. He looked like he'd know about those things.

Oh-oh. If she cut herself loose with her good hand, she'd have no way to catch herself when she fell.

Hooking her legs under the seat, she slashed the harness and hoped for the best. She hit the ground like a ton of bricks.

Still, she managed to get herself upright. She was
sitting on a chunk of fuselage and working on her map
when Jackson reached the wreck.

■■▶

The next morning Amelia
was with Katherine at her oak dining table. She was
dressed in a freshly washed flight suit. Her shoulder
was back in place, her arm in a sling.

Patton sat across from her, sipping coffee, chewing
on a cigar. Richard Sheckly wore a buckskin Indian
shirt and denim pants. His dark shoulder-length hair
was in a ponytail. Jackson wore a collarless butternut
shirt and a gray bandanna. Like Sheckly, he drank sassafras tea.

"I'm not sure the camp itself has any ammunition,"
Amelia said, looking around the table.

"Because they didn't fire on you?" Patton asked.

"Yes, and because I didn't see rifles or handguns."

"But you're estimating an army of twelve thousand
men?" Jackson said, studying his copy of her notes.

"There were six thousand *yurts.* I figured two families
apiece. That's twelve thousand warriors, maybe more."

"Horses?" Jackson asked.

"They had around four thousand in their remudas."

"Our reports," Patton said, "indicate they'll be
bringing back another ten thousand head."

There was a respectful silence.

"What about infantry?" Jackson asked.

"Inside their tent city is a second Horde," Amelia
said. "Darrell sometimes called it 'the Dirty Horde.'

These are the conscripts. They're filthy, ragged, louse-ridden. When they aren't being used in human wave assaults, they function as slaves."

"How many did you count?"

"It was hard to estimate. I would figure upwards of five thousand."

"Twelve thousand horse soldiers and five thousand infantry against a bunch of old cars," Katherine grumped.

"There are more problems," Amelia said. "The troops may be low on firepower but hill number 2 isn't. Its southwest slope—the one facing the basin—is fissured by a deep arroyo with boulders. The boulders make excellent defilade, and Tamerlane has placed howitzers behind them."

"What size?" Patton asked.

"I've looked at your sketches and studied Darrell's reports. Given the length and shape of the barrels—as well as the shock absorbers along the sides—they appear to be old 105s."

"Those are awfully big guns," Jackson said.

"They probably carried them up in pieces," Patton said, "and reassembled them in their pits."

"How much damage can they do?" Katherine asked.

"They can't hit the Citadel," Patton said, "but they can rake the basin at will."

"Which means," Jackson said, "they'll raise hell with our troops and tank corps."

"Provided they have the ammunition," Patton said.

"They do have some powder," Amelia said. "I saw plenty of shell casings beside the caissons. I also drew machine gun fire from their enforcement units near the summit."

"Any artillery on number 1?" Katherine asked.

"No, it was like you said. A big radio bunker with lots

of antennae. The slope is steep, probably impassable, and so fortified I don't see how you can dislodge them."

"I don't suppose we could wait them out," Katherine said.

"We have to stop them on those flats," Patton said. "My tanks require open terrain."

"Then we have to knock out Monte de Roca," Amelia said, "and its 105s."

"We'd have to fight our way through their entire army to get to them," Jackson said.

"We could try a surprise assault on the eastern face," said Amelia.

"I've had Apache scouts reconnoitering those canyons for weeks," Jackson said. "I was there too. Even our Indians got lost."

"Amelia thinks she found a way," Sheckly said.

They all stared at him.

"She had an advantage over us. At ground level you can't really see where the intersecting canyons lead, but she could get closer to the top. She had a good overhead view."

"I was also deep enough into the gorges to check for landmarks," Amelia said. "I even sketched a map from memory."

She pitched the hand-drawn map onto the middle of the table.

"That's crazy," Katherine said.

"I know topographical mapwork. I've flown by pilotage half my life."

"And I know those canyons," Sheckly said. "I think she's done it."

"Well, you still can't get up that cliff—not without them seeing you and hearing you," his mother argued. "Those pitons of yours have saw-toothed edges."

"But the chocks don't," Sheckly said. "They expand *inside* the crevices. You don't have to hammer them."

"I'm not sure Tamerlane would spot them anyway," Amelia said. "The cliff face juts out. You can't really see *down* all that well. And early in the day the sun's blinding."

"That whole cliff face is honeycombed with ridges, fissures, chimneys, old volcanic vents," Sheckly said. "We'd be climbing inside those half the way up."

"This is insane," Katherine said.

"I better be getting back," Sheckly said. "I have to discuss this with Spirit Owl. He can help us with logistics—verifying which water holes are still good. His scouts will have to cache water cans and supplies for us along the way."

"We'll still need a diversion," Patton said.

"I've been thinking about that," Sheckly said. "When I took John and Elizabeth spelunking, we explored those crevices on the cliff face. She was smaller then and made it all the way to the main fault line."

"You're not suggesting—?" Katherine said.

"If someone was small enough, they could load the fault with dynamite, set the fuse, then get out before it blew."

"And bring down half the mountain," Katherine said, "killing themselves and everyone else in the process."

"Do you have someone?" Patton asked. "Someone who knows those vents and can locate that fault?"

"Of course, he does," the old woman shouted. "His own daughter. He's going to kill himself with this harebrained scheme. Why not murder everybody else in the family."

She got up and stomped out of the room.

PART XXI

No beast so fierce but feels some touch of pity.
But I know none, and therefore am no beast.

—RICHARD III

The sun was at zenith. Forsythe lay spread-eagled on his back, the breeze whispering eerily over his naked body, the blazing desert sun raising huge bloody blisters on his skin.

He no longer tried to move. His hands, neck, and feet were lashed to crisscrossed stakes. Any movement drove the rawhide thongs deeper into his skin.

For awhile a scorpion had been studying him with rapt fascination but finally even he got bored. Arching his stinger high over his back, he scuttled off out of sight, as if even a scorpion couldn't stand to watch so wretched a sight.

All in all, Forsythe tried to forget the world around him. Most of all he tried to forget the blinding sun which was scorching his skin and searing his very soul.

It was imperative that Forsythe not think about his plight. To think about it was to compound agony with insanity, and he suffered enough without the added burden of serious psychosis.

Madness would not make his situation any easier.

2

At dawn he heard the Cuddler scream. The old man was staked out less than a dozen feet from him, but up till now he had been silent.

Forsythe turned his head to look, driving the thongs deep into his neck. The pain was awful but he had to know.

For ten days they had forced Forsythe to work on Old Mustafa, using hot coals and knives. When he had finished, Legion had rewarded him by staking him out beside the old man. For two days the two men had endured their torture in silence. But no more.

Forsythe saw why the Cuddler was screaming. The old man's face and genitals had been smeared with maguey syrup during the night. Now flies and ants swarmed his eyes, mouth, nose, and groin.

Somehow the old man found his voice. Spitting out a mouthful of red ants, he shouted hoarsely:

"Repent, ye blasphemers, ye whoremongers, ye fornicators. Ye shall be cast into the lake of everlasting fire. Allah will have ye in the end. He will cast ye down into the pit of hell. Ye shall eat thorns and rocks and devil's fruit and boiling oil. Ye shall be—shall be—"

Sayyid Amir Khar, the camp's new chief torturer, walked up to the Cuddler. He was an ugly man in a blood-smeared *caftan* and *kaffeiah*, missing both front teeth and one eye. He ladled more sticky maguey juice over Mustafa's face and crotch. The red ants redoubled their efforts. Again, the old man screamed.

Sayyid gave Forsythe an ugly grin. "Our Cuddler will be gone soon. Then we'll give you some juice."

Forsythe managed a weak smile. "Take your time, sport. I've got no place to go."

"By Allah, that is the truth," Sayyid said. "This is one appointment you will definitely keep."

As he walked away, Forsythe shuddered.

3

Legion stood on a brush-covered hill. She pulled her black robe tight against the dawn chill and studied the *bok*. Below her were bivouacked thousands of yellow *yurts,* and along the camp's perimeter was tethered the horse herd.

The remuda contained animals of every size, shape, and color. Wiry cow ponies, line-back roans, blaze-faced bays, grullas lighter than seven hundred pounds, snuffy colts, rawboned sorrels, and platter-footed braying mules.

Tamerlane joined her on the summit.

"How does our camp look to you?" he asked.

"The women look fit, my Lord."

"But not our men."

He was right. The soldiers, drunk on *kumiss* and the local *mescal,* were strewn around the camp, passed out in their own vomit and urine.

"Barbarism's hard work," Legion said.

"Not if the men are properly motivated."

"You do not trust their loyalty, sire?"

"I trust fear. Since we staked out Old Mustafa and Forsythe, there has been no one to keep them in line, only that toothless, one-eyed imbecile. Now they run wild."

"Our Cuddlers were justly punished. They let the Scribe escape the pit-cage."

"Yes, but they also dispensed discipline," Tamerlane said.

"Mustafa won't. Never again. The ants have him."

"What about Forsythe?"

"His own Cuddling's just begun," Legion said. "It amused me to postpone his death—to have him work on the old man, knowing the same fate awaited him."

"What's his condition?"

"A severe sunburn, some stiff joints, that is all."

"Grant him a reprieve. He can help us eliminate those renegade Apaches."

"The ones who keep running off our horses?"

"As fast as we can steal them. We haven't broken their chief scout—the one we captured last week—and he knows the location of their camp."

"Face it, sire, he has been interrogated by amateurs. That broken-toothed fool now running the Black Tent just doesn't have the stuff."

"He's no Mustafa," Tamerlane agreed.

"He's no Forsythe either."

"We better find that camp soon. At the rate those Apaches are running off our stock, we'll be fighting the Citadel on foot."

"They run off two head for every one we round up."

Tamerlane nodded wearily. "Let's visit the Englishman."

4

Old Mustafa's breath now came in rattling, ant-choked gasps. *Clear dereliction of duty* was Forsythe's only thought. Had he been in charge, he would have prolonged the old man's agony another month.

Then he remembered he was next. That thought snapped him back to reality. Soon his eyes and groin would be smeared with syrupy maguey, after which the fire ants would feed on *him*.

Forsythe gritted his teeth and tore at his stakes. He wondered whether he could strangle himself on his neck thongs.

Suddenly, Legion was straddling him.

"How long you been here, friend?" she asked.

He squinted at the sky and shook his head.

"I really can't say."

"I know. It's hard telling time by the sun. Those blisters must really hurt."

"It was worse in the British public schools. That's what my grandfather used to say. God, he was a sadistic old bugger. Claimed to have flogged those youngsters mercilessly."

"You'd have fit right in," Legion said.

"I'm afraid so," Forsythe said with a terse nod. "How are things with you, my Lady?"

"Not too good. The Chiricahuas are hiding up in the hills. They plunder our own raiding parties at will."

"Must be hard on morale."

"Nothing Old Mustafa couldn't have turned around," Legion said. "You could have whipped those troops into shape too."

"With both hands tied behind my back," Forsythe said.

"Not anymore," said Tamerlane. "Your recent experiences have softened you."

"Quite the contrary," Forsythe said. "My *esprit de corps* has reached an all-time peak."

"You don't look so tough to me," Tamerlane said.

"Never underestimate the power of negative reinforcement, sire," Forsythe said.

A red-robed baby-faced assistant Cuddler named Ahmad Al-Amin approached Mustafa with a gourdful of maguey syrup.

"Time to feed the ants," Ahmad said.

He groaned to see that Mustafa had expired.

"Hold it there, youth," Legion ordered, turning to face the boy.

Ahmad fell to his knees and began beating his forehead in front of their feet.

"Forsythe," Legion said, disgusted by the boy's incompetence, "you sure you're up to Cuddling again? It's a foul business, I'm told."

"No more foul than fornication," said Forsythe.

"We may ask you to torture innocent men," Tamerlane said.

"As you once proclaimed, sire, there's no such thing as an innocent man."

"If I dribble this syrup on your face, the ants will burrow into your brain," said Legion.

"If we splash some on your crotch," Tamerlane said, "they'll castrate you like a steer."

"I'd like another chance, my Lord. You won't be sorry."

"You're no Mustafa," Tamerlane said.

"The old man was an artist," Legion agreed. "He knew the music as well as the words. Forsythe, by comparison, you're a talentless hack."

"I resent that, my Lady."

"Resent *this*," Legion said.

She kicked the prostrating boy, then pointed at his crotch. Rising, Ahmad ladled maguey syrup on

Forsythe's groin. Flies swarmed, and fire ants attacked.

"Are you sure you remember how to Cuddle?"

"Do vampires forget how to bite?" Forsythe gasped.

"I say you lack motivation," Tamerlane said.

"I feel a new manic dynamism already," he shrieked.

"Your heart's not in it," Tamerlane said.

"I'll do AN-Y-TH-I-I-I-NG!" Ants were now gnawing at his crotch.

"Please, Forsythe," Legion said. "No shameless bootlicking."

"Anyway," Tamerlane said, "I like you here. Pegged out like a green hide."

"AN-Y-TH-I-I-I-NG!" Forsythe ululated.

Tamerlane glanced at Legion and nodded. She slashed the thongs with her belt knife, and Forsythe was free. With pain-racked arms he slapped at his genitals.

"Get up," Legion growled. "Time to get your fingernails dirty."

"I still say this won't work," Tamerlane said.

"Then he'll curse his mother for giving him birth."

"Just point me at them," Forsythe said, still slapping at his groin. "You won't be sorry."

"Something tells me we won't," Legion said under her breath.

5

Forsythe—again swathed in the red robes of his trade—entered the Black Tent. He was accompanied by the young baby-faced Ahmad. Two dozen men and women were in various

stages of bloody torture. Some were flayed, others
writhed on fiery gridirons. There were castrations and
dismemberments of every description. Four men were
stretched on vertical racks.

Forsythe limped through the tent, leaning on an
ebony cane. When he glanced at a victim, he felt only
professional disdain. He could not believe the incompetence of his replacements. Haste! That's what
Forsythe saw all around him. Red-robed Cuddlers
rushing through their work, impatient to get it done.
They did not have the faintest notion what their jobs
really entailed. Cuddlers were supposed to linger over
their victims, make their suffering *last.* He'd always
seen Cuddling as artistically inspired—containing
hints of the Eternal, echoes of the Divine.

He'd settle with these would-be torturers later.
Like Old Mustafa, he preached the gospel of stern
professionalism. These amateurs had stained his code
and mocked his craft.

In the far corner he spotted his victim—a Mexican
Apache in a breechclout. The man hung from the
elbows—which angled high above his head—in a
modified version of the ancient strappado. His stomach was a mass of burns and cuts. His eyes were rolled
back, and his mouth worked in mute agony.

"Why do we have him facing the rest of the tent?"
Forsythe asked.

"Our former Cuddler thought the sight of all that
suffering would break his spirit," Ahmad said.

"So you Cuddled him in front of his mates? You
gave him an audience? You made him an actor on a
bloody *stage?* You were boosting his morale, you
imbecile."

Ahmad quickly draped off the Apache's corner

with a frayed blanket. He filled a canvas water pail from an *olla* and splashed it in Red Shirt's face.

"Who are you?" Red Shirt asked, squinting at Forsythe.

"The Terror That Walks in Darkness."

"Why are you doing this?"

"I've come to save you from yourself."

Forsythe dropped a stone in an ankle basket, which dangled from the Apache's foot, inches above the ground. The man's elbows cracked. His screams filled the tent.

"God—no—"

"No point in calling on God," Forsythe hissed. "He can't help you now. You're in a world without the Almighty. In this tent the blind don't see, the lame don't walk, and the dead don't rise."

Forsythe dropped two more rocks in the ankle basket, and, again, the man shrieked.

"God— Please—"

"Don't you understand?" Forsythe said. "*I* am your God now: Allah, Krishna, Buddha, Jesus, even the ghosts from your bloody Spirit World—all rolled into one. *I* alone stand between you and everlasting night."

Red Shirt shut his eyes against the pain.

"There is only one way out," Forsythe said. "Tell me where your camp is. Where your red-skinned horse-thieving friends are hiding."

The Apache shook his head, no.

"Look, my friend," Forsythe said, "as much as I admire blazing patriotism, this time it will win you nothing. You shall not pass the needle's eye."

"I want to die."

"Death would not even save you now," Forsythe

said. "I'd carve my name on your tombstone. I'd follow you into your grave. I'd meet your soul in hell."

Red Shirt slowly opened his eyes. He nodded his head once, twice—and again mouthed mute words.

"Good boy," Forsythe said. "You can tell me. Our own little secret. No one else need know."

Red Shirt whispered slurringly.

"Now that's what I call a positive attitude," said Forsythe. "Here. Whisper it in my ear." He lowered the strappado till his ear was next to the Apache's mouth.

"Kiss my ass," Red Shirt whispered.

"Blindfold him, then expand that maze of burns and cuts."

Ahmad went to work on Red Shirt's stomach. The Apache passed out three times.

"Where am I?" the blindfolded man asked after being revived.

"Where the Christians feed the lions," said Forsythe.

Red Shirt tried to spit, but the red sputum only ran down his cheek.

"Time to rock and roll," Forsythe said.

After the fourth rock, Red Shirt again passed out.

"Well done," said a voice from the rear.

Legion, decked out in a black shirt and tight matching jodhpurs, walked up to Forsythe. Her riding boots were heeled with glittering buzz saw rowels. A double-plaited quirt was looped to her wrist.

"Who are you?" the blindfolded man asked, coming to.

"Who is *she?*" Forsythe said. "This poem of a girl? This flight of angels?" He pulled off Red Shirt's blindfold. "Take a closer look."

"She's dressed in black," the Apache said, confused.

"Black as your heart," Forsythe confirmed.

"Is she a *bad* woman?" Red Shirt asked, disoriented.

"Of Babylonian proportions."

"Who *is* she?" Red Shirt said.

"She's our Lady Legion."

The Apache passed out.

Ahmad hit the Apache with more water.

"I want to die," Red Shirt sobbed.

Legion's wrist quirt sang through the air, cutting the Apache's cheek to the bone. His body convulsed.

"Give it up, friend," Forsythe said. "They all do in the end. Do you really think you can stand up to us *both?*"

"He apparently does," Legion said.

"What is needed then," Forsythe said, "is a more authoritative voice, the touch of the master's hand."

He pulled a red-hot flaying knife from a smoking brazier. He severed the Indian's breechclout with one slash and went to work on his groin.

The Indian's screams echoed through the night.

6

Through his binoculars Forsythe scanned the rancheria. He counted over sixty wickiups in all, pitched on the rim of a deep redrock canyon. The gorge was spanned by a single rope bridge. The blanket-wrapped, sleepy-eyed sentries leaned against the outlying rocks, snoring through their watch. Even the dogs were still.

Forsythe studied the rancheria, relieved. In order to find it, he had had to work on that damnable Indian day and night. It had been the ultimate test of his craft. But he had succeeded. Even Legion had been impressed.

Forsythe surveyed the surrounding ridges, where Tamerlane's men had positioned themselves. The Apaches had yielded the high ground to be closer to the rope bridge.

Forsythe glanced at Legion. "They cross that bridge, they're home free."

"And the buzzards will breakfast on your eyeballs."

"Aren't we bloody tonight?"

"Great beauty is always bloodthirsty," Legion said. "That's what the Scribe used to tell me."

"Well, he won't be telling you that anymore."

"He won't be baiting Old Mustafa either."

"No, he won't."

She glanced at her watch. 0400 hours. She pointed toward the surrounding ridges.

"There," she said. "Watch."

Long columns of *Ordu* horse soldiers lined the ridges surrounding the Apache camp. Cavalry officers were flanked by foot soldiers, their arrow quivers slung across the horses' withers. The only sounds were the distant creaking of boot and saddle leather, and the muted clink of bits and bridles.

The archers lit their torches. Fire arrows poured down on the rancheria, and *Ordu* horse soldiers charged down the ridges at a swinging gallop.

Camp dogs yelped and sleepy sentries leaped to their feet. Braves, squaws, and children flooded out from the wickiups. The footrace to the bridge was illuminated by burning lodges and the endless rain of fire arrows.

A dozen women and children started out over the canyon. The fragile bridge swayed and shook under their weight but held. For a long moment it looked as if they would make it.

Then the Horde's hydraulically jacked crossbows released their fire arrows. The dry hemp bridge burst into flame, and its load of Apaches plunged screaming into the gorge.

The rancheria was a chaos of blazing lodges. *Ordu* horsemen, closing in on three sides, dispatched the dismounted Apaches with slashing saberwork.

"Which do these savages fear most?" Forsythe mused, watching the camp fall. "Death? Mutilation? Or their heathen afterlife?"

The sun flared over the eastern rimrock, the black sky turning deep red.

"They fear the light of day. They fear what will happen to them *if* they survive this night. In short, dear Forsythe, they fear you."

The two rose and headed down the hill.

That morning, as Forsythe and his Lady strolled through the charred remains of the rancheria, Legion seemed pleased.

"Forsythe," Legion said, "you've done well. You've given the men new purpose and discipline."

"They've learned the true meaning of *salaam*."

"Indeed. They are now free to obey."

"And to understand the wisdom of unswerving obedience."

"Yes, now there is wisdom enough to spare."

As if to emphasize her words, the body of a nearby Chiricahua was dragged, kicking and naked, to the center of the camp. He was placed on a pile of rocks so that all might enjoy the spectacle. His various orifices were packed with black powder, then fused and ignited. The simultaneous blasts silenced his resistance.

"A little too flamboyant for my refined tastes," Forsythe said, "but time was of the essence."

"At least, our men were amused," Legion said. "They even left off their whoring to watch."

Forsythe glanced at the canyon's rim, where several dozen spread-eagled squaws were being raped. Tamerlane and his half-naked officers were standing up. They had indeed stopped to watch.

"The Scribe would have lectured us on our lack of sympathy," Forsythe said.

"Yes, I remember that little speech. It was most amusing."

"I wonder if those squaws think we lack sympathy?"

"I can't imagine why. We liberated them from such a boring existence."

"And gave them something to remember us by."

"Memories ringing with terror."

As they crossed the razed camp, they came to a freshly dug ditch, filled with firewood. Around it were herded the babies, children, and old people. Forsythe nodded to Ahmad, who lit the tinder. The ditch burst into flames.

One by one, troops pushed the shrieking survivors into the conflagration.

"I would have preferred boiling them in oil," Forsythe said idly, "but we had no pot."

"We could have plucked their eyeballs out and replaced them with burning coals."

"We lacked the staff," Forsythe said bitterly.

"I know," Legion commiserated. "It's so hard to find good help these days."

The victims howled in the flames.

"All in all, you did well," Legion said.

"What next?" Forsythe asked, already bored.

"Tamerlane heads south after more men, more horses. You and I return to the main camp and prepare for the Citadel. What we do there will make this little *auto de fe* look like a day at the beach."

"Shall I have a go at the old woman, Katherine Magruder?" Forsythe asked.

"Her whole sorry clan."

"Good," Forsythe said. "I never got a chance to ply my trade on the Scribe. Perhaps I can requite myself on his sainted Grandma."

Legion smiled. "We do think alike, Cuddler, don't we?"

PART XXII

Once more into the breach . . . once more . . .

—HENRY V

PART XVII

It was coming together now, and nobody was more surprised than Katherine Magruder. Men and women from the quartermaster corps appeared on the Citadel's plank sidewalks daily, drawing up plans, issuing invoices, requisitioning matériel. Hundreds of mule-drawn freight wagons clogged the dirt streets, hauling arms and equipment from the train depots to Patton's supply dumps. Riggers poured through the town on the way to the fields and the refineries. The New Oklahoma pipeline was already pumping thousands of gallons of crude each day. The new three-hundred-foot distilling towers west of town smoked and seethed, red-orange flames shooting from their tops.

The war effort had even attracted new volunteers. Men and women streamed into the Citadel from as far away as East Texas and New LA. They came by train, by stagecoach, by wagon and horseback—faster than the Citadel could process them.

The training camps in the hills teemed with men, and the target ranges boomed with gunfire. The new tank and truck plants were finally on-line and dozens of vehicles poured into the camps daily.

The Citadel was finally coming around.

2

The days flew, and the legends grew. Newspaper articles on the war effort abounded. When the Citadel's leading paper, the *News-Sentinel*, ran out of genuine news, they made it up.

The ages of Patton, Jackson, Amelia, and Katherine were the cause of much humorous speculation:

"Inside sources report that the Citadel is now being run by a 100-year-old woman, two 500-year-old generals, a 300-year-old airplane pilot, and one baby dwarf. Together, they've conquered a cave full of hydrophobic bats, brought in sixty gushers, and are about to spit in Tamerlane's eye."

Elizabeth held her brother responsible for the the "baby dwarf" crack.

But as to the real events, Elizabeth knew better. She was out there every day watching the Generals and her grandmother inspect the troops. The army camps now were processing technicians of every kind. Blacksmiths, gas fitters, mechanics, wranglers, and stable hands.

Patton—with his riding breeches, tight-fitting cavalry jacket, and shiny ivory-handled pistols—drew the most attention. According to the stories he had an almost psychic ability to be at the right place at the right time. If, on a training maneuver, a tank broke down, he was there. He'd bang on the turret hatch, hammer at the cowling, and scream into the speaking tubes for the men to come out. He'd get down under the universal joints and the wheels for a closer look.

"You lack complete combustion," he'd shout back up to the men. "Skips in the high gear, doesn't it?" And of course, he was right. It *had* been skipping in fourth gear. He'd laugh. "Hardly premium-quality fuel we got here, but still we'll get it running. Let's raise the compression, that'll do it. High compression runs better in this heavy basin air." He'd crawl out from under the car. "Give me a screwdriver, and let's get under that hood. Got to open up the carburetor."

Every one of these lessons included a famous Patton talk. The men would gather around by the hundreds, and he would speak about everything—the importance of maintenance, the eccentricities of their M-60 turret guns, the art of tank-driving in battle, their overall strategy.

Examples of his speeches filled Elizabeth's notebooks.

"The secret to whipping these sonsofbitches is to hit and hit hard. You advance, advance, advance, and advance—always as rapidly as you can. Remember that the longer you're under fire from that big hill there, the more of you will die. So you always keep moving and keep firing. You close with them and murder them. You attack, attack, attack—till the last drop of gas is gone, and your last shot is fired. Then you exit your vehicle, fix bayonets, and advance some more. Slow down, meander—don't even dream of stopping—that'll buy you nothing but a quick grave."

The old woman's only quibble with his generalship was his use of four-letter words, and she told him so once.

It was the only time that Elizabeth saw Patton abrupt with her grandmother.

"I don't understand your obsession with decent

language. Anyway, it is impossible to run an army without profanity. It's a proven fact."

Occasionally, his dark side became more pronounced. Once, while inspecting the Citadel's largest and newest machine shop—containing over eighty metal lathes alone—he found one of his soldiers doubling as a machinist because of the Citadel's labor shortage. It should have been easy duty—except that this one, instead of running his lathe, was hiding behind a broken drill press, sleeping off a hangover. In front of God, the old woman, Jackson, and Elizabeth, he kicked the man's hind end all over the shop, shouting:

"These brave men are busting their butts, working eighteen-hour shifts, in 130-degree heat so you can saw wood? Not hardly. Sergeant," he screamed, "send this man to the stockade. And bring him up on charges. And when the shooting starts, I want him in the thick of it, right up at the front."

He turned to the owner who had been escorting them through the shop.

"I've never seen such slipshod management in my life, and I promise you this. You miss your quota, and you won't have to worry about Tamerlane or Legion coming for you. I'll come after you myself."

The next week the shop's production was up forty percent.

But for every dressing-down, there were, by Elizabeth's count, five hundred compliments which left the men literally aglow. Every speech he gave, including the bawlings-out, ended with a statement as to how proud of the men he was. Often he would single out one of them before leaving, as he did in the machine shop.

"What were you, son, before we shanghaied you into this outfit."

"Sir, I picked lettuce and fruit mostly."

"Well, you're a machinist now, and in a few more weeks, we'll send you back to the infantry. And I can't tell you how proud you—all of you—are making us. With men like you we'll whip those sonsofbitches." Then, in his best parade-ground voice, he shouted to the rest of the soldier-machinists. "I would be lacking in gratitude if I did not say that leading you men has been an unparalleled honor."

3

Yet late at night, all by himself, Patton knew melancholy. He would think of his wife, Bea, and how he'd left her a hundred years behind and how unbelievably alone he was.

Then he would worry about strategy. Like Jackson and the old woman, no matter how he tried to enthuse about their battle plans, he was skeptical. Entrust the most important part of the fight to renegade savages, a one-hundred-year-old war shaman, and Richard Sheckly?

But there was nothing he could do about that part of it. He had to trust to God, to Fate, to Destiny. That's what he'd done so far, and they had not let him down yet.

Funny, Patton thought, he had sometimes worried about his Destiny—when he was in between wars. That was always the hardest part for him—when he was lying idle, terrified of going to waste.

Well, his Destiny had come through this time. Like gangbusters.

But what was his Destiny? What was he doing? Making tanks out of fifty-year-old junked cars? Airplane fuel out of parboiled crude. Bombs made out of bat guano and heathen savages for shock troops?

Such thoughts made him tired. He tried instead to think about his last war. Damn, he would have like to have met his other nemesis—that bastard, Erwin Rommel. Always said he wanted to fight him tank-to-tank, one-on-one. Or pistol-to-pistol. Anyway the old boy wanted it. Bowie knives and barrel staves, if that was the way. Settle all the killing with just the two of them.

And he liked old Erwin too. About as much as he hated the psychotic paperhanger who murdered him.

Speaking of which, what about Tamerlane? Would he get to face him. He had been haunted by his face since childhood, since before Time itself. Him, he truly hated. And feared. Yes, feared. He had to admit it. Privately. To himself.

Maybe that's why I never got to meet you, Erwin. You, I liked.

Tamerlane, on the other hand, was something more than his enemy, more than his nemesis. Tamerlane was his Fate, Karma, Destiny, call it what you will.

Tamerlane, he had to kill.

I kill you, perhaps this vision-quest comes to an end.

My wars come to an end.

What would I do then? he wondered.

God, his head hurt. Ever since that horse fall in '35 he'd been plagued with headaches. Hurt even worse when he drank. Well, all those presents of whiskey were what did in Grant. With these headaches, wasn't much chance of that for him.

Could be worse. Could be Stonewall. Following an Apache trail through canyons, desert, heat, and dust.

If the desert didn't kill Tom, the Horde would.

Don't think that way. Tom will make it. He always has.

At least, until Chancellorsville.

You just worry about your end. Tom'll hold up his. He smiled. Imagine. Worried about Stonewall Jackson. Might as well worry about God.

Sleep now. Good. Head didn't hurt so much. Kicked by too many horses. Shot too many times. How many car crashes? Plane wrecks? Battles? Was that really me? At Thermopylae? Tyre? Crécy's field? Waterloo?

Of course, it was, General. Who else?

Oh, Tom, I hope you're all right. What have we gotten ourselves into this time?

Worry about Stonewall Jackson? What a laugh. Your idol, your God.

Might as well worry about God.

Slowly, the ache in his head subsided.

Yes, might as well worry about God.

The neck muscles relaxed. His mind was free. He dreamed of Gaul and Cannae, of Rome's fall and Battle of the Bulge.

Worry about Stonewall.

Worry about God.

What a laugh.

What a laugh.

General Patton slept.

4

Jackson sat in his dark tent, alone with his thoughts.

He was on the edge of Arroyos dos Noches, the Canyons of the Night. He was about to lead his army of twelve hundred men against a mounted force almost ten times that size.

Not that the odds bothered Jackson. Throughout the Virginia Campaign he'd been the underdog and had not cared. The truth be known, it had made the battles more interesting.

No, what bothered Jackson were his doubts. He felt he no longer understood war.

War, as Jackson fought it, had involved pride and honor, but no longer. Now men bounced around in motorized fortresses and attacked each other with machine guns. They flew through the air like iron birds and dropped bombs. It was the machines that mattered, not the men.

In his day a single soldier with a rifle—with only a bayonet—had made a difference.

Night fell. A quartet of soldiers gathered in front of his tent and sang Civil War songs. They were performing "The Night They Drove Old Dixie Down."

Jackson hated that song for the way it sentimentalized the South's defeat. Yes, the South had lost the war, and he also recognized that in many circles he was honored *because* of that loss. It seemed incomprehensible to him, yet some people actually glorified defeat. They romanticized it out of all reality. They made it trivial.

Jackson sat slumped on the edge of his cot. The song appalled him. Not only did people's attitudes toward the Civil War upset him. It was the nature of war itself. War had become so vast, so unwieldy, so destructive.

At Sharpsburg he'd glimpsed war's future horror. The fighting began in the misty drizzle of dawn and ended only after dark—with the dying of the light and the rattle of small-arms fire, with the smoke heavy in the air and the screams of the wounded.

The battle raged over croplands and woodlands, in valleys and hills, in Antietam Creek and in Sharpsburg town. He remembered the battles for that cornfield— thirty acres in all, harvested by cannon, its crop men. The Yankee guns were rifled Parrotts loaded with canister and case shell, and old-time Napoleons filled to their muzzles with grape. The Yankee gunners, black with smoke, raked the field at will.

Oh God, how men had suffered in that corn. When his troops finally fled, they were covered with blood, reeking of urine, bootless, sobbing, the split rail fences littered with their dead.

Something inexorable was happening even then. Jackson had glimpsed it at Antietam, all of it—the Somme, Ypres, Stalingrad, Hiroshima.

The End of Days—something horrendous that could not be stopped.

Jackson turned to the Bible—to John of Patmos. Why he took comfort from so frightening a work was puzzling, yet somehow the book soothed Jackson's soul.

He saw it as the culmination of all the prophesies—of Daniel, who had seen the kings of earth cast down before the Ancient of Days, of Isaiah, who had seen God in his Temple seated upon his throne, and who had prophesied the birth of the Suffering Servant, Jesus Christ.

In Revelation, the Lord was seated on a heavenly throne amid a rainbow. Before Him burned seven lamps of fire and beyond Him loomed a sparkling sea.

Then came the Lamb of God, escorted by ten thousand times ten thousand singing angels. He opened the Seven Seals to the roar of thunder, freeing

the Four Horsemen of the Apocalypse, the White
Horse of the Eastern Barbarians, the Red Horse of
Revolution and Strife, the Black Horse of Famine,
and the Pale Horse of Death. With the Fifth Seal the
Souls of Martyrs Slain rose up, and with the Sixth
Heaven was shaken.

With the Seventh came Hail and Fire, Darkness
and Death. The sea turned to blood, the sun and
moon and stars went out. The Abyss gaped, and
plagues swarmed the earth.

Then came the war between Michael and the Great
Dragon. In the final battle, Lucifer and all his hosts
fell flaming to the earth. The angels sang to God:
"Babylon is fallen, is fallen."

The earth was purged with the Seven Golden Vials
of Heaven's Wrath, with Plagues of Blood and Fire, of
Darkness and Death.

All that Jackson understood—and, in fact, it had
come to pass. An Antichrist had descended. The earth
had been scourged, and plagues followed.

But what came after that? John of Patmos next
wrote that the New Jerusalem had come down from
Heaven on High and become the City of God.

Jackson stared at the text, dumbfounded. Where
were the ten thousand times ten thousand victorious
saints? The shouts of *Alleluia?* The sea of glass? The
seven trumpets? The river of life? Where was the New
Jerusalem? The Mount of Zion?

They had not appeared—only hunger and darkness, pestilence and death. There was no tree of life.

Sheckly had told him a nineteenth-century philoso-
pher named Nietzsche had declared God dead. One
of his successors—a man named Lenin—had enslaved
Russia, and a man named Stalin had massacred it. An

Adolph Hitler had almost conquered the world, all the while proclaiming the demise of the Lord.

Were the madmen right?

He fought against despair.

> *The Lord is thy light and thy salvation.*
> *Whom shall I fear?*
> *The Lord is the strength of my life;*
> *Of whom shall I be afraid . . . ?*
> *A thousand shall fall at thy side*
> *And ten thousand at thy right hand;*
> *But none shall come nigh thee. . . .*

He did not know if he believed that any longer. He wanted to return to the Faith. He wanted to believe in God on High—Who had meted out the heavens with a span and whose goodness was from everlasting to everlasting—but he had doubts.

Suppose there was no God?

His course would remain the same.

If he could not have God, he could still fight men like Tamerlane.

He got out his maps.

He stared at the detailed drawings with empty eyes.

He prepared for the long march to come.

5

Elizabeth sat at the kitchen table late into the night.

She realized now her priorities had been all wrong. Throughout the buildup she'd kept a solemn look on her face, but, in truth, she'd never been happier. She was surrounded by glamorous men in uniforms. People hung on their words and jumped at their commands.

God, she loved it! She would never again be so happy.

Everyone else sacrificed. Her father and Stonewall Jackson might die in the canyonlands, on the mountain. Patton, Matthew, Amelia—they might be shot out of the sky. Her grandmother had subjected her eighty-five-year-old body to enormous strains—how could she survive this war?

The more she thought about it, the more Elizabeth knew she could not watch them pay the price while she wrote about their exploits and took bows.

Elizabeth turned to her paper and pen. She wrote:

> *Dear Grandma,*
>   *I know I promised, but I just couldn't stay behind . . .*

Thou shalt not be afraid for the terror by night;
nor the arrow that flieth by day.

—Psalms 91:5

PART XXIII

We few, we happy few, we band of brothers. . . .

—HENRY V

The bearded man in the gray tunic and forage cap trudged up the sloping canyon toward the mountain. The trek was hot, and the officer wiped the back of his neck with his gray bandanna.

He opened his B.W. Raymond railroad watch. A gold timepiece with an eight-day movement, it featured an anachronistic IIII and a winding key that hung from the chain. Since it had come through the hole with him, Katherine dubbed it: "The watch that transcended time."

It was 0930 hours. While their march was still concealed by rock cliffs and shadows—as well as the morning sun blinding the *Ordu*'s sentries—they would not be hidden long.

He snapped the watch lid shut. Digging in his walking staff, he continued upslope. His thighs and calves ached from the exertion, and his breath came in gasps. He was a man who'd spent his life leading marches on horseback. He was not used to strenuous walking.

He stared longingly upslope and pressed on. According to his map he would soon have his first unobstructed view of Monte de Roca. He could then decide whether to march for another hour—possibly betraying their position to the mountain lookouts—or halt in the lee of these canyons.

Major Thompson would be helpful. Born to these canyonlands, he had a good eye for terrain and defilade.

Jackson reached the top of the slope, panting and sweating. Before him lay the crimson cliff face of Monte de Roca, looming unbelievably huge, while behind him staggered two thousand men. On each side of his troops soared red canyon walls.

The General stared back at the mountain, dismayed. He was not even sure how far away it was. As the crow flies, it was a dozen miles.

But his crows had to march over ridges and rises, chasms and cacti, carry rifles, machine guns, mortars, and munitions.

Major Thompson was at his side. He looked a mess. His threadbare khaki blouse and pants were saturated with sweat and dust. His square-toed double-soled boots were down at the heels. His gray bandanna had long since rotted away. The men behind him were all in the same shape.

Jackson did not even give him time to catch his breath.

"Can we reach the *llano* by tomorrow?" Jackson asked. "It's twelve miles on the map."

Thompson stared upslope.

"If we press on, we might pick up another hour. We might also lose everything."

There it was. They would camp in the lee of the canyon.

"Major, night-marching will be brutal. To flank the Horde at dawn, we're going to have to *fly* over that ground."

"We could lose half our men from the march alone."

"I know. But we start at sunset."

"At sunset." The Major waved his orderly forward. "Pass the word down. We're making a cold camp. We start again at dusk."

2

Dusk in the canyonlands.

Jackson led his fifteen hundred troops up the canyon. On all sides his men saw nothing but red shadowy cliffs. The rock walls were scorchingly hot, and the air seared Jackson's throat.

Rounding a sharp bend, he caught another twilit glimpse of the mountain. From the east it was nothing but a sheer crimson cliff, and, once again, he prayed that Sheckly had scaled it.

But he did not worry about Sheckly long. He had other concerns. The 9 mm on his belt was again sliding down his hip, and there was no time to take it off and readjust the load, not with the pace his point men were setting.

Even worse, the next stretch of canyon looked impassable. He was approaching not so much a canyon floor as a succession of gorges and crevices, saddles and slopes, which twisted and turned—some rising three hundred feet here, dropping two hundred feet there—and now night was falling.

Tugging at his gunbelt, he tried to readjust it in midstride. It would look bad, indeed, if the General himself were unable to keep up.

He fought the slippery scree, struggled to catch his breath, and picked up his pace.

3

Richard Sheckly squeezed out of the chimney and climbed up onto a three-foot outcrop. He was now halfway up the mountain and had a lot of heavy hauling to do. He decided to risk a piton. He would need a standing belay.

He found a crack and, with a rubber-tipped mallet, drove in the spike. He bolted on the pulley and threaded his towline through it.

It not only had been hot on the mountain—and murderously hot in that rock chimney—it had been hell in those canyonlands. Down there, he had been cut off from the world by time and the desert, by scorching days and freezing nights, by an incomprehensible maze of sweltering slickrock gorges.

He began hauling up the rope. The pain in his back and shoulders was excruciating. What had Spirit Owl called such pain? The agony that dulls danger. *What the hell,* he thought. *Just take it one pull at a time. It couldn't hurt as bad as the old shaman's sun dances. Nothing could hurt as bad as those.*

He dragged the transmitters onto the sandstone ledge, then started back up the cliff face, free-climbing without belay, all his weight on his arms.

He was still more than a hundred feet from the summit before he spotted his first really solid foothold. By the time he got there, he was trembling so violently he could barely get a boot into it.

Two years ago he'd taken Elizabeth into the volcanic vent, and he hadn't done a lick of climbing since. He was paying for it now.

This'll teach you to get out of shape, he thought.

Less than ten feet from the top. Might as well be ten years. Richard was stunned by pain and fear—especially fear.

It seemed as if he had been afraid all his life, that fear had been his constant companion. Stuck on that cliff face, like a fly on flypaper, he struggled to shake it off. *Do it, man, you aren't getting any younger. Get your sorry hide up there.*

Richard pulled himself toward the peak an inch at a time. When he got there he hooked his hands onto the edge and jackknifed over the top.

He'd beaten the mountain.

Flipping onto his back, he stared up at the night sky. The Milky Way was a broad swath of white light, and the moon was startlingly huge, giving off enough light to read newsprint by.

Rolling over onto his stomach, he crawled across the fifty-foot mountain peak on throbbing arms and bleeding hands. He peered over the other side.

From across the *llano,* the Citadel's tanks crept toward the peak. There, gunfire flared and rattled. Near the mountain the *Ordu*'s horse herd grazed.

For the moment his position seemed safe enough. Cliff face behind him. Another drop-off in front. Halfway down the promontory the Horde's Death Squads were camped, while below them—in a gaping mountain arroyo—were bunkered the 105s.

Time to get started. His towrope was clipped to his belt, and the rest of his gear was still down there on the ledge. Time to torture his arms again. He crawled back to the far rim, took a standing belay on a rocky outcrop, and hauled up his radio transmitter.

Richard carried the bag to the far side of the peak. He took out the sniper scope, sat cross-legged on the summit, and reexamined the scene below.

This was his second look at the big guns. Damn, they were bunkered down tight, encased in solid rock.

He began to assemble his transmitter to call in those mortar strikes.

◀━━━ 4

Night in the canyonlands.

Jackson stared into a twisting gorge of red rock and black shadows. The gorge was about to grow even blacker.

"Tell them to move it out," Jackson said to Major Thompson. "And tell them to move it quietly. This is supposed to be a surprise."

Jackson reached the top of the rise. Taking a deep breath, he started down the talus-strewn slope. The scree was rough, the footing constantly rising or falling. Sometimes the slope even seemed to tilt sideways.

Behind him the brigade followed, thousands of footsteps merging into one dull drone.

Still the General was luckier than most. He only carried his canteen, a 9 mm, and three extra clips. The other men were burdened with rifles, ammunition, canteens, rations, forty- to fifty-pound mortar sections. They all struggled to balance the weight on their shoulders or keep it under their arms—anything to reduce the strain on their fingers.

Jackson's gunbelt was still weighted by his pistol,

clips, and canteen, and it was sliding down his hips.
This caused his pants belt—to which he'd tied his
map case and sheath knife—to ride down beneath it.

They were marching so fast that if he stopped even
for a few seconds to readjust his gear, he would, in
pitch-darkness, crash into more heavily burdened
men.

They were now on the edge of the *Ordu* lines. A
loud yelp or a lit cigarette could alert the enemy. So
could the unavoidable noises—metal banging on
metal, rocks accidentally kicked down a slope, the
rumble of footsteps.

Even worse, his calves were now starting to cramp.
Despite the pain and nearness of the enemy, he still
tried to hurry the men up. He passed that word down
the line. To lag now meant death. They couldn't even
wait for fallen comrades.

Jackson came to a vast black dropoff. The scouts
and point men were going over, one by one. Each
hung from the rim by his hands, then let go, disappearing into the blackness.

God only knew how the mortar men would manage.

It was his turn. He swung his legs over the abyss,
braced, then pushed off. He dropped, he reckoned, at
least fifteen feet before rolling onto a rock shelf. He
crawled to its edge, dropped over, hit another, then
another sloping edge. It gave way under his boots,
and he went bouncing, rolling, and sprawling till he
was facedown in a dried-up creek bottom, sweating
and in pain.

Keep moving, he said to himself. *You've got to keep
the men moving.*

On one side of the streambed were the canyonlands.

On the other, the mountain, in front of which was a scattering of boulders that offered some cover.

Jackson ordered his men up the dry streambed. Now it was just a matter of walking. The creekbed was flat enough that he did not have to brood about his cramping calves. He even found time to tighten his two belts.

This was the sort of marching he understood. He even tried to enjoy the view—the stars, the waning moon, the boulders and mountains and cliff walls.

As he rounded the next turn, he caught a side view of the big mountain guns. Three *Janizaries* were silhouetted along the line of the hill less than three hundred yards away.

At the next boulder he found his scouts and point men, waiting. Beyond that boulder, less than a mile off, twelve thousand enemy horsemen were lining up. He could hear the stamping of hooves mixed with the blowing and snorting of horses. From across the basin he heard the rumble of the approaching tanks.

He opened up his timepiece. 0355 hours. God only knew how long it would take his men to get their mortars and machine guns over that obstacle course.

Jackson's calves throbbed. He hoped his men were in better shape than he was.

"Get back there and warn the men to keep still," Jackson said. "At dawn, when the attack begins, this is the point from which we'll begin *our* assault."

Major Thompson was at his side. "I just hope Sheckly has reached that peak. If he hasn't, we're shooting blind."

"Look to your men, Major. They're the ones you have to be concerned about now. One way or another, we're striking Tamerlane on his flank."

5

Elizabeth paused halfway up the cliff face, clinging to the opening of the old mine tunnel. She stared into the 2' x 2' shaft and shuddered. It was dark, rat-infested, and stank of methane. In the glow from her carbide helmet lamp, shale dust glistened and swirled.

The mine was a firetrap. She deliberately placed her tin box of matches and candles in the shaft head's entrance.

Elizabeth crawled into the mine. Her elbows and knees were heavily padded. Her eyes were protected by spelunking goggles, her head by a leather helmet and the helmet lamp. In her backpack was the forty-pound bag of blasting gel, which she'd just hauled up the side of the mountain with a climbing pulley. From her waist hung her hammer and pitons.

She worked her way though the shaft, stopping here and there to clear away some of the deadfall and to replace collapsed shoring timber. Mines are never quiet places, and in this one the *dripdripdripdripdripping* of water and the groaning of rock faults and shoring timbers were continuous.

As she crawled, she also listened to the scurrying of the mine's inhabitants—beetles, spiders, snakes, scorpions, and centipedes. What frightened her most, however, were the shrieking mine rats. Given their record as plague carriers, she felt her fear was justified.

The main sump was coming up next, which she knew would put her near the lateral vent. If she could still squeeze through that, then she would be directly

above the 105s and on top of the mountain's main
fault.

Elizabeth took the crampons from her belt and
fixed them to the soles of her climbing boots. Using
chocks and handholds, she worked her way around
the cylindrical sides of the methane sump. It was a
thirty-foot climb to the lateral vent, and the sump was
hot. She could not stay near the core for long.

The lateral vent was less than three feet high. A
dozen mine rats froze in her helmet lamp's beam, then
shot screaming up the vent.

Elizabeth shook off her revulsion. Grabbing the
tunnel's rim, she jackknifed into the shaft and banged
her head on an overhead outcrop, smashing her carbide lamp.

The world went black.

Fighting panic, Elizabeth grabbed the flashlight
from her belt. Thank God it was still there. Now,
God, make it work.

The beam was unexpectedly powerful. Rats and
bugs, which had endured a lifetime of pitch-darkness,
scattered up the vent.

Good, Elizabeth thought, *just keep away from me.*

The vent angled twice, and at the second bend she
found the old volcanic fault. It was a black crack, over
fifty feet long, which ran just above the 105s. If she did
this right, she would bring down half the mountain.

She began widening the crack with her rock pick.
It was sweaty work. She was close to the subter-
ranean fires which had thrust up this hill thirty million years ago. If she did not clear the fault quickly,
plant her blasting gel, and get out, the heat and gas
would kill her.

She hurried with her digging. After two hours she

had dug out nearly a quarter ton of deadfall from the fifty-foot sector of fault line. She unfastened her pack and removed the gelatin.

After another half hour she'd packed the fifty-foot fault line with high explosive—almost one pound per foot. She crimped the caps and set the detonator, allowing herself four hours to get off the mountain.

Her entire body ached from digging and crawling, but, at last, she backed out of the vent. Dangling her legs over the sump, she swung out over the abyss.

The climb around the methane sump was even harder. Her helmet lamp was gone, and her flashlight, shoved down in her pants, flickered fitfully.

Somehow, she reached the old mine shaft. She grasped the lip with both hands, got a foothold with her crampons, and pulled herself up into the tunnel.

The flashlight hit the shaft's rim, flipped free from her belt, and spun, flashing, into the vent. The shaft was plunged into everlasting night. Elizabeth took a deep breath and tried to fight off panic. She told herself none of this was happening.

But it was.

Just get out. She clenched her teeth, put her head down and crawled furiously through the tunnel. Deadfall, rats, timberwork, none of it mattered. She just had to get out of that shaft. She dug and clawed, pushed and crawled.

She might have made it too—if she hadn't smashed into the shoring timber at the far turn. Suddenly, the entire tunnel was crashing down in front of her.

She backed up into the twisting shaft. Her shoulder ached. Her lungs burned from the gas and dust. Behind her lay the methane sump. She could retreat no farther.

She lay there still as death, listening to the *dripdrip-dripdrip* of the mine water, the interminable groaning of the timbers, and the shrieking of the rats. The noise was driving her crazy.

Calm down, she said to herself. *Keep your head. You can do it.*

The panic subsided, and she felt herself almost relaxing. *You can do it, you aren't afraid. You're a Magruder. You're a Magruder.*

To drown out the din, she began to sing. It was an old refrain her grandmother used to sing to them.

> *Amazing Grace,*
> *How sweet the sound*
> *That saved a wretch like me.*
> *I once was lost*
> *But now am found,*
> *Was blind but now I see.*

6

It was 0400 hours, and Amelia stood alone in the hangar. The big hut was awash in busted propeller shafts, ancient piston heads, coiled cable, tubes, tires, pipe of all sorts, parts of wings, dead batteries, fuel cells, lengths of longerons, sets of wrenches and screw drivers, wheels, flaps, radios, and hundreds of other parts that had been sifted through and in some instances cannibalized.

To the hangar's rear was the unsalvageable Jenny. This one had a cracked engine housing that they'd never been able to fix, as well as a dozen other ailments.

It was surrounded by a bizarre assortment of tools and spare parts—a sewing machine, three bolts of cloth, several stacks of wood slats, and four bales of chicken wire.

Is this how I'm fighting the Horde? she wondered. *With sewing machines and chicken wire?*

Amelia walked out the hangar's back door and looked over the airstrip. Patton and his pilot, Matt Magruder, were in helmets and flight suits, already heading for the Electra. Noonan waited for them.

Time to go.

She crossed the strip. Four dust devils twisted across the runway. Tumbleweed blew past her. The mountains to the east were turning pale gray in the false dawn. The stars were vanishing, one by one.

Noonan, her gunner and copilot, annoyed Patton with last minute questions.

"Anything special you want me to shoot at down there? I could hit one of your tanks by mistake."

"Those tanks have armor," Patton growled.

"Should he shoot at jackrabbits?" Amelia asked, walking up to the hardstand.

"Anything that moves," Patton said.

"The General would shoot an Angel of God if he could get a bead on it," Matt Magruder said.

Patton scowled. He opened the Electra's hatch and pulled down the gangplank. Amelia followed Matthew and the General halfway up.

"Matt," she said. "Tell me one thing. How old are you *really?*"

"Twenty-five," he said.

"Elizabeth told me you're sixteen."

"Grandma should've taken that knotted plowline to her, telling all those lies."

"General," Noonan said, "you're picking your copilots pretty young these days. If you'd asked, you could have had me."

Patton shuddered at the thought.

The Electra's radio began to squawk. Patton picked up the microphone. "Electra, over."

"That you, George?" Katherine Magruder snarled. "I've been trying to raise you all morning."

"Want to speak to your grandson?" Patton asked.

"What for?"

"Hey, Katherine," Amelia shouted across the cockpit, "how old is Matthew?"

"Old enough to know better."

Matthew turned on his transmitter. "Grandma, Noonan's worried he'll hurt a few *Janizaries*."

Her voice was a rasping roar. "They're going to be living in a whole world of hurt, we get done with them."

Beyond the hangar the tanks were halfway across the basin.

Amelia and Noonan climbed down the gangplank and waited for Matt to start it up. He had to hit the engines four times before they turned over. They misfired badly, smoking, coughing, and jerking.

"The Electra's still knocking," Noonan said. "After all that work."

Amelia clapped him on the shoulder. "There was nothing you could do. She was built for 189 octane fuel, and all we had was distillery gasoline. I'm happy she's flying at all."

The Electra went lurching down the runway. The engine knock was devastating.

"Those engines sound like somebody's hitting a fifty-five-gallon drum with a ball peen hammer," Noonan said.

The Electra rolled down the runway and somehow lifted off. Noonan and Amelia watched in awe.

"Well, as the General always says, time to saddle up."

"Afraid so."

Amelia climbed into the rear cockpit of the Jenny, while Noonan untethered her from the hardstand and took hold of the propeller.

7 ━━━━━

Betsy Ross perched on the corral gate, watching her son with narrowed eyes. Harry the Triceratops stood spraddle-legged—snorting, shaking his massive head, his shoulder muscles twitching in rage.

Harry was having a bad dream. In it, he was being menaced by a black forbidding shape. As the creature approached, it began to take on feature and form. It had broad wings, arching feet, and a gaping mouth full of fangs. It roared like thunder and was devouring Harry's cow.

Harry's heart hammered, and his eyes jerked open. This was no dream. The Demon was rolling down the runway with Harry's cow sticking out of its belly.

Harry had finally grown up. He stood twelve feet tall and was thirty feet long. This time when he crashed into the corral full of inward-slanting shafts, they shattered like twigs.

Circling the camp once, the Fiend soared over the basin.

Harry stared at the broken shafts. This was his chance—to get the awful Fiend and even up the score.

Just then his shrieking, flapping mother leaped off her corral block and onto his neck. She grabbed onto his frill with her talons and whaled at him with her ten-foot pinions.

So be it. Harry was going to get the Demon no matter what—even if his mother beat him half to death.

With Betsy Ross aboard, Harry galloped over the broken stakes and headed across the *llano*.

◀ 8

Mann and Hardy slogged across the battlefield behind a long row of tanks. Their khaki uniforms were dust-caked and smoke-blackened.

"The whores of war," Hardy said, "that's what we are. First fighting for New Salt, then Tamerlane, now the Citadel. Who do we fight for next?"

A shell hit nearby. It obliterated the tank to their left and knocked Mann to his knees. He got up slowly.

Hardy continued talking as if nothing had happened.

"God knows who we'll be fighting for tomorrow. Maybe Satan himself. Wouldn't surprise me to end up in hell fighting on a bed of hot coals."

Mann thought that sounded plausible. Even with the tanks in front of them—using their turret guns as a shield—the present battle was infernal.

The 105s were especially terrifying. Their ears rang from the din of incoming shells, the screams of men, and the screech of ripping metal when a tank took a hit.

Then there was the stink. Tank combustion was notoriously inefficient. The choking gas fumes and black exhaust combined with the dust and powder smoke to make the air sickening, nearly unbreathable.

"Any sign of the command car?" Hardy asked.

"The big Jeep with the twenty-foot antenna?"

The whistling roar of an incoming 105 drove both men to their knees. It exploded behind them, and afterward Mann pointed out the charred remains. All that was left was billowing smoke, twisted steel, and a single twenty-foot coaxial antenna, miraculously intact.

"There aren't any other command cars on the field?" Hardy asked.

"Not around here."

"Well, the General told us to advance. That's a standing order."

"Terrific."

"We could head for Mexico."

"Tamerlane would find us there."

"Patton would too."

"I be your witness there."

Another incoming shell detonated less than forty yards in front of them. The screams of the wounded were frighteningly close. Hardy approached one of the victims. He was hemorrhaging badly. A corpsman struggled to change his bloody bandages.

"You catch yourself some shrapnel?" Hardy asked.

"'Fraid so," the man said through gritted teeth.

"Save the metal for the kids. They love that war hero stuff."

Mann dragged Hardy forward. It wasn't a pleasant walk. Everywhere they turned there were more wounded. Canvas stretchers were little more than bloody rugs.

The tank in front of them suddenly swerved to avoid a wounded man. The prostrate soldier muttered to his blown-up litter-bearer:

"Listen, buddy, pick up the stretcher. I said pick it up."

"Hey, fella," Hardy said to him. "It's a bad habit, giving orders to the dead."

"What?"

The bleeding man stared at them, his eyes unfocused. He had a sucking chest wound. A broken shaft protruded from beneath his collarbone. He tried to say something, but the words rattled in his throat. Hardy pointed at the shaft and yelled to Mann:

"Look, an arrow. He got shot by Tonto."

The air filled with a weird, high-pitched harmonic hum. It grew in intensity, turned terrifyingly shrill, and then culminated in an awful clattering crash. Arrows vibrated all around them, thrummed in the earth, skewered tank turrets nearby.

Hardy dropped to his knees and fell on his side. An arrow had gone through his right eye and exited his neck.

Oh, my God, Mann thought, *they finally got Hardy.*

An arrow-riddled tank chugged to a halt beside him. The front of the turret had over a dozen arrows protruding from it. The driver stuck an arm through his eye slit and pointed at his dead turret gunner.

"You know how to use this thing?"

Mann wanted to get off the *llano.* He was too damned exposed on foot.

"I was born knowing," Mann yelled.

He and the driver opened the turret hatch and pulled the gunner out. An arrow had penetrated the steel combing and trepanned his skull.

They pitched him onto the *llano* beside Mann's friend. Two men killed by arrows.

He stared at Hardy one last time. *Keep hell hot for me, you insane sonofabitch.*

He climbed into the turret and pulled the hatch shut.

His relief was short-lived. Shrapnel and rounds whined off the tin box, and he grew frighteningly claustrophobic in the turret.

The driver yelled into their speaking tube: "Here they come!"

Another volley of steel-jacketed arrows hit, and, again, their tri-bladed broadheads pierced the turret from all directions.

He heard the whistling scream of an approaching shell. It grew in volume, till it roared like an express train, then exploded to their rear with a shuddering crash.

"I think I'm going to hate this war," the driver shouted up at him.

"It missed, didn't it?" Mann shouted back.

"You sound like you like this stuff."

"It's better than getting staked out on an anthill," Mann answered.

"I can't hack it anymore. I can't. I don't pack the gear."

"Shut up and drive."

"You aren't scared?"

"We don't have time to be scared."

Arrows droned like deathbirds. Shell bursts cratered the landscape with numbing regularity, and Jake, the driver, had to swerve all over the battle-ground to avoid them.

Through his firing slit Mann saw a dozen horse sol-diers emerge from the smoke and dust, slung low over their mounts. The horsemen grew bigger, bigger, bigger—and he opened up with his M-60.

The first four went down, then three more, then the rest. The horses piled up like cards, many of the soldiers still in their saddles.

"Well done," Jake yelled up at him.

Another shell hit, a horse screamed in agony. Mann shot it.

"Be careful with that ammo," Jake yelled.

"I'll be careful in hell."

There was another high-pitched harmonic hum, and a score of arrows blasted the tank. At least forty broadheads now stared Mann in the face.

"What are you gonna do after this war?" Jake called up to him. "I mean for fun?"

"Find someone to shoot arrows at us."

Jake peered through his firing slit.

"Oh God," he screamed, "I think we just found them. There must be a thousand of them coming at us."

"Welcome to the horrors of war."

Mann shoved his last belt into the M-60.

"Hope you get a clean wound," Jake shouted.

When he was done with the belt, the turret was filled with smoke, and the *llano* was littered with dead men.

"No more bullets," Mann yelled down to Jake.

"Guess what?"

"No more gas?"

"There you have it."

"What did Patton say?"

"Advance, advance, advance."

"Close with the bastards."

"Cold steel."

The two men opened their hatches. Hearing the whistling scream of a 105, they closed the tank back up.

When Mann came to, he was lying outside the tank. His first impression was of charred twisted steel: The tank had a big hole ripped in its side. Somehow he'd exited that hole. He could not figure out how.

On the ground beside him there was an empty M-16. Miraculously, his bayonet was still in its back sheath. Mann fixed it to the rifle and threw away the sheath.

He started forward again. Another artillery barrage drove him to his knees.

Nothing seemed to stop those 105s. Stonewall must be in trouble.

He started toward the big mountain—to lend Jackson a hand.

9

General Jackson stood on the low rise overlooking the *llano*. From there he could see the entire *Ordu* army—over twelve thousand strong.

He turned around and wearily studied his own troops. The long march through the desert canyons had cost him six hundred out of his original force of fifteen hundred men. His remaining troops were so exhausted they could barely stand.

"Here they come," Major Thompson shouted to him.

Jackson turned to the Horde's northeast flank. Three thousand horse soldiers were lining up for a cavalry charge.

"Major, mount those M-60s on this ridge and back them with riflemen. We can't let their horsemen flank us."

"Yes sir." Thompson sent a runner jogging off down the slope.

Jackson raised his field glasses. The *Ordu* horsemen were assembled by company and spread out along a two-mile front. Like the rest of their army, they rode every kind of animal imaginable. Wiry cow ponies, big roans, deep-chested blaze-faced bays, northern broncs, Appaloosas, grays, palominos, as well as an assortment of cantankerous mules.

The riders had shed their black robes. They now wore iron armbands, breastplates, and steel helmets linked under the chin. They carried double-curved steel-backed bows slung over their shoulders and *Shimsir* swords.

In between these horse soldiers lined up the archers, naked to the waist. They carried three to four bows each. Massive quivers hung over the horses' hindquarters.

A bugler blew "Charge," and the horsemen started out at a slow walk. The archers trotted beside them, clinging to the stirrup leathers.

Jackson's machine gunners were mounting the ridge and hammering in their tripods. Out of his original 150 machine guns and mortars, he was down to fewer than a hundred, thinly strung out over two miles.

Jackson's officers prodded the stunned and exhausted with pistols.

"Fall in! Close ranks! Get in line!"

Meanwhile, *Janizary* cavalry picked up their pace and trotted toward them. The archers, still clutching stirrup leathers, broke into a run.

Jackson's milling men dug in.

Well, he thought, *it's a good day to die.*

He stood, ramrod-straight, on the rise and faced the *Janizaries.*

He did not like the terrain. The ground rose and fell in gentle swells. The enemy horsemen, still trotting toward his lines, ascended one rise only to vanish beneath the next. Jackson turned to his adjutant.

"Major Thompson, the Horde is still too far away to fire on. We have to hold off till they ascend the last slope. Our only chance is to pile their mounts."

"Yes sir." Thompson passed the word to his officers.

The *Ordu* bugle call drifted toward Jackson from three hundred yards away. At the sound their archers appeared above the crest of the far rise, bows lifted. At the next bugle call a bright red banner flew.

Jackson estimated there were six thousand archers behind that rise—two for every horseman. When the bugle call rang out a third time, the red banner fell. Their arrow volley rose in a cloud, soared to over two hundred feet, then arced. The arrows plummeted on Jackson's troops at a steep angle, wailing shrilly, striking with a deafening clatter.

Men were going down all around Jackson. A shaft thrummed in a mortar man's chest, and a sergeant took an arrow through the knee. Blood burst from the severed carotid artery of a machine gunner like water detonating from a hose.

The three-foot steel-tipped arrows protruded from

everything and everyone—from heads and torsos, arms and legs, feet and hands.

The sight of the victims unnerved even Jackson. He did not believe his men could stand a second assault.

He had to do something.

"Bring up the mortars," he shouted at Major Thompson. "Give those archers a taste of shellfire."

"Sir, the men say the mortars are too hot from blasting the 105s. The men can't carry them."

"Wrap them in blankets. Drag them with ropes. Just get them up here. Place them up behind our M-60s."

The *Janizary* cavalry was less than 150 yards from the bottom of that slope. Again, the bugle call rang out. The banners waved, and the bows were lifted.

The arrow cloud rose.

More men lay bleeding all around the General.

Now a dozen mortars were dragged atop the ridge, wrapped in charred blankets. It was hard to gauge distances amid the rise and fall of those ridges, but Jackson estimated 325 yards.

Damn, he hated to take pressure off those 105s.

"Bracket the archers at 325," he shouted to the Major.

Thompson passed the order down the line.

"Now sir," Thompson said to the General, "please stand down."

Jackson wasn't listening. He instead watched the *Ordu* horsemen, who stood back, waiting to launch the next arrow volley.

"The archers are bracketed, sir."

"Tell our mortar men to fire at will."

The signal went out. The shells hit, and the archers fell back.

"The archers are regrouping, sir. You can come down now. The men are asking you to. They won't break."

Jackson ignored his adjutant's request. "Let's keep those mortar tubes hot, Major. Lay a barrage on those horse soldiers."

The *Janizary* cavalry halted in the lee of the last steep rise.

"Ninety yards," Jackson estimated.

The Major shouted his orders.

His two mortar companies shelled the horse soldiers, giving the *Janizaries* only two choices. They could charge or retreat. They could not stay put.

Three thousand cavalry poured over the rise. They all knew what would follow—another arrow cloud.

Again, Major Thompson implored Jackson to come down from his ridge.

"Sir, you have to stand down. For the good of the men. None of us will make it if you're shot."

Jackson didn't move. "Tell the gunners to hold their fire till the cavalry hits the bottom of that slope. Then they should blister them. We have to pile those horses."

The horse soldiers were now less than seventy-five yards away, and the archers were reascending the rise. Their next arrow cloud rose above the ridge, arced sharply, and roared down on Jackson's men with angular precision.

"Down, General, down," the Major screamed.

An arrow struck Jackson just above the right bicep and spun him around, knocking him off the rise. He pulled himself to his feet and climbed back up the ridge.

"Their horsemen are at the bottom of the slope," Jackson shouted. "Major, fire at will."

The Major, mounted on a runaway horse, waved a saber. He charged up and down their lines, screaming:

"Fire at will! Fire at will!"

The enemy horsemen charged into their fire in drillbook fashion, at a swinging gallop. Fifty yards, forty, thirty-five.

Jackson drew his own 9 mm. He wasn't very good left-handed, but he took aim. Thirty, twenty-five, twenty. At fifteen his men started to break from the ridge.

Suddenly from the south he heard a strange eerie rumble. Out of the smoke and dust, coming in at under fifty feet was Amelia's Jenny.

Jackson's radio was exploding. Patton screamed at him: "Stand down, General! I'm ordering you to get off that ridge."

"Sir, I respectfully decline to—"

Major Thompson galloped up the ridgeline on his commandeered mount and, with the flat of his saber, knocked Jackson back down the slope.

The Jenny raked the *Janizaries* with her M-60.

◄■ 10

Watching the action through the Lockheed's viewing port, Patton shouted into the transmitter:

"Twelve o'clock high on the flank. Rake incoming cavalry."

"Roger, affirmative," Noonan answered.

Patton saw the Jenny bank hard. Circling the enemy's flank, the Jenny strafed the attacking horsemen

laterally, piling horse after horse after horse, most of
the falling riders still mounted.

"Great shooting, Noonan," Patton yelled. "That's
the way. We'll make a man of you yet."

Jackson had been on the ridge up to the last second, until Major Thompson knocked him down with
the flat of his saber.

*Good man, that Thompson. Remember him for a pro-
motion.*

Jackson was getting up now, the arrow still in his
arm. He was eating dirt, but Patton still called him on
the radio.

"Tom," Patton shouted, "keep up the pressure on
those 105s. Move the mortars back around. Bracket
those guns. Blister 'em."

"The mortar tubes are awfully hot, General."

"Fire them till they burst. Fire everything you've
got—throw spears, chuck rocks, pull hair, kick dirt.
Do something, anything. They are blowing our tanks
to Kingdom Come."

"Yes sir."

"Noonan, how is your ammunition holding up?"

"Three hundred rounds, sir."

"You're our last best hope. Do something."

"Okay if I shoot a few *Janizaries?*"

"I got nothing against dead people," Patton
shouted. "Some of my best friends are dead."

Patton glanced over Matthew's shoulder. They'd
lost another hundred feet according to the altimeter.
And they were now below one thousand feet. From
the way the engines shook there was no telling how
long they'd remain airborne.

Patton cursed their low-grade fuel. They'd lost so
much compression they were now only hitting on half

their cylinders, and with all that rotten combustion both engines were awash in hot gas and oil.

The Electra's spark knock was louder than the Horde's 105s.

That they were airborne at all Patton credited to Matthew. Amelia had said the boy was the best natural pilot she'd ever seen—a talent Patton now fully appreciated. The kid was bucking the headwinds, kicking rudder bars, punching the throttles, riding out the thermals—somehow keeping the engines alive.

Again, Patton raised his binoculars. His tank corps was in shambles. Most of the field was shrouded in dust and smoke. Half the soldiers were milling about helplessly, his remaining command cars were stuck or out of gas. Half the tanks were twisted wrecks—black smoke coiling high above their charred remains. Spread-eagled among the fire-blackened tanks were the bodies of at least a thousand men.

The 105s were reloading, the Horde regrouping for another charge.

"General," Matthew yelled to him, "we got more trouble coming from the mountain. Those guns look ready."

"Noonan, you lazy bastard, how many rounds have you got?"

"Two-fifty, sir."

Suddenly, the mountain guns erupted—all three dozen of them at once.

Meanwhile, the sky over their southern flank turned black with arrows, and the *Janizary* cavalry charged his tank corps—pistols blazing, jampot grenades flying under the tanks, shells bursting all around.

Patton's vision blurred. His head throbbed ferociously, and the Electra's engine shook and pounded like a road grader. He thought his brain would explode.

"Sir," Matthew said, "you have to do something."

Christ, he thought he would faint from the pain.

He returned to the radio.

"Amelia," he said, massaging his temples.

"Yes sir."

"You see those horsemen."

"Yes sir."

"They fooled us. They didn't wait for the guns and archers to do their work. They went straight in. You have to go after them. Can you do that, Amelia?"

"Roger, affirmative."

"Don't use up all your ammunition, Noonan. We'll need some later."

The mountain erupted again. Another three dozen supersonic shock waves jolted the Electra.

Matthew bucked the blasts and dropped two hundred feet.

"We're losing compression in the number one engine, sir."

"Losing it?" Patton shouted. "I didn't think we had any." Patton got Jackson on the horn. "Tom, I'm counting on you. The south flank is collapsing under that artillery fire. You have to put pressure on that mountain."

Patton looked out the belly port in time to see Jackson in the midst of another arrow cloud. He was hit a second time, same arm, this time in the shoulder. But he got back on his feet. He remounted the ridge and faced the Horde.

The Horde charged, but Jackson's men were now joining him on the rise. His nine remaining mortars scored hits on the 105s.

Along the southwestern flank Patton saw the Jenny buzz a *Janizary* charge—just as their bugler lifted his horn.

Patton instantly saw Amelia's error.

"Amelia," he yelled into the radio, "you're under fire."

It was too late. *Janizary* arrows blackened the southwest quadrant of the sky. The cloud arced, then descended on the plane.

As Sheckly free-climbed down the cliff face of Monte de Roca, he pondered Jackson's mortar assault on the 105s.

He had called in the bombardment on his radio.

"Seven o'clock and a hundred yards short," he shouted to Stonewall's mortar men. "Bring 'em home to me. They're fixed targets, sitting ducks. Keep it up. You'll find them."

With himself calling in the coordinates, Stonewall's mortar men bracketed the big guns with pinpoint accuracy.

But it was not enough. None of it was. The guns were encased in solid rock. Their crews hung in, pouring shellfire on Patton's tanks.

Sheckly was now approaching the shaft head of an old silver mine. Gazing into the shaft, he wondered if he could have made it through that old tunnel, found the vertical vent, located the old volcanic fault, and packed it with blasting gel. No way.

Then he saw it. The tin firebox full of matches and the paraffin candles—Liz's firebox. His daughter was in that shaft.

Oh God.

He roared into the mine shaft.

"LIZ! LIZ!"

Silence.

Oh no. God, no.

Belly-down, he crawled into the tunnel. Liz was in there, somewhere, somehow.

12

Jackson stood on the ridge scanning the air strike to the south with his telescope. He could not believe his eyes. Somehow the Jenny had survived the arrow cloud. Badly hit—torn up by scores of heavy shafts—she had managed to crash-land in a stream a mile or two beyond the airstrip.

Amelia was on the radio to him.

"Hang in there, Tom. Just hang in. I'll get that second Jenny up. You hear me? If I have to kick her tail east to west to crossways. We still have some blasting gel back at the hangar. I'll be back with bombs. You hang in."

Tom knew then God had sent him His sign.

He had let Amelia live.

Stonewall Jackson slowly returned to the top of his ridge.

13

Amelia stood by the hangar door. Glancing over her shoulder, she glared at the second Jenny. Noonan was struggling with its cracked

engine housing. After he finished, busted or not, she
would take it back up. She had no other choice.

Their first Jenny was gone.

*Guy wires snapping loose, fabric flapping, the old Jenny
had piled up in a waist-high stream two miles from the airstrip.*

*Amelia had cut Noonan out of his harness and dragged
him to shore. As the Jenny's wreckage floated downstream,
Amelia said:*

*"That's what the insurance companies call 'a complete
write-off.'"*

*She commandeered braying mules, which they'd ridden
back to the hangar.*

Outside the hangar door she saw another muzzle-
flash from the hidden battery on the second mountain, Monte de Espinas. The shell thundered out of its
bunker. Arcing over the *llano,* the round took a full
minute to complete its nine-and-a-half-mile trajectory. She could follow it every foot of the way.

The shell missed the main house by a quarter of a
mile and left a hole big enough to bury a grain eleva-
tor in. If they ever bracketed the main house, there'd
be hell to pay.

The hangar radio had three speakers and nine work-
ing channels. Amelia listened to Katherine's reports.
She piped them in from all over the front. It seemed to
Amelia that the whole war was wired for sound.

She heard Patton call her name. "Earhart, do you
read? Earhart, do you read? Over."

"Yes sir, I read."

"What's happening on Monte de Espinas?"

"They have a 155 up there. They're trying to
bracket the Citadel."

"We can see it from up here," Patton said. "Over."

"What do you think, George?" Katherine asked.

"It's a tough shot," Patton said. "They'll have to be good."

"What else is happening, Amelia?"

"I'm going to take the second Jenny up."

"What then?"

"I'll take some gelatin with me."

"George, does she know what she's doing?" Katherine yelled.

"Amelia," Patton shouted, "what *are* you doing? Over."

"I'm going to advance, attack, disrupt, improvise."

"With blasting gel?" he asked incredulously.

Amelia clicked off the set. She left the hangar and jogged to the munitions shed. She came out with a water bucket full of gel, caps, and a detonator. She hastily covered the pail with oily rags and headed for the hardstand.

Noonan had towed the Jenny onto the strip. He was wiping the dirty grease off his hands.

"The engine housing's still cracked. I wrapped some baling wire around it. You sure you want to take it up?"

"Let's do it."

When Noonan's back was turned, she slipped the bucket into the copilot's cockpit. She strung the detonator wires back to her own controls.

The engine turned over on the fourth spin. Amelia immediately caught a headwind and taxied up the runway.

"What the hell?" Noonan shouted.

He raced up the strip after her. The plane was slow on takeoff, and he caught her easily.

"Where are you going?" he shouted.

"After that 155," Amelia yelled back. "Gonna see a lady about some snakes."

"What do you have in my cockpit?"

"A new copilot," she shouted back. "The last one was a drunk. Let go of the fuselage."

"Come on. Cut it out. Let me up there." He took the rags out of the bucket and saw wires, a detonator, gelatin. "Hey, what is this? Some kind of nuclear war?"

Amelia clubbed him with her .45. Noonan dropped from the plane like a hammered steer.

She hit the headwind and fifty yards later was airborne.

14

Elizabeth didn't mind being cramped, dusty, and hot. She didn't even mind the anoxia, dehydration, and sheer exhaustion. But it was lonely in the mine shaft, and that got on her nerves.

She continued to sing.

> When your back's against the wall.
> When your towns and cities fall.
> Black powder and alcohol.
> Black powder and alcohol.

As she drew her breath for another verse, she heard from down the tunnel:

"What kind of song is that for a little girl?"

What was her father doing here? Was she insane? Dreaming? Dead? She decided it didn't matter which, so she went along with it.

"It's one of Noonan's, Dad."

"Sounds like something your grandma would sing. She always liked her songs bloodthirsty. By the way, what happened to you?"

"Had a mining accident. I hit one of the shoring timbers, and some of the hanging rock came down. There's no place to back up except the sump."

"Are you hurt?"

"No, just kind of stuck."

"Yeah, I'm finding it tight in here myself. Can you clear any rubble out on your side?"

"Nowhere to put it. It's really close in here. And dark."

"Dark here too. I didn't want to risk those matches—still too much gas and dust. And I don't have a flashlight."

"I lost mine in the methane sump."

"Well, sit tight. I'll start clearing out this rock, work in a few shoring timbers as I go."

Elizabeth could hear him clearing away the rock and jamming in the supports.

"Dad, did you ever hear Grandma laugh?"

"She used to. Before Grandpa died. Of course, she wasn't very good at it. But sure she laughed. Grandpa made her laugh."

"I wish I'd known Grampa Frank better."

"Grandma used to call him frivolous."

"Because he made her laugh?"

"Because he made her laugh."

"Could you make Grandma laugh?"

"Not anymore. In case you haven't noticed, your grandma and I don't get along."

"Do *we* get along?"

"Would I be in here otherwise?"

"Oh my God, I just realized. Dad, do you have your luminous watch on?"

"Sure do. The time is 1442 hours."

"Dad, you have to get out of here. Really. Don't worry about me. You're leaving *now*."

"Why would I want to do a thing like that?"

He continued to dig rock and shove in shoring timber.

"Because I made it to the fault and loaded it with blasting gel. I capped it off and set a timer to it. It's due to go off any second now."

"Not till I clear this rock out."

"Please, go. I'm definitely dead. You're almost definitely dead."

"Too much rock to dig."

"I'm begging you. Go. I want to stay here."

"Why would anyone want to stick around here?"

"I don't know." The anoxia was severe now. Rapture of the deep. The methane didn't help either. "Maybe I want to be like Darrell and Rachael. Die like a Magruder. With my boots on."

"'Black powder and alcohol?/ When your towns and cities fall'?"

Elizabeth smiled. "Noonan sure likes weird songs, doesn't he?"

Suddenly, the rock was out, and the last shoring timber in. Sheckly reached into the darkness. She grasped his hand.

"I got you, Dad."

"I got you, kitten."

"Dad, I'm not a kitten. Don't call me that."

"I got you, killer."

"That's better."

She tried to crawl, but couldn't move.

"Nothing's happening."

"Are you pinned?"

"I don't think so."

"It's lack of oxygen. I'll get you under the armpits and give you a tow. Good thing you don't weigh much."

"Dad, you don't have time. I tell you this mountain is going to blow."

"Here we go. When I say breathe, you exhale, and I'll pull. Now *breathe*."

Elizabeth exhaled, and miraculously, her body began to move around the tunnel's bend.

"Dad, don't kick any timbers."

"I'll be careful."

"You knock down any hanging rock, I'll start singing again."

"We wouldn't want that."

Mine rats were scurrying around them, their red eyes glaring angrily.

"I sure don't like those rats, Dad."

"Well, it *is* their mine. We didn't ask them whether they wanted us here. Or if we should blow it up."

"Dad, are we going to make it."

"What do you think we're doing?"

"I mean I was all ready to die back there. It was like I was *prepared*. Do you understand that?"

"Maybe, but you're not going to die."

"What am I going to do?"

"Fly planes, marry bullfighters, write the Great American Novel, break hearts around the world."

"What's the Great American Novel?"

"Something people used to talk about. Your grandmother remembers."

"Are we going to see Grandma again?"

"She'll take a knotted plowline to us if we don't."

Elizabeth almost split her sides laughing.

"Don't laugh so hard," her father said. "I can't get you out when you laugh."

"The thought of Grandma taking a knotted plow-line to *anyone!* Did she ever do that?"

"She never touched any of us. Neither did Grandpa. They didn't even own a knotted plowline."

"She sure talks about it enough."

"Yes, she does."

"Why's she so mad all the time?"

"She made a mistake once. She never got over it."

"Wow, it must have been a whopper."

"She sure doesn't like to talk about it."

"What it was?"

"Don't ask."

"Why not?"

"She wouldn't want you to know."

"Dad, we're going to die here. It's not like it matters anymore."

"What difference does that make?"

Elizabeth thought over the question.

"Dad, if I did something bad, would you promise not to tell anyone? If I didn't want you to?"

"You wouldn't need my promise."

"Why?"

"When you love someone, you don't tell."

Elizabeth considered his statement.

"You never said that before, Dad."

"Said what?"

"That you loved me."

"Magruders aren't very good at that sort of thing, are they?"

"Grandma doesn't even know how to say 'Thanks.'"

"Never complain and never explain. That's her motto."

Suddenly, sunlight was streaming over her father's

head and shoulders. He was backing them out of the tunnel.

"What do we do now?" she asked.

They were both blind as moles in the sunshine.

"When we get our eyesight back, we go up. There's a ledge about thirty feet up with an old piton hammered in under it. We'll tie up there. If you're right, and this mountain starts to blow, it might block some deadfall."

"Shouldn't we try to get down first."

"That's a three-hour climb back down. If the mountain blows, we'll never make it."

He took off his belt and tied her limp wrists together.

"What's that for?"

"You can't climb. I'm hauling you up."

He threw her tied hands around his neck, then slung her over his back.

"Can you haul me that far?"

"What's that Matt calls you?"

"A baby dwarf."

"I can haul a baby dwarf thirty feet."

He worked his way off the tunnel ledge and started up the cliff face.

"Dad, back there in the tunnel, you didn't leave me."

"Did you think I would?"

"I—I didn't know."

"Well, I didn't."

She looked up. "Hey, that ledge isn't any thirty feet. It's more like two hundred and thirty."

"We'll make it."

"You sure we have to go up there?"

"With forty pounds of blasting gel in that fault line? The deadfall's going to rain on us like hail."

He was climbing hand over hand now. His hands were bleeding.

"Can you make it?" she asked.

"I've got motivation."

Hanging from her father's wide shoulders, breathing clean air, feeling the sun and the wind, seeing the sky, she was suddenly sleepy. She shut her eyes.

"See that ledge?" her father finally said, waking her up. "We're almost under it. There."

He swung her around so she was between himself and the cliff. He clipped her harness to the saw-toothed steel piton under the ledge. Her wrists were still tied around his neck.

She was safe.

"You didn't leave me, Dad. In the mountain. You went in after me."

"Try to rest."

"Hold me, Dad."

"I've got you. You're not going to fall."

"I love you, Dad."

"I love you."

"See, you said it. It wasn't so hard."

"I guess not."

"I love you. I love you. I love you. See it's not hard at all. You came back for me, and I love you."

"I love you too."

She shut her eyes and went back to sleep.

Arms outstretched, he spread himself over his daughter and the face of the cliff.

15

Jackson stood on the ridge.
The slope before him was littered for two miles

with the piled-up carcasses of men and horses, many of whom were already being ripped apart by vultures.

The General's bloody arm was discolored, distended, and—given the Horde's affinity for filth—undoubtedly gangrenous.

Luckily, there had been no further assaults from the far ridge. His men were out of water, out of bullets, and whipped to the bone. Their next engagement would be the last.

Well, at least he wouldn't have to face another amputation.

The *Janizary* archers and horsemen were inching their way up the rise. He heard the first stirring notes of the bugle, saw the red banner go up and the bows lift. At the second bugle call, the bows bent.

The enemy horses were now starting to stamp and snort.

He waited for the sky to blacken with the arrow cloud, for the awful harmonic hum and then the rain of death.

Instead he heard a rumble behind him. It started as a soft *boomboomboomboomboomboomboomboom!* followed by a protracted thunder roll, succeeded by a whole series of *ka-whummmp! ka-whummmp! ka-whummp-whummmp-whummmps!* culminating in a truly earth-shaking roar. Then the air stank of brimstone.

Jackson tried hard not to take his eyes off the enemy. He believed implicitly in facing the foe and never yielding an inch. However, when the Horde lowered its bows, and their horses began to buck off their riders, he had to turn around.

Monte de Roca was coming apart at the seams.

16

When it came to watching fireworks, Patton had the better view. From his plane he could see it all: Monte de Roca, with blood in her bowels and fire in her mouth, was screaming in her death-agony.

Hundreds of tunnel entrances were blowing wide-open, spewing bright tongues of flame and long serpentine cables of black smoke. The winds sweeping through the mountain's innards—a series of superheated, fire-breathing storms, fueled by rock-dust, seams of oily shale and the bottomless sump of methane—were now reaching cyclonic proportions. Patton doubted that the firestorm would ever go out.

He had never seen anything like it. The mountain was no longer simply in flames, she was howling.

Suddenly Electra began to lurch and shake. Their starboard engine burst into flames, windmilling helplessly.

"Sir," Matthew yelled to him, "I think we're going down."

"We'll go down when I tell you we're going down."

Then the second engine flamed, its exploding propeller shaft shattering the wing.

"Hold on tight," Patton yelled. "We're going down."

17

Not everyone, however, was obsessed with the mountain. Harry the Triceratops had other things to do. For four hours he had been hunting the Winged Demon, chasing its rumbling growl and cruciform shadow from one end of the *llano* to the other.

His mother was still riding the top of his neck-frill. She beat him with her massive pinions, not only cooling him off but fanning away the noxious smells.

Harry needed that breeze. He was facing some weird creatures—fire-breathing steeds that emitted awful fumes as well as all those four-legged and two-legged animals. As he pounded through the smoke and dust, blackened and fire-scorched, many of them pointed at Harry and screamed:

"Beelzebub! He's here! He's here to judge us all! Hell has opened up! Beelzebub has come!"

Their screams did nothing to improve his mother's disposition. Her cries were ear-cracking.

Then Harry saw Amelia—overhead, off to his left—on the back of the Demon.

He veered left to head the Demon off.

More creatures pointed at him, screamed, and raced away.

Ignoring them, Harry continued his pursuit of the Fiend.

For the first time in his career, Stonewall was baffled. The *Ordu* guns had blown up. The enemy was retreating from the field, and he couldn't figure out why. He couldn't even give chase. They were running too fast.

Finally Major Thompson came up to him with a captured enemy soldier and the man explained:

"Beelzebub," the man gasped, "with horns and beak and flapping wings. He's come to scourge us all. Hell is boiling over. Beelzebub will rule."

"Beelzebub?" Major Thompson was confused.

Suddenly, it was all clear. Jackson took the Major aside, put his finger to his lips, and whispered one word: "Harry."

◀── 19

When Patton came to, the first thing he saw was the Electra's nose pancaked into a ridge. The broken windshield—smashed hard against the rise—revealed little else. One mangled prickly pear, a pulverized yucca, a lot of red dirt and shattered rock, and two twisted propeller shafts. The port wing had sheared off.

The Magruder boy was coming to. Thank God. The old woman already held Patton responsible for Elizabeth's running off. If Matthew had bought the farm, there would have been real hell to pay.

He checked his own strapped-down body. He felt the usual postcrash stiffness and the standard pains. Otherwise he seemed to be in one piece. No skull fractures this time. He didn't think he could take another one. Even when he was healthy, his head bothered him now.

Pulling out his belt knife, Patton cut his safety harness.

"How you feeling, sir?" Matthew asked him.

"Like my head was run through a hammer mill. What I don't understand is why we didn't catch fire."

"Wasn't enough fuel. We were running on vapor."

Patton peered out a smashed porthole. Through a spiderweb of broken glass, he saw a squad of horse soldiers clearing the far rise. He recognized Jackson.

The radio crackled.

"You mean that thing's still working?" Patton asked, amazed.

"It's a good radio, sir. It was built for finding ships lost at sea."

Patton put on the earphones.

"Patton, here. How is the Citadel holding up? Over."

"The Citadel is going to hell, George."

"The Horde is in full rout, Kathy Jane. What's the problem? Over."

"That 155 on the hill has us bracketed. Another five rounds and there won't be anything left of this place."

"Tom and I will mount a force."

There was more crackling static. By the time Matt tuned the old woman back in, she was shouting. "There isn't time, George. I tell you the Citadel is falling."

"We'll get that gun."

"Forget the gun. We need you here. Now. Both of you—and every man you can muster."

"I don't understand."

More static.

"Tamerlane is in the cornfield," she said. "He's flanked us and breached our southern perimeter."

"It's wired and mined. We have machine guns there."

"He's got Mexican conscripts clearing those mines—thousands of them—and all we have to man those guns are small children and old men."

"Mrs. Magruder?" It was Fred Noonan on the hangar radio. "Amelia's got the second Jenny up."

"And you're not with her?" Patton said.

"She laid me out with a .45, General, after I turned over the prop."

"What's she doing?" Katherine asked.

"She has a bucket full of blasting gel and a detonator. She's going after that 155. She thinks Legion's up there."

"George?" the old woman shouted.

"Yes."

"Get back here as fast as possible. I'll raise Amelia on the radio and try to talk her down."

"Do you want me to—"

"Just get back here," she shouted. "They're in the corn. Do I have to do *all* your thinking for you? Tamerlane's sacking the Citadel."

"We're on our way. Over and out."

"Over and out."

Patton and Matthew climbed down out of the wrecked Electra. Major Thompson had horses ready for them.

20

Amelia's plane was in bad shape. Noonan had tried to secure the engine's cracked housing with baling wire, but the propeller shaft still slipped and the motor wobbled on its mount.

Amelia doubted she would stay airborne another ten minutes.

In the distance the big 155 boomed, and she heard the whistling shell. Its eerie vibration rose in volume till it screamed overhead and rocketed away, leaving her to buck the shock waves.

Still Amelia felt good. The Citadel had beaten their nemesis, and now she was going to whip hers—Legion.

She knew Legion would be there. She would personally supervise the 155. That big gun was Legion's *raison d'être*—the thing she had been born for—her chance to destroy the Citadel.

The radio was crackling. Katherine had located her frequency.

"What is it?" Amelia said.

"Turn that crate around," the old woman ordered. "We need you at the Citadel."

"Couldn't do it if I wanted to. You hear that engine banging? That's gen-u-wine structural damage. The rubber band's about to snap. I got no way home."

"I said put it down."

"And I said no-can-do."

Katherine lost the frequency, and the radio went dead.

Amelia was pleased to have the solitude. Up there alone—bucking the thermals, Monte de Espinas in the distance—she finally know what she was doing. She had been heading toward this moment all her life. Even when she had escaped the Horde—lashed to Stonewall's saddle—she had been pointed this way, toward this landing.

Well, old girl, it's time to set this crate down.

She banked toward the mountain, fighting a headwind. The Jenny's acceleration was maddeningly slow, and the sun was angling into her eyes, diffracted by the spinning prop.

The sun ought to be at your back, she thought.

Too late for that.

Steady on, old girl.

Amelia trimmed for her descent—the big gun dead ahead—when the radio crackled again.

"What *are* you doing?" Katherine screamed.

"I'm headed for glory, old lady."

"You've got a job here."

"Never happen. The wheels came off."

"Tamerlane's in the cornfield."

"The cornfield's eleven miles from here, and I'm leaking like a sieve—down to my last buck's worth of gas. You should hear this engine knocking. Sounds like a drop forge."

"Why are you doing this?"

"Got a meeting with an old friend of mine. You've heard of her. Legion."

"That's insane."

"Probably. My father always told me to look for something sensible—nursing, stenography, cost accounting. But you know me—my warrior soul."

Noonan was back on. "Amelia, come down. *Please.*"

"No way, Freddy. I'm back to my old trade. What did Patton call me? Troubler of the Peace?"

"And I'm telling you it's over," the old woman said. "We can't stop them."

"Maybe not, but I can stop that 155 from hurting the Citadel."

"It'll hurt you a lot worse."

"I'm living in a whole world of hurt, Kathy Jane. It just doesn't matter anymore."

"Yes, we all hurt, Amelia. But now it's over. The important thing is that we did our best, and we're still alive."

"That's right, old lady. I'm still alive, and I'm free, and I'm not afraid. You taught me that. You hear me, Kathy Jane. You taught me that."

"I lost Rachael, Darrell, Frank. Now Elizabeth. I even lost Harry and that idiotic bird. I'm not losing you!"

"It's too late."

"Please, don't. Please."

"Just watch my smoke. I'm taking out that gun. I got Legion in my sights."

"They'll blow you to bits."

Amelia's laughter was wild and carefree. "Who dares to shoot the girl who rides the tiger?"

She clicked off her radio and descended for her first tentative pass, gauging the thermals, checking for headwinds.

She had to do this one right.

21

A fourteen-year-old boy, in a khaki scouting uniform, stood on a ridge overlooking the Citadel's southern flank. An Eagle Scout, he'd earned the rank of Captain in the Youth Militia. Below him was a deep gorge—filled with grain, boobytraps, and coiled barbwire—and beyond that was a hundred acres of corn, likewise wired and mined.

The boy studied the endless expanse of what had once been chest-high corn. It was no longer chest-high, but cropped short by Citadel machine guns and red with Mexican blood.

Still the Mexican conscripts pressed on—wave after wave—peons in white homespun cotton, wielding machetes and ancient muzzle-loading rifles. Nothing stopped their advance. There were too many of them.

The first wave of conscripts tore out of the cornfield and descended, screaming, into the canyon. Captain Davies shouted to his Lieutenant:

"Bring up the machine gunners. We'll stop them in the gorge."

Then he heard it—a shrilling bugle, an eerie whistling scream followed by a strange harmonic hum and the sky overhead turned black. Next came an ear-shattering clatter.

When he pulled himself to his feet, his Lieutenant, a Life Scout, was impaled by four arrows.

He grabbed the officer's tripod M-60 and dragged it to the rim of the gorge. He screamed to his remaining platoon.

"Stop them at the gorge!"

The Captain's company of old men and young boys pounded in their tripods and sighted their guns on the mass of men below.

The *Ordu* bugler repeated his shrill call, and the sky, once again, blackened with arrows.

Captain Davies prayed that his men would not break.

◄■ 22

Tamerlane stood on a high hill, knee-deep in bloody corn. Before him lay a sloping arroyo and beyond that the Citadel. Through his binoculars he studied the slaughter in the gorge.

A batallion of his best *Janizary* enforcers were driving two thousand Mexicans into the canyon with automatic rifles. The slopes were wired and mined. The rate of conscript attrition was staggering, but the Mexicans still kept charging.

There was nothing else they could do.

The Citadel was now on the verge of collapse. Tamerlane could see that now. They were reduced to small boys and old men. For weapons they had broken-down carbines, ancient breechloaders, lever-action .30–.30s, and an occasional machine gun.

Time was on Tamerlane's side.

Still it had not been easy. Conscripting this peon army had been a living nightmare. He'd had to scourge the Mexican countryside, shanghaiing those he wanted. Most had entered his Horde semiconscious, shackled, and chained.

The journey north had been hard. Before they started back, a scout described the terrain as "mighty sudden country." Tamerlane assumed that the man referred to the suddenness with which men died and vultures circled.

Now, however, Tamerlane was convinced that the suddenness had also referred to the land itself. Every time he turned his head, it seemed he was in a totally different world. You could be crossing a desert, half-dead with heat and thirst, then just over a rise you would be confronted by an impassable mountain chain. Half a day's ride, and you would be lost in logging-style forests of ponderosa pine, salt cedar, and live oak. Then you descended from the mountains into chasms thousands of feet deep, and once more found yourself in scorching desert country.

Thousands of Mexicans had died during that march, and though he tortured his scouts, none knew a better route.

The old woman had chosen her battleground well.

Tamerlane turned to his adjutant, Major Rashid.

"Tell our enforcement battalions to elevate their line of fire. Time to drive those small boys and old men off that ridge. When the last of the peons emerge from the gorge, we go in."

23

Harry charged through the drifting smoke. His arrow-riddled hide was blackened by gunfire and drenched in blood, but he held his horns high, and his red eyes blazed.

The Fiend was, again, in sight—diving toward the great fiery tree on the mountain—and Harry hoped to cut him off and kill him.

It looked like a tough job. His final charge would be uphill, and at the summit stood a woman in black, swathed with snakes, who defended the blazing tree with a fire-stick.

He gave it everything he had, but her bullets hit like sledgehammers. They slammed him back on his hind legs, blowing off the top of his frill, catapulting Betsy Ross high into the air.

To Harry's surprise, however, instead of tumbling head over talons back to earth, she caught a thermal updraft. Flapping her wings three times, she then soared high above the hill.

Funny, Harry never knew his mother could fly.

The bullets stopped, while the woman in black fed a long snakelike vine into the fire-stick.

With a trumpeting roar, Harry renewed his charge.

24

For two hours she had seen and heard men fleeing the field, screaming:

"Beelzebub! Beelzebub!"

That the winged demon—her Father-in-Darkness—had taken the field she could not accept. The soldiers' panic was clearly due to some mass hallucination.

Then Legion saw him thundering straight at her—with wings, horns, and fire-blackened hide. Standing her ground, she quickly shoved a fresh cartridge belt into her tripod machine gun. The big Kalishnikov hammered in her fists, rocking the beast back on his haunches, ripping the massive wings off his neck-frill, which, to her amazement, caught a mountain thermal and flapped, screaming, into the sky.

Suddenly, she recognized the wing-flapping thing, circling overhead. Those were not *shaitan* wings. This was no devil. It was— It was—

An eagle.

The beast before her wasn't Beelzebub. He was a fake fiend, a stupid brute. Streaming blood, shot full of arrows, he was, in fact, already at death's door. Her men had been deceived.

Unfortunately, their panic was now irreversible. Even her gunnery captain was crying: "Beelzebub! He's come! He's come!" As for the rest of the Horde, they still fled the field, unchecked.

And now there was a second adversary. An old biplane, banking out of the east, angled toward her, bent on mischief.

Forsythe shouted at her: "Get the plane. Get the plane."

All the while, her gunnery captain continued to cry: "Beelzebub! Beelzebub! Save us!"

They were all cracking up, deserting her, and she hated them for it. Even Forsythe was screaming:

"Let's get out! Let's run for it!"

When they could take it no more, when Forsythe and her gun crew finally did run for it, she turned the Kalishnikov on them with real pleasure.

God only knew what she would do next. She could operate the big gun herself, but only after she'd eliminated the two attackers.

The plane was going to hit first. She studied the angle of its descent, estimating both trajectory and speed.

Then she locked eyes with the pilot. She should have guessed. Amelia.

Without hesitation, Legion lifted the Kalishnikov out of its bunker, tripod and all. She sighted in on the old Jenny and squeezed off the first burst.

◀━━━ 25

Patton split from Jackson's force just north of the Citadel, taking two men with him. He cut through the base camp toward the old stronghold.

They reached the Citadel's forward breastworks. Two hundred zigzagging trenches—eight feet deep and six across—protected the north wall. Their former defenders—a ragged army of old men and small boys—were gone, making their last stand in the Citadel's southern cornfield.

Patton approached the old fort over a succession of

makeshift trench bridges. Built of heavy adobe blocks, the north wall, looming high above them, was gessoed a scintillating alabaster.

Instead of a gate, the wall was breached by an underground tunnel barricaded at both ends by thick steel doors. Two ancient sentries opened the tunnel gates, and they rode through.

Inside sprawled a curving courtyard five hundred feet across and lined with cottonwood and piñon. It was presently empty.

Patton led his two men up to the main house. He swung down off his mount and tied it to the hitchrack. He gave the hacienda a long careful look.

Had the Horde breached the big house? He could not tell.

The Citadel was eight stories high, constructed of white adobe with a heavy red tile roof. In the front of it was a great white porch with matching columns and swings.

Patton and his men went up the front steps. He motioned them to each side of the door. Ignoring their protests, he was the first one in.

The front door opened into the grand hall, a vast room filled with white gessoed walls, two cut-glass chandeliers, dark ceiling beams, and teak floors.

He quickly crossed the room, stationing himself beside the entranceway to the sitting room. He motioned his men behind him, pivoted around the corner with his M-16 at his shoulder and on full-auto. But there were no enemy inside.

A dozen narrow, straight-backed chairs were scattered around the room. Carved oak, they were upholstered with dark leather. Next to the chairs were delicately carved mahogany tables.

The drawers were not pulled out and emptied. The old woman's silver crucifixes hung, unmolested, on the walls.

There were no bullet holes in the ceiling or blood on the floor.

The Horde had not been here.

Patton crossed the *sala* to a big dining hall where the council met and where the Magruder clan and friends met for family celebrations. The teak dining table, at the moment, was strewn with books and maps.

Nothing had been disturbed.

Still . . . ?

Lieutenant Rowdy gestured that he was going in. He motioned for Sergeant Harris to follow. Patton hesitated. Something was wrong. There was a balcony, just off the east wing, Patton remembered it now. The perfect place for—

An AK-47 stitched Rowdy vertically from his eyes to his crotch. Two more clips took out Harris—four rounds in his face alone.

Patton wheeled around the doorway and sprayed the balcony with his M-16. The railing broke. One *Janizary* crashed on the floor. Another wrecked a coffee table. The third smashed an antique Castilian couch.

Except for the drifting smoke and the ringing in Patton's ears, there was nothing. No screams or gunfire or grenades. No *Janizaries* raced from the far end of the house to finish the job. The whole house seemed, once again, empty. He'd nailed their advance scouts.

Patton crossed the smoky *sala* and glanced down the long hallway. The radio room was the third door on the right.

The front and back entrances to the radio shack—having been set up as the Citadel's control-and-command—were barricaded with steel doors and crossbars. He prayed there were no enemy inside and knocked.

He heard a boy's voice from behind the peephole. "General, that you?"

"It's me."

The boy opened the door, then slammed it behind Patton replacing the crossbar. The command Post was unbreached.

Patton surveyed the room. Two big tables were covered with radio equipment. Katherine Magruder—wearing denim work clothes, a headset, and a .45 in her shoulder holster—operated the transmitter.

Her assistant was a fifteen-year-old niece, who tirelessly turned a hand-cranking generator. Nobody looked up.

"Take a seat, George," the old woman said, "and keep out of the way."

One of her other assistants, a freckle-faced boy of twelve named Joel, said: "We're not having much luck, General. We can't reach the command cars."

"They were knocked out," Patton said.

He did not bother telling Joel there was nothing left to command.

The front door shuddered.

"What was that?" Joel asked.

"A battering ram," said Patton.

"That's a good door," Katherine said. "I designed it myself."

After ten more thuds the battering stopped.

The silence was oppressive.

It was followed by a strange burning smell.

"Fuse smoke!" Patton yelled. "Get down!"

He motioned to her niece to get Katherine onto the floor, then he hit the deck himself. With one hand shielding his eyes, he set his M-16 to *semi*, intending to make every shot count.

For another instant the room was perfectly still, then the black-powder charge blew the door to splinters.

Janizaries rushed the room, but Patton had them in his sights. He shot five of them dead before the rest backed off.

Then they threw in a jampot grenade, which Joel lobbed back.

If it hadn't been for the sulfurous stink of the black-powder smoke, Patton might have enjoyed himself.

Finally, a white flag fluttered though the smoky hole. Behind it was a fourteen-year-old boy.

"What is it, son?" Patton yelled to him.

"There's a man here. He wants to talk to you and Aunt Katherine."

"That's my great-nephew, Harold Davies," the old woman said. "Let him in."

"We held them as long as we could, General," Harold said. "We fought them all the way. There— There— There were just too many of them."

His voice broke. He dropped the white flag and ran to the old woman. She folded him in her arms.

Behind him, through the smoke and flames, walked a solitary soldier.

"He's the one who sent me in," Harold said, pointing at him.

Patton was on his feet. The two men stared at each other. No one had to tell Patton who this one was.

Ignoring Patton, Tamerlane stared at Katherine Magruder.

"The old whore?" he said in plain English.

She spit at him.

Tamerlane looked at Patton. It seemed to Patton that he had the deadest, flattest eyes he'd ever seen.

In fact, he was about to say just that when Tamerlane shot him in the head.

26

The mountain thermals slammed the Jenny up and down, and the setting sun glared in Amelia's eyes. Still she managed to chop her throttles. Easing the stick forward, she braced it with her knees—no small feat with all the pitching and yawing.

She was not apprehensive. Patton had said he'd felt the hand of God in this. Amelia felt it too. She was Destiny's Child. The destruction of Legion and that big gun had always been her appointed end. As the sunlight flared in her eyes between the propeller blades, she knew she would do it.

She had known it before she'd soloed the Atlantic, before she'd ever seen her first plane, before she was hurtled through Time. This was *her* moment—the supreme expression of her being, the high tide of her life, the moment she had been born for.

She was not in time but *of* Time.

Between the guy wires and the whirling blades she could now see Legion's face. *I got your name, girl. I got your number. You hear me? I own you.*

The muzzle of Legion's machine gun lifted, but the Lady in Black was too late. Even as Amelia stared into

the Kalishnikov's flaming muzzle and felt the rounds
scream past—the first burst wide, the second low—
Amelia knew that Legion had run out of time.

*But I haven't. I've got all the time in the world. I own
time. I am Time.*

She came in low—closer, closer, closer. The wind
shrieked through the struts, and the 155's muzzle
looked like Hell itself.

It was only during her last seconds that she felt a
small shudder of fear.

"'Thou shalt not be afraid for the terror by night nor
the arrow that flieth by day,'" she prayed, half-aloud.

She reached for the detonating wires.

27

Stonewall Jackson rode
through corn that was flattened by guns and drenched
in blood. Surrounded by the echoing cries of the dying,
his own arm was hugely swollen, its stench gangrenous.

This was as bad as the General had ever seen it,
and that was going some. Jackson had spent a lifetime—two lifetimes, in fact—learning the cruel art of
killing, but now he felt he'd learned nothing. If he
had, it wouldn't have ended like *this*.

Nor was it the first time he'd seen bloody corn.
He'd seen it at Antietam.

*This field, in some ways, was not all that different from
Antietam—barbwire aprons instead of split rail fences,
machine guns instead of muskets—but the crop was just as
bloody, and the corpses just as dead.*

The soldiers were different. He'd never seen them this

young or old. Boys strung on the wire, shot down in their youth. Old men killed in their dotage.

It was not supposed to be this way. Jackson had always conceived of the Universe as a smoothly running clock with God as the Divine Watchmaker. In such a Universe there were rules. God had a Plan, the Plan was sacrosanct.

But no more.

Now the mainspring had shattered and the hands snapped.

And who was the Watchmaker? What was Time? Jackson no longer knew.

Too late for such thoughts now. It was taking all of his strength and concentration to stay upright on his horse.

He was not sure he had the will to ride through the south gate, let alone reach the Citadel.

28

When Amelia came to, she was, upside down, staring at Richard and Elizabeth Sheckly. Her head throbbed, and she couldn't see them all that clearly. Her right cheek bled into her eyes, and the crankcase oil, once more, splattered her smashed goggles.

Richard had her by the shoulders, while Elizabeth sawed at the leather harness with her jackknife.

Then Amelia remembered the eagle. The Jenny had been on the final leg of its descent. She had pushed the stick forward with her knees, preparing to cross the wires, when out of nowhere Betsy Ross rocketed straight at the plane's nose.

Without thinking, Amelia dropped the wires, kicked the right rudder bar, and yanked the stick back.

The Jenny promptly crashed.

Elizabeth finished sawing through the harness, and Richard eased Amelia out of the cockpit. The ringing in her ears was now a dull roar.

"What happened to the battle?" Amelia asked.

"I'm not sure," Richard said. "We met Private Mann here by the plane. He says Harry and Betsy Ross took off across the field, apparently after you, Amelia. The Horde seemed to think Harry was some ancient fiend. He scared them off."

The Private rode up to them, leading two extra mounts.

"They called him Beelzebub," Mann said.

"There's renewed fighting at the Citadel," Richard said. "Patton and Jackson returned to join my mother. Let's get going."

Mann rode off to rope a third mount. It wasn't hard. Thousands of *Ordu* war ponies were rein-standing across the *llano*.

Suddenly out of the smoke and dust, Harry appeared. His hide was smoke-blackened and drenched in blood. Scores of arrows dangled from his tough hide. His nose-horn was broken off, and he was riddled with bullets.

"I'm staying here," Amelia said.

"You and Elizabeth should both stay," Sheckly agreed.

"Why me?" Elizabeth asked.

"Harry needs you."

"But—"

"Liz," he said, "you did your share on the mountain."

Amelia was already limping toward the bloody dinosaur.

Elizabeth followed her, grudgingly.

29

Jackson, less than forty yards from the Citadel's back porch, found himself surrounded by nearly a thousand *Janizaries* and Mexicans. They were all armed, but not one of them made a hostile move.

The Citadel's few survivors were stumbling around like zombies. They seemed to understand the situation no better than Jackson.

He had no time for them anyway. Drugged by fatigue, blood loss, and the crucifying agony in his gangrenous arm, it was all he could do to dismount and climb the back-porch steps. He had time to find the radio room—and Katherine Magruder.

One step, two, three—the north face of the Eiger could not have been harder. By the eighth step he was swaying badly. Major Thompson had him by his right shoulder.

"We're almost there, sir."

"What's happened to the fighting, Major?" Jackson asked.

"There seems to be a truce."

"What?"

"It's just a guess, sir. I really don't know. None of us speak their language."

Then they were at the radio room, and Major Thompson pushed open the door. He and Jackson entered cautiously.

The first thing Jackson noticed was the black-powder smoke. The windows had been sealed off because of the battle, and the air was almost unbreathable.

Then there was the black-robed soldier spread-eagled in the center of the room, his chest shot away.

Patton sat in a straight-backed chair, eyes glazed and unfocused, his head swathed in bandages. Katherine's great-nephew, a fourteen-year-old boy, stood behind him, tying on the last strips of cloth.

"General Patton's going to be okay, sir," the young boy said, without looking up. "The bullet just grazed him."

Katherine sat hunched over her staticky radio, twisting the dials and punching buttons.

"This radio never did work right," she snarled. "It's those vacuum tubes. If we had some transistors now, we wouldn't have these problems."

"What happened?" Jackson asked.

"We won, Tom, that's what happened," the old woman growled, her eyes still fixed on the dials. "Couldn't you figure that out? You *are* a general. Now if I could only get this blasted thing to work, I'd let everyone know."

"We won?" Jackson was delirious.

The story came rushing out of Harold while he dressed Patton's bloody head.

"Tamerlane came through that door and shot the General. But when he called Aunt Katherine this bad name—God, I'm never going to call her any names—you should have seen her."

"Slow down, son," Major Thompson said. "What happened?"

"Aunt Katherine had the General's .45—the one with the four stars and the white grips—out on the radio table. She had it all ready, sir, cocked, and—and—and—" The boy was stammering.

"Take your time, son," the Major repeated.

"Boy, I never want Aunt Katherine mad at me, sir. She wasn't kidding about those knotted plowlines. She just kept shooting him and shooting him and shooting him. Even after Tamerlane was down there on the floor, dead, she kept firing. She shot him eight times, sir, till the slide went back and the gun was empty. Then those other officers turned white as sheets and ran out of here."

"He was a foul-spoken man, Tom," the old woman said, still working her dials, "and I do not countenance profanity. You know that. Certainly *never* in the presence of children."

"But *eight times?*" Jackson said.

"That's all the gun held." Katherine shrugged. "If I'd had eighteen bullets, I would have used them."

"Why did they give up?" Major Thompson asked.

Patton slowly raised his bloodied head. "They thought he was immortal—some sort of a god. When Katherine proved they were wrong, she destroyed their cause. She—" Patton froze, staring at Jackson. "Tom, your arm—"

For the first time Katherine looked up from her radio.

"Tom. Oh, my God."

Just then the front door opened, and Richard Sheckly was there.

"Mom, Elizabeth and Amelia are all right. They're looking after Harry right now. He was still alive when I left, but shot to pieces. I want you to know— General Jackson. Oh, God—"

"Richard," the old woman said, "do something."

"But I don't know how to—"

"*DO SOMETHING!*" she screamed.

Richard Sheckly took a deep breath. "Major

Thompson," he said quickly, "get me some hot water."

"There's coffee brewing," Joel said. "The pot's been on that burner all day, sir."

"That'll do. I'll also need something sharp."

The Major handed him his bowie. "It has an edge, sir. I honed it myself."

"Joel, get that burner down here on the floor. Put Major Thompson's knife in the flame, and heat some more knives. Boil bandages in that coffee. Major Thompson, get some of your men in here. Mother, do we have—"

She handed him a bottle of brandy from her desk drawer.

"General, drink some of this," Richard said.

"Don't lecture us on temperance, Tom," Katherine said. "Just drink."

Jackson swallowed close to a pint.

Sheckly drenched one of the boiling rags with the brandy.

Major Thompson placed soldiers on each of the General's limbs. He personally took his head.

Harold was honing and heating more knives.

He prised a lead slug out of a .45 shell and placed it in the General's mouth.

"Bite on this, sir."

He stripped off the General's shirt and moved the tourniquet up under his arm to his armpit. He drenched the shoulder with brandy. Jackson stared fixedly at the ceiling.

Sheckly glanced up at Harold. "Better heat some more knives, son."

He removed the Randall bowie from the flame and began to cut.

30

High on a distant hill a woman lay by a pool of bloody water. Her body was crisscrossed with slashes, and her left arm was permanently crippled. Her face was horribly lacerated.

She could still remember the eagle—plunging and screaming, flogging her with its wings. The screams had pumped out of her, over and over, till her lips streamed vomit and blood. But the beast continued to swoop, shredding her, ripping out an eye, pursuing her high into the hills.

The woman gazed into the bloody pool. She had lost everything—her empire, her army, and her Lord—but she did not despair. She was not broken. Tamerlane might be captured or killed, their armies scattered, but she would find others. She could no longer entice them with her ravishing beauty—the eagle had taken that from her forever—but she would find a way. She still had her hate, and for Legion that was enough.

She would find other causes, other leaders, other wars. She did not care how long it took—if it took a lifetime, a thousand lifetimes.

If it took forever.

She stared again into the pool. The water was crimson with her blood, and her red reflection frightened even her. Still, she recognized in her raw, gaping socket a certain power. She would hold men with that blind slashed eye, while she harangued and prophesied—and rallied them to her Cause.

On this Golgotha, this hill of skulls, her hate would take root. Her song of death would never cease—not while flower bloomed or wind blew free.

The Citadel would pay. God, how they would pay. You could count on it. The woman in black was nothing if not persistent.

Legion would be back.

PART XXIV

Violence shall no more be heard in thy land, wasting nor
destruction within thy borders . . . The sun shall be no
more thy light by day; neither for brightness shall the moon
give light unto thee: but the LORD shall be unto thee an
everlasting light, and thy God thy glory.

—ISAIAH 60:18–19

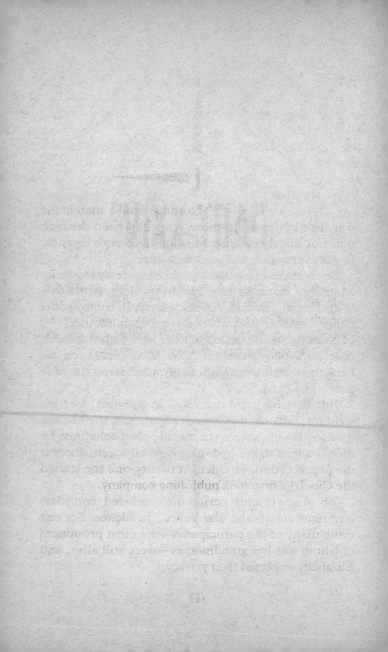

Nothing could match the war. For better or ill, those years had been the high point of Elizabeth's life. She had lived with legends, flown with eagles, and mastered Time.

She was the one who had single-handedly blown up Monte de Roca, and she had been there, with *them*. With Patton, Jackson, Amelia, Harry, Betsy Ross, her father, brothers, and, of course, her grandmother.

Nobody was interested in what Elizabeth was doing now. Everybody wanted to know what it had been like back then. Some people actually considered the little girl "a has-been."

But Elizabeth did not dwell in the past. Her life went on. Following in Darrell's footsteps, she became a writer. By age sixteen she was the chief columnist for the Citadel's major newspaper. At eighteen, she was the paper's editor-in-chief. At twenty-one she started the Citadel's first book publishing company.

Throughout this period she endured countless questions about "the War Years." In silence. For one thing many of the participants—the most prominent of whom was her grandmother—were still alive, and Elizabeth respected their privacy.

She did, however, keep a journal in which she chronicled the war and its aftermath. She researched the events she had not witnessed herself—took some liberties with thoughts and dialogue, action and descriptions—but on the whole her history was accurate.

Elizabeth never had any trouble detailing Stonewall's subsequent life. Her father's bowie knife surgery was a complete success. Afterward Stonewall was made Commandant of the Citadel's newly established military academy. During his tenure the academy prospered, and some later maintained that one of the General's greatest contributions to Citadel security was his ability to wring money out of its parsimonious council.

He taught the academy's course on tactics and strategy personally. He was a perfectionist, a strict disciplinarian. He believed cadets were there to study, to soldier, and not to be coddled. He was not always popular.

In his private life, however, he was loved. He courted and won Amelia, believing her to be the most courageous woman he had ever met. She was equally devoted to Tom. They had three children and thirteen grandchildren.

Not everyone was that fortunate. Elizabeth's father never adjusted to the peace, and he grew increasingly despondent.

Particularly when his father-through-choice lay dying. When he visited the old Apache on his deathbed—when he saw him pale, weak, emaciated, he started to cry. Spirit Owl was merciless.

"You do not cry for me," the old man said. "You cry for yourself."

Sheckly knew the old man was right.

"You believe it was my medicine, not yours, which opened the hole in time. That is not true. I merely gave you the faith to succeed. The medicine was yours—yours alone. It was you—who roped the thing the white-eyes call Time and broke him to your saddle and rode him like a horse—not I. You can do it now. You can do it tomorrow. You can do it for-all-tomorrows."

That night Spirit Owl died, and when Sheckly came down from the mountain, he knew what his vision-quest required of him. His medicine dream had been quite specific.

It was laid to his charge to break Time-To-His-Saddle-And-Ride-Him-Like-A-Horse, but he was frightened. Such a vision required a faith and power he was not sure he possessed.

But in the end, he had no choice. Patton made the decision for him. The General had a problem—a problem Sheckly was responsible for. Sheckly had brought Patton through the hole in time but had now taken away from him his reason for living.

The General no longer had his war.

Without war, Patton was nothing.

Eventually word of Patton's discontent reached the old woman. She called her son to her backyard and told him something had to be done for the General.

"After all," she said, "we brought him here."

Sheckly had been reviewing his theories and had arrived at some shattering conclusions. He spoke unflinchingly of infinitely dimensioned worlds, paralleling one another across the length and breadth of Time, worlds he could probe and explore.

"You mean there's one we could send Patton to?" his mother asked.

Sheckly told her about his conversation with Spirit Owl, but was frank about his doubts. He felt that he had no vision, that he lacked faith and power.

"Then show your kids how to turn those dials and knobs, whatever it was *you* did," his mother said. "I'll take Spirit Owl's place and do whatever is necessary. Somehow, I'm getting Patton back through that hole."

Sheckly briefed his kids on the equipment, showed them how to calculate coordinates, then prepared for his ordeal—self-purification, self-knowledge, self-sacrifice.

The fasting, sweat baths, and sun-dancing were crucifying, but finally Sheckly pinpointed what he thought was an appropriate world for Patton. FDR survived in this world, but the Manhattan Project had failed. Roosevelt was forced to take on Stalinist Russia, and without nuclear weapons. Since Patton had, in that world, been burned beyond recognition in an auto accident, Roosevelt lacked a general tough enough or smart enough to take on the Red Army.

"When the ambulance comes," Elizabeth explained to Patton, "they'll find you standing outside the burning wreck, with a case of temporary amnesia."

"If Dad can get you there," Matt said.

Sheckly gave it his best shot. He composed his own chants, prayers, and incantations. He slashed his arms, legs, and sides in the agonizing ritual of the Scarlet Blanket.

At dawn the sun's first rays ignited the sacred cliff face. The fire flared, forked, and exploded in blinding incandescence. The hole slowly opened.

They all knew the rest: George S. Patton was interred on a wet fog-bound morning on December 24, 1945 in the American Military Cemetery in

Hamm in Luxembourg. There, under the sod he joined 5,076 of his men.

In the driving rain thousands thronged the cemetery streets, waiting to pay their respects to the man who had come to save them.

His was a spectacularly beautiful resting place—with wrought-iron gates, a white stone chapel, lush woods, and endlessly curving rows of white marble headstones.

For decades to come trains would slow when they passed, then blow their whistles.

But Elizabeth also knew that in a different place, on a parallel plane, in a desperate time, drums beat, bugles blared, tanks rolled. And another man—with four gold stars blazoning the butts of his ivory-handled pistols—goes to war.

Nor did their forays into Time end there. Two days before Sheckly's mystic ritual, he took his daughter aside and explained to her his True-Vision.

After Patton entered the hole, she had punched in a new series of coordinates. The hole closed, and the lightning blazed again. The hole opened into the infinite future.

Her father—in accordance with his secret vision—strode through the hole in time.

The old woman was a long time forgiving Elizabeth for her betrayal.

"Dad wasn't happy here," her granddaughter tried to explain. "Don't you understand? He didn't care about our time, not anymore. He believed he was needed more *out there*. In that Great Beyond."

Her brother phrased it more succinctly. "There was nothing for him here."

Finally, late one night, her grandmother told Elizabeth the real reason for her anger.

"I was never mad at you. It was him. Richard was my favorite, the one I loved best. The child a parent sometimes gets that special feeling for. But he didn't care. He never cared. My feelings meant nothing to him. The way he walked through that hole without so much as a fare-thee-well, without even looking back. He never cared about *me*."

Elizabeth had stared at her grandmother's angry eyes and felt sorry for her. But she also realized that her grandmother would recover.

Katherine Magruder always recovered.

Elizabeth's father had broken the old woman's heart for the last time.

2

It could be said the old woman had sustained another loss. She no longer had Betsy Ross bird-hopping around her backyard.

But her loss was the Citadel's gain. Eagles are not only high flyers, they have spectacular vision, and the sight of Betsy Ross circling the Citadel was apparent to more than earthly mortals. She was visible to creatures of the air.

Soon scores of eagles flocked to the Citadel. When they weren't nesting in trees or on the nearby crags, they circled overhead.

Betsy Ross, of course, roosted atop the fifty-foot saguaro cactus in the old woman's backyard, and her nest overflowed with eggs and eaglets.

It is said the sight of a soaring bald eagle with its white head and wedge-shaped tail glistening in the sun is one of the most stirring scenes in nature, but to the citizens of the Citadel, their eagles transcend such paltry adjectives as "stirring" or "thrilling." Their presence lifts hearts and touches people's souls.

There are some outside New Arizona who view the birds less romantically. Throughout the surrounding desert country wander *bedouins* with dark eyes, high cheekbones, and black mustaches. With double-curved bows strung across their backs and their broad *shimsir* swords gleaming in the belts of flowing robes, they wring a precarious existence from this harsh and barren land.

A one-eyed gray-haired, obscenely scarred woman also roams these wilds. She harangues all she meets on the need to unite, to form a fire-forged alliance, to wreak bloody revenge on those who had slaughtered the *Altyn Ordu*, the Golden Horde.

But the nomads invariably point to the Citadel's guardians, circling overhead, and patiently explain that they are not birds at all. They are too large, too formidable, too ferocious. They are, in fact, emissaries sent by Beelzebub, from the ether and the astral of the Everlasting Night, the black bottomless void where the Fallen Angels dwell under Hell's shadow.

And if anyone dare once again to challenge their clan, Beelzebub will open that awful pit and unleash his *shaitans*. Never again will the Gates of Darkness be closed.

This is no idle threat. To these wanderers, Beelzebub is no myth. They have witnessed his fire-blackened hide, heard his trumpeting roar, seen his bloody horns, thrashing wings, and slashing talons. They had been singed by his fiery breath.

They are not about to challenge him again.

3

To the extent that there was a true victor, the hero was Harry. But he did not triumph unscathed. His left foreleg was maimed. His chest and high frill were bullet-torn. His right eye was an empty socket, and he was missing his nose-horn.

Still his spirit was undaunted, and his appetite had returned. He now consumed eight hundred pounds of provender daily, and each day he could be found trotting around his private cornfield—donated to him by the Citadel—chomping on cornstalks, frolicking with his friends.

Amelia, Stonewall, Elizabeth, and the old woman had now been permanently installed in Harry's herd. As a consequence, they were forced to set up housekeeping nearby. Eventually, the Triceratops even made his peace with Amelia's planes.

If the citizens of the Citadel viewed Harry as a genuine hero, among the Apaches he attained the status of a legend. By a sacred cliff, high up in the Chiricahua Mountains, the Indians honored him with a stone statue. This unflattering likeness depicted Harry as a horned demon, sprouting massively flapping wings. He was portrayed as rearing back on his hind legs and flinging a huge tripod machine gun over his shoulder.

They needed an inscription for the statue's base and asked for suggestions. Someone on the council suggested assigning the inscription to "an inscription committee." The old woman's scowl was awesome.

Instead she asked Elizabeth to try her hand. Katherine intuited that her granddaughter had been hurt in the war. Not in any way that showed; nor was it evidenced in anything Elizabeth said. But the girl had witnessed too much violence not to have come away with scars of the soul.

One night in the old woman's backyard, Elizabeth asked her about the war and what it all meant. Her grandmother stared at her a long hard moment.

"You know what always stuck in my craw? Something young Darrell wrote in his dispatches. He said that Legion liked to refer to Tamerlane as 'the Wrath of God.'"

"Wasn't he?" There. Elizabeth let it out.

The old woman averted her gaze. "He couldn't have been. God isn't wrathful, child, neither is life. Life *is*. That's all. Human beings make it loving or hateful, generous or mean."

"What was Tamerlane then?"

"He was Tamerlane. Who else?"

"Didn't God make him?"

"God made the baby. Tamerlane and those around him—including us—made the man."

"But God still created the world, didn't he? And the people and the conditions that shaped the Tamerlanes and Legions?"

"Go get me Patton's pistol."

Elizabeth fetched the General's nickel-plated ivory-handled pistol for her grandmother. The old woman pulled back the slide, then handed it to her grand-daughter.

"There. You're still mad at God? Gun down a mountain lion. Blast a diamondback. Waste wildflowers while you're at it." She pointed up at the billions of stars glittering in the night sky. "There's Sirius, Cassiopeia, the Big Dipper. Shoot bullets at the stars."

Elizabeth returned the gun. "It wouldn't do any good."

"It never does any good getting mad at God. You can hate Him, curse Him, lay waste to His works, but you're still stuck with him."

"Is He stuck with us?"

"Ask Stonewall, Patton, Amelia. Ask Harry or your father. They crossed the Gulf of Time."

"Then what do I do about it? All the evil in this world—all the horror and pain, the disease and death?"

"If you were practical, you'd raise sheep, plant crops, and forget about it. If you were real smart, you'd cure cancer or invent Time Machines. Being Elizabeth Magruder, you'll probably write books about it. And since you're sensible, you won't waste time hating God."

"Should I hate Tamerlane?"

"No. Kill him if you can, but you should never hate him."

"Whom should I hate, Grandma?"

"No human, child. Certainly not God."

"I love you, Grandma."

She ruffled the child's hair. "Now where did you learn talk like that? Not from your grandma, that's for sure."

"What's wrong with it? Don't you love me?"

"Why shouldn't I love you? You're the only Magruder left I can whip."

"You don't know how to say 'I love you,' do you? You've never said it to anybody. You never thanked anybody either. Isn't that right?"

"Never thought I had to. But I was wrong. Patton taught me that, and I still owe him for it. Not every day somebody can teach me something."

"I assume you thanked him?"

The old woman's stare was hard enough to hurt.

4

That night the little girl composed the inscription, which was subsequently engraved on the statue's base:

If Tamerlane Was God's Wrath, Harry Was His Deliverance.

The rocky soil around the statue is so arid that no one has ever commemorated the monument with flowers. However, the Apaches say that from time to time a circling eagle folds her wings and dives toward the monument. Two feet above the statue, she spreads her pinions and comes to a heart-wrenching halt. At the base, she deposits a morsel of organ meat.

With three wing beats and a hard back kick, she rejoins her mate. In the harsh blue sky, they resume their courtship of life and love, of mating and nesting, of dying and being born.

The eagles, with effortless ease, drift slowly apart, then double back, almost touching but not quite. On motionless wings they ride the desert thermals in ever-rising ever-widening spirals.